Santa Monica Public Library
I SMP 00 2785498
P9-BZR-148

THE BEST OF INTENTIONS

Books by Susan Anne Mason

COURAGE TO DREAM

Irish Meadows

A Worthy Heart

Love's Faithful Promise

A Most Noble Heir

CANADIAN CROSSINGS

The Best of Intentions

CANADIAN CROSSINGS

BOOK ONE

BEST OF INTENTIONS

SUSAN ANNE MASON

BETHANY HOUSE

a division of Baker Publishing Group

Minneapolis, Minnesota

Published by Bethany House Publishers
11400 Hampshire Avenue South
Bloomington, Minnesota 55438
www.bethanyhouse.com

Bethany House Publishers is a division of
Baker Publishing Group, Grand Rapids, Michigan

Printed in the United States of America

ISBN 978-0-7642-1983-2 (paper)
ISBN 978-0-7642-3204-6 (cloth)

Library of Congress Cataloging in Publication Control Number: 2017963694

Unless noted, Scripture quotations are from the King James Version of the Bible.

This is a work of fiction. Names, characters, incidents, and dialogues are products of the author's imagination and are not to be construed as real. Any resemblance to actual events or persons, living or dead, is entirely coincidental.

Cover design by Koechel Peterson & Associates, Inc., Minneapolis, Minnesota/Jon Godfredson

Author is represented by Natasha Kern Literary Agency.

18 19 20 21 22 23 24 7 6 5 4 3 2 1

For my dear friend,
Sally Bayless,
fellow writer and valued critique partner,
who shares this writing journey with me.
Our friendship has been a wonderful
and unexpected blessing.

"My grace is sufficient for you,
for my power is made perfect in
weakness."

2 Corinthians 12:9 NIV

PROLOGUE

May 1919

Grace Abernathy stood at the rail of the SS *Olympic*, staring out over the calm expanse of sea as the last trace of sunlight disappeared over the horizon. Darkness spread outward to encompass the water, pierced only by a single beam from the masthead light. All traces of warmth vanished with the sun, and Grace shivered within her new wool coat—the one Mum had insisted she buy for the trip.

After her second full day at sea, Grace forced herself not to stare longingly back toward England, her beloved homeland, but instead concentrated on her destination with a mixture of excitement and trepidation. Toronto, Canada, the city where her sister had settled five years ago. So much had happened in those five years to both of them.

Would Rose have left home that spring of 1914 if she'd known the world would soon be engulfed by war and that her life would be forever changed? Grace gripped the rail in front of her as a wave slapped the hull, sending a spray of cold water droplets upward. The churning sea below mirrored the emotions surging beneath her calm demeanor. Rose needed her help, and Grace would not let her down.

She reached inside her coat to finger the small gold cross Rose had given her before she left.

"Wear this close to your heart, Grace, and remember I love you. We'll be together again one day, I know it."

Now a war widow with an infant to care for, Rose had begged Grace in her letters to come to Canada, but the danger of sailing during wartime and the responsibility of caring for their ailing mother had kept Grace from leaving their Sussex village. Once the travel warnings had been lifted, Mum insisted Grace go to Rose and convince her to come home, since the hope of seeing her grandson was the only thing keeping her alive. And so, with Aunt Violet agreeing to take Mum in, Grace had finally purchased her ticket to cross the sea.

The cry of a gull overhead drew Grace's focus back to her surroundings. With the wind on her face and the rush of the water beneath her, she felt free for the first time in her life. Free of the constraints of her hometown, free to pursue the adventure she'd always longed for, and almost free—but not quite—of the guilt that chained her soul. She prayed that bringing Mum's only grandchild home would be the key to loosening those chains once and for all, and at last allow Grace to pursue her own dreams. Her own goals.

But first, there was Rose.

"How about a kiss for a soldier, darlin'?" A rough voice cut through the night air.

Goose bumps erupted over Grace's body at the slur of the man's words. The fact that she was alone at the ship's rail at this late hour made matters worse. The lay passengers shared the ship with many soldiers returning to Canada, and though the crew worked hard at keeping the two groups separate, it wasn't always possible to corral the military men. Most of the soldiers were respectful, but the captain said he couldn't guarantee the women's safety and had warned them to remain belowdeck after dark.

Yet, unable to sleep in her stuffy quarters, Grace had craved the fresh sea air and had dared to risk coming up alone. Bracing herself, she faced the uniformed man. "My husband wouldn't appreciate you talking to me that way, sir. Kindly leave me alone." She turned back to the water, hoping her quaking knees would not betray her.

"Husband, eh? What kind of man would allow his lovely wife to run around on a ship full of soldiers—alone?"

A heavy hand landed on her shoulder. She jerked and attempted to step away, but the man pulled her closer. His breath reeked of spirits and tobacco. His jawline was covered in several days' growth of beard that didn't hide the angry red scar marring his face.

Her heart thumped hard against her ribs. Why hadn't she worn her hat instead of tying a kerchief around her hair? At least then she'd have a hatpin to use as a weapon.

"If you value your hand, you'd best remove it from the lady. Now."

Another masculine voice issued the challenge from behind her.

The soldier whirled around, scowling. "Mind your own business, pal. My lady friend and I are looking for some privacy, if you get my drift."

Grace turned to see a tall man dressed in a fedora and trench coat, standing perfectly still. His dark brows were drawn together in a frown, and a pulse ticked in his clean-shaven jaw.

"I highly doubt that, since the lady is my wife." His gaze never wavered.

Grace fought to keep her jaw from dropping.

The soldier's eyes narrowed. "If you're her husband, why haven't I seen you together? I've been watching her since we boarded yesterday, and she's been alone the whole time."

Grace's heart thudded. *Since we boarded?* She gripped the lapels of her coat together.

The stranger didn't blink. "I've been in our cabin. Feeling a bit under the weather. But I've got my strength back now." He took an intimidating step closer. "I suggest you return to the other soldiers where you belong. And don't think about bothering any of the other women on board." Another step brought him within striking distance. He towered over the man. "Do I make myself clear?"

The soldier regarded him for a few seconds, as though deciding whether or not to engage in a fight, then spat a stream of brown tobacco juice onto the deck. "Can't blame a guy for trying." With a humorless laugh, he stuffed his hands in his pockets and strolled away.

The stranger moved to Grace's side, not taking his focus off the soldier until he was out of sight. Then he turned his attention to her. "Are you all right, miss?"

"Yes, thank you." She released a breath and allowed her stomach muscles to relax. "I appreciate your help."

Up close, the man's eyes radiated compassion and kindness.

Thank you, Lord, for sending a protector.

"It's the least I could do . . . for my wife." He chuckled.

Grace hoped he couldn't see the heat in her cheeks.

"My name's Quinten Aspinall. It appears we'll be traveling companions."

"Grace Abernathy." She pulled her collar up around her neck. "I probably shouldn't have come here alone, but I had to get out of the cabin. I was going stir-crazy, not to mention that my roommate snores rather loudly."

"That's why I'm out here as well. And—"

"Quinten?" a female voice said. "Is everything all right?"

For the first time, Grace noticed a young woman standing in the shadows. She came toward them, her brow furrowed. As she drew nearer, Grace was awed by her beauty. Flawless skin, ebony hair, and striking blue eyes. Unlike Grace in her sensible gray coat, this girl was the height of fashion, dressed in a matching red cape and feathered hat.

"Everything's fine, Emmaline."

Grace frowned at the man. "You left your wife to help me?"

"Oh, he's not my husband." The girl trilled a perfect laugh. "We met yesterday on the ship." She strolled over to them. "My traveling companion hasn't found his sea legs yet, so when Quinten saw me up here alone, he gallantly offered to serve as my protector until Jonathan rallies."

Grace did her best not to gape. This girl was traveling with a male companion? How unconventional.

"It seems my services might be required here as well." Mr. Aspinall winked at Grace. "May I be so bold as to suggest we form an alliance while on board?"

"What sort of alliance?" Grace didn't bother to hide her skepticism. A woman traveling alone couldn't be too careful.

"You have to admit there's safety in numbers. And I, for one, could use some friends on this voyage."

Emmaline laughed. "You might as well agree. He'll only hound you until you do. Trust me, I know from recent experience." She held out a gloved hand. "I'm Emmaline Moore. And I'd be happy to have a friend on board too."

"Grace Abernathy." She smiled as she shook the girl's hand, finding her infectious good humor as soothing as a tonic. "I'd like that." She hesitated a moment, then offered her hand to Quinten. "Very well, Mr. Aspinall. It appears you've made another friend."

"Friends it is. And please call me Quinn."

A spray of salt water showered the deck. Quinn led her and Emmaline to a more sheltered spot and gestured to the deck chairs. "Why don't we have a seat and get to know each other better? I'd love to hear why you're traveling to Canada. And why Emmaline has a mysterious male companion who is neither a relative nor a husband."

Grace settled into her chair. "I'll admit I'm curious about that as well."

"It's no big mystery." Emmaline perched daintily on the edge of one of the lounges. "Jonathan and I grew up together. We're like brother and sister. When I told him I intended to travel to Canada to find my father, he insisted on coming with me—in separate cabins, of course."

"How fortunate you are," Grace said. "I wish I had someone to travel with."

"What's the reason for your trip, Grace?" Quinn's face was shrouded in shadows.

"I'm going to visit my sister. Her husband died in the war, leaving her alone with a new baby." She fingered the cross hanging from her neck. "I hope to convince her to come home with me."

"I'm very sorry for your sister." Emmaline's expression grew sad. "This war has been such a terrible waste of lives."

"That it has." Grace breathed in the salty air. "You said you're looking for your father?"

"Yes. It's a long, rather gloomy story." She pulled her cape up under her chin. "I'd believed my father to be dead all these years, but when I discovered he's alive and living in Canada, I had to find him."

"I don't blame you." Grace thought of her own father, gone these many years. She'd sail to China if there were a chance to find him alive. "And what about you, Quinn?"

A sudden gust of wind threatened to lift the hat from his head. He removed it and held it on his lap. "My story is similar to both of yours in that I'm searching for family members. Siblings actually." His jaw became tense, his eyes stormy. "I'd rather not get into the details though."

Grace feared his was not a happy tale. It seemed they each had their own obstacles to overcome on this trip. Yet for the first time since she left home, she didn't feel quite so alone. "Well, I'm grateful to have you both as traveling companions. And I pray that once we reach the shores of Canada, we'll find the answers we seek."

Quinn nodded, his face grim. "God willing. I only hope we can live with whatever we discover."

Grace shivered, burrowing further into her coat, wishing to dispel the ominous tone of his words. Only God knew what was in store for each of them. Faced with such an uncertain future, all Grace could do was rely on her faith to sustain her through the journey.

CHAPTER 1

April 1914
Dearest Grace,

I made it! I've arrived in Toronto. The month of April is still cold here with only the barest hint of spring. Reverend Burke has helped me find a lovely boardinghouse in the heart of the city. Mrs. Chamberlain, the proprietress, is a kind, generous woman. She's taken me under her wing, along with several other girls from back home, and has made me feel most welcome. Living here, I can almost forget I'm thousands of miles away from you. Almost . . .

Toronto, Ontario
May 1919

"Here's your address, miss. That'll be two dollars and fifty cents."

Grace paid her fare, alighted from the vehicle, then stood on the sidewalk, clutching her valise with trembling fingers.

She could scarcely believe that after a six-day ocean voyage, a journey by train from Halifax to Montreal, and another train from Montreal to Toronto, she had finally reached her destination.

Her first impressions of Canada were as varied as the three cities she'd visited since her arrival at the Nova Scotia port. Cold, gray

Halifax still harbored remnants of winter with traces of snow that hugged the landscape. Foreign and vaguely frightening, Montreal was filled with tall buildings and strange, lightning-fast snatches of the French language. And now, Toronto. Having been in the city for less than an hour, she'd yet to form a complete picture. On her ride from Union Station, she'd passed an eclectic mix of buildings, from office towers to historic churches, until they'd finally come to a residential neighborhood with tree-lined streets.

It was hard to believe that a mere three weeks ago Grace had been at home in Sussex, caring for her mother, her life as normal as could be expected after the ravages of war. She and Mum had been slowly coping with the news of her brother Owen's death in one of the last battles before peace had been declared. Her mother had not dealt well with the blow and had sunk into a deep depression at the loss of her son. Nothing Grace said or did seemed to lift her spirits.

Which was why so much depended on this trip.

Grace drew her attention back to the lovely redbrick house before her—a far cry from the fleapit she'd imagined. Rose and the baby must love living in this charming home. The first leaves were beginning to bud on the trees in the yard. A welcoming pot of pansies decorated the wide front porch. Above her, an upper balcony ran the length of the house, interrupted by a jutting turret room. Where did Rose stay? Likely on the third story, where an appealing dormer window peeked out over the roof.

Grace inhaled deeply and pressed a palm to her stomach, which rolled and tossed as though she were still aboard the ship. Would Rose be surprised to see her at the door? Even if the telegram had reached her by now, Rose wouldn't have any idea how long it would take Grace to get from Halifax to Toronto.

She walked up the stairs and knocked on the front door, praying Rose was right and that Grace would be welcome at Mrs. Gardiner's, at least until they'd sorted out their plans. Her sister seemed genuinely fond of the woman who had taken Rose and the baby in when she could no longer stay at the boardinghouse. For the moment, however, Grace forced her worries aside and focused instead on the long-awaited reunion with her sister. Tingles of anticipation shot through her. She could hardly wait to hug Rose and hold her new nephew for the first time. Kiss his sweet cheeks and catch up on all her sister's news.

Several seconds went by with no response. Was everyone out? Grace knocked again, but no one appeared. Disappointment sat heavy on her shoulders. She set her suitcase on the porch and turned to look back at the street. Only then did she spy a For Sale sign almost hidden by a wide tree trunk. Rose hadn't mentioned that Mrs. Gardiner was planning to sell her house. Perhaps that was the reason Rose had talked about getting a place of their own as soon as Grace managed to find work.

She swallowed the metallic taste of guilt. Rose didn't realize that Grace had no intention of procuring a job or renting a flat, because she planned to do everything in her power to persuade Rose to return with her on the next ship home.

After another knock with no response, Grace picked up her suitcase and descended the front stairs. Her frazzled mind struggled to come up with a new plan. She'd never even entertained the possibility that Rose wouldn't be here.

Next door, a woman stepped out onto the front porch.

Grace's steps slowed. Perhaps a neighbor might know something about Rose or her landlady. She headed across the lawn.

The plump woman wearing a flowered dress shook a mat over the railing. She glanced up as Grace approached. "Good afternoon. Can I help you?"

Grace put on her friendliest smile. "I hope so. I'm looking for Mrs. Gardiner. She doesn't appear to be home."

The woman's hands stilled. "I guess you haven't heard. She moved to Vermont to live with her daughter. I'm keeping an eye on the house until it's sold."

Moved to Vermont? What about Rose and the baby? Surely she hadn't put them out in the street. "Do you know if Rose Ab—I mean Easton—is still living here? She and her baby have been boarding with Mrs. Gardiner for a few months now."

The woman paused. "I remember a young woman and a baby, but I don't know what happened to them after Cora took ill. I'm sorry. Wish I could help you, dear." She laid the mat over the railing. "Why don't you try Reverend Burke, the rector at Holy Trinity Church? He used to visit them quite often. He may know where they went."

"Thank you. I'll do that." Grace bit her lip, realizing she had no idea how far away that might be. "Can you tell me where to find the church?"

"It's about ten blocks away." The woman pointed to the next crossroad. "Just follow Sherbourne Street. You can't miss it."

Grace held back a sigh. Ten blocks sounded far, but it might be good to get some exercise after all the time spent on trains lately. "Thank you again," she said, and with a lift of her chin, set off.

The ten blocks didn't take nearly as long as she'd imagined. When the landscape changed from residential to urban, the streets became more crowded. People walked at a fast pace and jostled Grace, who struggled to keep up with the flow. A flash of homesickness went through her as she thought longingly of the uncluttered roads in her village where the only obstruction to a pedestrian's stroll might be a farmer's cart halted by a stubborn mule.

As she fought to navigate her way through the newness of the city, worry for her sister plagued her. What had happened to Rose and little Christian? Surely Reverend Burke had found them an alternate place to live. Perhaps with another kind soul from his parish.

A church tower came into view, and as Grace got close enough to read the sign, she was relieved to find it was indeed Holy Trinity. She stepped out of the flow of pedestrians onto the church walkway.

Would anyone be here on a Wednesday afternoon? She tugged the handle of the large wooden door. It gave easily under her hand, and she entered the building. Once her eyes adjusted to the dimness, she moved farther into the church and scanned the rows of pews. A few women sat scattered throughout. Nowhere did Grace see a clergyman. She was about to leave when someone touched her shoulder.

"Can I help you, miss?"

Grace turned to find a regal-looking woman staring at her with undisguised curiosity.

"Yes. Do you know where I might find Reverend Burke?"

"At this time of day, he's probably at home."

"Oh. I see." Grace felt suddenly foolish. She had no idea of the etiquette involved in calling on a minister at his place of residence, but since she couldn't afford to wait until Sunday, she'd have to figure out a way to see him.

"Would you like me to take you to the rectory?" The kind woman smiled.

"Yes, please. If you wouldn't mind."

"Not at all. It's right next door. Follow me."

She led Grace to the little bungalow that sat back from the street, almost hidden from view. The woman marched up to the front door and knocked.

Grace's heart began to thump when the door opened, and a rather rumpled older gentleman answered.

His gaze toggled between the two women. "Mrs. Southby. This is an unexpected surprise." His eyebrow raised in a question.

"This young woman would like to speak with you, Reverend. I offered to bring her over."

The minister looked down at Grace's suitcase, then back at her face. "Are you here about our Newcomers Program?"

"N-Not exactly." Her tongue seemed to tangle as she searched for a way to begin. She'd hoped for a little privacy, not eager to spill her story on the minister's stoop.

"One moment," he said. "Let me get my jacket, and we'll go across to my office."

Mrs. Southby smiled at her. "You've come to the right place. Reverend Burke is a godsend for so many people new to our country. I'm sure he'll be able to help you too."

Grace supposed that because of her suitcase and her British accent the pair had jumped to a logical, albeit erroneous, conclusion.

Five minutes later, Reverend Burke said good-bye to Mrs. Southby and offered Grace a seat. He then took his place in the wooden captain's chair behind the cluttered desk. "Now, what can I do for you, my dear?"

On the wall, a cuckoo clock struck the top of the hour. Every chime jarred Grace's nerve endings. She must be tired from the long trip or unsettled over the unexpected turn of events.

She licked her dry lips and attempted to pull herself together. "My name is Grace Abernathy. I'm Rose Easton's sister."

Instantly, the man's smile fell away, and sorrow filled his blue eyes. "Oh, my dear. I wondered if you'd come when you received my telegram."

"Telegram?" Icy prickles rippled down Grace's spine, erasing all thoughts of what she wanted to say.

"Yes. The one I sent to your mother in England." The chair creaked as he leaned forward. "Did she not receive it?"

The sudden desire to bolt seized her, but her feet seemed glued to the wooden floor. "No, she didn't. I'm here because Rose asked me to come."

He stood and came around to sit in the chair beside her. A loud sigh escaped his bulky frame. "There's no easy way to say this, Grace. I'm sorry, but Rose came down with the Spanish flu. She passed away about three weeks ago. It was all very sudden and tragic."

Grace's throat constricted, the air backing up in her lungs. "No," she whispered. "It can't be true. Someone would have . . . I would have known. . . ."

He shook his head sadly. "I sent a telegram to the postmaster in your village as soon as I could. I don't know why you didn't receive it."

Grace tried to recall where she'd been three weeks ago. That was about the time she'd moved Mum to Aunt Violet's where she would stay while Grace was away.

"I . . . it . . . no, it can't be." She covered her mouth with her hand to still the trembling of her lips. "I was supposed to bring

Rose home. Home to Mum." Her whole body began to shake. The thought of her mother receiving such terrible news without Grace there to comfort her brought the hot rush of tears to her eyes.

"I'm so very sorry, Grace." A warm hand squeezed her shoulder.

She stared at a knothole in the wooden floorboard. The handle of her purse bit into the flesh of her hands.

All her plans to take Rose and little Christian back to England, to reunite their family and make them whole again, vanished in an instant. Her chest filled with heat that burned up her throat and clogged her airway. With shaking fingers, she pulled a handkerchief from her purse and wiped her streaming eyes. "What am I going to do now?" she whispered. "I planned to stay with Rose at Mrs. Gardiner's. She wanted us to be together. . . ." A strangled sob escaped.

"This has come as a terrible shock." The minister went to the credenza, poured a glass of water, and handed it to her. "Might I suggest that I take you to my friend, Mrs. Chamberlain? She runs the boardinghouse where Rose first lived when she came to Canada. I'm certain Harriet will be able to offer you a place to stay while you decide what to do next."

Grace could only blink as tears continued to blur her vision, her mind too fuzzy to absorb his words.

He must have taken her silence for agreement, for he nodded. "Right. I'll telephone Harriet and let her know we're coming."

Grace sipped the water and fought to gain control of her emotions. Amidst the haze of grief, one question screamed through her mind. Why had God brought her all this way, only to learn that her sister was gone? That little Christian had lost his mother?

Grace snapped to attention, her fingers tightening on the glass. "What happened to the baby? He's not in an orphanage, is he?" She would never allow her nephew to be raised in such a place. He belonged with his family—or what was left of it.

Reverend Burke paused, the telephone receiver in hand. "No need to worry. Christian is being well cared for."

But the guilty expression on the man's face did nothing to reassure Grace.

"Who's looking after him? Someone from the church?" It couldn't be Mrs. Gardiner if she'd moved to Vermont. Grace's hands shook, sloshing the water as she set the glass on the desk. "Tell me and I'll go and get him right away."

She had no idea how she'd care for an infant, but she would figure it out soon enough. And in the meantime, Christian would be safe with someone who loved him.

The minister set the receiver back in the cradle with an apologetic shrug. "The hospital officials were going to call the Children's Aid Society unless I could provide a family member to care for him. With you and your mother so far away, I didn't have much choice."

A sickening sense of dread formed in the pit of Grace's stomach. Not Rose's dreaded in-laws. The ones who had disowned their son because he married Rose. The ones Rose specifically tried to hide the baby from after her husband's death.

She squared her shoulders. "Tell me where he is."

"I did the only thing I could. I contacted the boy's grandparents." A look of regret crept across his broad features. "Christian is living with the Eastons."

CHAPTER 2

Andrew Easton peeked into the open doorway of the second-floor nursery and held back a grin. His usually ladylike younger sister was bent over the crib, making ridiculous faces at her nephew in a blatant attempt to make the child laugh.

"Take care, Ginny. Your face might stay like that if you're not careful." Andrew laughed as he stepped into the room.

Virginia's head snapped up, two patches of red blooming in her cheeks. "How long have you been standing there?"

"Long enough to see your eyes cross."

"Hmph." She wrinkled her nose, one dark ringlet falling over her forehead. "Well, Christian likes it. He gave me a big smile. Didn't you, sweetheart?" Virginia reached into the crib and lifted him out. When she bent to kiss his cheek, the child made a grab for her nose and squeezed.

"Ouch. For a little one, you sure have an iron grip." She shifted the boy in her arms. "What brings you here at this time of day, Drew? Shouldn't you be at the office?"

"I'm working at home this morning, so I thought I'd see how our nephew is doing." He crossed the carpeted floor. "Does he seem to be adjusting to his new home?" Christian had been with them for three weeks now, ever since the flu had taken his mother's life. For a child to lose his father before he was born, and his mother shortly thereafter, was a tragedy Andrew could barely comprehend.

Frank's son deserved a carefree childhood and a happy life, and as the boy's newly appointed guardian, Andrew was determined to provide it for him.

Virginia handed Christian to him, then moved to open the draperies at the window. "He's slowly getting used to us, I think. But he still wakes up crying for his mama at night. Poor little darling." She came back to stroke the boy's head, smoothing down the tufts of dark hair. When she raised her head, tears filmed her gray eyes. "I wish Frank could have seen him."

"I know. He would've been so proud." A rush of sadness tugged at Andrew's chest. Would he ever accept the fact that his brother was gone?

She let out a sigh. "If only his wife could have come here after he died. Maybe then . . ."

Andrew stiffened. Ginny knew their father would never have allowed such a thing. Not when he blamed Rose Abernathy for ruining Frank's life. "There's no use wishing for the impossible, Gin. Let's be glad we have a chance to get things right with Frank's son. We'll do our best to make sure he has a happy childhood."

"On that note, I have something I'd like to discuss with you." She plucked Christian from his arms and bounced the tyke on her hip.

"What is it?"

"I've been thinking about my plans for the summer, and . . ." She drew in a breath. "I've decided to cancel my trip." She darted a nervous glance at him, then turned back to the baby who had grabbed a fistful of her long hair. With a playful tug, she pulled the strands free and went to sit in the rocking chair.

Andrew followed her over, studying her face for some clue to this sudden change. Did it have anything to do with her new attachment to their nephew, or were there deeper motives at play? "You promised Basil you'd accompany him and his family to Europe. He won't be happy if you back out now."

"But I'm needed here. I can't abandon Christian just when he's getting used to me. It's too cruel."

His sister was anything but cruel. Andrew had never encountered a kinder young woman.

"Children adjust quickly to new situations," he said soothingly. "And hiring a nanny is at the top of my list. If we find a suitable person soon, you'll have lots of time to ensure a smooth transition before you set sail."

Unshed tears brightened her eyes, highlighting the golden flecks within the gray. "I hate to leave him, Drew. He's captured my heart already. If only Basil would consider—"

"Ginny." Andrew bent to gaze directly into her anxious face. "I know you love Christian, but you can't give up your entire future for him."

"Why not?" Her eyes flashed in challenge. "Aren't you planning to do just that?"

"Not at all. I'll have the help, and if I marry—" Why did he hesitate every time the subject of marriage arose? "When I marry," he said more forcefully, "my wife and I will assume the role of his parents. And Christian will have the continuity of the same nanny." He did his best to smile. "It will all work out for the best. You'll see."

Virginia rested her chin on the boy's head. "I hope you're right. Though I can't help thinking I might be better off to raise him on my own." She stared across the room, her wistful expression tugging at his heart.

"Is this about Christian?" he asked gently. "Or about your relationship with Basil?" He'd sensed his sister's less-than-enthusiastic feelings about this match, one that their father clearly wanted. Yet Andrew doubted she would ever go against Father's wishes. Not after the disaster that had ensued when Frank had done so.

She lowered her gaze to the floor. "Perhaps a bit of both."

Andrew rose from his crouched position. "That's something you'd best resolve before you agree to marry him, sister dear. If he ever gets off his duff and proposes, that is. Now if you'll excuse me, I have to ensure our advertisement for a nanny will run in the newspaper for another week." Laying a soft kiss on his sister's head, he straightened and moved to the nursery door.

"Drew?"

"Yes?"

"Don't find a nanny too soon. I still have eight weeks before we sail, and I want to spend as much time as possible with this little one."

Andrew's heart melted at the sight of her rocking the child, a breeze stirring the curtain at her back. She would make a wonderful mother one day. Too bad Basil Fleming couldn't see how much it would mean to Virginia to raise the boy. Not only would it be better for Christian, who would surely thrive under Virginia's devotion, but it would solve Andrew's issues with Cecilia as well. "Don't worry. You'll have plenty of time alone with him. Finding a nanny who meets Mother's standards could take some time." He sent her a wink before closing the door behind him.

On his way downstairs to the library, he offered a silent prayer that the Lord would provide the perfect candidate for his orphaned nephew. Someone who would give the child all the love and attention he so rightly deserved.

After a brief stop at the newspaper office, Andrew steered his automobile toward the Easton Towers Hotel. How he loved this city, the wonderful mix of old and new. It never failed to inspire him. As he motored past the college buildings on University Avenue, a wave of nostalgia hit him. Even years after his graduation, he still missed his time on campus and the camaraderie of his fellow students. But those carefree days had ended with the onset of the war that summer. Andrew had no way of knowing then how much his life would change.

A few minutes later, he pulled his car to a stop outside the front of the hotel, set the brake, and got out. As he entered through the revolving doors into the lobby, his chest filled with pride. The Easton Towers Hotel was the epitome of elegance, Oscar Easton's pride and joy. Sometimes Andrew thought his father cared more about these bricks and mortar than he did his own family.

Nevertheless, Andrew had to admit the hotel was indeed an outstanding achievement.

He nodded to the staff behind the reception desk on his way to the elevator that would take him up to the company offices on the tenth floor.

Once there, Andrew knocked on his father's door and waited for an invitation to enter before stepping into the opulent office. "Good afternoon, Father."

"Ah, good. You're here." Oscar Easton looked up from the papers on his desk. "I didn't realize you'd stayed home this morning. Is everything all right?" The overhead light glinted off the silver threads running through his father's dark hair, another sign of the toll that recent events had taken on him.

Yet Andrew wasn't fooled by the false concern, for he understood the veiled criticism beneath the words. *Why weren't you at your post where you should be?*

"I chose to work from home this morning. Sometimes a change of scenery is good for productivity." He moved across to the wall of windows overlooking the downtown core and allowed the magnificent view to relax him. If he stared straight ahead, he could almost see the sunlight glinting off Lake Ontario. How long had it been since he'd gone to the beach? Or taken a boat out on the water? Now that the good weather had arrived, he should make such an outing a priority.

He turned back to see his father frown.

"Don't make a habit of it. We need you here in the trenches." One eyebrow rose, and for an instant, Frank's reflection stared back at him. It was uncanny how much Frank had resembled their dark-haired father, while Andrew took after his mother's lighter-haired side of the family. Perhaps that was part of the reason Father had favored Frank. Nothing like a mirror image of oneself to bolster the ego, especially when that image could charm the socks off a hobo.

Father leaned back in his chair. "By the way, how is the search for a nanny going?"

Christian's arrival into the family had been a shock to everyone, but his father seemed to be having an exceptionally hard time. Andrew suspected the boy was bringing up a lot of guilt for the way his father had disowned Frank, and more specifically for the way he'd treated Frank's wife.

Andrew, on the other hand, viewed the child as a gift, one he hoped would be a source of healing for the Easton family. The glue that would fill the cracks and bind them back together.

"We haven't had much luck so far. Mother's strict requirements have proven somewhat daunting. This morning, I rewrote the advertisement and dropped it off at the newspaper office on the way in."

"Good." The lines in his father's forehead eased. "I'll feel a lot better once the boy has the proper staff to care for him. I don't want this situation to cause a setback in your mother's health."

Andrew wished his father could see that little Christian was the one thing keeping his mother from drowning in grief over Frank's death.

"Right now, however, we have a more important issue to discuss." Father rose from the desk and adjusted his vest.

"Such as?"

"Such as the soirée at the Carmichaels' tomorrow evening for Cecilia's birthday."

"What about it?"

"I hope you're planning to attend. You need to be present to stake your claim, because if you don't, plenty of others will be ready to step in."

Andrew suppressed the urge to roll his eyes. "I'll be there. Cecilia's already instructed me when to arrive and which suit I should wear."

"Splendid." A genuine look of approval lightened his father's features. "I'm delighted you and Harrison's daughter are getting along so well. I assume we'll hear news of an engagement soon?"

Andrew's hands curled into fists, but he forced himself to relax.

"We're nowhere near that point yet, Father. I'm taking things slowly."

"Time waits for no man, Andrew. If you don't act soon, someone else will snatch her up. A beauty like Cecilia, with intelligence to match, is rare."

"I realize that." Andrew crossed the room. "However, I need to be sure before I commit to something as serious as marriage."

Father paused from pouring himself a cup of coffee from the ever-present carafe on the credenza. "Sure about what?"

"That she isn't still in love with Frank." The bitter taste of jealousy rose in his throat. Would he ever accept the fact that Cecilia had initially chosen his brother over him? If it weren't for Frank meeting that flirty English girl and subsequently breaking his engagement to Cecilia, they would have been married.

Andrew certainly hadn't forgotten, and it made him suspicious that Celia could have now formed such a strong attachment to him, when she'd barely noticed him before.

His father came forward to grip Andrew's shoulder. "You have the chance to do one last thing for your brother—fix his mistake and return honor to our family name. Marrying Cecilia will go a long way to restoring good relations with the Carmichaels." His eyes hardened. "You've always been a man of integrity, more so than your brother turned out to be."

Andrew allowed the rare compliment to seep in. Yet the approval he'd sought for so long now tasted sour on his tongue. Why did it take Frank's death for his father to utter these words of praise? "I understand what's at stake, Father. But I won't rush things."

His father gave Andrew a long look. "I think it's time I told you about the deal Harrison and I have been negotiating." He gestured to the guest chairs that surrounded a round table in the far corner of the room, and they both took a seat. "What I'm about to tell you is highly confidential." Father removed a cigar from the box on the table. "Harrison is considering joining forces with us to open more hotels. With the power of his development firm behind us, we'd have all the leverage we need to open several more hotels on an even grander scale than this. We're looking into a few potential sites in Ottawa and Winnipeg. Possibly as far out as Vancouver."

Andrew ran a thoughtful hand over his beard. "Is this the right time for such a move? The economy is still reeling from the effects of the war. People aren't traveling when they can barely make ends meet. It could be a risky endeavor."

"Perhaps. Or perhaps men with the right vision for the future can take advantage of everyone else's reticence and make a bold move." His father struck a match and lit the cigar. "If all goes well, I'll need a man to oversee the new hotel at the location we choose. And who better than my son? Someone I trust implicitly, who knows the business inside out, and who's been by my side all this time."

Stunned, Andrew shifted on his chair, hardly able to believe what his father was saying.

"Your marriage to Cecilia would be the icing on the cake, linking our families in a more permanent way. It would all but guarantee Harrison's investment."

A cold chill slid down Andrew's spine. "Are you using this promotion as a bribe? So I'll marry Cecilia to further your business deal?"

"Of course not. I'm simply stating the facts. Your marriage could benefit us both greatly." Father blew out a ring of smoke. "Think about it, Andrew. A beautiful wife. Your own hotel in our country's capital city. What more could you want?"

Andrew's dream shimmered before him. Everything he'd been working toward suddenly seemed within his reach. Not only would he have his father's respect, he'd get a huge promotion in the process, one with new responsibilities and challenges.

But could he leave Toronto? Move a day's journey away from his family, from the home where he'd grown up?

"You've given me a lot to think about."

"Don't think too long, son. As I said before, time waits for no man." His father's steely expression made his point better than any spoken ultimatum.

If Andrew didn't follow through with his plan, he'd be letting his father and the company down. Before Frank's estrangement from the family, Father had been grooming his eldest son for just such a promotion. Now Andrew was expected to step in to fill the vacant spot. Be the dutiful son. Marry Cecilia and bridge the gap that had been created between two of the most powerful families in Toronto when Frank had rejected Cecilia for another woman.

Andrew held the key to giving his father everything he desired. Yet the nagging question remained. Was he prepared to submit to his father's demands at the potential cost of his own happiness?

CHAPTER 3

April 30, 1914
Dear Grace,

I have wonderful news. I've found a job at a grand hotel, not far from the boardinghouse. In nice weather, I can walk to work, and other times the streetcar takes me practically to the front door. Because of my skill on a typewriter, I earned a position in the secretarial pool of the hotel's administrative offices. Mr. Easton Sr. is a strict taskmaster, but thankfully his son more than makes up for it.

In the third-floor bedroom of Mrs. Chamberlain's boardinghouse, Grace unpacked her few items of clothing and hung them in the narrow closet. It had been more than twenty-four hours since Reverend Burke had brought her here. The gracious landlady had taken note of Grace's traumatized state and had shown her right to her room. Other than bringing up a tray of toast and tea, the woman had let her grieve in private.

After hours of weeping, Grace had fallen into an exhausted sleep, the stress of the whole voyage finally catching up with her. When she awoke early this morning, feeling hollowed out from crying, she'd taken a hot bath and dressed in fresh clothes, while trying to sort out her thoughts. For now, the future was too difficult to focus on. Instead, Grace concentrated on what she would do today. She needed to see Rose's gravesite, and she wanted to talk to Reverend Burke and Mrs. Chamberlain about meeting her nephew. She wouldn't rest until she knew Christian was all right.

After making the bed, Grace stored her valise in the closet, then looked around the room. If she weren't so emotionally numb, she might be better able to appreciate the hominess of the space. A handmade blue-and-white quilt covered the single bed, and piles of colorful pillows sat on top. They matched the ones in the corner window nook. A vanity, dresser, and nightstand rounded out the furnishings. Had Rose stayed in this room when she first arrived in Toronto? If so, no wonder she'd been delighted with her accommodations.

Grace pulled the packet of Rose's letters out of her purse and sat in the window seat. From her high perch, she had a lovely view of pedestrians walking along Jarvis Street below. She opened the last letter she'd received from Rose, as though by reading it again she might find some clue as to when Rose had fallen ill. But nothing her sister wrote had hinted of any pending health crisis.

"Oh, Rose," she said aloud. "Didn't I warn you that coming to Canada wouldn't turn out well?"

But nothing had swayed her decision to leave home, certainly not her little sister's advice. In that moment, their roles had reversed, with Rose acting impulsively and Grace, for once, being the voice of caution.

Grace stowed the letters back in her handbag and checked her watch. Surely Mrs. Chamberlain would be up by now, preparing breakfast for her boarders. It was time Grace faced reality and made a plan to go forward. But she would need Mrs. Chamberlain's help.

With determination, she descended the main staircase and made her way to the parlor where she'd briefly met her landlady yesterday. Today, seeing the space with fresh eyes, Grace could appreciate the cozy décor. Floral sofas and high-backed wing chairs surrounded the fireplace. Pictures on the wall depicted scenes from back home: green English meadows and a cottage much like the one Grace had grown up in. A gray tabby lifted its head from the cushioned window seat, blinked lazily, and dropped back to its previous position.

"Good morning, Grace. It's good to see you up and about." Mrs. Chamberlain appeared in the hallway. She wore a floral apron over her dress and held a large teapot. Her kind eyes radiated unspoken compassion. "I'm serving breakfast if you'd care to join us."

"I'm not very hungry, but tea would be nice." Grace walked toward her. "And afterward, I could use your help with something, if you have time."

"By all means. Once I finish the dishes, I'm all yours."

At the far end of the Holy Trinity Cemetery, Grace bent to place a bouquet of daisies atop a mound of fresh dirt. Then she straightened, wrapping her arms around her, as if by doing so she could shield herself from the crushing weight of her grief. Rose's grave bore no marker, not even a simple wooden cross. Reverend Burke told Grace that the members of the congregation all felt badly for the young widow and were raising money for a headstone to give her a decent resting place.

How did this happen, Rose? If I'd come sooner, could I have saved you from this horrible fate?

The cool spring wind tore at the hem of Grace's skirt and loosened strands of her brown hair, which blew about her cheeks. "How will I ever make things right with Mum now?" she whispered.

Memories of her last conversation with her mother crept into her thoughts.

"You owe me, girl. You know you do." From her sickbed, Mum's hard eyes had pinned Grace to the spot, unearthing the guilt that always sat just below the surface. *"The least you can do is to bring Rose and my grandson home where they belong."*

Looking down at the stark burial site, Grace dashed the traces of tears from her cheeks. "I promise, Rose, I'll do everything in my power to see that Christian's safe. I'll make sure the Eastons are treating him properly. And if they're not, somehow I'll find a way to fix it."

How she would accomplish that feat, she didn't know. She'd have to trust the Lord to provide her a way when the time came.

With a final glance at the pile of dirt, she crossed the cemetery grounds to the church where Mrs. Chamberlain had gone to give Grace some privacy.

As Grace reached the steps, she heard her name called.

"Yoo-hoo, over here." Mrs. Chamberlain waved from the rectory next door. "Come in for some tea to warm up."

Slowly Grace headed over. She welcomed the chance to speak to Reverend Burke and see what more she could learn about the Eastons in order to determine her next course of action. Anything to take her mind off the raw sorrow that tore at her chest.

Mrs. Chamberlain held the door for her and ushered her into the hallway. The delicious scent of yeast and cinnamon made Grace's mouth water, reminding her that she hadn't eaten much over the last twenty-four hours, too consumed with grief to have any appetite. It almost felt wrong to be hungry now.

"Reverend Burke found me in the church and invited me in. There are fresh rolls if you're hungry." The sympathy in Mrs. Chamberlain's voice warmed the hollow places inside Grace.

"Thank you. That sounds wonderful."

Grace entered the homey kitchen where Reverend Burke stood at the stove. "Welcome, Grace. Please have a seat. My cinnamon scones are almost ready."

Grace sat at a round table covered with a plain red cloth. "You bake your own bread, Reverend?"

His smile created crinkles around his eyes. "It's a skill I had to learn after my dear wife passed on. Since I enjoy eating"—he patted his round stomach—"I had no choice. Harriet here was kind enough to give me a lesson or two." He winked at Mrs. Chamberlain, who chuckled.

Grace stared, not sure what to make of their easy talk of death. For her, it was far too painful a subject to banter about.

He opened the oven door and reached in with a dish towel to pull out a baking tin.

When Mrs. Chamberlain had poured the tea and laid two scones on her plate, Grace searched for a way to begin the conversation. "Have you both lived in Toronto long?" she asked. Perhaps getting to know these two a little better was a wise place to begin.

"We have." Reverend Burke gestured for Mrs. Chamberlain to answer first.

"I came to Canada as a young woman, but I lived through unhappy times before I met my dear husband. Thankfully we started attending this church, which became my source of strength when poor Miles passed on." Mrs. Chamberlain refilled her cup and set the pot back on the table.

Reverend Burke sat down. "I was a boy when my parents moved here. I felt the calling to a life of ministry and attended Wycliffe College in the city. I've been pastor of Holy Trinity Church for sixteen years now." He waved a butter knife toward Mrs. Chamberlain. "Learning of Harriet's struggles upon coming to Canada was instrumental in us starting the Newcomers Program. A place for immigrants to meet and get aid in finding a job or a place to live."

Mrs. Chamberlain nodded. "Most people are terribly homesick at first. It helps to be around others from their homeland, which is why my husband opened the boardinghouse. He saw a real need for immigrants to have a decent place to stay until they got their feet under them." She added a spoon of sugar to her tea. "Once he passed away, I wanted to keep the business going in his memory, although I take only female boarders now. A woman alone can't be too careful."

Reverend Burke lifted a brow. "I'm only a few blocks away if you ever need me."

"I know." She gave him a warm smile. "It's a comfort to have good friends around."

Grace set her cup down, bracing for the topic to come. "Speaking of neighbors, do the Eastons live nearby?"

Mrs. Chamberlain gave her a wary look. "Their hotel isn't far from here. But the family's residence is a good streetcar ride away."

"I understand the hotel is quite fancy." Grace had almost forgotten about the place where Rose had first met Frank.

"The finest in the city." Mrs. Chamberlain patted a napkin to her lips. "The Eastons are one of the most influential families in Toronto. And from what I hear, their house is a mansion—as grand as a castle."

Something in Grace shrank at the woman's words. She'd never really thought about Rose's in-laws being so well-regarded, but Mrs. Chamberlain made it sound like they were pillars of the community. How could she compete with that?

Grace reached for her handbag and took out one of Rose's letters. "They may be rich, but it doesn't mean they're honorable. If you hear what Rose had to say, perhaps you'll understand my reservations about them." She unfolded the well-worn pages and skimmed down to the pertinent paragraph. "'Now with Frank gone,'" she read, "'I worry that his family will try to take Christian from me. I can't allow my son to be raised by such people. Ones who disowned Frank because he chose a different life than what they expected. How could any parent treat their son like that? Promise me, Grace, if anything happens to me, you'll take Christian and raise him as your own.'" Grace's voice gave out, forcing her to stop. Had Rose already been ill when she wrote this? Had she worried even then that she might never see her son grow up? Grace folded the pages and raised her head. "Rose begged me to come, many times. If only I'd come sooner, she might still be alive."

"Oh, my dear, you mustn't think that way." Mrs. Chamberlain laid her hand on Grace's arm. "I've blamed myself as well, thinking I should have done more to help her."

"Now, Harriet. You did your best." The minister turned to Grace. "Rose was a very independent woman, determined to take care of herself and not accept charity. I did what I could to help, but in the end, God's will is all that mattered." A shadow passed over his features.

How could it be God's will that a little boy be left an orphan? Grace clutched the paper in her hand and struggled to rein in her emotions. "Was Rose . . . was she alone at the end?" The thought of her dear sister dying by herself in a strange hospital was almost more than she could bear.

"No, I was with her. I'd gone to give her a blessing, but when I saw how low she was, I decided to stay and pray. She woke once more before the illness finally took her. Looked right at me and asked me to tell her mother and sister that she loved them. Then she asked me to make sure Christian would be taken care of."

Tears spilled down Grace's cheek. She dashed them away. "Which is why I need to make sure my nephew is being treated the way Rose would have wanted." She leaned over the table. "Will you help me?"

"I would if I knew what to do." Compassion shone in his eyes. "It's not like you can march up to the Eastons' door and demand they hand the child over. They're Christian's legal guardians now."

Grace bit her lip, her mind spinning. "What if I hired a barrister? To see what rights I might have."

Reverend Burke eyed Mrs. Chamberlain who gave a subtle shake of her head. "I'm afraid the law will be on the Eastons' side. Short of proving them unfit, I don't see what good it would do. A legal battle would be expensive and wouldn't likely change anything. The Eastons are not only rich, they're powerful. They have connections with lawyers, judges, and politicians in the city and across the province."

The minister rose from his chair, his mouth set in a grim line. "I'd be very carefully around Oscar Easton if I were you. He's not a man to be trifled with."

Grace sagged on her chair, the air whooshing from her lungs, along with her hope of ever being able to bring Christian home.

Mrs. Chamberlain patted her arm. "Geoffrey's right. I'd think long and hard before taking on that family, Grace dear. It would only lead to heartache for all involved."

Grace swallowed her disappointment. "Very well," she said, more to appease them than anything else. "I'll give the matter due consideration before I take any action."

Reverend Burke smiled, the lines of concern around his eyes easing slightly. "And a big dose of prayer wouldn't hurt either."

Perhaps he was right. Perhaps challenging the Eastons legally would be a futile endeavor. Yet she couldn't just forget she had a nephew. Rose would never forgive her for going back on her promise. Not to mention her mother, who wanted her grandson in England more than ever after learning of Rose's death.

But what else could she do? If Grace were to call the Easton house or simply show up on their doorstep, what kind of information would she learn? Even if they invited her in, a brief visit wouldn't reveal the true state of affairs in the household. She needed a more long-term way to check on Christian.

For now, she would do as the minister suggested and think long and hard about her next move. In the meantime, she'd need a temporary job to support herself while planning a way to determine if the Eastons were indeed suitable guardians for Rose's son.

CHAPTER 4

In the Carmichaels' parlor, Andrew sipped the cocktail Cecilia had foisted on him and held back a grimace of distaste. Much to his father's chagrin, Andrew had never developed a taste for spirits, which made the endless rounds of social engagements his father attended each month all the more tedious.

"Oh, come on." Cecilia pouted while twisting a blond curl around her finger. "It's my birthday. Can't you please relax a little?" She frowned. "And for heaven's sake, get rid of these."

Before Andrew realized her intent, she lifted the spectacles from his face.

Heat spread up his neck. "Sorry. Forgot to take them off." She always hated when he wore his glasses. Said it made him look too bookish. He shoved the frames into the breast pocket of his jacket. One more reminder of his imperfections. He tried not to squint as he scanned the room, finally spotting his father who stood talking to Harrison Carmichael.

"What did you get me for my birthday?" Cecilia's flirtatious tone drew his attention back.

"You know it's not polite to ask." Andrew managed to summon a playful smile. "You'll have to wait and open it with the others." He gestured to the table against the far wall, laden with wrapped gifts.

"You sure you don't want to go somewhere private and open it alone?" She ran her hand down his arm.

He raised a brow. "I don't think that would go over well with your parents. Or the other guests."

Disappointment flashed over her attractive features, sparking a pang of regret in Andrew. He knew that she, as well as both sets of parents, had been hoping they would be engaged by now. But with the whole business of becoming Christian's guardian, Andrew's life had been more hectic than usual, and it hadn't afforded him much time to spend with her lately.

"Have I mentioned how lovely you look this evening?" Perhaps he could charm his way out of the situation. "The blue of your dress matches your eyes perfectly."

A coy smile bloomed. "Lovely enough for you to dance with me? I believe the orchestra is about to start."

With great effort, Andrew suppressed a cringe. Being the son of Toronto's biggest hotel mogul, he should be used to being the center of attention, yet it still chafed—every time. He pushed back his discomfort, set his drink on a nearby table, and bowed over her hand. "I'd be honored."

She laughed and pulled him onto the dance floor. As the music floated over the air, Andrew tightened his arm around Cecilia's slim frame. The scent of some new and likely expensive perfume drifted upward. Her fair curls tickled his jaw. Yet Andrew felt nothing. No zing of attraction. No quickening of the pulse. Nothing but a slight flutter of affection. He'd hoped by now his old feelings for her would have rekindled, yet so far they remained dormant. Could such a weak bond grow into one of love? Or at least into something that could sustain a marriage?

He smiled down at her. She was so beautiful. She could literally have the pick of all the eligible men in the city. But for reasons he couldn't fathom, she seemed bent on having him. Andrew held back a sigh. He owed it to her and his family to muster up more enthusiasm for this relationship.

As soon as the song ended, Cecilia tugged him over to the side of the room. "There's Rosalyn and Danica. We must say hello."

Andrew swallowed a groan. Cecilia's best friends were two of the most annoying gossips he'd ever encountered, but for some reason Cecilia held them in the highest regard. They'd been friends since their school days, all attending the same private girls' academy, and as such, he could not afford to alienate them.

After the women had hugged and kissed, he pasted on the expected smile. "Good evening, ladies."

"Good evening, Andrew. You look especially handsome tonight." Danica, an attractive brunette, dropped a mock curtsy in front of him.

"And you both look lovely as well."

Rosalyn laid a hand on his arm, giving him a coquettish smile. "Celia dearest, if you ever change your mind about this one, I'd be happy to step in and mend his broken heart."

"I would too," Danica added. "He wouldn't be lonely for long."

Andrew forced his lips to stay smiling, though his insides clenched. Never in a thousand lifetimes would he court the likes of these two. Yet could he honestly say Cecilia was any different?

"That won't be necessary for I don't intend to change my mind." Cecilia wound her arm through his in a possessive manner, laying her cheek against his shoulder.

"Does this mean we might expect a certain announcement tonight?" Rosalyn's eyes widened as she stared at them.

Cecilia laughed. "You'll have to ask Andrew. He *was* being mysterious about my birthday gift."

The women giggled, and Andrew struggled to hold on to his growing temper.

Did everyone believe an engagement was about to happen? If so, they were in for a huge disappointment. Andrew's gaze swung out over the crowd and landed on his father. He raised his glass to Andrew, then turned to say something to Mr. Carmichael. A sick feeling swirled in Andrew's stomach. Surely his father hadn't insinuated such a thing to Cecilia's parents. If and when he proposed, it would be in his own time and in his own manner. Not in front of hundreds of strangers. He'd better head off this problem before the situation got out of hand.

"Excuse me, ladies. I need to speak with my father for a moment."

"Hurry back, darling. It's almost time for the cake and presents."

He bent to kiss Cecilia's cheek. "I won't be long."

Andrew caught up with his father near the entrance to the room and waited for him to finish a conversation with one of his colleagues.

When the man drifted away, Father spotted Andrew and smiled. "There you are, Andrew. Having a good time?"

"Not especially. You know how I dislike these affairs."

"Think of it as part of the job. It's good business to mingle outside of work." Father leaned closer. "Speaking of mingling, I'm happy to see you and Cecilia spending so much time together. Harrison is hoping for an announcement soon."

Andrew fisted his hands into balls. "We've already discussed this. When I'm ready, you'll be the first to know. Other than Cecilia, that is."

His father shot an almost nervous glance across the room to where Harrison Carmichael stood and gave a slight shake of his head.

Andrew's temper simmered. "I don't know what you two are plotting, but this is *my* life, and I will determine when and *if* I marry." The band started up again, the jarring of the trumpet creating a line of tension at Andrew's temple. "If you'll excuse me, I've developed a raging headache. I must go and make my apologies to Cecilia."

"You can't leave yet. The cake hasn't even been served."

"No one will miss me, I'm sure. Don't bother sending for the car. I'd prefer to walk."

Andrew set his jaw as he made his way through the crowd to find Cecilia, bracing for her displeasure. It would be worth her annoyance to escape this infernal gathering. He'd send her some flowers as an apology in the morning.

Minutes later, after a chilly good-bye from a decidedly unhappy Cecilia, Andrew let himself out the front door and was soon striding down the Carmichaels' long drive. Once on the street, he loosened his tie and undid the top button of his shirt. Finally, he could breathe again. He inhaled deeply, relishing the hint of chimney smoke in the crisp night air. Springtime in the city was one of Andrew's favorite times of year, when the world awakened from its slumber to begin anew.

Exactly what Andrew hoped to do.

But which direction to take?

Until a few weeks ago, Andrew's course had seemed certain. He'd worked alongside his father in the hotel business since he graduated from university and was poised to take over whenever his father decided to retire. Granted that wouldn't be for some time yet. Father was still in his prime with no intention of slowing down. Especially not before he saw Andrew properly settled with a family of his own.

The news of Rose's death, however, had thrown the whole Easton family off-balance. Just when they'd been recovering from the shock of Frank's death, they'd learned he had a son. And now that son had lost his mother too. What else could they do but take the poor child in?

Andrew hadn't counted on the toll his guardianship of Christian would take on Cecilia, who had soon made it plain she resented the boy's intrusion in Andrew's life. Another reason why he had cooled their relationship temporarily until the situation with Christian became more certain. The baby had quickly found his way into Andrew's heart, and he couldn't imagine letting anyone else, save Virginia if circumstances allowed, raise the boy. If Cecilia wanted a future with Andrew, she would have to learn to accept Christian as part of their family. He hoped in time she would.

But for now, he was taking it one day at a time.

Andrew turned the corner onto a side street, deserted at this time of night, and looked up at the evening sky. A multitude of stars winked back at him. He paused to exhale, content to simply admire God's handiwork—something he hadn't done in a long time. Vivid recollections of his boyhood came to mind, when he used to lie out on the back lawn at night and try to memorize the constellations. It was during those moments of peace and awe that Andrew had felt closest to God.

Regret and a touch of guilt rippled through him. He needed to get back to those simpler pleasures. And he needed to pay more attention to his prayer life as well. He'd been remiss in seeking the Lord's guidance lately, a practice he needed more than ever if he was to become a parent to his orphaned nephew.

Andrew was so intent on the beauty of the sky that he almost walked past a lone figure sitting on the curb.

A loud sniff caught his attention. He stopped and glanced across the street, astounded to find that it was a young woman. What was she doing out here alone at this hour?

The slump of her shoulders screamed dejection. She clutched a purse on her lap, and one shoe lay discarded on the patch of grass beside her. The brim of her hat hid her features, all except her trembling bottom lip.

Immediately, Andrew's chivalrous instincts kicked in, and he crossed the road. "Excuse me, miss. Are you in need of assistance?"

Her head whipped up, revealing traces of tears on her cheeks. She dashed a gloved hand across her face. "Yes, thank you. I think I've sprained my ankle."

A distinct British accent laced her soft words.

He bent down in front of her. "May I?"

"Are you a doctor?" She blinked luminous brown eyes at him.

"No, but I've experienced my fair share of sprained limbs." He smiled. "I was a terrible athlete in school. Sat on the injured bench more than actually playing." He ran his fingers over her foot. Definite swelling. "May I ask what you're doing out here alone?"

"I was taking a walk and got turned around. I seemed to be going in circles and couldn't get my bearings. Then I went off the curb and twisted my foot. I tried to go on, but it's no use. I can't put any weight on it." She winced as he touched the bruised area. "Do you think it's broken?"

"Unlikely. But we should probably let a doctor determine that."

Andrew scratched his beard. "I don't live far from here. Let me get my car and drive you home."

"Oh no. That's too much trouble. If you could call me a cab, I'd be most grateful." She shivered and pulled her arms tighter around her middle.

"I doubt you'll have much luck getting a cab at this hour. They tend to congregate near Union Station. By the time one arrives, it could be ages. Besides, my conscience would never allow it." He rose, removed his jacket, and draped it over her shoulders. "Promise me you'll stay right here. I'll be back as soon as I can."

CHAPTER 5

May 15, 1914

I have met a wonderful man. His name is Frank. He's handsome and funny, and he's crazy about me! He's taken me out a few times, though I've never let him come back to Mrs. Chamberlain's. She doesn't approve of gentlemen callers. But I think even she would approve of Frank if she got to know him. As Mum would say, he can charm the birds from the trees.

Grace tried to ignore the throbbing in her foot and figure out another solution to her dilemma. One that didn't involve getting into an automobile with a very attractive stranger. If she were back in her hometown, she wouldn't hesitate to accept his offer. But here in this urban labyrinth, where a person couldn't discern north from south, accepting help from a strange man didn't seem a wise idea.

But what other choice did she have? She couldn't walk with her injured foot, and not one person had come by in the past hour. Except for this gentleman.

And a gentleman he was indeed, offering her his jacket. The warmth from his body still clung to the material that hugged her shoulders, and the woodsy scent of some type of soap or cologne surrounded her. Surely someone so kind wouldn't have ill intentions toward her.

She dropped her head into her hands. What had she been thinking, going out alone at night? Mrs. Chamberlain had tried to dissuade her, but once again, Grace's reckless nature had taken over. "I'll be fine," she'd said. "I just need a bit of fresh air."

While I find the Eastons' house.

She wanted to at least see where Christian was living and hoped she might catch a glimpse of him through one of the windows. Instead she hadn't been able to get near the fortress, so high were the stone walls surrounding it, and she didn't dare walk up the drive for fear of being caught.

After waiting for over twenty minutes for someone to come or go through the large iron gates, Grace had given up and attempted to return home. Only to become hopelessly lost in the maze of streets, then injuring her foot on top of it.

A car swung around the corner and headed toward her. She sucked in a loud breath and murmured a quick prayer for protection.

The auto came to a halt, and the man jumped out. He dashed over and offered Grace his hand. "Here, let me help you stand."

She hesitated, but finally placed her hand in his. With his assistance, she rose awkwardly on one foot, teetering until his other hand wrapped around her waist to steady her. He helped her over to the car and into the passenger seat.

Once he secured her door, he rounded the front and got inside. "All set?"

She leaned back and nodded.

"What's the address?" He shifted gears and the car lurched forward.

Pain shot up her leg. "Jarvis Street. Near Isabella."

He turned the most startling blue eyes on her and gave a low whistle. "You did get lost, didn't you? Where were you headed?"

"Nowhere in particular." She could hardly admit she was spying on one of the wealthiest families in Toronto. For all she knew, this man could be the Eastons' next-door neighbor. "I was out for a bit of exercise and fresh air. I should have been more careful, being new to the city."

"Judging by your accent, I'd say you're from England?"

"I am."

"What brings you all the way to Canada?" The intensity of his gaze scattered her thoughts like a bunch of spilled marbles.

Grace focused out the window at the dark street, illuminated by the car headlights and a few well-spaced street lamps. She certainly wouldn't discuss her private affairs with a complete stranger. "I've always wanted to travel, and I'd heard great things about Toronto." Not a total falsehood. Rose always did praise her new home.

"So you came here by yourself?"

Grace fought a sudden surge of homesickness and merely nodded.

"Quite a brave thing to do."

"I suppose." She didn't feel very brave at the moment. More foolish than anything else. How was she going to look for work now with a sprained ankle? She'd have to wait for it to heal.

"My name's Andrew, by the way. And you are?"

"Grace." Despite his friendly manner, something held her back from revealing too much. She had no wish to talk about the real reason she came here or about her sister's death. "You have a lovely automobile. What kind is it?" She knew nothing of cars but talking about it might keep him from questioning her.

"It's a Rolls-Royce. My father gave it to me when he ordered a newer model for himself, though it's a little ostentatious for my taste. I prefer something simpler, like a Model-T."

"I'm afraid I don't know much about cars." She shrugged. "Not many people own them in the town I come from."

"Then Toronto must seem overwhelming to you."

"It does indeed."

"Are you working here or on vacation?"

She studied his handsome profile, the sweep of his golden brown hair over his forehead, the regal nose, and the strong jawline emphasized by a precisely trimmed beard. He wore an air of confidence, like one who knew his place in the world. What would he think of a woman who'd journeyed halfway across the globe with little or no planning, who now found herself adrift on a sea of uncertainty?

"I'm doing some work for the church. The minister has been very kind. He's offered to help me find a more permanent position."

"I'm sure you'll find something soon." He turned onto a street that at last looked familiar. "This is Jarvis," he said. "What number are you?"

Grace peered up the road. "You could just drop me at the corner."

Andrew frowned. "Not with that ankle. I'll take you right to the door."

"There's no need, I assure you."

"And how will you walk the rest of the way?"

"I'll be fine."

"Really? Are you planning on hopping on one foot?" His faintly amused gaze caught hers.

"It's just that . . . I'm already past curfew, and if my landlady sees a man bringing me home . . . well, I don't want her to think badly of me." Heat flooded Grace's cheeks. What would dear Mrs. Chamberlain think of her after this escapade? Would she ask her to leave for breaking the rules of the house?

Andrew slowed the car to the curb. "I'm sure she'll understand when she sees your ankle. I'd be happy to come in and explain."

"No, really. You've been more than kind already. You can bring me to the door, but I'll go in alone." She held his stare, willing him to yield.

He let out a loud breath. "Very well."

She gave him the address, and he continued down the road until he reached the boardinghouse. As soon as he pulled up the brake, he ran around to assist her.

With his help, she made it up the walkway and the few steps to the door. She leaned against the entrance while she fumbled in her purse for the key. Despite her unsteady hands, she managed to open the door, and then turned to him. "Thank you ever so much. I don't know how I'd have made it home without you."

A slow smile spread over his handsome face. "Glad to be of assistance. You're sure you can make it from here?"

"Yes, thank you."

"Then I will bid you good-night." He tipped his hat and started down the walkway. At the gate, he looked back at her. "I hope you enjoy your stay here, Grace. For future outings, though, you might consider buying a map of the city." He winked and turned toward the car.

At a complete loss for words, Grace watched until he pulled away, then limped inside the house.

The next morning, Andrew tapped his pencil on his desktop, his thoughts consumed with the stranded girl he'd helped last night. Why he should be giving her any further consideration was beyond his comprehension. But every time he forced his mind back to Cecilia, where it belonged, an uncomfortable comparison kept creeping in. Cecilia, attired in her beautiful evening gown with jewels glistening at her throat and ears, and Grace in a plain wool skirt and jacket that were neither fashionable nor particularly flattering. Yet even in her simplicity, with only a hint of dark brown hair peeking from beneath a straw hat, Grace had appeared almost noble. And when he stared into those intriguing brown eyes, he'd barely been able to look away.

Andrew's door opened, and his father stalked in. At the scowl on his face, Andrew straightened in his chair. "Good morning, Father. What can I do for you?"

"You can find a way to make up for the mess you created last night." His father didn't bother sitting but stood with his arms crossed.

"I assume you're referring to my leaving the party early?"

"You let a fine opportunity slip through your fingers, Andrew. Once you'd left, all the bachelors swooped in to rain attention on Cecilia." He leaned over the desk as if to emphasize his next point. "One man in particular monopolized her for the rest of the evening." Father paused, obviously waiting for a reaction.

Andrew kept his expression bland. "I didn't expect Cecilia to sit in a corner all night because I'd gone home. It was her birthday, after all."

"Then I guess you don't care that Paul Edison spent the rest of the night dancing with her."

Andrew's fingers tightened on the pencil in his hand. Of all people, why did it have to be Father's new junior executive? Bad enough the guy was trying to impress Father at the office by attempting to undermine Andrew whenever possible and showcase his own work in a more advantageous light. But moving in on the girl Andrew was courting was low, even for him. Andrew's jaw clenched.

"Ah, that finally got your attention." His father's satisfied smirk only added to Andrew's annoyance. "I trust you'll do something about it. A nice bouquet of flowers might go a long way to restoring Cecilia's good graces." He paused. "But an engagement ring would be even better."

With a last pointed look, his father left the room.

Andrew dropped his head into his hands. He'd forgotten all about sending flowers this morning. It seemed a personal apology was in order. If he were lucky, a bouquet of roses might smooth out Cecilia's ruffled feathers. If not, a new piece of jewelry should do it.

Anything other than an engagement ring.

CHAPTER 6

May 31, 1914
Dear Grace,

Tonight Frank kissed me for the first time. I'm floating on air.

I've never felt this way before. I think I might be falling in love.

On Mrs. Chamberlain's insistence, Grace spent the first two days after spraining her ankle on the sofa in the parlor with her foot on a pillow, while the poor woman waited on her hand and foot. On the third day, when the swelling had lessened and Grace could get around better, she'd sat at the kitchen table and helped peel potatoes and chop vegetables.

Mrs. C.—as the woman insisted Grace call her—was kindly allowing her to stay for a reduced fee until she got a proper job. And Reverend Burke had been most understanding about her injury, saying not to rush her recovery, that the chores at the church could wait until she was on the mend.

After dinner on the fifth day of confinement, Grace helped her landlady with the dishes in the homey kitchen. Her ankle, though still tender, was improving every day and she looked forward to attending church on Sunday.

"You're not required to do manual labor, you know." Mrs. C. handed her a plate to dry.

"I don't mind. There's only so much sitting with my foot up I can stand without going mad."

"Your ankle seems much improved."

"It is." Grace smiled as she stacked the clean dishes in the cupboard. "Your nursing skills have proven very effective."

"I'm glad." Mrs. C. dried her hands on her apron. "If you're up to it, how would you like to join us at the Newcomers' meeting tonight?"

Grace's hand stilled on the glass she was drying. "It's kind of you to offer, but I don't think so."

"I know you're still grieving for Rose, but getting out of this house for a couple of hours will do you a world of good. Who knows? You might even make a new friend." Sympathy softened her landlady's features. "Everyone can use more friends, Grace. Especially ones with a similar background."

Grace doubted she'd have anything in common with those people, yet she couldn't bear to disappoint Mrs. C., not after she'd been so kind to her. She summoned a smile. "All right. I'd be happy to go with you."

An hour later, seated on a hard folding chair in the church basement, Grace balanced a teacup on her lap and looked around at the diverse group. Reverend Burke had led the meeting with a short prayer service and then spoke about some job opportunities in a local factory. Some of the members shared their experiences over the past few weeks, both good and bad. Grace gradually relaxed, realizing it did feel good to be around people from home, though not everyone was from Britain. Some were from Italy, and a few came from Poland and the Ukraine. Yet everyone laughed and chatted like old friends.

"I can't believe you're from Sussex and I had to come all the way to Canada to meet you." The man on her left, one Mrs. C. had introduced as Ian Miller, regarded her through very thick lenses that distorted the appearance of his eyes into tiny pea holes.

"That is a coincidence." Grace turned her head, trying to shrug off her discomfort at the intense attention.

"I've been coming to these meetings for five years now. I never imagined meeting anyone as lovely as you." He gave a nervous laugh.

Grace smiled and scanned the room for Mrs. C., who waved at her from the other side of the room where she and another lady served the refreshments. If not for Grace's ankle, which had started to ache as it often did later in the day, she'd have hopped up to help them.

"Are you looking for work, Miss Abernathy?"

"As a matter of fact, yes. Though this ankle injury has set me back a bit."

"I work in the CPR building on Yonge Street. I can keep an eye out for jobs if you like."

She frowned. "What is a CPR building?"

"Canadian Pacific Railway." Mr. Miller fished in his jacket pocket and pulled out a small card. "I actually work in the telegraph office on the second floor. If you ever need to send a telegram, I'll make sure you get the best possible service. Maybe even a discount." He pressed the card into her hand with a myopic wink.

Despite herself, Grace laughed. "Thank you, Mr. Miller. I'll keep that in mind." She placed the card in her purse while he watched, just to prove she meant it.

"I hope you don't think me too forward, but I know what it's like to be new in a strange city, so far from home. If you ever need a friend to talk to . . . or for anything really, please think of me."

The sincerity in his voice touched Grace's heart. It brought to mind her brother, Peter, who was always so thoughtful and attentive to others, and she berated herself for thinking unkindly of the man simply because of his looks and his overeagerness. She smiled at him. "That's very kind of you. I might take you up on that one day."

"Good. I'll hold you to it." He beamed at her as though she'd just promised to marry him.

When the gathering came to an end, Mr. Miller helped her to her feet. "It was very nice to meet you, Miss Abernathy. I hope to see you at our next meeting."

As he tipped his hat politely and walked away, warmth spread through Grace's chest. Mrs. C. had been right about coming tonight. You could never have too many friends.

During her week of recuperation, Grace hadn't managed to come up with a single new strategy to meet her nephew. Because of that, as soon as she was able to walk without a limp, she'd resorted to spying on the Easton estate again. Not exactly a crackerjack plan, but short of breaking into the house, she couldn't think of anything else. Surely if she persisted, she'd eventually catch a glimpse of her nephew, though what good that would do, she didn't know.

Today was the third day in a row Grace had spent hours lurking on the street across from the mansion. The previous two days, she'd come in the morning with no luck, so today she decided to try the afternoon. She'd just about resigned herself to giving up for the day when the iron gates opened and a young woman dressed in a stylish plum jacket and matching hat pushed a pram onto the sidewalk.

Grace's heart began to race. Every instinct told her that Christian was inside the pram.

As discreetly as possible, Grace followed on the opposite side of the street, grateful her ankle was healed enough that she could keep up. Several blocks later, the woman turned onto a side street. Before she could lose sight of her, Grace crossed the road and trailed her at a respectable distance until they entered a park.

Grace followed her in, slowing her stride to make it appear like she was out for a leisurely stroll. Thankfully, there were several people around—some walking, some sharing a picnic on a blanket under the trees, others playing ball with their children. Enough activity that Grace wouldn't seem out of place.

She kept a close watch on the pram as she strolled. After two times around the park, the woman stopped to sit on a bench. Grace slowed her gait and meandered past, using all her self-control not to stare. Instead, she headed to the next bench and sat down. The beginning of an ache in her ankle told her she would pay for overdoing it today.

Grace pretended to watch the activities of the children playing on a swing set, while stealing side glances at the woman who had taken out a book to read. Was this Christian's nanny? If not, could it be Rose's sister-in-law? Grace tried to recall any details Rose had written in her letters. She had mentioned Frank had a brother and sister but little else, talking mainly about the overbearing Mr. Easton, who had disowned Frank for marrying a penniless foreigner.

A few minutes later, a baby's cry sounded. Grace's attention snapped to the pram. The woman laid her book on the bench and reached into the carriage. Smiling, she lifted the child out. She kissed the baby and snuggled him to her chest, arranging a blanket around him. Within seconds, the child quieted. The two seemed to share an intimate bond that would indicate more than a few weeks' acquaintance. Maybe this wasn't her nephew after all. Maybe this was the woman's own child.

Grace had to find out somehow. Before she could talk herself out of her crazy plan, she rose and approached the pair.

The woman looked up as Grace neared. With her raven hair and wide gray eyes, she was quite beautiful.

"Hello." Grace pasted on her friendliest smile. "I couldn't help but notice your lovely baby. He's adorable."

The woman beamed back. "Thank you. We certainly think so."

"Your husband must be very proud." Grace held her breath and waited for the response.

The woman shook her head. "No husband, I'm afraid. This is my nephew."

Grace's knees began to shake. She moved closer and sat on the edge of the bench, leaving a good space between her and the woman. "How wonderful to be such a doting aunt." She peered over at the perfect little face, and her breath seized.

Large blue eyes, exactly like her sister's, stared back at her.

This was Rose's son. Grace knew it as surely as she knew her own name. Foolish tears sprang to her eyes, and she blinked hard to keep them at bay.

The woman studied her. "Do you have any children?" she asked.

"Not yet, but I hope to someday."

The lines of concern on the woman's forehead eased. "Me too. A whole houseful of them. In the meantime, little Christian is the next best thing. Aren't you, darling?" She gazed at the child with absolute adoration.

Grace's heart squeezed. She'd been thinking of the Eastons as the enemy. It never occurred to her that she could have so much in common with one of them. Yet she and this woman had both lost someone dear, and both loved this little boy—the only tie they had left to their siblings.

Grace squared her shoulders and shook off the sentimentality. She couldn't afford to lose sight of her goal. "Are you sitting for the baby's parents?" She kept her focus on the child's cherubic face.

After several seconds, a soft sigh escaped. "Tragically, no. Both his parents are dead." She pressed a kiss to the top of his head. "But we will make sure Christian grows up with all the love he needs." She laid her cheek against the boy's until he started to squirm.

Grace swallowed the lump of emotion that blocked her own throat. "I'm so sorry for your loss." *And for mine.*

"Thank you."

"It's quite a responsibility to take in your nephew. Are you going to raise him yourself?" Grace couldn't imagine Mrs. Easton, a wealthy middle-aged woman, wanting to take on such a formidable task. She'd likely leave it to her daughter.

"Actually, my older brother has become Christian's guardian."

"Oh." Grace couldn't hide her surprise. She'd never considered that possibility. Maybe her brother was married and felt he and his wife would make the best guardian for the boy.

"If it were up to me, I would take Christian in an instant." A shadow of sorrow passed over the woman's pretty face. "However, circumstances in my life dictate otherwise." She gave a shrug. "I'll have to wait for a child of my own one day."

"Did his parents die in an accident?" Grace asked softly.

"No. His mother died recently from the flu, and my brother . . ." Her voice broke. "He died in the war." She sat the boy up straighter and hugged him.

For the first time, Grace's heart filled with compassion for the Eastons. No matter what family rifts had ensued, they must have loved Frank very much and mourned him as much as Grace mourned Rose. "I'm so sorry. I lost a brother in the war too, so I know a bit of what you're going through."

Horror flooded the woman's features. "Oh, forgive me. Here I am going on about my own troubles when you've been through the same thing."

"No need to apologize. We're among thousands who lost someone we love in the war. I'm glad this wee boy has family to look after him. An orphanage is no place to grow up." Without thinking, Grace reached out a finger and touched the soft satin of the baby's cheek. Just a quick brush, then she pulled her hand away before the temptation to linger could take hold.

"Well, I shouldn't take any more of your time." Grace rose from the bench. "I'm glad I found this park. I've been taking my daily walks on the streets, but it's much nicer to stroll among the trees and watch the children playing."

"Are you new to Canada?" The look of sadness was replaced by one of curiosity.

"Yes, I've only been here a few weeks. So far I'm finding Toronto to be a fascinating city."

"That it is. I, however, am excited to be traveling to Europe later this summer."

"Europe? How . . . how nice." Grace fought to calm a spurt of panic. Were the Eastons leaving Toronto? Would they take Christian with them? "Is your family going on vacation?"

"No. I'm going with friends of the family. It will be hard to leave this little fellow though, now that I've become so attached."

She kissed the baby's cheek and placed him back into the pram. "We're in the process of hiring a nanny before I go." She arranged the blankets, then straightened. "Not having much luck, I'm afraid. All the candidates are unsuitable in one way or another. My mother has very high standards."

Grace's palms grew damp as a thousand thoughts flew through her mind at once. She pressed her lips together. Should she say anything? The woman might think her too forward. Yet if she didn't take advantage of the situation . . .

"It so happens I'm looking for a full-time position." The words burst forth of their own volition.

"Really?" The woman gave Grace a curious stare. "Do you have any experience with children?"

"A little. I've minded my neighbor's children and taught Sunday school in my home parish." Grace's nerve endings shimmied like an electric charge had passed through her.

"Sunday school? So you're a churchgoer then?"

"I am. In fact, right now I'm doing odd jobs for the rector of Holy Trinity Church. I'm sure Reverend Burke would give me a reference, if that would help." She held her breath, a hand pressed to her stomach.

"It would." She studied Grace. "You obviously love babies or you wouldn't have stopped to talk. Would you want to be a live-in nanny?"

Grace's pulse raced. Living in the Easton household? She'd never dreamed of such a possibility. She thought of her cozy room in the boardinghouse and the unexpected friendship she'd developed with Mrs. Chamberlain. She'd miss their cups of tea in the evening before they retired. But for a chance to be close to her nephew, Grace could do almost anything.

"It sounds like the perfect job to me." She gave her best smile, hoping to convince the woman that despite being a total stranger, she would be a good candidate for the position.

"You know, you might be just the type of person we're looking for. What's your name?"

"Grace A . . ." She bit her lip. She couldn't give her surname or they'd connect her to Rose. Yet the idea of lying had acid rising at the back of her throat. For the time being, she would have to shove her conscience aside. "Foley. Grace Foley." The only name that came to mind was her aunt's married name.

"Foley. Isn't that an Irish name?"

Grace froze. "It is. There's some Irish on my father's side." She gave a nervous laugh, and the woman nodded.

"Well, Grace, I'll see if I can arrange an interview with my mother. Is there a phone number where I could reach you?"

"I can give you my landlady's number. Her name is Mrs. Chamberlain." Grace took a pencil and a scrap of paper from her purse and quickly jotted down the number that Mrs. C. had insisted she memorize. "I'm usually home in the evenings."

"Wonderful. I'll call you tonight with a time and the address. And don't forget to bring that reference." She smiled as she gripped the pram's handle and swung it onto the path. "Oh, by the way, my name is Virginia Easton."

"Thank you, Virginia." Grace waved as the woman headed out of the park, then sank back onto the bench, her head swimming with the ramification of her deception. She hated not being honest with Virginia, but if she'd given her real name, she'd never have been considered for the position and would have lost the opportunity to learn the true circumstances of Christian's life. Surely something as simple as hiding her identity was justified under the circumstances.

Lord, I don't know if this is a miracle or the biggest mistake of my life, but I'm going to have to trust you to guide me through it.

CHAPTER 7

June 9, 1914

Did I mention Frank is the son of Mr. Easton, the owner of the hotel where I work? We're trying to keep our relationship a secret for now. Frank recently ended an engagement to someone his father wanted him to marry, and Frank wants to wait before telling him about us. He's worried it might affect my job. Isn't he thoughtful?

Andrew stopped outside his father's office and paused to let his temper settle. Paul Edison had summoned him for an unscheduled meeting, wreaking havoc yet again with Andrew's timetable. He'd hoped to finish up his work and get away early in order to sit in on the nanny interview his mother had scheduled this afternoon. But this interruption meant that likely wouldn't happen.

What scheme did Edison have up his sleeve this time? Something designed to make Andrew look incompetent in his father's eyes, most likely.

He ran a hand over his hair, adjusted his spectacles, then entered the office.

Edison lounged in the chair across from Father's desk as if he owned the space. His slicked-back blond hair and light blue eyes gave him the look of a playboy. Handsome enough to turn the ladies' heads and charming enough to sway the men.

"Andrew, come in. Paul and I were just discussing an idea, and we'd like your input."

Paul's arrogant expression brought flashes of Frank's smirk to mind. Frank had always been the golden boy, his father's pride and joy. The one who could do no wrong.

"Why can't you be more like your brother?" Father used to say. *"Talk to the customers, make them feel special. Watch how Frank does it and try to imitate him."*

His father could never understand that Andrew didn't have the kind of gregarious personality his brother did. That while Frank craved the limelight, Andrew preferred to remain in the background, quietly going about his business.

As painful as Frank's estrangement had been, at least Andrew no longer had to face constant comparisons that proved him lacking. Foolishly, he'd believed he would now have his father's full attention, the chance to gain his approval at last—a notion that had lasted only until Edison had joined the company as a junior executive.

Andrew took a seat. "What is this idea?" Whatever it was, it had better not require a large infusion of cash.

"I'll let Paul explain." His father sat back in his chair, his hands folded across his stomach.

Edison stood and straightened his jacket as though preparing for a theatrical performance. "Now that the war's been over for six months, people are ready for a celebration. I think we should host a gala—a victory celebration, if you will—in honor of our winning the war, and in recognition of the soldiers who fought for our country." He got more enthused as he went on, his expression animated. "We'll invite a few key veterans and make a show of presenting them with some sort of tribute. We'll charge an exorbitant entry fee, which no one will mind, because it's for a good cause." He winked at them. "It will be a great way to bring the community together and boost the city's morale. Not to mention an opportunity to raise a lot of money."

Andrew's gut tightened. "So you want to exploit the soldiers who have survived the horrors of war—something we can't even imagine—for your own selfish purposes."

Edison's face darkened. "Of course *you* couldn't imagine it, staying here in the comfort of your family estate. But speaking as one who experienced a taste of battle and lived to tell about it, I can assure you I won't be exploiting anything."

Andrew clenched his back teeth together. Trust Edison to poke at Andrew's sore spot—the fact that the army had turned him down because of a physical limitation, while everyone else he knew had passed with flying colors.

"The profits would be split evenly," Edison continued. "Half for the veterans, half for the hotel. A benefit to everyone involved. And, as I said, it would bring the community together in a positive way."

"I, for one, am in full support of the idea." Father leaned forward over the desk to focus his attention on Andrew. "And I expect you to extend Paul your full cooperation. We'll need to set a date, and get some of the other staff involved. But first and foremost, we'll need to set up a budget. That's where you come in, Andrew. I want you to work with Paul to decide how much capital we'll need. Give him whatever funds are necessary to get this event off the ground."

So this was why his father had brought him in. Not because he valued Andrew's opinion, since it was obvious he'd already decided to go ahead with Edison's proposal no matter what Andrew thought. He pushed to his feet with a grunt. "Fine."

Edison raised a hand. "Before you go, I have one other idea." He turned, a smug glint in his eye. "I believe Cecilia Carmichael might be the perfect one to work with me on this project. She has a flair for the dramatic and is used to throwing lavish parties. This would only be on a slightly grander scale."

Steam built in Andrew's chest. He clenched his hands at his

side. "We have employees who are far more qualified than Miss Carmichael. I fail to see—"

"A splendid idea," Father said. "And I'm sure we'd all enjoy having Cecilia around."

Before Andrew could protest further, a knock sounded at the door and their secretary entered. "I'm sorry to interrupt, sir. There's a call for Andrew." The woman had taken to calling him by his Christian name because it was too confusing with two Mr. Eastons on the same floor.

"Thank you, Martha. I'll be right there."

As he stalked into his office seconds later, he paused for a breath before picking up the receiver. Whoever it was did not need to bear the brunt of his foul mood. "Andrew Easton here."

"Drew, it's Ginny. I need a favor."

Grace walked up the long drive toward the Easton estate, tension twisting her stomach into knots. This could be a disastrous idea on so many levels, yet she couldn't pass up the chance to possibly become Christian's nanny and see for herself that the boy was well cared for. She owed it to Rose and to their mother.

Even if she didn't get the position, she'd have managed to see inside the house where her nephew now resided. That would be worth all these nerves. She hoped.

Her pace slowed as she approached the front entrance. Afternoon shadows filtered over the house and surrounding property, giving it a slightly ominous feel. The building, even more imposing close up, was as far removed from her tiny cottage back home as the stars were from the moon. Three stories of grand white walls towered above her. A portico with two stately columns sheltered the entrance. She climbed the few stairs and stared at the impressive carved door. Not wishing to be late for the appointment Virginia had so kindly arranged with Mrs. Easton, Grace smoothed down her jacket. She hoped the navy blue suit she'd chosen would give the impression of a trustworthy woman. With a last deep inhale, she knocked.

A few seconds later, a middle-aged woman dressed in a uniform answered. "May I help you?"

"Good afternoon. I'm Grace . . . Foley. I have an appointment with Mrs. Easton."

The woman opened the door wider. "Please come in. I'll inform Mrs. Easton that you're here."

"Thank you." Grace stepped into the impressive entranceway and waited on the mat.

While the woman disappeared down a hall, Grace took in the elegant interior of the residence. Rich burgundy carpets lined the wooden floors. Warm oak railings framed the staircase. Every wall showcased paintings of all sizes, landscape and still-life mixed with what appeared to be family portraits. She'd never been inside such a grand house before. Squeezing the handle of her purse, she prayed for God's strength to sustain her through this interview.

The housekeeper reappeared. "Right this way. Mr. Easton will see you now."

"Mr. Easton?" Grace forced her feet to follow the quick-moving woman. "I-I was supposed to meet with *Mrs.* Easton."

"I'm afraid Mrs. Easton is under the weather, so Mr. Easton will be filling in." She reached an open door and poked her head in. "Miss Foley, sir." Then she gestured for Grace to enter.

Grace had only a moment to swallow her panic at having to face the dreaded patriarch of the Easton family—the one who'd disowned his own son for marrying beneath him and who'd caused Rose such despair. Squaring her shoulders, she entered the room.

Her gaze swung from the floor-to-ceiling bookcase to the massive oak desk that dominated the room, then finally to the man sitting behind it. He wore a charcoal gray suit and striped tie. A shock of light brown hair swept back off his forehead, and dark-framed eyeglasses highlighted a pair of unforgettable blue eyes.

Her jaw dropped open. The same man who had rescued her last week stared at her now, appearing as stunned as she.

He removed his glasses, set them on the desk, and rose. "You're Miss Foley? The candidate for the nanny position?"

"I . . . Um, that is . . . yes." Her tangled thoughts fell over one another as she attempted to make sense of the situation.

Andrew gave her a warm smile. "What a pleasant coincidence. Please sit down."

"Th-thank you." She stumbled forward and sank onto the chair, grateful to be off her shaking legs.

"So, I understand you met my sister at the park. Mother told me Virginia was the one who presented you as a potential candidate." One eyebrow quirked. "A somewhat unorthodox manner to get an interview, I must say."

She held her gaze steady under his scrutiny, and despite the perspiration dampening her back, attempted a light laugh. "Yes, it was most unexpected. I stopped to admire the baby, and we struck up a conversation. When I found out she was looking for a full-time nanny, it seemed like a God-given opportunity."

"I remember you told me you were seeking work." He frowned suddenly. "How is your ankle? You didn't walk all the way here, did you?"

"It's fully healed, thank you. And I took the streetcar most of the way."

"That's good news." The lines in his forehead eased. "Well, let's begin the interview, shall we? Do you have a letter of reference?"

"I do." Grace opened her handbag and pulled out the envelope containing Reverend Burke's glowing report. He'd been kind enough to write it for her last night on very short notice.

Andrew removed the letter and began to read.

Grace tried to breathe normally as she waited, while her mind whirled with the implication that this handsome stranger, the one who had rescued her that night, was little Christian's uncle and guardian. No wonder he was so quick to retrieve his auto. He'd been only a block or two from home.

Andrew laid the paper on the desk. "Reverend Burke certainly has nothing but the highest praise for you."

"He's been very kind."

"His letter speaks to your work ethic and your character, but do you have any experience with children?"

This time Grace was prepared for the question. "Not formally. But I did teach Sunday school at our church for several years. And I've minded a good number of the neighbors' children."

"What about babies in particular?"

Grace hesitated. She desperately wanted this chance to spend time with her nephew, but she couldn't outright lie and claim to have experience that she didn't. "I adore babies," she began. "Some of the neighbors' children I looked after were infants, and though I might not be an expert, I can surely learn whatever I need to. I'm more than willing to be trained."

"Fair enough." He picked up a pen and poised it over the paper in front of him. "Why don't you tell me a little of your background."

"Right." She clasped her handbag tighter. "I grew up in a small town near Southampton. My father worked in the shipyards, but he died when I was fourteen. I had planned to go to college, but my mother became ill and needed me at home to care for her." Grace paused. She wanted to give a semi-complete picture of her life in England, yet certain details she would keep private. Most especially her connection to Rose.

"Did you have a job there?"

"I worked part-time in our town's general store when I could, depending on how Mum was faring. They were very understanding about the situation."

"I see." He tapped his pen, a wrinkle forming between his brows. "What made you leave home and travel all the way to Canada then?"

Grace licked her dry lips, willing the answer she'd rehearsed to come out with ease. "I came at my mother's insistence. I suppose she felt bad for all the time I'd spent looking after her, putting my life on hold to care for her." There, not a lie. Everything she'd said was true.

"So her health is improved?"

"Somewhat. She agreed to stay with her sister. It was the only way I'd leave her."

"And what was your plan when you arrived?"

Beads of perspiration snaked down her back. "I was initially to stay with a relative but that . . . fell through." She gestured to the letter. "I'd heard of Reverend Burke and went to meet him. He does his best to provide assistance to newcomers to the city."

"Sounds like a good ally to have." Andrew tilted his head, lips pursed. "If I might be so bold, what about romantic attachments? There's no husband or suitor you've left behind, is there?" His gaze narrowed on her naked left hand.

A bolt of indignation shot through her. "I hardly think that's relevant."

He held up a hand. "Forgive me. I don't wish to invade your privacy, but I must be sure you don't have reason to leave, such as a potential suitor showing up to entice you back home."

Aware of her racing heart and her rising temper, Grace inhaled and released a slow breath. "I assure you, I have no romantic attachments. No one who might come after me as you insinuated."

Crimson stained his cheeks. "I beg your pardon for making you feel uncomfortable, but I had to ask."

She gave a tight nod.

Andrew cleared his throat. "May I assume then that you're planning to stay in Canada?"

Grace hesitated. What were her intentions? She hadn't thought any farther ahead than this interview. But if she managed to get the position and developed a bond with her nephew, she'd stay as long as necessary. "I hope to, yes."

"Good. Because I couldn't let Christian become attached to a caregiver only to have her disappear. Not after losing his mother." A shadow passed over his features.

"I would never do that, Mr. Easton." She leaned forward in her earnestness, fighting the rise of emotion in her chest. "I would treat that child as a most precious gift from God." All she wanted to do was cuddle that sweet boy and shower him with all the love Rose would have given him.

"I believe you would." His smile eased the lines of tension on his face. "And please call me Andrew. When anyone addresses me as Mr. Easton, I always look to see if my father is in the room."

She laughed. "Very well, Andrew."

As the tension in her muscles began to relax, guilt seeped through her system. Andrew seemed like a good person, someone who might understand why she felt it necessary to perpetrate the deception she was planning. The honest thing to do was to tell him the truth and ask her questions about the boy in a straightforward manner. Make it clear that she only wanted Christian to be raised in a loving family.

She bit her lip and rolled the handle of her purse between her fingers.

But what if Andrew wasn't as nice as he appeared? What if he would be furious that she'd come here under false pretenses? What if his father showed up and had her removed from the house before she could even explain herself?

That would mean leaving her sweet nephew here and returning to England, never being part of his life.

She couldn't take that chance. What she was doing wasn't entirely honest, but she couldn't give up this opportunity.

She lifted her gaze to find Andrew studying her.

He quickly looked down at the papers on his desk and cleared his throat again. "I believe in being upfront about things," he said, "so I'll tell you that Mother and I have interviewed at least a dozen women for this position. While many appeared to have wonderful qualifications, each had some quality I didn't care for. I'm looking for a younger person with enough energy to play with Christian and take him on outings. Someone who would be the next best thing to a mother." He pressed his lips together and seemed to fight to collect himself.

She shifted on her chair. "May I ask a question?"

"Certainly."

"I presume you're not married?"

"Correct."

"What would happen if you were to marry one day?" If he could question her long-term plans, she could do the same.

"You're worried about the security of the position?"

"Yes."

"When the time comes, I hope my future wife will love Christian as much as I, and want to be a mother to him. But getting married wouldn't necessarily negate having a nanny. Many members of our social circle employ nannies or governesses for their children." He paused. "However, in the event that I no longer required your services, you would be well compensated and given ample time to find a new position."

She drew in a full breath and released it. "That seems more than fair."

Andrew rose and came around from behind the desk. "I will have to discuss your application with my family. How may I contact you once we've reached a decision?"

"You can telephone me at my landlady's. Or leave a message with Reverend Burke."

"Fine. If you would leave me your landlady's name and number, I think we can conclude our interview." He passed her a piece of paper and a pen.

She quickly jotted down Mrs. Chamberlain's phone number, then rose and smoothed the wrinkles from her skirt.

He held out his hand. "Thank you, Grace. I'll be in touch as soon as we've made a decision."

She placed her hand in his. Warmth surrounded her, leaving her with a feeling that Andrew Easton was someone trustworthy and good. "Thank you. I look forward to hearing from you."

As she made her way back to the streetcar, Grace inhaled deeply, willing her nerves to abate. Despite her shock at Andrew's identity, she'd made it through the interview well enough. Her fate now rested in God's hands. She would have to accept whatever the Eastons decided. So far they appeared to love her nephew very much.

But it would take living in the same house with him to ascertain how they treated him. Would they hand him off to a nanny and have little contact with him? Or would they love him unconditionally and treat him as a treasured member of the family?

These were the questions Grace needed to determine for herself in order to have any peace of mind about Christian's future.

Andrew closed the front door and expelled a loud rush of air from his lungs. He'd never expected to see Grace again, and now he was thinking of hiring her for a live-in position in his home. What were the odds?

He ran a hand through his hair, recalling how attractive she looked in her blue suit and the matching hat perched on top of her dark hair. Once again he'd found himself riveted by her warm brown eyes, which at times glowed with sincerity and other times hinted at possible secrets.

Was he crazy to even consider hiring her?

Footsteps alerted him to someone coming down the stairs. Seconds later, Virginia appeared in the hallway. "Well?" she asked, her face alight with hope. "What did you think? Grace seems perfect, don't you agree?"

"I wouldn't say perfect. She does lack credentials and actual experience."

"Pishposh. I can tell a person's heart right away, and I know she would love little Christian as much as we do." Virginia crossed her arms. "Besides, we've had nothing but a parade of credentials so far, and where has that gotten us? Nowhere."

"True." He shrugged one shoulder. "I'll have to talk it over with Mother and see what she thinks before I make a decision."

Virginia smiled and patted his arm. "I'm sure you'll weigh all the pros and cons until you decide on the most logical course of action," she teased.

"You make it sound like a bad thing."

"Not always. But sometimes a little spontaneity goes a long way. Sometimes you have to follow your instincts."

"And what do your instincts tell you?"

"That Grace is a good person, kind and compassionate, with a heart for children."

"I'll keep that in mind when I talk to Mother." He bent to kiss her cheek. "I take it Christian is napping?"

"Yes. I'm getting a cup of tea, and then I'll take him out for our usual walk when he awakens."

"If I do decide to hire Grace, you'd have no problem teaching her everything she needs to know?"

"Of course not. I'm not going to abandon Christian just because he has a nanny. Especially when I'll miss so much time with him when I leave for Europe." Sadness dulled the light in her eyes.

"Ginny," he said quietly, "if you don't want to go, you don't have to."

"Yes, I do. Basil expects it." She pulled herself up to her full height, barely reaching his chin. "Don't worry about me, Drew. I'll be fine."

Yet Andrew couldn't help but worry about his baby sister. She'd lost the man she cared for at the beginning of the war, and he hated to see her settle for less than a true match. At least now she was open to the idea of marrying. It had taken her nearly three years to get over Emmett's death. Andrew should be happy she'd found someone she would even consider sharing her life with. She deserved a family of her own, children of her own.

With a shake of his head, he pushed such useless thoughts away and concentrated on the issue at hand. Best to find Mother and learn her opinion on the matter of the nanny.

CHAPTER 8

August 14, 1914

Has the world gone mad? I cannot believe we're at war! Mum writes that she's devastated because Owen is thinking of joining. I know how she feels. Frank is determined to enlist as well. I've never seen him so passionate about a cause, yet I'm scared. Oh, Grace, what will I do if he goes? His parents found out about our relationship a few weeks ago, and it caused a huge fight. He told me he didn't care what his parents thought, that I meant more to him. But if that's true, would he really leave me to go to war?

"Are you certain you want to do this?" Mrs. Chamberlain stood in the doorway of Grace's bedroom.

Grace looked up from her suitcase, and a pang of regret twisted her stomach. The kind woman wore a worried frown, her eyes glazed with a hint of tears.

"I'm certain, Mrs. C.," she said. Grace crossed the room to lay a reassuring hand on her arm. "The only thing spoiling my delight at getting this job is that I'll miss spending time with you. I've enjoyed my stay here so much."

Tomorrow Grace would begin her new assignment as Christian's nanny. She still couldn't believe the Eastons had decided to take a chance on her, even with her limited experience. The phone call from Andrew had come as a wonderful surprise—one that, in her mind, confirmed she was on the path God meant for her to follow—and she had gratefully accepted the position.

As long as the Easton family never learned about her connection to the boy, this job could prove a blessing to them all. A chance for her to be part of her nephew's life—maybe not as a guardian—but as someone responsible for his day-to-day care. This way, she could give the boy as much love and guidance as she saw fit, for as long as she could, and Rose could rest in peace, knowing her baby was well cared for.

The only drawback was that Mum wouldn't be at all happy about her staying in Canada for an extended period of time. But Rose's child had to be her main priority. She only hoped her mother would understand.

Mrs. Chamberlain moved into the room and picked up the framed photo from Grace's dresser, the one Grace had taken of Rose the day she'd left for Canada. "Oh, my dear. Your leaving is like losing Rose all over again. She became like a daughter to me. Little Christian was born right here in this house." She sniffed and took a handkerchief from her pocket.

"You're not losing me, I promise." Grace gently lifted the photo from her hands. "I'm only a streetcar ride away. I'll come and visit whenever I can." She ran a finger over the glass, then carefully laid the treasure in her suitcase, where it would have to remain hidden for the foreseeable future.

"What about Sundays?" Mrs. Chamberlain asked. "Will you be able to join us for church? I know Reverend Burke will miss seeing you too."

"I don't know yet. I'll have to see what the family expects." She hadn't told Mrs. Chamberlain or the reverend where she was working—or more importantly *who* she was working for. Somehow she didn't think either would approve. And no matter what their opinion, she would not change her mind about this. "If it's at all possible, I'll try to attend services with you." She would certainly miss the little parish that had started to feel like home.

Grace leaned over to embrace her landlady. "What would I have done without you? I thank God every night for leading me here."

"The Good Lord always manages to make the best out of the worst situations." The woman gave her a watery smile.

Then, while Grace returned to filling her suitcase, Mrs. Chamberlain flitted about the room like a nervous bird, pausing to dust the furniture with the corner of her apron. "Wouldn't it be better to wait until the morning to leave?"

"I'd like to get settled tonight, so I'm fresh for the morning. Besides, the family is expecting me." Grace placed a blouse in the suitcase.

"I suppose that makes sense. Would you at least let Reverend Burke drive you? I don't like the idea of you traveling alone on the streetcar at this hour."

Grace laughed. "Mrs. C., it's not even seven o'clock. There's no need to bother him."

"But you'll have your suitcase to lug all the way." Her brows pinched together. "Where exactly is this place again?"

"On Spadina Road." Grace busied herself emptying a drawer, trying to ignore the weight of the other woman's stare.

"Please don't tell me you're working for the Easton family."

Grace's hand stilled. She should have known the shrewd woman would figure it out. She squared her shoulders. "Yes. I'm going to be Christian's nanny."

Mrs. Chamberlain sat down heavily on the bed, the springs creaking under her weight. "Good grief. I'm not sure that's a smart idea."

"I think it's perfect." Grace stood in front of her. "I can get to know my nephew. Make sure he's loved and well looked after."

She pinned Grace with a direct stare. "But you're deceiving them, aren't you? Not telling them who you are."

"How could I? They'd never let me in the door if they knew I was Rose's sister."

The woman shook her head. "Nothing but heartache will come from this. Mark my words."

The criticism stung. A little too reminiscent of Mum chastising her for another rash decision. She clutched her hands together, searching for a way to make Mrs. Chamberlain understand, a way to alleviate her guilt at the deception. But there was nothing she could really say.

"What exactly do you think this will accomplish, dear? You'll only fall in love with that baby, and the day you have to leave him will break your heart."

"You're probably right." Grace walked to the window under the sloping roof and stared down at the street below. "All I know is I can't ignore this God-given opportunity. I feel certain it's where He and Rose want me to be. If I don't go, I'll always regret missing this chance to spend time with Christian." She turned back to the bed. "In my last letter to Rose, I promised I would take care of her son. This is the only way I can see to do that."

Mrs. Chamberlain released a weary sigh. "You have a point. Well, there's another ten minutes added to my nightly prayers." With a huff, she pushed off the mattress. "I may not agree with you, but I know your intentions are good. You can count on my support."

"Thank you, Mrs. C. That means a lot." Grace's throat burned with the sudden rush of tears. She gave the woman another quick hug, then lifted her suitcase off the bed. "Well, I'd best be off before it gets dark."

"God speed, Grace dear. And don't let those Eastons push you around."

"Miss Virginia, there's a gentleman to see you." Mrs. Green made the announcement from the open parlor doorway.

Virginia looked up from her book. "Who is it?"

"Mr. Fleming." A flicker of disapproval flashed over the housekeeper's face before she schooled her features.

Virginia held back a sigh. Why did everyone seem to dislike Basil? True, he could be overly dramatic and a bit rambunctious, reminding Virginia of an overgrown puppy. Annoying at times, but harmless. "Send him in, please. And have Mrs. Hopkins prepare a pot of coffee." Basil swore Mrs. Hopkins made the best brew he'd ever tasted.

"Right away, miss."

Virginia fluffed her skirt and straightened her posture, crossing her legs daintily at the ankle. The way a perfect lady should.

"Good evening, Virginia, my dear. How are you today?" Basil bowed over her offered hand.

"Very well, thank you. What brings you by?"

"These." With a dramatic flourish, Basil whipped something out of his breast pocket and laid it on the table before her.

"They look like tickets."

"You're smart as well as beautiful."

Virginia held back a laugh. Perhaps that was what had won her over. The fact that Basil truly thought her beautiful, while the majority of men viewed her as a washed-up, twenty-four-year-old spinster. After losing her beloved Emmett, Virginia had believed she'd be alone forever, until Basil Fleming had come into her world and offered her the first glimmer of hope for the future she'd always wanted: a husband and children of her own.

"I've booked our passage to Europe. We set sail in eight weeks' time."

Virginia managed a smile. "Wonderful." When Basil had first mentioned the idea of her accompanying him and his family on this trip, she'd been filled with excitement. Traveling abroad. Seeing the wonders of the Louvre, the Eiffel Tower, the ruins of Rome. Something she'd always dreamed about doing one day was becoming a reality.

However, that was before Christian had come into their lives. In the few short weeks since his arrival, the boy had wormed his way into her heart like no one else ever had.

Virginia had tried to convince Basil to let her bring the baby with them, but he would have no part of it.

"I want your undivided attention on this trip, sweetheart. I won't share you with anyone. Not even an infant."

In some ways, his possessiveness thrilled Virginia. Who wouldn't bask in such adoration? Yet his slightly superior attitude often rankled. If he truly loved her, wouldn't he want her to be happy, even if it meant raising her brother's child?

Basil came to sit beside her on the sofa and gathered her hands in his. "I have a fantastic idea." He waited until she met his gaze. "What if we were to marry before we leave? This trip could double as our honeymoon. Wouldn't that be perfect?"

Virginia's heart thumped uncomfortably in her chest. Though she'd known their unconventional courtship was leading to marriage, she hadn't thought it would come so soon. "I don't know what to say."

He raised a brow, studying her. "I sense this has come as a shock."

"It has, yes." Virginia tried to smile but feared it came out more as a grimace.

"I see. Well, I'd best give you time to digest the idea—before I propose for real." He pulled her to him then and kissed her. It wasn't the first time he'd taken such liberty, yet this time the embrace held a possessive quality that caused a spurt of apprehension to rush through her.

"Now I'm afraid I must be off. I'm meeting some associates for drinks at the club. Keep those tickets in a safe place, darling. I will see you soon. And think about my idea."

"But your coffee . . ."

"Tell Mrs. Hopkins I'll make it up to her," he called over his shoulder as he exited the room.

Virginia fell back against the sofa, feeling as though a tornado had just whirled through the room and out again. With a sigh, she picked up the tickets. First-class accommodations, of course. Had he booked two staterooms or only one, confident she would meekly follow his suggestion that they get married before the trip?

Be careful what you wish for, Virginia. The result might not be entirely to your liking.

The main-floor windows of the Easton estate glowed from the lights within, giving the residence a welcoming air—one Grace appreciated all the more at this moment. She switched her suitcase from one hand to the other, the walk from the streetcar seeming longer than it had the first time she'd come here, most likely due to the weight of her bag.

She climbed the stairs, set her suitcase on the ground, and knocked on the door. Not wanting to interrupt the family meal, she'd purposely waited to arrive until she believed dinner would be over.

The housekeeper answered her knock. "Good evening, Miss Foley. Please come in."

"Thank you." She retrieved her bag and stepped inside.

The large-framed woman held out a hand. "May I take your coat?"

"Certainly. Thank you." Grace slipped off her coat and gave it to the woman.

"Welcome to Fairlawn Manor. I'm Mrs. Green, the housekeeper. If you need anything, please don't hesitate to ask." Though her tone was friendly, she did not offer a smile or any indication of warmth.

Perhaps that was part of her job.

"You may leave your bag here. One of the maids will bring it to your room. Now if you'll come with me, Miss Virginia is waiting for you."

Grace nodded and followed the woman down a wide hallway to a set of double doors.

"Miss Foley has arrived," the woman announced, then stepped aside for Grace to enter the room.

Virginia shot up from her seat on the sofa, her face alight with enthusiasm. "Grace, welcome. Come in and share some tea with me."

Grace surreptitiously scanned the room, surprised to find none of the other family members there. She relaxed a little, glad for a reprieve from meeting the infamous Mr. Easton. As she walked in, she couldn't help but be charmed by the elegance of the décor. The dove-gray walls presented a perfect backdrop to the blue sofas and patterned side chairs. "Thank you, Miss Easton. A cup of tea would be lovely."

"Please, you must call me Virginia."

"Is that appropriate for an employee?" Grace took a seat on the sofa opposite to where Virginia had been seated, reading a magazine.

"Very well, in front of the others you may call me Miss Easton, but when we're alone, it's Virginia." She poured tea from a silver service.

"I thought I'd be meeting your parents when I arrived," Grace said as she took the cup Virginia handed her.

"I didn't want to overwhelm you on your first night here. After our tea, I'll show you around the house and take you to your room."

Half an hour later, Grace followed Virginia on a tour of the residence, which seemed more like a castle than a home. Room upon room of expensive furnishings and fabrics, paintings and sculptures, crystal and velvet. She could scarcely believe she would be living in such a palace.

"And here is the nursery." Virginia pressed a finger to her lips. "We must take care not to wake Christian. Once he rouses, he's impossible to get back to sleep."

She opened the door wide enough for the light from the hallway to illuminate a bit of the interior. Grace made out a crib against the wall, a rocking chair, and a dresser before Virginia slowly closed the door.

"Your room will be next door. It connects with the nursery by a two-way door. I always leave it open so I can hear him if he wakes in the night." She pushed into the adjoining room and flicked a switch.

Grace was pleased to note the house had electric lights.

"I've been staying here ever since Christian arrived because my bedroom is too far away to hear him. We'll switch rooms as soon as I feel he's comfortable with you. Right now it might scare him if a stranger came in to tend him."

"Of course. I understand."

"For now I've put you in this guest room." Virginia moved across the hall. "I hope you find it satisfactory." Once again she turned on the light as she entered the room.

Grace glanced around the most beautiful bedroom she'd ever seen. The walls were decorated in a pale blue flocked paper. Feminine white furniture and thick carpet gave the room a homey feel.

"It's lovely. Thank you."

Virginia smiled. "I'll let you get settled in. If you need anything, just ring the bell and one of the maids will assist you." She pointed to a tasseled rope in the corner. "Breakfast is at seven thirty. I'll come and take you down to meet the rest of the household. Everyone should be there, unless Father has an early meeting at the office."

Nerves flittered in Grace's stomach at the prospect, but she managed a smile in return. "Thank you, Virginia. I don't know how I'll ever repay your kindness in helping me get this position."

"You're welcome. If everything works out, you'll be doing me a favor, putting my mind at ease so I can go off and enjoy Europe." She headed to the door, pausing to give Grace another smile. "It's good to have you here, Grace."

Then she slipped out into the hall, leaving Grace on her own in the strange new house that would now become her home.

CHAPTER 9

Seated with his parents in the dining room the next morning, Andrew sipped his first cup of coffee and attempted to ignore the tingles of anticipation coursing through his system. Every five seconds, he glanced at the doorway, expecting to see Virginia arrive with the newest member of the household.

He was being ridiculous. The fact that a new employee had moved in should not cause him a minute's thought. However, the fact that Grace Foley now resided at the opposite end of the hall from him had cost him almost a full night's sleep.

At the far end of the table, his father sat reading the morning newspaper. He snapped the paper closed and looked up with a frown. "Well, where is this girl? Sleeping in on her first day? That doesn't bode well for her future here."

Father had been opposed to hiring Grace from the start, mainly because she hadn't come recommended by an employment agency, but from a chance meeting in the park. Only Virginia's persistence and Andrew's added recommendation made him relent. Mother, on the other hand, seemed rather indifferent, which puzzled Andrew, since she'd insisted on interviewing all the previous candidates personally. Perhaps she was still feeling under the weather. Yet she looked as well-groomed as always in a cheerful pink blouse with her hair neatly pinned. She must be expecting the ladies in for tea today.

"I imagine Virginia will bring her down any moment." Andrew laid his napkin on the table.

"Did I hear my name?" His sister's cheerful voice floated into the room, announcing her arrival. She glided forward to kiss Father's cheek. "Good morning, Daddy. Mother. I'd like you to meet Christian's new nanny, Miss Grace Foley."

Andrew and his father rose from their chairs. Grace entered somewhat cautiously, as though trying to determine whether the atmosphere was fair or hostile. She wore the same navy suit she'd worn for the interview, paired with a white high-necked blouse. Her hair was pinned in a bun at the nape of her neck. Even in her simplicity, she exuded charm.

Andrew smiled. "Welcome to Fairlawn, Gr—Miss Foley. We're pleased to have you as Christian's nanny."

"Thank you." Her nervous glance darted to his parents. "Mr. Easton. Mrs. Easton. It's a pleasure to meet you both."

Father's face turned a mottled shade of red. "You're British?"

"Y-Yes, sir."

"Why did no one tell me? I would have vetoed this unorthodox hiring at once."

Grace's lovely brown eyes widened in apparent distress. "I don't understand—"

"I'll make this very plain, Miss Foley. I've no love for immigrants—British ones, in particular. I made the mistake of hiring a young woman fresh off the boat to work in my office. And how did she repay me? She bewitched my son and turned him against his family."

Grace's face drained of all color. She swayed and grasped the back of a chair.

Andrew came around the table toward her as though he could somehow protect her from his father's outburst. "That has nothing to do with Grace, Father. Just because she comes from the same country is no reason to judge her unfairly."

"Andrew's right." Virginia looped her arm through Grace's in a show of support. "Besides, isn't it the height of society to have a British nanny? You'll be the envy of your friends."

His mother, silent until this time, rose from her seat. "The girl is here now, Oscar. We owe her a chance to prove herself." She turned to Grace and extended a hand. "Welcome, Miss Foley. Please do sit down and eat. You'll have a busy day ahead learning what's required of you."

"Thank you, ma'am."

A frown creased his mother's brow. "Who is watching the baby now?"

"Serena is with him while we eat," Virginia said as she took her seat.

"I see. In future, Miss Foley, you will take your meals in the nursery with my grandson."

Grace nodded grimly. "Yes, ma'am."

"Mother, you can't expect her to stay locked up there like a prisoner," Virginia sputtered. "Surely Grace can join us for dinner at least. Christian is usually asleep by then."

Mother pursed her lips. "I suppose that would be acceptable. Miss Foley, we eat promptly at seven thirty. If that hour doesn't suit your schedule, you may take your meals in the nursery or downstairs with the other servants."

Andrew's face heated. His parents' superior attitude had never felt so humiliating before. But somehow this time it seemed personal because of Grace's heritage.

He held out a chair for her. She flashed him a look of gratitude before sitting.

"Ellie, please bring Miss Foley a plate of eggs and bacon and a fresh pot of tea." He assumed being British she would prefer tea to the coffee he and Father drank.

The maid stepped forward. "Yes, sir. And for you, Miss Virginia?"

"I'll have my usual, Ellie. Thank you."

Andrew resumed his seat and looked up to see his father still scowling.

"I'm ready to head to the office. Are you coming, Andrew?"

With effort, Andrew kept his tone even. "I'd like another cup of coffee first. I'll be along shortly."

"I hope you haven't forgotten Cecilia is coming today to begin work on the fund-raiser. She'll expect you to be there waiting for her."

"And I shall. Knowing Celia, however, I doubt she'll arrive much before noon. I have plenty of time."

Father grunted, then bent to kiss Mother's cheek. "Have a good day, my dear. I'll see you tonight."

The tension in the room seemed to ease the minute Father left. Ellie came in with plates for Grace and Virginia and a pot of tea.

"Why is Cecilia coming to the office?" Virginia gave him a curious look as Ellie set her dish before her.

Andrew poured more coffee. "Paul Edison is having her consult with us for a fundraiser we're planning."

"Interesting." Virginia tilted her head. "After you left her party the other night, Paul stayed glued to Cecilia's side the entire time. You'd best make your move, big brother, before he steals her away."

Andrew set his cup down with a loud clunk. "When and if I make a move," he said sharply, "it will be on my timetable. Not because of Paul Edison's manipulations. Or anyone else's."

"Andrew!" Mother's rebuke sounded from the other end of the table.

His annoyance evaporated as quickly as it had arisen. "Forgive me, Ginny. Cecilia is a rather touchy subject lately. I had no right to take it out on you." He took another gulp of coffee as he rose. "I'd better be going before Father gives my office away."

Painfully aware of Grace's curious gaze, Andrew ducked his head to kiss his mother as he passed. "Have a pleasant day, everyone," he said, and then escaped into the hall.

On his way out the front door, he gave himself a stern lecture to get his emotions under control, especially around a certain brown-eyed beauty.

"Who is Cecilia?" Grace dared to ask as she and Virginia climbed the stairs after breakfast. She'd almost felt sorry for Andrew and his obvious discomfort at the turn the conversation had taken earlier.

Almost.

The other part was relieved she was no longer the focus of such intense scrutiny. The idea of taking her meals in the nursery suddenly seemed far preferable, yet she couldn't pass up the chance to spend time with the Eastons for an hour or so each day. She'd already learned quite a bit from her first meal with them.

Virginia's skirt swished about her calves. "Cecilia is the daughter of one of my father's colleagues. Andrew's been courting her on and off since Christmas." Her tone held a note of distaste.

"I see." Grace's chest tightened. Why did the idea of Andrew's courtship bother her? It was none of her business whom the man chose to date. Yet she couldn't help picking up on Virginia's disapproval. "You sound less than pleased about it," she ventured.

Virginia looked over her shoulder. "Cecilia and I tolerate each other, but there's no love lost there."

Grace longed to question Virginia further to find out why her brother would court someone his sister didn't care for. However, she feared she'd already overstepped her place.

They headed along the second-floor hallway toward the nursery. All thoughts of Andrew flew from Grace's mind as they neared Christian's room. Her heart began an uneven thrum in her chest. Soon she would get to hold her nephew in her arms.

"Let's see if the little darling is up." Virginia quietly entered the room.

A maid was seated in the rocking chair with the baby on her lap. A few toys lay strewn over the carpet.

"Serena, this is Grace Foley, who will be training as Christian's nanny."

"Nice to meet you." Serena rose and handed the baby to Virginia.

"Likewise." Grace smiled, trying not to stare at the boy.

The girl bobbed a slight curtsy and then exited the room.

Grace held her breath as she turned her attention to her nephew. He laid his head on Virginia's shoulder, his thumb firmly in his mouth.

"Christian, sweetheart, this is Miss Foley, your new nanny. Not that you have any idea what a nanny is." She laughed and swept the tangled hair off his forehead.

Grace's throat closed up. What a beautiful child. Rose's son. She moved closer, forcing a smile to her lips. "Hello, Christian. My, you're a handsome lad."

Christian turned his face into Virginia's neck.

"He's always a bit shy at first." She kissed his cheek. "Grace, why don't you sit in the rocker? I'll put him on your knee facing me so he won't be scared."

Grace took her place in the rocking chair, willing her pulse to settle. When Virginia placed the baby on her lap, Grace cautiously wrapped her arm around his middle. She leaned over his head, inhaling the scent of talcum powder. When the tiny body finally relaxed, warmth spread through her, melting her heart at the same time. It was all she could do to refrain from squeezing him tight.

Virginia made funny faces, and the boy gurgled with laughter.

The back of Grace's eyes burned. *Wouldn't Rose love to be here, laughing with her son?* She blinked hard to keep any trace of tears from showing. It was essential to keep her emotions tamped down and maintain a professional air.

Virginia handed the boy a teddy bear, and he promptly thrust one floppy ear into his mouth. She chuckled. "Christian likes to taste everything. We have to pay close attention now that he's becoming more mobile and can grab things." She began to collect the toys from the floor, placing them in a large wooden crate. "This box used to be Frank's. I thought it fitting that we use it for Christian's toys." She closed the lid with a sad smile. "I intend to teach Christian all about his father."

"What about his mother?" Grace asked softly.

Virginia paused. "I didn't really know her. I only met Rose a few times under . . . difficult circumstances." She moved to the dresser and picked up a framed photo. She studied it for a moment and handed it to Grace.

Grace's lungs froze. A smiling Rose, dressed in a fancy hat with a piece of netting covering her forehead, beamed at a handsome soldier. She looked so happy. Happier than Grace had ever seen her.

"This is my brother's wedding picture. It was with his things that the army returned to us. I had it framed for Christian." Virginia's chin quivered. "I wish I could have attended Frank's wedding."

Grace handed her back the photo. "Why didn't you?"

"Frank and Rose eloped, but Daddy wouldn't have allowed us, even if we'd known."

"Why didn't your father approve of her?" Grace rocked the chair, gratified that the baby appeared content with her.

"He blamed her for stealing Frank from us." Virginia grew pensive. "To be honest, I think the main reason he resented Rose was because the moment Frank met her, he had eyes for no one else. He lost interest in the hotel and broke off his engagement to Cecilia. Daddy had his heart set on the match."

Grace frowned. "The same Cecilia who Andrew is dating?"

"One and the same." She shrugged. "It's a complicated situation."

Grace didn't know quite what to say, so she remained silent.

"This whole affair has been very difficult for my mother. Losing Frank to the war almost killed her." Virginia placed the frame back on the dresser. "You know," she said as she turned back, "you bear quite a resemblance to Rose."

Grace's heart stuttered, and she stopped rocking. "Really?"

It had never occurred to her that someone might think they looked alike. Her mother had always remarked on their dissimilarity, constantly comparing Grace with her smarter, prettier sister.

"Yes." Virginia studied her. "The shape of your face and something about the eyes."

A sheen of perspiration dampened Grace's forehead.

"No wonder Daddy took an instant dislike to you. But don't worry. I'm sure he'll get over it soon enough." Sadness wisped across Virginia's delicate features. "I like to imagine that Frank and Rose are together in heaven, watching over their son. I hope they'd be pleased he's with us."

Grace bit her lip, certain from Rose's letters that she wouldn't be pleased at all. Still, the woman obviously loved Christian and missed her brother as much as Grace missed Rose.

"Enough of this melancholy." Virginia reached for the baby. "Let's give Christian his bottle, and we can discuss his schedule."

Grace reluctantly let him go, already ruing her empty arms. With determination, she set aside all sympathy for the Eastons. She would need to remain objective in order to ascertain whether Christian would be happy growing up in this deeply fractured family.

CHAPTER 10

Andrew tried to focus on the conversation going on at the conference room table, but his mind kept drifting.

Paul Edison and Cecilia sat together, poring over the papers Paul had brought to the meeting, detailing the basic premise for the fund-raiser gala. Enthusiasm radiated from Cecilia as she listened, interjecting ideas of her own from time to time. Neither seemed to notice, or care, that Andrew wasn't fully present.

In truth, he wasn't even needed at this meeting, since he doubted they'd be ready to discuss budgets at this point. They were too busy dreaming up bigger and better scenarios, each more grandiose than the next. He'd have plenty of time to bring them back to earth with the financial realities.

In the meantime, he couldn't help going over the morning and what had transpired before he left for the office. He'd been halfway down the street when he realized that in the frazzle of the breakfast conversation he'd forgotten some important papers in his bedroom. In a fit of frustration, he'd turned the car back home and rushed upstairs to retrieve them. As he'd been coming out of his room, he caught a glimpse of Virginia and Grace entering the nursery. Andrew had paused while his conscience waged war with his instincts. Spying wasn't the most ethical thing to do, but he needed to see how this woman—one he'd hired based solely on a gut feeling—would interact with his nephew. What if Christian couldn't tolerate her for some reason?

He made his way silently down the corridor to the nursery, where thankfully the door had been left ajar. He peered inside and was instantly mesmerized by the scene before him. Seated in the rocker, Grace appeared somewhat nervous, and when Virginia lowered the boy to Grace's lap, a maelstrom of emotions had whipped across her lovely face. Actual tears glistened in her eyes as she wrapped her arms about the baby's waist, securing him more firmly against her. Though she blinked hard, she couldn't disguise the fact that she was clearly overwhelmed. Her cheeks reddened, her lips trembled, and she laid her hand on his head with a reverence that someone emotionally attached to the child might—someone like a mother.

Andrew had pulled back from the door, his heart thumping. What could account for such an extreme reaction upon meeting a child for the first time? Had someone close to Grace lost an infant, or was she simply moved by the tragedy of Christian's story?

Andrew couldn't stop thinking about it all the way to work and now couldn't concentrate on the meeting. He tapped a pen on the ledger before him. Too many things about this new nanny remained a mystery. He needed to spend more time with her. Learn more about her. In the meantime, he'd ask Virginia for her impressions, and between the two of them, they would determine if Grace would prove suitable for the long term.

"Have you been listening to one word we've said?" Edison's sharp question broke Andrew from his thoughts.

Cecilia stared at him, her brows turned down, indicating her displeasure. An occurrence that was happening with regular frequency of late.

"Of course I was listening. To the key points at least." He flashed them a smile he hoped was convincing.

"Really, Andrew, this is too important for you to be daydreaming. We asked about the possibility of hiring a large orchestra. We'll need one with a good reputation in order to draw the best crowd."

"Of course. I'll allow a decent amount for music in the budget. Perhaps your parents could recommend a few potential groups."

She frowned. "The band my father hired for my birthday was pleasant enough but too small for a gala the size we're planning."

"I'm sure you'll find the best one available," Andrew soothed. Feeding Celia's ego usually helped avoid further arguments. "Just remember we don't want to appear too lavish after coming through four years of war."

"I disagree." Paul leaned back in his chair and crossed his arms. "We've been frugal for long enough. It's time to shake off the doom and gloom. Lavish is what the people want and what they deserve."

Andrew strived to keep his voice even. "Do you think the returning soldiers will share that sentiment?"

Edison glared in his direction. "If it raises money to benefit them, why should they complain?"

Andrew held his gaze in silent challenge. Despite having been in the war for a short time before getting injured, Paul didn't seem to really care about the veterans. They were merely a means to an end. A way to make him look like a philanthropist in front of Father. Andrew pushed away from the table. "I think you two can manage from here without me. If you have any financial questions, I'll be in my office."

"Fine by me." Paul's smug expression didn't help Andrew's mood. Neither did the possessive arm he draped across the back of Cecilia's chair.

Celia, however, seemed to take umbrage at Andrew's departure, and judging by the icy daggers she aimed at him, he would be in for a tongue-lashing later.

Virginia's warning from earlier echoed in his mind. *You'd best make your move, big brother, before he steals her away.*

Time to salvage the situation—and make his position clear to Edison in the process.

Relaxing his features into a more pleasant expression, he walked over to Celia. "I was wondering if you'd care to join me and my family for dinner tonight? My parents have been after me to invite you over."

"I'd love to." A smile transformed her face as she beamed up at him.

"Good. Dinner is at seven thirty. Come by earlier for cocktails, if you'd like."

"I'll be there."

"I look forward to it." Andrew leaned over and kissed her cheek. Then, ignoring Edison completely, he strode out the door.

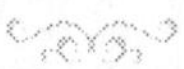

Grace descended the back staircase on her way to inform the cook of Virginia's preference for little Christian's lunch. As she entered the dimly lit kitchen where the maids scurried about their work, an idea bloomed. What better way to learn the secrets of the Easton family than to become friends with the other servants? After all, they were privy to the ins and outs of the entire household. If Grace could get in good with the cook and the maids, no telling what tidbits of information she might learn.

She pasted on a bright smile as she approached the sturdy woman in a white cap and apron. "Excuse me, Mrs. Hopkins. I'm Grace, the new nanny."

The woman lifted her head from her task of kneading dough at a long table. "Nice to meet you, Grace. I'll wager Miss Virginia sent you about Master Christian's lunch."

"That's right. She says it's to be mashed peas and stewed applesauce. Along with his bottle, of course."

"The wee tyke needs all the nourishment he can get." She wiped her floured hands on her apron.

A thread of worry wound through Grace. "Why is that? He seems healthy enough."

"He's better now, but he was quite underweight at first. Doctor Ballard is keeping a close watch on him to make sure he improves."

"That poor child. My heart breaks at what he's been through."

And what Rose must have been through. Grace hated the thought of her sister trying to cope with so many problems all alone.

"Aye. Such a shame." Mrs. Hopkins pulled the chair out for her. "Sit down a spell and have a spot of tea." She hustled over to the stove, where steam spewed from several pots on the burners, and poured tea from the large pot warming there. Two young girls washed dishes at the sink.

Grace took a seat and accepted the cup. "Tell me, Mrs. Hopkins. Do you have any advice on how to get along with Mr. Easton? I seem to have gotten off on the wrong foot with him."

Mrs. Hopkins resumed her kneading in silence. "I suspect it's your accent," she said at last. "You likely remind him of Master Frank's wife, who he blamed for ruining his son's life."

With effort, Grace held her emotions in check. She had to learn not to react to every criticism of her sister.

The woman shook her head and took out a baking pan from a lower cupboard. "Still, that has nothing to do with you. My best advice for getting along in this household is to work hard and don't cause any fuss. If Mr. Easton sees you're loyal to his grandson, he'll come around."

"Believe me, the last thing I want to do is stand out." Grace drank the rich brew, which brought an instant wave of homesickness to her chest. How she missed Mum's tea. No one else made it quite the same.

"You're welcome to take your meals with us, if you'd like," Mrs. Hopkins said as she transferred the dough into a loaf pan. "Unless you have to stay in the nursery."

"That's kind of you, but I'll be eating dinner with the family. I will try to come down for the other meals when Christian's schedule allows." Grace rose and took her cup to the sink.

Mrs. Hopkins's eyes widened. "That reminds me, I need Serena to set two extra places in the dining room tonight. Master Andrew and Miss Virginia are bringing guests for dinner."

Grace's stomach tripped with sudden nerves. Would she fit in with their visitors or would she feel like an imposter at the table?

"I suppose I'd better dress with extra care this evening then." She gave a light laugh and headed toward the door.

"One more thing, Grace."

"Yes?" Grace looked back to see Mrs. Hopkins' serious stare.

"Another way to gain Mr. Easton's favor? Stay far away from his son."

After Christian awoke from his nap, Grace changed the boy's nappy under Virginia's supervision and dressed him for their afternoon outing.

"Before we go to the park," Virginia said, "I want to show you around the grounds. Maybe introduce you to the chauffeur. Toby will take you wherever you need to go, as long as Father doesn't need the car."

"That's not necessary. I'm perfectly happy taking the streetcar."

Virginia gave her a horrified look. "My parents would never allow you to take Christian on the streetcar. You'll be expected to use the chauffeur."

"I see. In that case, I'd be happy to meet him."

"Wonderful. You'll like Toby, I'm sure." Virginia pulled a knitted bonnet over the baby's head, tied it under his chin, and picked him up with a smile. "Master Christian, your baby carriage awaits."

Five minutes later, Virginia pushed the pram down the path on the Eastons' back property, past the gardens to an enclosed glass structure Grace assumed was a greenhouse.

"This is where Collin, our gardener, can usually be found. He loves to tinker with new plants and flowers. Do you know he's determined to create the first blue rose?"

Grace laughed. "He sounds like an evil scientist in a lab."

"Not quite, though he does get distracted by his work." Virginia slowed the pram and stared at the greenhouse as though she could see right through to the man inside. She set the brake on the carriage. "Come on. Let's see if he's here."

"What about Christian?"

"He'll be content enough for a few minutes."

Not wanting to go against her wishes, Grace followed her in. Immediately, she was transported to a tropical paradise. The warm, moist air enveloped her with the perfume of a thousand flowers. Everywhere she turned, vivid green leaves and colorful blooms filled her vision.

They wound their way through the aisles of plants until she saw a tall, dark-haired man at a wooden worktable. He had smudges of dirt on his cheeks, and his fingernails were blackened with soil.

But he grinned when he saw them. "If I knew I was having company, I'd have cleaned up first." He winked. "Miss Virginia does love to surprise me."

A delicate shade of pink spread over Virginia's cheeks. "Grace, this is Collin Lafferty, our gardener. He is responsible for all the fresh flowers you see throughout the house. He also tends the orchard and the vegetable garden in the summer."

"How do you do, Mr. Lafferty? You have an amazing greenhouse here."

"Thank you. But please call me Collin."

"Very well. And I'm Grace." His light Scottish burr gave her a feeling of kinship. Another soul far from home.

He picked up a tool and began to fill a clay pot with earth. "Do you have a favorite flower, Grace? If so, perhaps I can make sure you have fresh ones in your room each week."

"Oh, please don't go to any trouble on my account."

He turned his hazel eyes on her. "Every woman deserves flowers. Don't you agree, Miss Virginia?"

The girl gave a ladylike snort. "I can think of a few who don't."

Collin laughed and moved to a nearby pot. He snipped off a lilac-colored rose and presented it to Virginia with a flourish. "For you, fair lady."

Her blush deepened.

"I'm attempting to create a blue rose. This lavender beauty is as close to blue as I've come. As rare as the woman who holds it."

"There you go, blathering on again." But Virginia brought the petals to her nose and inhaled. "We'd best continue with our walk. Christian will start to fuss if we leave him alone too long." She headed back toward the entrance.

"Nice to meet you, Collin," Grace said.

"Likewise. And if you decide on any flowers you'd like, please let me know."

Though he spoke to Grace, she noted his eyes followed Virginia's retreating back all the way out the door.

The next stop on their tour of the property was a building with a peaked roof. Enormous wooden doors spanned the entire front section.

"This is where Father and Andrew keep their autos." Virginia rolled the baby carriage to a stop. "Let me see if Toby is inside." She disappeared around the side of the building.

Grace stepped closer to the pram, intent on staying with Christian this time. It hadn't seemed right leaving him unattended earlier, even in his own yard.

A few minutes later, one of the large doors slid open. A well-built man in a white shirt with the sleeves rolled up to his elbows came out with Virginia.

He smiled as he approached. Auburn hair peeked out from under his cap, and his eyes were a vivid shade of green, reminding Grace of Collin's plants. "You must be Miss Foley. I'm Toby McDonald, the chauffeur." Grace made out a distinct Scottish accent, much stronger than Collin's.

"Nice to meet you."

"Ah, an English lass. Interesting." He glanced at Victoria. "I imagine your father was none too pleased."

"No. But he'll come around," she added hastily, glancing at Grace. "Once he gets to know you, he won't even notice your accent. Any more than he notices Toby's."

"Aye. Mr. Easton didn't appear to care much for Scots, so I was surprised when he hired Collin and me. He had great fun making our lives miserable for the first few months we worked here." Toby winked. "But now the man can't do without either of us."

Virginia laughed. "How right you are."

Toby moved toward the pram and peered inside at Christian. "And how's our wee man today?"

"Better than ever." Virginia acted as though the two were great friends. Not mistress and servant. What must her father think of that?

"That's good to hear." Toby turned his focus to Grace. "Miss Virginia wanted me to let you know I'm available if you ever need a drive. My only time off duty is Sunday afternoon once we're back from church. Other than that, I'm at your service." He gave a mock bow.

"Thank you, Mr. McDonald."

"It's Toby. And I'm pleased such a lovely lass has joined the household. I look forward to getting to know you better." He took her hand and raised it to his lips.

Warmth spread up Grace's neck to her ears. With a self-conscious laugh, she pulled her hand free and grasped the pram handle. "Shall we be on our way to the park?" she said to Virginia.

"Certainly. Thank you, Toby."

As they strolled along the sidewalk, Grace's breathing began to even out. "Goodness, is Mr. McDonald always so . . . forthright?"

Virginia sent her an amused look. "He's always friendly, but today he seemed especially intrigued, which is likely why he poured on the charm."

Grace bit her bottom lip. Having the attention of the family chauffeur would not be in keeping with her plan to remain unnoticed in the background. She'd have to do her best to avoid Toby McDonald before he caused her any problems.

As they turned into the park, Grace noticed the lavender rose sitting in a place of prominence on the lapel of Virginia's jacket.

Perhaps Mr. McDonald was not the only one with romance on his mind.

CHAPTER 11

After changing into her favorite teal dress with black lace trim, Virginia sat in front of her vanity mirror and tried to be patient while the maid fiddled with her hair. Mother had invited Basil to dine with them this evening, presumably because Andrew had told her that Cecilia would be joining them for dinner. The earth might cease rotating if the numbers of people at the table didn't match.

"That will do. Thank you, Alice."

"One more thing, miss." Alice opened the jewelry box on the dresser and removed an emerald pendant. "This will be perfect with your dress." She draped the necklace around Virginia and fastened the clasp behind her.

"It's lovely. Thank you."

Alice curtsied and quietly left the room.

Virginia studied her reflection in the mirror. Outwardly she portrayed the ideal upper-class woman. Elegantly coiffed hair, stylish dress and jewelry, perfect poise and grace. Yet somewhere deep inside, her soul yearned for more.

Marrying Basil would be considered a coup. He was a well-sought-after bachelor, wealthy, polished, and admired. And Basil was good to her, in almost every way that mattered. But life as his wife did not hold the appeal Virginia had once thought it would.

When Father had mentioned Basil's interest in courting her, she'd been flattered. After all, once a woman reached her mid-twenties, she was often overlooked for younger, prettier girls. Basil's suit seemed divinely timed as well, as though God had been showing her the direction she should take. Virginia had finally reached a place where she was able to put Emmett's death behind her and move forward with her life. Only she hadn't a clue where "forward" would take her.

And now Basil had made his intentions known. Virginia was afraid he might mention his plan to marry before their trip at dinner tonight in order to gain her parents' support. Would they favor such a quick wedding? Virginia believed Daddy would, and Mother would not likely disagree with him.

With a quiet sigh, Virginia rose from her seat and walked to her bedside table. She opened the drawer and took out the single lavender rose she'd received earlier. Over the course of their courtship, Basil had sent her numerous bouquets of flowers, yet none could compare to this single rose, chosen for her by Collin from his beloved plants. After sharing only a few conversations, Collin seemed to know the innermost workings of her heart, whereas Basil never bothered to ask her opinion or her preferences. Nor did he listen when she offered them.

Was she being too picky, wanting her future husband to care about the things she valued?

Like what type of wedding she wanted? Or where they would live once they were married? Or if they would have children?

These were significant issues a couple ought to discuss before leaping into marriage.

She lifted the flower to her nose and inhaled its subtle fragrance. Daddy would tell her she was far too romantic for her own good. Marriage was a partnership, much like a business merger. One had to be practical about such matters. Still, her heart yearned for what it could never have. A penniless Scottish gardener with kind eyes and a spirited laugh.

With measured care, Virginia opened her Bible and pressed the rose, along with several others already there, between the pages containing her favorite verses from the Song of Solomon.

My beloved . . . said unto me, Rise up, my love, my fair one, and come away. For, lo, the winter is past, the rain is over and gone; The flowers appear on the earth; the time of the singing of birds is come. . . .

Set me as a seal upon thine heart . . . for love is strong as death . . . the coals thereof are coals of fire, which hath a most vehement flame.

She ran her fingers over the faded print. This was the kind of love Virginia craved. Passionate, powerful, and at the same time, sanctioned by the Lord.

That was another thing she admired about Collin. He was a staunch Christian, who practiced his faith in his everyday life. She'd never seen him angry or out of sorts. He was always kind and quick to offer assistance in any situation that arose in the Easton household.

She returned the Bible to her bedside table, then pulled herself up tall. No matter how uncomfortable, she planned to have a serious talk with Basil very soon, and make sure he understood how their married life would be if she agreed to marry him. He needed to know that she would not be content to sit quietly in a corner. That she wanted a large family and intended, God willing, to start having babies right away.

And if this didn't suit him, he would have to find another woman who would fit more easily into his world.

Andrew had made a colossal mistake inviting Cecilia for dinner. Being included in such an intimate family gathering would give her the impression that he was ready to become more serious about their courtship, when in fact he was more uncertain than ever.

He ground his back teeth together, unable to deny that Paul Edison's apparent interest in Cecilia had played a part in the impromptu invitation. Lately, Edison's smug attitude had succeeded in getting under Andrew's skin, making him react in ways he normally wouldn't. It had to stop. From now on, he would simply ignore the troublemaker's flagrant attempts to undermine him at every turn.

Andrew peered at his tie in the bedroom mirror and attempted to straighten it. His attire had to be perfect if he were to endure Cecilia's scrutiny. He smoothed his hair back with a dab of petroleum jelly, making sure not one hair was out of place. When he felt his appearance would pass inspection, he removed his glasses and slipped them into the breast pocket of his jacket. No use riling her up by wearing those. He needed to set the proper tone for the evening right from the start.

He paused to consider one possible benefit of tonight's dinner. Perhaps his father would see that his relationship with Cecilia was on solid ground, and maybe then he would lessen the pressure he'd been placing on him.

Squaring his shoulders, Andrew headed downstairs to the main level. He found his father and Basil Fleming in the library, enjoying a drink before dinner. Knowing Mother, she'd invited Basil to even out the couples, which suited Andrew fine, since Basil's flamboyant personality would hopefully take the attention off him.

"Good evening, Father. Basil. Has Cecilia arrived yet?"

"I believe she's in the parlor with your mother and Virginia."

"Ah, good. That will keep her occupied for the time being." He took a seat in one of the wing chairs beside his father, since Basil had taken over the sofa.

"I must say I was pleased to hear you'd invited Cecilia tonight," his father said. "Spending more time together is the best way to move your relationship forward."

The dinner bell sounded, thankfully sparing Andrew from any further lectures. The men rose and walked into the hall, just in time to see the women exiting the parlor.

"Good evening, Andrew." Celia wound her arm through his. "I thought you'd forgotten about me." She pouted her painted lips at him.

"Good evening, Cecilia. You look lovely tonight." And she did. She wore a peacock-blue dress that hugged her figure in a manner bordering on risqué, tight at the bodice and hips but flaring out around her calves. Her blond hair was elegantly coiffed as usual with sparkly earbobs dangling almost to her shoulder.

She gave him a coy look. "I'm glad you noticed."

They followed his parents into the dining room. Father helped Mother into her chair, then stood behind his own seat at the head of the table, waiting for everyone else to take their place.

Footsteps sounded in the hall, and an out-of-breath Grace rushed into the room.

Father scowled. "Why is Miss Foley here when we have guests? She should take her meal with the servants tonight."

Grace froze. Color bloomed in her cheeks. "I'm sorry. I should have realized. Excuse me, please." She started back out the door.

"That won't be necessary." Andrew moved swiftly to take Grace by the elbow and guide her to her chair. "This is a casual dinner, Father. There's no reason for Grace to leave." He met his father's eyes and stared, unblinking.

Tension crackled in the air.

"Please don't leave on my account." Basil smiled. "One more lovely lady at the table will not be a hardship."

"This is my fault," Mother said. "I meant to inform Miss Foley about tonight's arrangement, but it must have slipped my mind." She wore a slightly bemused expression. "I'll just ring for another place setting."

Andrew frowned. Mother hadn't been right lately. Frequent headaches. Forgetting appointments. He made a mental note to check how much medication the doctor had her on.

Father cleared his throat. "For tonight, we'll let it pass. But in future, Miss Foley, if we're having guests, you will take your meal with the staff."

Andrew pulled out the chair for Grace with a smile, hoping to impart an unspoken apology for his father's rudeness. "Please stay."

"Yes, Grace, please do." Virginia leaned forward.

Grace nodded and took her seat, her eyes downcast.

Andrew hated that his father had made her feel beneath them.

"Leave it to Andrew. Ever the gallant one." Cecilia's forced laugh did not fool Andrew for a moment. He knew she was incensed at the fuss he'd created over a mere servant. On social matters, she and Father were of the same mind.

Andrew took his place at the opposite end of the table, dismayed to note that Cecilia sat directly across from Grace. But there was little he could do about it without making more of a scene.

"That's a lovely frock you're wearing," Celia said to Grace as the maids brought in the first course.

Andrew glanced at Grace. She did look lovely in a pale green dress adorned with a simple gold cross and chain.

Her cheeks were still quite flushed, but she managed a smile. "Thank you. When I heard there were to be guests for dinner, I thought I should wear something nice."

"Nicer than your uniform, you mean?" Celia's feigned casual tone didn't fool anyone.

Grace just blinked, a pucker forming between her brows.

"Grace doesn't wear a uniform," Virginia told her. "Though I did advise her to wear an apron. Babies certainly are messy creatures."

"Messy and noisy." Cecilia actually shuddered. "Thank goodness for nannies to take care of all that."

The maids began to serve the soup, and the conversation took a different turn, thanks to Basil.

Andrew breathed a little easier, yet his muscles remained tense, prepared for whatever else might arise. He barely tasted the clam chowder.

Soon the platters for the main course arrived, filling the room with the scents of roast beef and gravy.

"How are plans going for the gala, Cecilia?" Father asked once the food had been served.

Immediately Celia brightened. "We've made a great start so far. We'll have to meet a few more times before we have all the details ironed out. In fact, I may need access to the ballroom to take some measurements."

"Anytime, my dear. We are at your disposal."

"I have so many ideas swirling in my head," Celia continued. "It's hard to settle on one. I may bring my mother with me. She has such a flair for design."

"I have no doubt you'll choose the perfect décor for the event." Mother smiled at Celia. "You have the same good taste as your parents."

"Thank you, Mrs. Easton." Celia smiled, then turned to lay a hand on Andrew's arm. "We all know Andrew will be no help at all, except for trying to keep us on budget."

Her burst of overly loud laughter grated on Andrew's taut nerves. "Someone has to keep an eye on the finances."

"And no one is more qualified than Andrew, a fact his business diploma attests to," Virginia said with a glare at Cecilia.

"Thank you, Ginny. I can always count on your staunch defense."

"Speaking of defense," Cecilia said to the table in general. "I'd like to hear everyone's opinion on something."

Her cat-that-ate-the-canary expression had Andrew immediately on guard.

"What about, dear?" Mother's eyebrows lifted in question.

"I'm trying to convince Andrew to shave off his beard."

Andrew held in a groan. Not this again. He thought he'd put the subject to rest once and for all.

"A face this handsome shouldn't be hidden. Don't you agree?" Cecilia reached out to run her fingers over his beard.

He had to fight not to slap her hand away.

"It's bad enough him wearing those stodgy old glasses most of the time." She laughed and shook her head.

"I agree." Father gave Cecilia an approving nod. "Executives should be clean-shaven and neatly groomed. It's more professional and inspires trust."

Andrew's stomach clenched as he struggled to keep his temper from slipping. Of course, his father would side with her. When had he ever taken Andrew's side about anything?

"See, Andrew, darling, my idea has merit. Won't you do it? For me?" She pinned him with a pleading gaze.

Irritation stiffened his spine. She had some nerve, trying to get his family to join forces against him. Shouldn't a man be able to decide whether he shaved his face or not?

"I think Andrew's beard suits him. If he likes it, it shouldn't matter what anyone else thinks."

All heads swiveled in Grace's direction, Andrew's included. Her eyes widened in an almost apologetic look.

Cecilia scowled, and in the strained silence that followed, Father and Mother exchanged incensed glances.

"Thank you, Grace," Andrew said quickly. "I am very fond of my beard, and I intend to keep it." He was amazed at the courage it must have taken to speak out against everyone.

Cecilia tilted her head at a haughty angle that revealed her extreme displeasure. "I'll wear you down yet, Andrew Easton. Mark my words."

Though everyone thought she was joking, he knew she would keep badgering him until she got what she wanted. It was the way their whole relationship had gone from the start. And as he well knew, she wanted him to do a great deal more than shave off his beard. The fact that he hadn't proposed yet was partly a stubborn rebellion to resist her manipulations.

Basil rose and cleared his throat. "This might be a good time for me to change the subject."

Andrew could have kissed him for diffusing an awkward situation. Poor Grace still looked as though she wanted to crawl under the table.

"Go ahead, Basil," Father said. "The floor is yours."

The wattage of the man's smile rivaled the chandelier above him. "It's no secret that I have been courting Virginia for some time now. And that my family has invited her to join us on an extended trip to Europe this summer." Basil reached in his pocket and took out a small box. "Now that I have your blessing, Oscar, I would like to make this official." He opened the box to reveal a large diamond ring, then bent one knee to the ground. "Virginia, will you make me the happiest of men and marry me?"

A hush fell over the room awaiting her response.

Virginia pressed a hand to her mouth, her gaze remaining glued to the ring. Then she looked around the table in what seemed quiet desperation.

Andrew longed to jump in to help her, but he couldn't tell if she was pleased or panicked.

"Go on, Virginia," Mother said with a nervous laugh. "Don't keep the poor man hanging."

Virginia looked down at him and nodded. "Yes, of course, I'll marry you."

Basil's face burst into a relieved smile. He slipped the ring on her finger, then rose to kiss her.

A murmur of good wishes went around the table. Mother clasped Virginia's hand and kissed her cheek. Father stood and shook Basil's hand.

"How romantic." Cecilia leaned over to whisper in Andrew's ear. "Perhaps you should take a cue from your sister's beau."

Andrew's smile felt encased in cement, as if one false move would cause it to crack wide open. He went to offer his congratulations to his sister and Basil. Ultimately, it didn't matter whether Basil was his favorite person or not. If Virginia chose to marry him, Andrew would support her one hundred percent.

"I have one other idea to propose." Smiling broadly, Basil draped an arm around Virginia's shoulder. "I'd like us to marry before Virginia and I leave for Europe. That way the trip can serve as our honeymoon."

Virginia's smile faded. "We could never prepare properly in that short amount of time."

"I'm sure if we put our minds to it," Basil soothed, "we could—"

"No." Virginia stepped from under his arm. "I will marry you, but not then. We'll decide upon a date after our return from Europe."

Andrew recognized that inflexible set to Ginny's jaw. She'd made up her mind, and nothing would sway her now.

"Now, darling, let's not be too hasty."

Virginia crossed her arms. "My point exactly."

Father laid a hand on Basil's shoulder. "The first thing you need to learn, my boy, is when to back down." He chuckled. "Let's all retire to the parlor. I'll open a bottle of champagne to celebrate."

"That's a wonderful idea." For the first time in ages, Mother was smiling. Virginia's upcoming wedding would give her something positive to focus on instead of grieving for Frank.

Andrew should be relieved. He should be happy.

Yet as the group crossed the hall into the parlor, he couldn't ignore the tightening in his gut, the feeling that something was amiss. He looked around and realized Grace was no longer there. In all the uproar, she must have slipped away.

"Andrew, are you coming?" Cecilia's irritated voice snapped at his nerve endings.

He uncurled his fists, warring against the urge to seek Grace out and apologize for his family and Cecilia. After the rude manner in which she'd been treated, he couldn't blame her for wanting to escape. But to go after her would only cause more strife.

Reluctantly, he entered the parlor, unsettled to find that the rest of the evening held no appeal at all without her there.

Grace entered her bedroom and shut the door behind her. Only then did she release a breath from her bursting lungs. Perhaps it was rude to have left without saying good-night, but she couldn't tolerate another minute of Cecilia Carmichael's glares across the table. The woman seemed to take an instant dislike to her for some reason. And after Grace blurted out the comment about Andrew's beard, the woman's hostility had only increased.

Would Grace ever learn to hold her rash tongue?

She turned on the lamp by her bed and allowed the coziness of the room to soothe her shattered nerves. The chintz curtains, the pale pink quilt, and the plush carpet beneath her feet created a haven of comfort. Now that Christian was used to Grace, Virginia had returned to her own room, and Grace had moved into the nanny's quarters, delighted to find them as charming as the room she'd just vacated. It even had a snug window nook, perfect for reading. Best of all, she was closer to her nephew, able to tend to him during the night if he needed her.

With a contented sigh, Grace allowed the last traces of tension to seep from her body. She quickly changed out of her good dress—or "frock" as Cecilia had called it—and put on her comfortable brown skirt and a blouse. Then she opened the connecting door to the nursery and went to check on the baby. The glow from the small lamp beside the rocking chair afforded her enough light to see him. Asleep on his back, the child's perfect features were relaxed in slumber, giving him the look of an angel. She stood staring at the peaceful rise and fall of his tiny chest, then took a seat in the rocker, content just to be near him.

This was quickly becoming her favorite time of day, sitting vigil in his room for several hours before she went to bed. Sometimes she read, sometimes she knitted. But often she worked on the quilt Rose had started—one of the items Reverend Burke had turned over to Grace after informing her of Rose's passing.

Most of Rose's clothes had been donated to charity, but Grace had been happy to find her sister's pink shawl among the items the minister had kept. Now draped around her shoulders, Grace envisioned it as a hug from her sister. Alone in the silence of this room, with Rose's son sleeping beside her, Grace could drop all pretense and simply be an aunt and a grieving sister.

She opened the wicker basket at her feet and took out one of the squares, admiring Rose's impeccable stitching. Grace recalled her sister trying to teach her the finer points of sewing and embroidery, but no matter how hard she tried, she could never match Rose's skill. Still, she would do her best to finish the quilt Rose had been making for her son, certain that one day Christian would be grateful to have it.

Sometime later, Grace awoke from a light doze with a start. She blinked, trying to focus in the dim room, and was stunned to see Andrew standing by the crib.

"Andrew. Is anything wrong?" Grace straightened and smoothed a hand over her hair. Her cheeks heated at his scrutiny. How long had he been watching her sleep?

"Everything's fine. I only wanted to check on Christian before I went to bed." He put a hand on the rail. "Why are you here? Was he fussing?"

"Oh no. I just enjoy sitting here before I retire." She stowed the fabric back in the basket and rose.

Andrew gazed down at the sleeping child, and a tender smile crept across his features. "When he's asleep like this, I can see a strong resemblance to my brother. Frank would have been so proud."

Grace moved closer. "I'm sure he would have."

They stood in silence for a few moments. The faint glow of the lamp cocooned them in the cozy space. Grace could almost imagine they were Christian's parents, looking in on their child, and her heart gave a tiny lurch. This was how she'd envisioned her future. With a man who took an interest in his child, who wanted to be home every night to tuck him in with a story or a lullaby.

Andrew turned to her. "Why did you disappear after dinner? I thought you'd want to celebrate Virginia's good news."

"It was a family celebration. I'm far more comfortable up here where I belong." She reached to tuck the blanket around the baby's legs, and her arm brushed Andrew's. An odd tingle of awareness rushed through her.

"Virginia doesn't view you as merely an employee. She considers you a friend. She would have loved you to be there."

Grace's throat tightened. She too was starting to consider Virginia a friend, but certain boundaries should not be crossed.

"It was Cecilia, wasn't it? I know she made you feel uncomfortable and for that I'm sorry."

"No apology needed."

"She's sometimes too opinionated, but underneath, she has a good heart."

"I'm sure she must, or you wouldn't be considering marrying her."

He flinched. "Did Virginia tell you that?"

"It appears to be common knowledge among the household." She forced herself to stare into the blueness of his eyes.

A frown creased his brow. "Marriage is what both our families want, but for now, we're taking our time to see if we're a good fit."

Cecilia Carmichael seemed the last person who would *fit* with Andrew. Where he was steadfast and kind, she appeared superficial and shallow. Grace couldn't imagine him being saddled with such a wife. The urge to say something burned through her, and though she knew she should hold her tongue, she couldn't stay silent. "For what it's worth, I believe if someone truly cares about you, they shouldn't want to change you."

A muscle tensed along his jaw. Had she offended him with her directness?

Andrew ran a hand over his beard. "I've learned it's best to ignore some of what Cecilia says and things usually blow over." He turned his intense gaze on her. "By the way, I wanted to thank you for your support earlier. It took courage to speak up that way."

Heat flashed up her neck. "I tend to say what's on my mind, often to my own detriment. I hope I didn't cause any problems for you."

"Don't worry. I can handle Cecilia. And my father."

She moved to retrieve her shawl from the rocking chair. "Well, I should turn in."

"Before you go, there's something I've been meaning to discuss with you." Andrew stepped toward her, and the clean scent of his soap met her nose. "You're free to take Sundays as a day off each week. Virginia and I will take care of Christian on those days."

"Thank you. I've been meaning to ask about that."

"If you'd like to attend church, you're welcome to join our family at the cathedral. The architecture alone will take your breath away."

Somehow she couldn't picture Mr. Easton welcoming her in their family pew. "I would love to see the cathedral one day, but I've promised my former landlady I'd spend Sundays with her when I can. She brought me to her church when I first came here."

"Which one is that?"

"Holy Trinity. Not as grand as your cathedral I'm sure, but the parishioners were very welcoming. Quite a few people from Britain attend there."

He smiled. "I'm glad you've found somewhere you feel comfortable. Now I will go and let you get your rest. Good-night, Grace." He started toward the door.

"Andrew?" An inexplicable force urged her to prolong their connection for even a few more seconds. Did he feel it too?

He turned back. "Yes?"

"For the record, I don't think your glasses are stodgy. I think they make you look rather distinguished."

The intensity of his stare bore through her. "You're the first person to say that. I've always felt self-conscious wearing them."

"You shouldn't."

"Thank you. I'll try to remember that." His gaze locked with hers.

It seemed to hold her in place like a magnet until she couldn't catch her breath.

"Good-night, Andrew," she said at last.

Before he could respond, she slipped through the connecting door to her room and closed it behind her with a soft click.

CHAPTER 12

August 25, 1914
Dear Grace,

Remember when we used to plan our weddings? How we promised to be each other's maid of honor? Well, please don't hate me, but . . . Frank and I got married! Frank begged me to elope with him before he went away to war. He said he needed to know I'd be here when he returned and not run off with the first available bloke. To be honest, I couldn't bear for him to go without us being married. Now we're husband and wife and nothing can change that. I only wish Frank's parents had come around. Don't they realize what they're doing to their son?

On Saturday afternoon, Grace prepared Christian for their daily walk. Due to the threat of rain, she decided to stick closer to home. Virginia wouldn't be joining them since she had plans with her new fiancé. Grace tried to be happy for her, but something about Virginia's lack of enthusiasm unsettled her. Surely a woman in love should be glowing with happiness, her head in the clouds. But Virginia appeared strangely subdued, as though the light had gone out of her. As soon as Grace had the chance, she planned to talk to her friend about it.

Grace tied Christian's bonnet under his chin. "There's my big boy," she crooned as she picked him up. "Are you ready for your walk?"

Christian's answering smile told her he agreed wholeheartedly. The boy loved being outdoors.

She carried him down the back staircase to the side entrance where the pram was stored. The house seemed eerily silent today. Likely Andrew and his father had gone into the office. Saturdays were not always a day off for those two. Since Virginia had gone out with Basil, perhaps Mrs. Easton was catching up with some of her friends.

Grace placed Christian inside the pram and released the brake.

"How about we explore your grandmother's garden today? I'd like a better look at all those lovely flowers." She aimed the pram onto the path that led around the property.

They passed the greenhouse, where she imagined Collin Lafferty would be hard at work. Or perhaps, despite the threat of rain, he would be tending the outdoor plants on this warm June day. She circled the perimeter of the property to the rear of the house where the magnificent sunroom dominated the setting. The solarium had apparently been added at Mrs. Easton's request. In the winter, she loved to sit there and enjoy the sunshine, as well as the many indoor plants that mirrored the ones outside.

Grace headed toward the center of the fabulous gardens, eager to find the stone fountain. She'd caught a glimpse of it the other day and wanted to take a closer look. It didn't take long to locate the elegant statue of a lady swathed in flowing robes. From the middle of the fountain, she stretched one hand toward the sky. Her other arm held an urn tipped toward the ground where a stream of water poured out into the pool below.

"She's breathtaking," Grace whispered, marveling at the artist's talent. One could almost feel the soft flow of her garment, the gentle fall of her hair.

The fountain was surrounded by a low stone seating area, but Grace wasn't ready to rest just yet. She continued through the rows of flowering greenery until she came to the small orchard and a vegetable garden that she knew kept the house supplied with fresh produce. In the far south corner of the property, a gleaming white gazebo created another inviting space to relax. But she would explore that area another day.

Grace stopped the pram near an array of flourishing rosebushes. Blossoms in yellow, pink, and red filled the air with the most glorious scents. She lifted the baby from the carriage and held him up to share the beauty.

"Do you like roses, Christian? They're one of my favorite flowers."

"Ah, but don't forget to beware of the thorns."

Grace whirled around to see the chauffeur standing behind her. "Mr. McDonald. You startled me."

"It's Toby, please." He plucked a bloom from the bush beside her and held it out to her. "A beautiful flower for a beautiful lady."

Heat rose in Grace's cheeks as she accepted the blossom. "That's kind of you, but I am far from beautiful." She fingered the velvet petals.

"On the contrary. Your beauty has been the topic of much discussion among the staff."

"Then you all must be sadly lacking in conversation topics." She ducked her head, anxious to get away from this uncomfortable sensation. Flirting with the chauffeur would not earn her any favor with the Eastons.

Toby must have sensed her unease for he quickly changed the subject. He pointed to the boy in her arms. "How is Master Christian faring today?"

"He is doing very well under the circumstances."

A shadow chased the humor from Toby's face. "Such a sad tale. I guess we have to be thankful the boy had family willing to take him in." He swept a hand toward the house in the distance. "He'll certainly never want for anything living here."

She bristled. "Except for the love of his parents."

"Yes, of course. I didn't mean to minimize the tragedy." He cleared his throat. "And how are you settling in, Miss Foley?"

She almost corrected him to use her given name, but figured it might be better to keep a professional distance. She didn't want him to think she was interested in a personal relationship of any kind. "Quite nicely, thank you. How could I not in such a beautiful home?" She smiled, trying to keep the conversation light. "But more importantly, I get to care for this darling boy." She kissed Christian's cheek and was delighted when he giggled. "Well, if you'll excuse us, we should continue with our walk." She set Christian back in the pram.

"Don't stray too far. Those clouds look ready to let loose any second."

"I won't. Good day, Mr. McDonald."

He tipped his cap with a smile.

Grace's muscles began to relax as she headed toward the house. Even as the first drops of rain landed on her cheek, she couldn't resist the chance to check out the terrace that surrounded the sunroom. She left the pram in a covered area at the side of the house, lifted Christian out, and climbed the stairs to the verandah. The view from the rail overlooking the gardens was magnificent. She wished her mother could see this. Mum would never believe how far she'd come from their country cottage.

She turned and peered in the window of the solarium, expecting to find it empty. Yet amid the plants and wicker furniture, Mrs. Easton sat slumped in a chair, her face in her hands.

Grace took a closer look and alarm swept through her. She appeared to be weeping. Had the woman received some bad news? From various comments she'd overheard among the staff, Grace had determined that Mrs. Easton's health was quite fragile. Perhaps she should go in and make sure she was all right.

The rain had started coming down harder. Grace rushed to the side entrance, and once inside, she dabbed the moisture from her face and Christian's and turned down a hallway that she hoped would lead to the solarium.

"Let's pay your grandmother a visit." If anything could brighten the woman's spirits, it would be her adorable grandson.

Still unsure of the house's layout, Grace ventured through what she remembered to be the main sitting room and found an opening to the solarium. She entered quietly so as not to startle the woman.

The soft sound of weeping echoed in the space.

Grace hesitated. Maybe Mrs. Easton wouldn't thank her for intruding on her private grief. After all, she hadn't been overly friendly to her, perhaps out of loyalty to her husband, or perhaps because she felt a similar loathing for immigrants.

Still, Grace would feel terrible if she didn't try to help.

"Mrs. Easton? Is there anything I can do for you?"

The woman's head jerked up. "Miss Foley. What are you doing here?"

Grace moved farther into the room. The soothing smell of damp soil and flowers filled the air.

"I was walking with Christian in the garden and it started to rain. When I returned to the house, I couldn't help noticing you in here alone. I thought a visit from your grandson might be nice, since our outing got cut short."

Mrs. Easton blew her nose in a handkerchief, then motioned her in. "That was very thoughtful. Thank you."

Grace took a seat beside her with Christian on her lap. She bounced her knee until the boy giggled.

Mrs. Easton gave a watery smile. "Nothing like a child's laughter to brighten the day."

"So true. Would you like to hold him?"

"Yes, thank you."

Grace handed the boy to his grandmother.

Mrs. Easton hugged him to her chest, closed her eyes, and inhaled. "It's as if I'm holding my Frank again. He used to smell exactly the same." Her voice quavered.

"I imagine Christian will grow up to look very much like him." *With the exception of his mother's eyes.*

"I hope so. Maybe then I can learn to live with the sorrow of losing Frank."

Grace nodded. "I know exactly what you mean."

Somehow holding Rose's son helped ease the pain of Grace's loss. And wasn't that the reason she'd originally wanted to bring Christian back home to her mother? As a substitute for the loved ones Mum had lost?

Mrs. Easton set Christian on her lap, not even rebuking him when he grabbed her string of pearls. She looked Grace in the eye for the first time. "Have you suffered the loss of someone close to you as well, Miss Foley?"

Grace bit her bottom lip, willing herself to be strong. "As a matter of fact, I have."

Andrew didn't mean to eavesdrop. He was just so stunned to see Grace and his mother seated together in the solarium, having an apparently intense conversation, that he couldn't move away. Then curiosity got the better of him, and he edged closer, staying out of sight behind the heavy drapery by the doorway.

"I see you understand my pain," his mother said. "Who did you lose? A parent?"

"A parent and siblings. One of my brothers died when I was twelve. My father passed away two years after, which was hard on my mother, being left with three other children. But more recently, we lost my oldest brother, Owen. He died in the war, like your son." Grace's voice broke. "It almost destroyed my mother. She took to her bed for weeks after the news."

"I did the same thing. Strange to think our families live an ocean apart and yet have so much in common."

"Indeed it is, ma'am."

"Please, call me Lillian, when it's just the two of us. Of course when Mr. Easton is present, we must maintain our formal titles."

"Of course."

"You mentioned three children. Where is your other sibling? In England, with your mother?"

A long silence ensued.

"I'm afraid we lost my sister recently to . . . a sudden illness."

"Oh, my dear. I'm terribly sorry. So it's only you and your mother left."

"That's right."

The sorrow in her voice stirred something in Andrew's chest. He inched closer.

"Then may I ask," his mother continued, "why you left to come all the way to Canada? I would think you'd want to be near her after enduring such tragedy."

When another silence ensued, Andrew risked a glance into the room. Grace was frowning, biting her bottom lip as she often did when agitated. He ducked back out of sight, hoping she would answer since he wanted to know the reason as well.

"It was my mother's wish that I come to Canada. She wanted me to . . ."

"Find a better life?"

"Yes."

"And I imagine you didn't want to disappoint her. Still, it must have been hard to leave."

"Extremely hard."

Those two words, fraught with such sorrow, wrenched Andrew's heart.

"You're a devoted daughter, which I can respect. You remind me very much of my Virginia in that regard."

Andrew peered around the curtain once again and his throat cinched. His mother was bouncing little Christian on her knee. The child laughed with undisguised delight. How had Grace known to bring him in to cheer his mother on this difficult day?

Frank would have turned twenty-eight today. Andrew had left the office early when he realized Mother was home alone, knowing she would be grieving and would need her family around her. He also worried she might overmedicate herself to ease the pain.

He stepped out from behind the curtain and entered the solarium. "Well, what do we have here? A party and I wasn't invited?"

Grace's head snapped up. Her posture stiffened.

"Andrew darling, what are you doing home so early?" His mother smiled.

He bent to kiss her cheek and rested his hand on Christian's back. "When it finally hit me what day it was, I didn't want you to be alone."

"Thank you. The house was much too quiet."

"Is today a special occasion?" Grace frowned, her expression confused.

Andrew nodded. "It's Frank's birthday."

"Oh." Grace looked at his mother, then back at him. "You'd probably like some time alone as a family. I can come back later for the baby."

Her thoughtfulness was more than admirable.

"Thank you, Grace." Andrew held out his hand to help her rise. "I'll walk you out."

She stared at him, then nodded. "Good afternoon, Mrs. Easton. I hope you're feeling better."

"Thank you so much, Grace. I enjoyed our conversation."

Andrew put a hand under her elbow and led her through the parlor into the main hall. "I want to thank you for bringing Christian to see my mother. How did you know this was a bad day for her?"

She glanced up at him, her eyes awash with sympathy. "I happened to see her through the window and realized she was crying. I hoped a visit from her grandson might cheer her up."

"That was most kind. Especially since she hasn't been very welcoming."

Her eyelids fluttered down and the sweep of her lashes touched her cheek. Why did he find her every move so fascinating?

"I'll be back in an hour or so for Christian," she said.

"If he gets fussy before then, I'll bring him up. Take some time for yourself and relax."

"Thank you." She started up the stairs, then looked back. "I'm very sorry about your brother. If I can do anything more, please just ask."

He nodded, his throat too tight to speak. As he watched her ascend the stairs, he couldn't help but admire her compassionate nature. She too had lost a brother in the war, and a sister recently as well, it seemed, yet she went out of her way to offer comfort to others.

Cecilia, on the other hand, had not even acknowledged the day. She of all people should know what significance the day held for him. She'd supposedly been in love with Frank once. Shouldn't she be feeling some sort of sorrow or regret? Yet she'd come into the office to work with Paul Edison as though the day meant nothing, never inquiring about his parents' well-being or his own, for that matter. Instead she flirted and giggled all morning with Andrew's nemesis, their laughter ringing out over the halls with irritating regularity.

Another reason why Andrew had wanted to leave early.

With a last glance up the stairs, he shook off his dark thoughts and went to enjoy the extra time with his mother and nephew.

CHAPTER 13

October 2, 1914

My heart is breaking, Grace. Today I said good-bye to Frank. He's finished the first course of his training and has received his orders. The Canadian Contingent are heading overseas next week. They will receive further training once they reach England. It seems so strange that Frank will be making the journey to my homeland without me. I only pray that when this war is over, we can travel there together and visit you and Mum. I'm sure you'll both love Frank as much as I do.

On Sunday morning, Grace awakened early, eager to take the streetcar to Mrs. Chamberlain's house and accompany her to church. She'd missed her long chats with her landlady, as well as the wise counsel of Reverend Burke.

But when she pushed back the drapes, torrents of rain streaked her window, making the trip across town improbable at best. She'd be soaked by the time she reached the streetcar stop. And then to sit in the drafty church in wet clothes, she'd be asking for her own case of influenza for her folly. With a sigh, she straightened her bed and quickly got dressed.

As Grace entered the baby's room, her heart warmed to the soft gurgles coming from the crib. Lately, instead of awaking in a frenzy of tears, Christian would content himself with his rattle or looking at his fists as he waved them in the air. Perhaps he was starting to forget his mother—a thought that both comforted Grace and saddened her greatly.

Smiling, she bent over the crib rail. "Good morning, sweetheart. How are you today?"

A wide toothless grin brightened the boy's face. Grace bit her lip at the unexpected rush of emotion. Did she dare believe he had bonded with her this quickly?

She lifted him up and snuggled him close. "Let's change your nappy and get you dressed."

The bedroom door opened, and Andrew stepped inside. "Grace. I didn't expect to see you. I thought you'd be getting ready for church."

"I've decided to postpone my trip until next week because of the weather."

"That's probably wise." He moved toward her, and her heart gave a lurch. In his gray suit and navy tie, he looked more handsome than ever. She dropped her gaze before she stared too long.

"Why don't you join us at the cathedral this morning? We'll be going by car, so you shouldn't get too wet." His tone was teasing, his smile open.

Yet the idea of squeezing into the family auto with Andrew's whole family set her nerves on fire. "I don't think your father would approve. I'll be fine here."

"If it will make you more comfortable, I can take you, Virginia, and Christian in my car."

She hesitated, hating to refuse his kind offer.

"You said you've been missing church. Why not try the cathedral and see if it suits you? If not, you don't have to go again."

Christian wiggled in her arms. The wetness of his bottom had begun to seep through to her apron. "I would have to change . . ." Her working clothes would never do for a cathedral. The very word inspired thoughts of royalty.

"I can take him while you do that." Andrew reached for the baby, but she held on.

"Careful, he's soaking. You don't want to ruin your suit. Let me change him and then you can take him while I dress."

"All right." One side of his mouth quirked up. "I'm learning that tending to a baby requires teamwork."

Grace laughed. "I'm discovering the same thing."

An hour later, after feeding Christian his breakfast, Grace sat with the boy held tightly on her lap in Andrew's car. Virginia had chosen to ride with her parents, which sent a glimmer of alarm through Grace. It felt as though Virginia was trying to give them time alone on the ride over. Grace had no idea why she would do such a thing, even if she disapproved of Cecilia Carmichael.

She glanced over at Andrew as he steered the auto confidently down the rain-slicked streets. He'd added a dashing fedora to his outfit, which sat at a rakish angle over his brow. For a moment, Grace allowed herself to imagine they were a real family heading off to church together. What would it be like to have a kind, honorable husband and a lovely baby boy?

Grace quickly erased that mental picture. Spending time alone with Andrew was not a good idea. Their relationship needed to remain strictly employer and employee.

Nothing more.

The steeple of the church came into view and Grace could only stare. St. James Cathedral was as awe-inspiring as it sounded.

"It's beautiful," she breathed.

"Wait until you see the inside. I never tire of its grandeur." Andrew craned his neck to see the road. "I'm afraid I'll have to let you off. It appears everyone has come in their vehicles today. I'll meet you in the vestibule as soon as I find a spot to park."

Grace peered out at the rain. "Did you bring your brolly?"

"My what?"

"Oh, sorry. Your umbrella."

He grinned. "Yes, I have my *brolly* in the back seat. Thank you."

The car stopped, and Grace managed to open the door and

step out with Christian, whom she'd wrapped in a blanket. She pressed the boy's face into her shoulder as she ran for the steps of the church.

A man held the door open for her, and she dashed inside where a crush of people stood talking in the foyer. Grace shook water droplets from her jacket and hat and checked Christian to make sure he wasn't wet. Thankfully, the outer blanket had protected him from the brief shower.

"My, what a beautiful baby." A tall woman in a blue velvet hat and matching coat stepped toward her.

"Thank you." Grace shifted Christian to a more comfortable position. Something about the compliment seemed as false as the woman's cold eyes.

"Does he take after you or your husband?"

Grace pasted on a smile. "Oh, he's not mine. I'm his nanny."

The woman's brows rose to the brim of her hat. "His parents let you take him to church? I've never heard of such a thing." The woman scanned the group of people as though expecting his parents to come rushing forward and pluck the child from her arms.

"I'm waiting for his family. They should be here any minute." At this point, Grace would even be relieved to see Mr. Easton come through the doors, but she suspected he and the others were already seated, since they had left before her and Andrew.

Thankfully, the door opened and Andrew entered, shaking the moisture from his brolly. Grace lifted a hand to catch his attention. He smiled and headed in her direction, but as he neared, his expression became guarded.

"Mrs. Carmichael. How are you today?" He moved beside Grace and, in what seemed a deliberate action, adjusted the blanket around Christian's back.

"Andrew?" The woman's brows rose higher. "What is the meaning of this?"

"Allow me to introduce Miss Grace Foley and my nephew, Christian. Grace, this is Mrs. Carmichael, a close friend of the family."

Carmichael. As in Cecilia Carmichael? As Grace studied the

woman, the similarity became evident. The woman wore the same air of superiority that clung to her daughter.

Mrs. Carmichael inclined her head, then turned to Andrew. "I was just admiring the baby. I'm afraid I've been remiss in visiting since his . . . arrival."

"No need. I know how busy you are."

Grace glanced at Andrew. His tone seemed reserved, chilly almost. Why were things so strained with this woman, who in all likelihood would one day become his mother-in-law?

"You must sit with us, Andrew. Cecilia will be thrilled to see you."

"Thank you, but I'll be sitting near the back in case Christian fusses." His features appeared set in stone. "Mother and Father are in their usual spot. You should say hello on your way in."

Grace held her breath, willing the tension to ease.

The woman glared at Grace, then looked back at Andrew. "I hope we'll see you at the house again soon. I fear Cecilia has been feeling somewhat neglected of late."

"She knows I've been busy since becoming Christian's guardian. Helping him adjust to his new home has to be a priority right now."

"Yes, well, now that you have a new nanny, your time should be much freer." Her arctic tone matched her frozen features.

The organ music swelled, and people began filing into the church.

Mrs. Carmichael spared Grace one last disdainful glance, then headed inside with the rest of the congregation.

As soon as she left, the air whooshed from Grace's lungs. "Did I do something to upset her?"

"Not at all. Irritated is Charlotte Carmichael's perpetual state, I'm afraid. Don't let her get to you." He gestured to the interior of the church. "Let's find our seats, shall we?"

"Are you sure you want to sit with us? You'd probably be better off with the rest of your family."

"I'm not afraid of a little gossip, Grace. My place is with Christian. If anyone has a problem with it, they can take it up with me later."

Grace was certain Mr. Easton would do exactly that.

With a hand to her back, Andrew guided her into the church. She shook off the tension and concentrated instead on taking in her surroundings. The inside of the cathedral was as awe-inspiring as Andrew had described. Gorgeous stained-glass windows lined each side of the building. Rows of identical pillars marked the aisles all the way to the altar. The heady scent of flowers and candle wax filled the space.

She and Andrew sat in the second-to-last row so they could make a quick escape if need be. Grace became instantly aware of the blatant stares and whispers around them, yet Andrew appeared unfazed. With enormous effort, she held her head high and focused on the service.

Once she settled in, she found the minister to be an eloquent and uplifting speaker. But the greatest inspiration came from the remarkable choir, accompanied by a powerful pipe organ, which sent chills straight up her spine. The music rivaled something she might have heard in Westminster Abbey.

"How did you enjoy the service?" Andrew asked afterward.

Grace looked up from tying Christian's bonnet. "It was brilliant."

"Brilliant?"

"Marvelous. Incredible. Extraordinary."

He chuckled and stepped into the aisle. "Ah, I get the picture."

"I could stay here all day and listen to the singing." She lifted Christian and rose from the pew.

"I'm glad you enjoyed it. And this little man"—Andrew angled his head toward Christian—"was very well-behaved. He must have liked the music too." He held out his hand and Christian grabbed his finger.

Grace laughed. "All babies love music. It's inborn, I think."

Andrew's smile suddenly faded. "Brace yourself," he whispered.

She followed his gaze up the aisle. Mr. Easton marched toward them, a decidedly unpleasant expression reddening his face. Mrs. Easton and Virginia had stopped to talk to someone farther back.

"What is the meaning of this, Andrew? Why were you sitting at the back of the church like some sort of criminal?"

Andrew huffed out a breath. "I doubt many criminals come to church, Father."

Grace bit her bottom lip to contain a rush of laughter. She suspected Mr. Easton wouldn't share her humor.

"We've been invited to the Carmichaels' for lunch," Mr. Easton said. "Drop Miss Foley off and meet us there." He continued down the aisle without a glance in Grace's direction.

Andrew laid a hand on her arm. "Please excuse my father's rudeness."

"You needn't apologize. His anger is merely a mask for his pain."

His eyes widened. "That is a perfect description. How did you come up with that after so short a time?"

"I've lived with my mother's version of it for over a decade." She tucked the blanket under Christian's chin as they made their way into the vestibule. "It doesn't render the comments any less hurtful, but understanding the source makes it bearable."

"Why is your mother so angry?" Curiosity lit his blue eyes.

But Grace had no intention of telling Andrew about her own horrible character flaw—one that had led to such tragedy and was a constant source of friction with her mother. He might not trust her with Christian if he knew, and she wasn't willing to risk it. "That's a story for another day. Come on. Your father will be livid if we delay any longer."

CHAPTER 14

November 18, 1914
Dear Grace,

I don't know when Frank will be able to send his pay home. Mail is sporadic at best. So in order to keep our little flat, I've had to take a job cleaning houses. I'm also doing some sewing on the side for one of my neighbors. I only hope I can make enough to keep living here until Frank returns.

Much later that day, with Christian in bed for the night, Grace tiptoed to the door of the kitchen and peered inside. No sign of Mrs. Hopkins. Grace breathed a sigh of relief. As much as she adored the woman, if she were here now she'd want to talk, and talk, and talk. Usually Grace enjoyed her fanciful stories, but after a long day, all she wanted was a cup of tea and some solitude. Since she hadn't been inclined to go anywhere in the downpours of rain, she'd relieved Andrew and Virginia from their offer to mind Christian. Perhaps next Sunday she would get her day off and visit Mrs. Chamberlain.

Grace set the kettle on the stove and turned on the burner, then rummaged quietly in the cupboards for the tea. In the process, she discovered a tin of homemade sugar cookies. Soon she settled at the staff's table with two cookies on a plate and the warm cup between her fingers.

Her thoughts immediately circled back to the undercurrent of tension at the dinner table that evening over a discussion of an upcoming event at the hotel, the one Cecilia Carmichael had been helping with. Grace didn't understand the exact nature of the problem, but it was clear Andrew and Mr. Easton held vastly different opinions about it.

She finished her tea, rinsed the cup, and set it in the sink to dry. Not feeling any more ready to sleep, she nonetheless started up the stairs to her room. As she reached the main floor, the sound of music drifted over to her. Her curiosity got the better of her, and she followed the sound to the parlor. Someone was playing the piano.

She peeked around the doorframe, surprised to find the room shrouded in darkness. Only a small lamp over the keyboard illuminated the area, creating a halo effect around the player's head.

Her heart hitched. She had no idea Andrew was musically inclined.

Something about the soulful manner in which he played and the haunting quality of the melody riveted Grace to the spot. She waited, not wanting to interrupt the flow of the music.

Finally his fingers stilled on the keys, and his shoulders slumped. He seemed worn down, defeated.

Grace couldn't leave without at least trying to help.

"That was beautiful. I didn't know you could play."

He swiveled on the bench, surprise and perhaps pleasure lighting his eyes. "Thank you. It's all due to my mother, who insisted on mandatory lessons when we were young." He rose and came to stand by the sofa. "Now I only play when trying to solve a problem. I find it frees my mind."

"I could tell something was bothering you at dinner this evening." She took a seat in one of the armchairs. "I'm a good listener if you'd care to talk about it."

He studied her a moment, then nodded, his brow furrowed in thought. "Thank you. That might help." He turned on a lamp beside the sofa, which cast a warm glow over the area, then perched on the arm of a wing chair.

"Does it have anything to do with the benefit at the hotel?" Grace asked. "It seemed a bone of contention between you and your father."

His lip quirked up. "One of many, I'm afraid."

If Andrew considered it odd to be having such a frank discussion with one of his staff members, he didn't let it show, which gave Grace the courage to forge on. "I gather you don't agree with him about hosting the gala."

"It's not that. The idea for the benefit came from Paul Edison, one of my father's executives. It's supposed to be a tribute to the soldiers, a show of gratitude for their efforts in the war. But Edison's doing this for all the wrong reasons. He's using the gala to make himself look good in my father's eyes." Andrew rose abruptly and walked to the window where he pushed the curtains aside and stared out at the darkness beyond.

The clock on the mantel struck nine, the chimes echoing in the stillness of the room.

Grace folded her hands in her lap and waited for him to continue.

At last he spoke. "Edison's invited one token soldier as the focus of the event. The majority of people attending will be the usual upper class of Toronto, when it should be the veterans we're inviting. Yet the cost of a ticket is likely too expensive for a returning soldier to afford, and the goal is, after all, to raise money for the hotel as well as the veterans." He let the curtain drop back into place and ran his fingers through his hair. "I don't know what the answer is, but the whole affair is leaving a sour taste in my mouth. I'm sure Frank would be appalled at the idea."

Grace nodded. Owen would feel the same way. It would be different if this was a sincere attempt to pay tribute to the men who had sacrificed so much for the world's freedom. But there was no reason why that still couldn't happen.

"Have all the tickets been sold?" she asked.

"No. Why?"

"Could you not, as a show of good faith, purchase a number of tickets on behalf of the hotel and offer the seats to some local veterans?"

At his puzzled look, warmth bled into her cheeks. Perhaps he thought the idea foolish. "I don't begin to know the amount of money involved, but if it were feasible, wouldn't that be a fitting way of rewarding the soldiers?"

"An admirable thought, but where would we find the names of these people?"

She considered it for a moment. "At home, we have a Department of Veterans' Affairs that keeps track of all the returning and deceased soldiers." Grace pushed back the recollection of them coming to the door with tragic news about Owen. "There's also the hospital where the wounded soldiers were taken. The officials there kept meticulous records of every man who came through their doors."

His eyes lit with sudden enthusiasm. "We have the Toronto Military Hospital right here in the city. I could start there." He took a seat across from her. "Thank you, Grace. I think I can salvage this event and turn it into something positive. Something Frank would be proud of."

"I'm glad I could help." She hesitated. "Might I offer another suggestion?"

"By all means."

"I think it would be wonderful if you gave a tribute to your brother at the dinner. It would add a more personal touch to the event, and I'm sure the soldiers would appreciate hearing how the war has touched your family."

Andrew stared at her, a muscle working in his jaw. Had she gone too far suggesting such a thing? After all, his relationship with his brother had been strained at best. Still, Frank had given his life in service to his country, which had to count for something.

"That's perfect. It would be a way to tie the event to our family and provide a valid reason for hosting it." Andrew's gaze grew more intense. "You're brilliant."

Pleasure flooded her system at his praise. "But will your father agree to it?"

"I won't give him the chance to refuse. I'll add the tribute to the agenda myself—at the last minute, if necessary." His face became determined. "And if I do get more soldiers to attend, I may have to keep that as a surprise as well. If not from my father, then definitely from Paul Edison."

Grace wondered if Andrew's animosity toward this Mr. Edison was purely business or if it had anything to do with the other man's supposed interest in Cecilia? But his feelings about Mr. Edison didn't matter. Finding a way to make this gala more meaningful, instead of being simply about raising money, was the issue.

Andrew reached out and took her hand in his. Warmth spread up her arm and her pulse quickened. Flustered, she tried to pull her hand away, but he held it firm between his own.

"If I manage to pull this off, you must come to the gala. We both lost siblings in this dreaded war. My tribute to Frank will be a tribute to your brother as well."

"I don't think that would be appropriate," she said.

"It would mean a great deal to have you there." His blue eyes shone with sincerity, causing nerves to flutter in her stomach.

"I-I have nothing to wear to such an event."

He grinned. "Never fear. Virginia will come to the rescue, I imagine."

"But what will Miss Carmichael say?"

"She can hardly object to me inviting a friend."

A friend. Grace swallowed a sudden rush of disappointment. How silly to imagine she was anything more than that to him. "I'd have to see if one of the maids would be willing to watch Christian for me."

"I'm sure they will. And if they give you any trouble, I'll speak to them."

Grace's stomach sank. The last thing she needed was for Andrew to order one of her peers to do her work while she attended the ball. Visions of Cinderella came to mind, and while Virginia might be her fairy godmother and provide her with a gown, Cecilia Carmichael fit the role of the evil stepmother to perfection.

This affair could prove to be a roaring success—or a complete disaster.

When the day of the gala arrived, Grace still hadn't found a way to get out of attending the event. None of her arguments had swayed either Andrew or Virginia—his co-conspirator—from their determination that she come with them. Grace could have simply refused, but if she were being perfectly honest, part of her thrilled at the possibility of attending such an exclusive function at the Easton Towers Hotel. When would she ever have such a chance again?

And part of her looked forward to the chance to pay tribute not only to Owen, but to Rose's late husband too. Even though Grace had never met Frank, she felt like she knew him through Rose's letters.

Besides, it seemed important to Andrew that she be there, and she couldn't bring herself to let him down.

"I'm so excited you're coming," Virginia had told her earlier in the week while she forced Grace to try on gown after gown from her closet.

How did one girl possess so many beautiful dresses?

"I won't feel like such a lame duck at the table with Mother and her friends. Andrew and Father will of course be at the head table, along with all the other hotel dignitaries."

"What about Basil? Won't he be there?"

Virginia's features clouded over. "As usual, he has business of his own that evening. Though he did say he'd try to come for an hour or so."

Grace hid an expression of relief behind the ruffles of the dress she was trying on. It would be good to have Virginia there as a buffer, not only between her and Mr. Easton, who would likely be apoplectic when he saw her, but between her and Andrew as well. She had to remind herself that he was not her escort, that he'd only invited her out of a shared interest in the veterans being honored. Nothing more.

"I think this is the one." Virginia fluffed the sleeves of the frothy blue creation, then propelled Grace to the mirror. "It's fabulous, don't you agree?"

Grace could only stare at her reflection. She'd never worn anything so fancy in her life. With a slight movement of her hips, the fabric swung about her legs, the whole dress shimmering with reflected light. "It's beautiful. Are you sure you don't mind me borrowing it?"

"Absolutely not. This color looks great on you. Andrew won't be able to keep his eyes off you."

Grace stiffened. The last thing she needed was her friend's continued attempts at matchmaking. "Virginia, you have the wrong idea. Andrew only invited me because we've both lost brothers in the war. Don't forget, he'll be escorting Cecilia."

Undaunted, Virginia only grinned. "You can't blame me for wishing someone might take his focus off her."

"Well, that someone won't be me," Grace said sternly. "Can you imagine your father's reaction?"

Virginia sighed. "You're probably right. But one can always dream."

Dreams, Grace told herself now as she dressed for the event, were a ridiculous waste of time. Especially dreaming of something that could never be.

Lord, I ask for your help tonight. Keep my focus on what the evening is really about, and let me not fall into temptation.

She waited nervously in her room until Virginia tapped on her door, the signal that her parents had already left and that they should meet Andrew in the foyer. He was to drive them both over and pick the appropriate time to usher them into the ballroom. She had to trust him when he claimed his father would never make a scene in public, and, as he assured her, with the extra veterans arriving, as well as the speech Andrew intended to give, she would be the last thing on his father's mind.

Grace opened her door to find Virginia resplendent in a fuchsia silk gown and matching shoes.

"You look wonderful." Grace smiled at her partner in crime and closed her bedroom door behind her.

Virginia gave a mock curtsy. "Why, thank you. So do you. My maid did a fabulous job with your hair. You, my dear, will be the belle of the ball."

Grace patted the intricate sweep of curls on top of her head, still marveling at the way the other staff members had jumped in to help her. "I never imagined I could look like this. I'm not sure I'm at all comfortable with it."

Virginia wound her arm through Grace's, pulling her along the hallway. "Better get used to it. You're bound to have all the men swooning at your feet." She came to a sudden stop and leaned over to whisper in her ear. "Starting with my brother."

Grace's gaze flew up. Andrew stood several feet away, staring at her with his mouth open. Her pulse tripped at the sight of him. He looked incredibly handsome in a black tuxedo, his hair slicked back to one side, and his beard impeccably groomed.

She swallowed hard, but no words made it past her dry throat.

He took a few steps forward, meeting them at the top of the stairs. "Grace, you look positively stunning."

Heat stole into her cheeks at the unaccustomed compliment. "Thank you."

"What about me, Drew? Am I stunning as well?" Virginia's teasing tone brought a slash of red to Andrew's face.

"You're beautiful as always, Gin." He kissed her cheek, then cleared his throat. "I'll bring the car around. Meet me out front in five minutes."

"We'll be there," Virginia promised.

Grace took a deep breath as Andrew headed down the stairs. Already she'd failed to guard her heart. She'd have to try extra hard for the rest of the night to keep all romantic thoughts of Andrew at bay.

CHAPTER 15

Andrew's unexpected nerves were a result of the surprises he had planned for this evening. They had absolutely nothing to do with the way Grace looked in that dress or the fact that the mere sight of her made his heart beat double time in his chest. He continued to try to convince himself of that as he escorted the women into the lobby of the Easton Towers Hotel.

Once inside, he stopped to check his pocket watch, relieved to find they were a good thirty minutes early. With all he had in store for his father and Edison, Andrew wanted plenty of time to make sure everything went smoothly.

The first hurdle to cross—Grace's presence. He prayed his father would not embarrass her in front of Toronto's entire elite set. Another reason he was glad to be early. Most of the upper class tended to arrive late, wanting to make their grand entrance in front of as many people as possible.

When he reached the elevator, he found himself alone. He looked back to where Grace and Virginia had stopped in the middle of the lobby. He frowned and crossed the floor toward them. "Is something wrong?"

Grace's brown eyes were wide with awe. "Oh, Andrew. Your hotel is magnificent. I've never seen anything so grand before."

Andrew's chest swelled with pride—and a little remorse. He'd been so consumed with tonight's event that he never stopped to think this was Grace's first time to see the hotel—maybe her first time ever in such an opulent place. "I'm glad you like it. We're very proud, of course."

"Wait until you see the ballroom." Virginia looped her arm through Grace's. "It's even more impressive."

Grace seemed to hold her breath as they entered the elevator.

Andrew pushed the button. The cage jerked into motion, and she gasped. She gripped his arm with steely fingers, until they came to a stop and the doors slid open.

"I've only been on an elevator once before," she said. "That was . . . exhilarating."

He laughed. If only everyone was so easily impressed.

Andrew led the way to the ballroom entrance. A large sign reading *Veterans Ball, June 28, 1919* stood beside the open double doors. One of the hotel employees sat at a small table, ready to take tickets, and if anyone wanted, to check their coats. A bellboy would take all the wraps to the coatroom farther down the corridor.

Andrew handed their tickets to the woman with a smile. "Good evening, Martha."

"Good evening, Mr. Easton."

He placed an envelope on the table. "These are the tickets for the VIP guests. They should be arriving soon. You'll know them by their uniforms."

"Yes, sir." She beamed up at him. "And may I say what a wonderful thing this is that you and your family are doing. Honoring the veterans this way."

"Thank you, Martha. Say a prayer that all goes well tonight."

"Oh, indeed I shall, sir."

Andrew held out his arms to Grace and Virginia, and together they entered the ballroom. His mouth fell open at the sight of the transformed area before him. Dark blue and silver strips of material swooped down from the chandeliers in the ceiling. The walls were draped in similar swatches of fabric, as were the tables and chairs. Candles glowed in containers at each table, creating an intimate atmosphere. Huge arrangements of flowers graced the head table, with smaller versions at each of the other ones, scenting the whole room with a heady perfume.

Grace's head swiveled as she surveyed the room. "It's absolutely stunning."

"I agree," Virginia said. "As much as I hate to admit it, Cecilia has outdone herself."

"Indeed, she has." It rankled Andrew a bit to have to agree. Had he secretly been hoping the event would flop so Edison would look bad? Not a very Christlike attitude. He gave himself a mental shake. For the soldiers' sake, he was glad the room looked so elegant. They deserved nothing but the best. "Come on. I'll take you over to Mother's table. Then I have duties to attend to."

A smattering of early arrivals milled about the room. Andrew held back a groan as he approached the table closest to the front. How could he not have checked the seating arrangement beforehand? He should have realized Cecilia would seat the Carmichaels with Mother. Now Grace would be at the mercy of Charlotte Carmichael's caustic tongue. He'd have to hope Virginia would handle the disagreeable woman.

"Mother, you look positively radiant." Andrew bent to kiss her cheek. Then he aimed his best smile at her table companions. "Mr. and Mrs. Carmichael, good to see you." He shook hands with Harrison and kissed Charlotte's icy hand. "You look lovely, Mrs. Carmichael."

She gave him a slight nod, then peered past his shoulder. "You brought the *nanny*? Won't she feel terribly out of place at this type of event?"

Virginia took Grace's arm and propelled her forward. "I hope you don't mind, Mother, but I begged Grace to come with me. I didn't want to be the only youngster at the table."

Mother smiled. "Grace dear, this is a lovely surprise."

Andrew blinked, almost as stunned as Grace appeared to be.

"Thank you, Mrs. Easton. I'm honored to be invited and grateful for the opportunity to pay tribute to all those who served their countries in this war, my brother included."

"Well said, young lady." Mr. Carmichael, ever the gentleman, came forward. "I don't think I've had the pleasure. I'm Harrison Carmichael."

"Grace Foley. How do you do?" She bobbed a small curtsy.

"You're English?" A light of interest brightened Mr. Carmichael's face. "I adore the British accent. I could listen to you talk all night. You must sit beside me."

Andrew repressed a sigh at the obvious stiffening of the man's wife. Charlotte did not need another reason to dislike Grace.

"I'm sorry, Mr. Carmichael," Virginia said. "But Grace is my guest for the evening."

Harrison only laughed. "Fair enough, Miss Easton. I defer to your youth."

From the corner of his eye, Andrew saw Cecilia and Edison talking close together at the front of the room. "Excuse me, everyone," he said. With a subtle bow, he crossed first to the head table where his father stood. His heart thudding in his chest, he braced himself for his father's reaction to the changes he'd made.

"Andrew. Thank goodness." His father's heightened color accented the silver threads at his temple. "Paul and Cecilia are confused with two extra tables that were added at the last minute, apparently at your request."

Andrew smiled. "I've invited some guests who will make this night even more special."

A frown creased Father's brow. "Is the kitchen aware of these extras?"

"Of course. I do know a bit about the hotel business."

"Well, you'd better go and appease Cecilia before she has a fit."

"Leave her to me." A movement caught his eye. "Ah, here comes Harrison. Why don't you two keep him company and relax. Let me handle things."

As soon as his father and Harrison headed across the room, Andrew made his way to the corner where Edison and Cecilia were poring over some papers.

Celia's head snapped up the moment he approached. "Andrew.

What is the meaning of this change to the agenda? It says you're giving a speech."

"That's right," he said calmly.

"Since when do you give speeches?" Edison demanded.

"Since now."

"And what about these extra tables? Why didn't you tell us about this before now?"

"Yes, Andrew," Celia said. "Why the secrecy?"

"I have a surprise for everyone. Trust me. It's going to be wonderful." *He hoped.*

Both of them scowled at him.

With great effort, he kept his smile in place. "Remember, tonight is all about the veterans."

CHAPTER 16

August 1, 1916
Dear Grace,

I finally got a better job! In an office. I've also been volunteering with Reverend Burke at the church. He's recruiting people to make care packages to send overseas to the soldiers. We've been knitting socks and scarves. With every stitch, I picture my Frank getting something clean and warm to wear in those dreadful trenches. I can't believe he's been gone nearly two years.

Grace had never before seen a building of such opulence.

When they arrived at Easton Towers, the hotel lobby had taken her breath away, but it couldn't compare to the ballroom. A multitude of overhead chandeliers illuminated the large space, the crystal orbs shooting sparkling rays over the tabletops. The heady perfume of thousands of fresh-cut flowers permeated the entire area. Grace almost wanted to pinch herself to make sure it wasn't all a delicious dream.

The one thing marring her total enjoyment of the evening, however, was the obvious hostility emanating from Mrs. Carmichael. If only the woman knew she had nothing to fear from Grace.

Nothing at all.

Despite the tension, Grace managed to enjoy the meal, which was one of the best she'd ever eaten. Filet mignon, roasted potatoes, asparagus, and glazed carrots, topped off with an amazing chocolate soufflé for dessert.

Throughout the feast, Virginia kept Grace amused, murmuring little tidbits about the different people who stopped by the table to pay their respects.

Grace took a sip of her tea, her gaze moving—as it had so many times that evening—to Andrew at the head table. He looked so official up there, so handsome and self-assured.

And so very far out of her league.

Just then he rose and walked to the microphone at the dais. Two brass stands held places of prominence on either side of the wooden structure. One contained a large red flag, presumably belonging to Canada, the other, a Union Jack, the flag of the British Empire.

Andrew pulled out several sheets of paper and laid them on the podium.

Grace's heart raced. She gripped her hands together under the table, praying his speech would be as well received as the arrival of the soldiers had been.

"Good evening, ladies and gentlemen. I hope you've enjoyed this delicious meal as much as I have. A big note of thanks to Chef Morrow, who did such a great job with the menu."

The audience applauded.

"To begin, Mayor Church has asked me to extend his regrets that he couldn't be with us tonight because he had a previous engagement. But he has assured us of a large donation from city hall on Monday." The people clapped politely. "As you all know, the reason for holding this gala tonight is to pay tribute to the brave men who fought so hard in the Great War. Without them, heaven only knows where we would be today. To that end, I would like to introduce one of our guests for this evening. I invite Dr. Victor Fullman, the director of the Toronto Military Hospital, to come up please."

More applause sounded as a dignified gray-haired man rose from the veterans' table and made his way to the podium.

"You may notice that I'm not dressed in a military uniform," the man began. "That's because the army deemed me a little too long in the tooth for combat." Light laughter ensued. "I am, however, the director of the Toronto Military Hospital where hundreds of soldiers have come in need of healing. My esteem for these heroes has only grown since meeting such stoic patriots." He paused to look over at one table. "One such man has become a good friend and colleague, a man who served as an army medic and who was himself injured while attempting to save a fellow soldier. This man recovered in England and brought back with him some innovative therapy techniques, which he has put into practice at the hospital. He's a very private man, but I hope you'll help me encourage him to come forward and share a bit about his experiences. I give you Doctor Matthew Clayborne."

Grace applauded while a tall, handsome man in uniform rose slowly from his seat. He walked forward with a slight limp to shake Dr. Fullman's hand. From the way he stood staring over the crowd, focusing on no one, the medic seemed uncomfortable at being the center of attention. But then he began to speak, not about himself, but about the therapy techniques he used to help soldiers overcome their disabilities so they might go on to lead normal lives. His passion for his work shone through his words.

If Owen had survived his injuries, Grace would have wanted someone like Dr. Clayborne to treat him. The man exuded sincerity and integrity.

As did the man beside him. Andrew had done a fantastic job picking the men to honor tonight. Dr. Fullman and Dr. Clayborne took turns commending the soldiers at their table and highlighting their particular stories. Each one was more riveting than the next.

Grace's heart swelled. Andrew had done it. He'd turned this event into a real tribute for the soldiers. When he stepped forward to present Dr. Fullman with a sizable check for the military hospital, she could barely keep her tears at bay. She didn't think she could be any prouder—until Andrew began his next speech.

"The credit for this gala tonight must go to Mr. Paul Edison, who came up with the initial idea, and to Miss Cecilia Carmichael, who decorated this beautiful room." He gestured for them to stand and waited while they acknowledged the audience's applause. When the room quieted, Andrew shuffled the papers at the podium. "I would also be remiss if I didn't acknowledge a good friend who helped me when I was looking for a way to make this evening more meaningful." For a second, his gaze caught Grace's. "Her suggestions were wonderful and I thank her for them."

Heat rushed into her face. Surely he wouldn't mention her by name.

But he quickly turned back to his prepared speech, and Grace released a grateful breath.

"Many of you here have been touched by the war in one way or another," he continued. "The Easton family is no exception. When the war broke out, my older brother, Frank, was one of the first people in line at the recruitment office. Some called him reckless, some called him patriotic. Only Frank knew his true motivation, but as his brother, I suspect a big part was the lure of adventure." He smiled. "Frank always did seem too big for this world. Too filled with excitement for it to contain him." He halted, his Adam's apple bobbing.

Grace glanced at Mr. Easton. He stared straight ahead, his mouth set in a grim line. She couldn't tell what he was feeling except that she swore she saw the glisten of tears in his eyes.

Andrew cleared his throat. "I'm ashamed to admit it, but I was jealous of my brother. I tried three times in three different recruitment offices to enlist, but unfortunately due to some physical limitations"—he pushed his glasses up higher on his nose—"they deemed me unfit for combat. Frank made it seem like he'd won another contest, and this time his prize was a uniform and a helmet. If only his winning streak could have continued."

Mrs. Easton let out a quiet sob and pressed a handkerchief to her mouth. Virginia too was weeping softly. Grace reached over to squeeze Mrs. Easton's arm. She hadn't counted on the toll Andrew's tribute might take on his mother.

"Our one consolation," Andrew went on, "was that Frank died a hero. During a particularly bloody skirmish, he went back to help an injured comrade, and in the process, was hit himself. He managed to get the man to safety, but unfortunately Frank succumbed to his injuries." He stopped and took a quick sip of water, while the room murmured their sympathy. "Too many young men lost their lives in this conflict, but without them, we probably wouldn't enjoy the same liberties we do now. So tonight we remember their sacrifice." His focus moved to the table of veterans. "Once again, gentlemen, on behalf of the Easton family and everyone here, we thank you most sincerely for your service to our country."

The people surged to their feet in a standing ovation. Mrs. Easton rose as well, clapping enthusiastically. Virginia and Grace followed suit, Virginia seeming unashamed of the wetness staining her cheeks. When Mr. Easton shook Andrew's hand and clapped him on the shoulder, Grace bit her lip to contain a fresh surge of emotion.

"Thank you for that fine tribute, Andrew," he said in a gruff voice. "And now let us continue the evening with a celebration of victory and the end of the war. The orchestra is ready and waiting to entertain us, and those of you who wish to dance are invited to. And please help yourself to the dessert table, which shall remain available until midnight. Now, maestro, since everyone is already standing, let's begin with the royal anthem."

After the last strains of "God Save the King" faded, the orchestra began a waltz, and Mr. and Mrs. Carmichael were one of the first couples to join in the dancing. Grace sat back against her chair, content to watch all the colorful pairs swirling around the floor. The whole evening had been something out of a dream for her. She truly felt like Cinderella at the ball—except the handsome prince would never come for her.

Virginia nudged Grace from her musings. "Don't look now, but I think Mr. Edison is heading your way."

Grace glanced up. "He's probably coming to speak to your mother."

"Judging by the gleam in his eye, I'd say not."

Mr. Edison strode up to the table and gave a small bow. "Good evening, ladies. I trust you're enjoying yourselves."

"We are indeed, Mr. Edison," Mrs. Easton replied. "You and Cecilia have done an excellent job."

"Thank you, ma'am." He bowed to Virginia. "Miss Easton, you look beautiful as always. Where is your esteemed fiancé this evening?"

Virginia's smile dimmed. "I'm afraid business has kept him away, although he may show up yet."

"If I had such a lovely fiancée, you'd be hard-pressed to keep me away." He turned his intense gaze on Grace. "I don't believe I've had the pleasure of an introduction to your friend."

The man was charming enough, but because Grace knew Andrew's dislike of him, she didn't allow his attention to sway her.

"Forgive my manners," Virginia said. "Paul Edison, this is Grace Foley."

"Pleased to meet you, Miss Foley. Would you do me the honor of a dance?"

Grace's throat tightened. She didn't want to be rude, but how could she get out of this situation without insulting him?

"I'm afraid she's spoken for." Andrew's cool voice came from behind her shoulder, sending a cascade of shivers down her spine.

She turned slightly to see his blue eyes trained on Mr. Edison in what could only be described as a challenge.

Mr. Edison's features hardened. "Shouldn't you be dancing with the woman you hope to marry?"

"Cecilia has a queue of partners waiting for her. And besides, I owe this lovely lady a dance since I was the one who convinced her to come tonight." He held out his hand to her.

The tension between the two men stretched like a slingshot.

Beside her, Virginia coughed, hiding a grin behind her napkin.

Grace repressed the urge to smack her arm. "Thank you, Mr. Edison," she said, "but I must take advantage of Andrew while he's free." She smiled and placed her hand in Andrew's. "However, I'm sure Virginia would love the opportunity to dance." She winked at a flustered Virginia as she stepped away from the table.

With a hand at her elbow, Andrew led her toward the dance floor.

"You never told me you have a wicked side," he whispered in her ear.

The warmth of his breath sent goose bumps along her arms. She turned to him with a light laugh. "I'm full of surprises once you get to know me."

"Then I look forward to discovering all the intriguing facets of your personality."

With a flourish, he whisked her onto the floor, placing one hand at the small of her back. Her breath caught in her lungs, his nearness doing crazy things to her pulse. As they moved to the melody, Grace gave thanks that her father had taught her to dance, even if it was only for the parish socials they used to attend. It meant she could at least keep pace with an accomplished dancer like Andrew.

She gazed up into the warm glow of his eyes and smiled.

"I hope you're enjoying yourself," he said. "That the evening hasn't been too tedious."

"Not at all. I've loved every moment, especially your wonderful speech. I'm so proud of you, Andrew. You've made this night very special for everyone involved."

A hint of color infused his cheeks. "All thanks to you. Your suggestion was the spark I needed."

His praise expanded within her, filling the hollow spaces with warmth.

"Was your father upset?" Surely the man could see how meaningful the evening had become with the additional guests and speeches.

"I don't know. I'll likely hear about it tomorrow though. He's not the kind of person who appreciates surprises."

His hand splayed at her back as he guided her around another couple. The music flared, and when the dance floor grew crowded, he pulled her closer. Heat from his body sent flutters through her midsection. With the scent of his woodsy aftershave filling her senses, she had to fight the urge to lean into the solid wall of his chest and lay her head on his shoulder. Her face grew heated at the direction her thoughts had turned. It wouldn't do to show how he affected her. Especially if Cecilia happened to be watching.

She pulled back slightly and attempted to concentrate on their conversation, despite the intensity in his eyes that wreaked havoc with her senses.

Andrew gazed into Grace's upturned face, so near and so alluring that he imagined tasting those perfect lips. The subtle floral fragrance of her perfume scented the air around them, intoxicating him.

"Andrew?"

He dragged his attention back. "Sorry, my mind wandered."

"I asked if you think your father's reaction to your speech was genuine?"

Andrew relived the moment where his father had praised him and actually given him the first show of affection since Andrew's graduation from university. His chest tightened. "I believe it was. At least I hope so, since it might indicate that his view of my brother is softening."

"That would be wonderful. Your mother was also greatly affected by your tribute." Her eyes shone with moisture.

Once again, Andrew marveled at Grace's deep capacity for compassion. Despite Mother's aloofness toward her when she first arrived, Grace had treated her with the utmost respect.

"I hope it wasn't too painful for you, remembering your brother," he said softly.

"Just the opposite. It made me feel closer to Owen. He would have been very proud to see his fellow soldiers being honored in such a way. In fact, I might suggest doing something similar at home. Maybe not in a grand ballroom like this, but our community hall would do nicely."

"You're not planning on leaving us, are you?" Though he kept his tone light, his heart constricted at the thought of her returning to England.

"Not as long as Christian needs me. I intend to honor my commitment to you."

The shimmering glow of her eyes held him captive. *My commitment to you.* The idea of her committing to him in a more personal manner warmed him to his core. What would it be like to have the love and respect of such a wonderful woman?

Andrew had noticed a slight softening in his father's attitude toward Grace recently, even asking her several questions about her life in England at dinner one night. Could he eventually accept someone from a different social class into the family? Someone as thoughtful and kind as Grace?

The music ended and everyone stopped to applaud the orchestra's performance. Andrew, though, could not make his arms release Grace to follow suit. They stayed locked together, staring at each other for several heart-stopping seconds until someone cleared their throat behind him.

Virginia moved into his line of vision. "Cecilia is headed this way," she whispered, "and judging by the scowl on her face, you're in for it."

He suppressed a groan. Grace didn't need to witness the scene that would likely follow. He bowed to her. "Thank you for the dance, Grace."

"It was my pleasure." She gave him a sad smile. "Time for Cinderella to return to the castle."

With that odd comment, she slipped away through the crowd, leaving him to face Cecilia's displeasure on his own.

CHAPTER 17

The next evening at dinner, Andrew waited for his father to comment on the changes he'd made to the gala. It was the first chance he'd had to speak with him all day. The morning had been taken up with church, followed by brunch with the Carmichaels, and his father's usual Sunday nap before dinner.

Once the main course had been served, Father looked down the table at Andrew. "From all accounts, last night's event has been deemed an overwhelming success. And a large part of the credit must go to you, Andrew. Inviting those extra soldiers was a brilliant tactic. After hearing their stories, most of the guests lined up to donate money and to buy Victory bonds as well."

Andrew released a breath. "So you don't begrudge the cost of their tickets?"

"If you'd asked me in advance, I probably would have vetoed the idea. But once again you've proven that we can't focus solely on money. That sincerity and goodwill count for a lot."

Andrew glanced over at Grace. Words were not necessary to convey her feelings. He could tell by the admiration in her eyes. "I owe a great debt to Grace. It was her idea to include more veterans. All I did was implement it."

Mother set down her fork. "Grace, why didn't you say anything? You're far too modest for your own good."

"I'm only glad my ideas helped make the night more special for everyone involved." Grace smiled, then continued to cut her beef.

Perhaps Andrew shouldn't have mentioned her part in the plan, but to take credit for the success of the evening without acknowledging her input would be wrong.

For once, Father studied Grace without animosity. "Well, Miss Foley," he said. "That was a fine idea. Thank you for suggesting it."

"You're welcome. But it was really Andrew who made it such a success." She gave him a quick smile that did strange things to his pulse.

"With all the fuss over the gala," Virginia said, breaking the ensuing silence, "it seems we've overlooked the upcoming holiday. Are we going to Hanlan Point for Dominion Day this year?" She looked expectantly at her parents.

Andrew held back a sigh. Could she not have waited until dinner was over before broaching a topic that would surely incite more controversy? Their family had gone across to the Hanlan Point amusement park every year on the first of July since he, Ginny, and Frank were young. But after Frank's estrangement from the family, his parents had made excuses not to go back.

"Perhaps, if the weather cooperates." Her father picked up his water glass.

"I can't wait to bring Christian," Virginia said. "He will adore the children's zoo and the carousel."

Andrew chuckled at his sister's eagerness. "He might be too young for any of that, Gin."

"Pishposh. It's never too early to introduce children to animals and amusement rides."

"The place isn't the same since the hotel burned down." Mr. Easton shook his head.

Not one for amusement rides, Father used to spend a large portion of the day in the lounge at the Hanlan Point Hotel. But the building had been destroyed by fire several years ago and had not been rebuilt, although the roller coaster and the baseball stadium had.

"We still have the games and the rides," Virginia argued. "I'd love to take Christian on the miniature train. I can just see him clapping his little hands as we go."

"May I ask what Dominion Day is?" An adorable frown puckered Grace's brow.

Andrew smiled. "Sorry. Of course you wouldn't know. It's our national holiday, commemorating the formation of Canada as a dominion of Great Britain. It's celebrated on the first of July each year. Most people have outdoor parties or picnics, and there are usually fireworks once it gets dark." Surprisingly, Andrew found himself growing enthused at the prospect of a day of fun. No work, no budgets, and no Paul Edison to rattle him. He hadn't been to the island for several years and found he missed the excursion.

"You must come with us," Virginia said to Grace. "We always stay until the last ferry. It's wonderful."

"Ferry?" Grace's eyes grew wider. "How far away is it?"

"Only a twenty-minute boat ride. Part of the whole experience."

"I hardly think it appropriate to include the staff on a family outing." Father sent Virginia a stern look. "Christian will have plenty of people along to watch him. And I'm sure Miss Foley would enjoy a day to herself."

Grace glanced over at him. "Yes, sir. A day off would be lovely." She sounded sincere, yet Andrew sensed her underlying disappointment.

Virginia's gray eyes sparked with anger, but thankfully she remained silent. There was no use arguing with their father when he was in this mood. Better to bide their time and figure out another way for Grace to go.

After seeing her disappointment, Andrew was now determined that she would, in fact, join them. Grace would love the park and the fireworks. Andrew stole a look at her as she picked at her food. Who was he kidding? He wanted Grace there because it would be more enjoyable for him. She'd made the gala last night so much better, simply by knowing she was in the audience. As for the dance they'd shared, he couldn't remember enjoying a waltz more.

"You should invite Cecilia along," Father said. "I'm sure she'd love to join you."

"Perhaps Basil will go as well," Virginia added. "I'll ask him later."

The gravy curdled in Andrew's stomach. He could only imagine how Cecilia would react. She'd be concerned about the wind messing her hair or the sun being too strong, and he doubted she would venture on any of the rides. She certainly wouldn't care to spend time with Christian. She'd made that abundantly clear.

Maybe, if he were fortunate, she would decline his offer to go with them.

The morning of July first dawned sunny and warm, a perfect day for the Eastons' outing to the park. Grace sighed as she looked out her window to the gardens below. The idea of amusement rides, games, and a picnic sounded heavenly. She would have loved seeing it all through Christian's eyes.

Resolutely, she pushed aside her disappointment. After all, what did she expect? She was an employee, not a member of the family—at least not one the Eastons were aware of.

A wave of remorse swamped her as she turned from the window. Lately she'd been feeling more and more guilty about hiding her true identity from Andrew. After everything they'd shared, she'd come to know him as a fine, upstanding person, and the fact that she was deceiving him tore her up inside. But how could she ever admit the truth now? Andrew would hate her. He'd fire her immediately, and she would lose all contact with Christian.

No, she couldn't risk it. Not yet.

Maybe it was a good thing she wasn't going to Hanlan Point after all.

Mrs. Hopkins had invited Grace to join the other servants for a picnic at a nearby park. She'd gratefully accepted, not wishing to spend such a beautiful summer day indoors. Still, she would be thinking of Christian . . . and Andrew . . . every minute.

Grace entered the nursery, intent on getting the baby ready for his outing. She'd have to pack all the necessities he'd need for the entire day. Extra nappies and blankets, several bottles, a change of clothes, his little woolen jumper—or sweater as they called it—in case it got cooler in the evening.

He was still asleep, so she went about collecting the items, humming under her breath.

The door opened a few minutes later, and Virginia entered, attired in a simple white day dress and button-up boots. With her raven hair fashioned in loose ringlets that flowed over her shoulders, she looked positively stunning.

"Good morning, Grace." Two dimples appeared in her cheeks.

Grace smiled at the girl's perpetual cheeriness. "Good morning. All set for your outing?"

"I am." Virginia peered into the crib. "But there's been a slight change in plans." She winked over her shoulder at Grace.

Immediate suspicion rose in Grace's mind. "What are you up to, Virginia Easton?"

"Not a thing. It's Father. An emergency has come up at work, and he's already left for the office."

Grace closed the dresser drawer. "Will your mother go without him?" She would hate for Mrs. Easton to miss the outing because her husband couldn't attend.

"Oh, yes. Father made sure Andrew and I would take her. It's the only reason he didn't insist Andrew join him at the hotel. He knows Mother would enjoy the time with Christian."

"Are Basil and Cecilia going?" Grace bent to retrieve Christian's favorite stuffed bunny, keeping her face averted lest Virginia read anything into the question.

"Basil said he'd meet us later. Some business obligation he needs to take care of first. And I believe Cecilia has declined Andrew's invitation. Probably too rustic for her tastes." Virginia giggled.

A ridiculous wave of relief washed through Grace. Yet she couldn't help but wonder about Virginia's cavalier attitude toward her fiancé. "Don't you mind that Basil always puts his work ahead of you, even on a holiday?"

A shadow crossed Virginia's pretty face.

Grace instantly regretted the bold question. "Forgive me. It's none of my business."

Virginia crossed to her side and squeezed her arm. "There's nothing to forgive. You're my friend, and you care about my welfare."

Her admission gave Grace the courage to speak up. "It's just that you don't seem very happy, like someone in love should be."

"Oh heavens. I'm not in love with Basil." Virginia's eyes lit with amusement.

"Then why are you marrying him?"

"Most people in our social circles don't marry for love. They marry for a title, for social position, or to unite two wealthy families. And for many other reasons that have nothing to do with love."

"It sounds so cold. You deserve to be with someone you truly care for." Grace couldn't fathom marrying a man she didn't love.

"Thank you." Virginia reached over and gave Grace a quick hug, then pulled back, her expression somber. "The truth is, my chance for happiness ended with that dreadful war."

Understanding dawned. "You lost someone you cared about?"

Virginia nodded. "Emmett and I were supposed to be married as soon as he returned from the war. But that never happened."

"I'm so sorry. If I'd known, I never would have brought it up."

"It's fine. I've had my time to grieve, and now I'm being practical. Marrying Basil will give me the stability of a good home, and God willing, lots of children to dote upon. Besides which, it will make my father very happy. The fact that I'm not crazy in love works to both our advantage, since I don't begrudge coming second to Basil's career."

It seemed such a sad way to live. "What about Collin Lafferty?" The question slipped out before the thought had fully formed.

The color drained from the other girl's face. "What do you mean?"

Grace hesitated. Had she mistaken the interest between them or was it only one-sided? "It's just that you two seem to share . . . a special bond."

Virginia frowned. "Collin is our gardener, Grace. Do you really think anything could come of a relationship with a mere employee? Father would never allow it."

Grace's stomach dropped. "I didn't mean to—"

"It's time to get this young man ready for his big day." Virginia turned to pick up the sleepy boy from the crib.

Grace blinked. How did she always manage to say the wrong thing?

"Grace?"

"Yes?"

"You'd better get ready yourself . . . since you're coming with us." Despite her annoyance of a moment ago, Virginia's voice was light as she hugged Christian.

"But your father—"

"Daddy won't be there, and what he doesn't know won't hurt him. If he gets grumpy when he finds out, I'll say it was my idea." Virginia winked again.

"Are you sure?"

"Absolutely. In fact, Mother insists on it."

"With a little persuasion from you, no doubt." Grace chuckled, a sudden surge of anticipation lifting her spirits.

"I may have suggested you could be helpful to have along, and Andrew heartily agreed." She laughed. "Let's go have a wonderful time celebrating Christian's first Dominion Day."

CHAPTER 18

Andrew stood at the rail of the Bluebell Ferry as it crossed to Toronto Island, his hat clutched in his hand. The breeze was just powerful enough to whisk it from his head if he wasn't careful. The feeling of freedom without it was exhilarating, the wanton locks flying about his forehead with complete abandon.

He lifted his face and let the sun warm his cheeks. Before them, the blue sky stretched out toward the horizon, while gentle waves lapped at the hull. They couldn't have asked for a more perfect day.

Andrew peered over his shoulder to make sure Mother was comfortable on one of the benches. She appeared quite content with Virginia and Grace on one side of her and the pram between them.

His gaze rested on Grace, so pretty in a blue dress with a tidy white collar. She too had forgone her usual straw hat and instead had tied her hair back with a colorful scarf. He still couldn't believe Ginny had talked her into coming. And that Cecilia had declined his invitation, as he'd hoped she would. He should feel guilty about preferring Grace's company to Celia's, but he simply didn't. Instead he planned to enjoy every minute of this fine day that was free from his father's critical eye and Cecilia's complaints.

Grace came to join him at the rail. "This ferry ride is a far more enjoyable experience than crossing the ocean." Her brown eyes sparkled. "The view is so pretty. Look at the way the sunlight dances over the water."

The wind whipped some loose strands of hair about her face. His fingers itched to smooth them back, but he stuffed his hands in his pockets before he gave in to temptation. "It is beautiful. I haven't taken the time to enjoy a day like this in a very long time."

"What is your favorite thing to do at the park?" Her enthusiasm rolled off her in waves as big as the ones that crashed against the boat.

"Not the roller coaster, that's for certain."

"No? Not a thrill seeker?" She was teasing him, and he found he liked it.

"Definitely not." He gave an exaggerated grimace. "I suppose I enjoy the carousel best. I also like the shooting gallery and the games of chance."

"I used to love those as well. My brother always tried to win me prizes." A hint of nostalgia seemed to dim the light in her eyes.

"The one who died in the war?" he asked gently.

"No. My other brother, Peter." She bit her lip and turned toward the water, visibly working to contain her emotions.

"I didn't mean to upset you."

"It's all right." She smiled, but her eyes remained sad. "Peter and I were very close. I still have the stuffed poodle he won for me the last time." She swallowed hard.

"What happened to him?" Andrew couldn't help asking.

She shook her head, blinking back tears. "He died . . . in an accident."

"I'm so sorry." Andrew kept his hands tight in his pockets. The urge to put his arms around her and comfort her was almost a physical ache.

"Thank you." She inhaled and released a long breath. "Even though it happened a long time ago, the grief still sneaks up on me."

Andrew gave himself a mental slap for stealing her joy. He needed to dispel the gloomy mood he'd created—and fast. "Well, perhaps I'll have a chance to match his skill today. I'm pretty good at the bottle toss, if I do say so."

His ploy worked, and she laughed. "You want to win me a prize?"

"What better incentive than to make a pretty girl smile?"

Grace's eyes widened. A blush stained her cheeks, and she quickly looked away.

The sharp *toot* of the ferry's horn sounded, indicating that they would be docking shortly.

"We'd better sit down," he told her. "It could get bumpy."

With a hand at her back, he guided her to the bench, and they squeezed in beside his mother and Ginny. Andrew did his best to ignore the speculative stare of his sister.

Not even Ginny's meddling was going to bother Andrew today.

Anticipation thrummed through the crowd as the passengers lined up to disembark from the ferry. Grace thrilled at the sight of the park before her—the rails of the roller coaster rising high above them, the music from the carousel competing with the hum of voices, and the smell of cotton candy and pretzels floating on the breeze.

Right now she didn't care how incensed Mr. Easton would be when he discovered she'd come along. She intended to soak up every inch of this delightful experience and store it away as a wonderful memory for the years ahead.

Andrew insisted on pushing the pram. They made their way down the main thoroughfare at a leisurely pace, in keeping with the movement of the crowd. After a while, the throngs dispersed in different directions and Grace could breathe again.

"Where shall we head first?" Virginia asked.

Andrew pointed ahead. "How about the carousel? Even Mother can join us on that."

Minutes later, they boarded the ride, and Grace scurried to find a seat. Mrs. Easton sat on one of the benches with Christian on her lap. Virginia ran straight for an elephant. Grace laughed, watching her try to mount the wide animal while keeping her skirts about her calves. Grace chose a multicolored horse, and after several unsuccessful attempts to climb into the seat, Andrew appeared beside her. "Allow me."

She blinked as he gripped her by the waist and lifted her onto the painted saddle. Sitting sideways, she grasped the pole and held on for dear life, laughing. "Thank you, gallant sir. Which one will you choose?"

"I believe I like the view from here." With his hands still on her waist, his eyes never left her face.

Grace held her breath, unable to look away. Her heart pumped at a furious rate. Did she imagine the suggestion behind his words?

"You can't stand the whole time, Drew," Virginia called. "Grab a seat."

Andrew gave a cheeky salute and climbed onto the jet black stallion beside Grace. "I think this one is manly enough for me."

Grace couldn't help but laugh at his wry expression. "I don't know. You could try the duck." She pointed to a cartoonish white bird with a yellow bill, where a young girl was climbing up, assisted by her father.

Andrew narrowed his eyes at her. She only laughed harder.

A voice came over the loudspeaker warning patrons to hang on tight and keep all limbs inside the carousel. A few seconds later, the organ music grew louder, and the ride began to move.

Grace's horse chugged, then started to rise as the carousel gained speed. Her scarf, tied securely under her chin, whipped out behind her.

Virginia waved at her. Grace waved back and twisted to see how Christian was faring. He and Mrs. Easton both wore wide smiles. Grace darted a glance at Andrew, who held his hat on with one hand and grasped the pole with the other. He grinned over at her. She'd never seen him so relaxed, so carefree. The carousel picked up speed, moving faster and faster in dizzying circles. The crowds surrounding the ride cheered and waved, speeding by in a blur.

All too soon the ride slowed to a halt.

Andrew jumped down and came to help her dismount. The

feeling of his strong arms sent a surge of electricity though her, leaving her strangely breathless.

He cleared his throat and stepped back, shoving his hat back on his head. "I think I should have left this at home today. I fear I'll lose it before the day is out."

"Why don't you store it in the boot of the pram? There's plenty of room there."

"An excellent idea. Come on. Let's see how Christian enjoyed himself."

The morning passed quickly as they explored the park and the petting zoo, which Christian adored. His wide eyes and giggle of glee when Grace laid his hand on a sheep's furry back had been priceless. Around noon, Mrs. Easton insisted they find a picnic table in the shade to eat the lunch Mrs. Hopkins had prepared for them. The cook must have made enough food for Mr. Easton and Basil Fleming as well, for the basket was filled to overflowing with sandwiches, fruit, and strawberry tarts.

"Are you enjoying yourself, Mother?" Andrew asked after they had eaten their fill.

"Very much so." Mrs. Easton smiled.

Grace gave her credit for putting on a brave face when she must surely be missing Frank.

Andrew removed the trash from the table and spread a blanket over the grass. "It's time for us men to have a nap." He lifted Christian from Virginia's lap and laid him on the blanket. The boy instantly stretched out his feet and arms as if relishing the freedom. Andrew flopped down beside him, pillowing his head on his arms.

"Where is Basil, Virginia?" Mrs. Easton asked as she repacked the basket. "I thought he'd be here to share lunch with us."

Virginia sipped her bottle of lemonade. "He said he'd try. I guess he wasn't able to get away."

Grace studied her. She certainly didn't seem upset that her fiancé hadn't come to the picnic as promised. If Grace were in Virginia's shoes, she'd be madder than a wet hen.

Mrs. Easton closed the hamper. "We'll wait a while longer before we leave the picnic area in case he arrives."

"I don't want to hold up everyone on his account. Why don't you all head out and I'll stay here with Christian? He can have his nap on the grass in the open air."

Andrew sat up on the blanket, frowning. "I don't like the idea of leaving you here alone. We'll stay until we can all go together."

Half an hour later, Christian started to fuss, and Virginia seemed on edge. She kept looking up and down the long expanse of grass, as though nervous. But what would she be nervous about? Did she fear Basil would appear and ruin the outing for her?

Grace looked around. "Who wants to try the roller coaster? Virginia, you seem the type who would love those daring rides."

Virginia's dark curls swung as she shook her head. "Not me. I prefer my feet on the ground, thank you very much."

"Oh, come on. Live dangerously." Grace tugged on her arm.

"No, thank you. I enjoyed my lunch, and I don't care to lose it." With a laugh, Virginia picked the baby off the blanket and laid him in the pram. "I think Christian needs a diaper change anyway. Drew, why don't you take Grace on the ride?"

Andrew's eyes widened with mock horror. "Have you seen how high that thing is? A guy would have to be crazy to risk his neck that way."

"I'd be happy to take you, Miss Foley. I happen to love roller coasters."

Grace whirled on the bench to see Collin Lafferty and Toby McDonald standing behind the picnic table. Both were wearing vests and matching caps, their white shirt sleeves rolled up to the elbow. But while Toby was smiling, Collin's features were pinched and pale.

"Mr. McDonald?" Grace rose from her seat, conscious of Mrs. Easton and Andrew's attention on her. "What are you doing here? I thought you were spending the day with the other staff members." Grace hoped her pleasant tone would ease the instant tension that had fallen over the small party.

"A change in plans. When we spotted you here, we couldn't pass by without saying hello. And it seems we're just in the nick of time." Toby winked at Grace.

Her cheeks blazed with heat that had nothing to do with the sun. "That's most kind of you, but—"

Andrew jumped to his feet, brushing some pieces of grass from his pants. "I was joking, Grace. I'd be happy to escort you on the roller coaster." He moved to her side, laying a hand at her waist.

If Grace's spine grew any stiffer, she'd snap in two.

The men exchanged heated stares for a second or two, then Toby tipped his cap. "Another time then, Miss Foley. Mrs. Easton, Miss Virginia, have a pleasant day."

Collin nodded and shot a glance at Virginia as Toby pulled him back onto the walkway.

Virginia bent over the pram, busying herself with Christian.

"Is it me, or was there something odd about that whole encounter?" Mrs. Easton pinned Grace with a pointed look.

"It did seem strange. But I assure you I had no idea those two were coming to the island today."

"So you didn't ask Mr. McDonald to meet you here?"

"No, ma'am. I didn't even know I was coming until Virginia invited me this morning."

The woman's shoulders relaxed. "Just a coincidence, then?"

"Yes, ma'am." But as Grace looked over at Virginia, suspicion dawned. Perhaps Basil had never agreed to join them. Perhaps Virginia had been biding her time to sneak off and meet Collin.

Grace turned to Andrew. "You don't have to take me on the roller coaster. Why don't we try our hand at the games instead? I just might give you a run for your money at the shooting gallery."

The relief that spread over his face was almost comical. "You're on, Annie Oakley."

"Who is Annie Oakley?"

He only laughed harder.

CHAPTER 19

Andrew had never had a better day.

And without a doubt, it was because of Grace. Her enthusiasm for everything she encountered in the park was contagious. Through her eyes, he experienced all the attractions as though seeing them for the first time.

Despite her bold assertion that she was a skilled markswoman, her attempts at the shooting gallery had been hilarious, resulting in fits of laughter on both their parts. That was another thing he appreciated about Grace, her ability to laugh at herself. And her ability to make him laugh too—something he didn't do nearly often enough.

When he won her a kewpie doll at the bottle toss, she seemed as thrilled as if he'd handed her a diamond necklace. He could only imagine Cecilia in the same position. She'd likely keep the doll long enough to please him, and then toss it in the nearest trash receptacle as soon as he wasn't looking.

Andrew gave himself a stern reprimand. Nothing could be gained by comparing the two women who were as different as chalk and cheese.

After enjoying hamburgers and potato chips for supper, the group had taken a seat by the water, content to simply enjoy the view.

Andrew glanced at the sky. Still several hours before the fireworks would begin. He doubted his mother or Christian would last that long. Even Virginia seemed unusually subdued. Perhaps it was time to call it a day. "If everyone is ready, I suggest we head down to the dock to catch the next ferry home."

His mother gave a weary sigh. "That might be best. I fear I've worn myself out."

Grace rose at once. "I can accompany you back, Mrs. Easton. I need to take Christian home anyway."

"That's most thoughtful of you, Grace."

Grace smiled as she adjusted the blankets in Christian's carriage. "I've had such a wonderful day. Thank you all for including me."

When she turned her grateful gaze on him, Andrew's chest tightened. If only everyone could be so appreciative of the little things in life.

"This is silly." Virginia suddenly bolted up from the ground. "Grace, you can't miss the fireworks. They're the best part of the day. I'll take Mother and Christian back. Andrew, you stay and show Grace how Canada celebrates our national holiday."

"No, really," Grace protested. "I don't mind."

"I insist. I have the start of a headache anyway. The noise will only make it worse."

Andrew looked to his mother, ever the one for propriety. "What do you think, Mother? I don't mind leaving early."

Mother got to her feet and brushed off her skirt. "Virginia's right. It would be a shame to miss the fireworks. And you certainly won't be alone with all the people here. Not that I don't trust you to be a gentleman." She smiled and patted Andrew's cheek. "Thank you for escorting us. It couldn't have been easy putting up with us females."

"It was no hardship. Besides, I had Christian along to even out the male side. Imagine how excited he'll be next year. We won't be able to contain him."

Mother chuckled. "Yes. I'm sure. Well, good-night then. We'll see you tomorrow."

Grace pulled her wrap and Andrew's jacket and hat from the boot of the baby carriage.

"You don't have to do this, Andrew." Grace's brow furrowed as she watched Virginia and his mother retreating down the boardwalk. "I don't want to be a nuisance."

He looked into those brown depths and felt the pull clear to his toes. "I'm happy to stay," he said softly. "And don't worry. You could never be a nuisance, Grace Foley."

Grace and Andrew strolled along the boardwalk, searching for the perfect spot to view the fireworks. Andrew, she discovered, fancied himself quite the fireworks expert and claimed to know the ideal location to get the greatest effect.

Halfway along the planked walkway, he stopped and tugged Grace over to the railing. "Other than being out on the water in a boat, this is the best place to watch the fireworks." He pointed to the middle of the lake. "Right out there is where they'll begin."

To their left, the sun was a red ball, hanging just above the water, casting a reddish-orange reflection over the lake.

"It's so beautiful. I love watching the sun set over the water, don't you?"

He looked down at her and smiled. "I do. Though I don't take the time often enough to appreciate it."

Crowds of onlookers began to press in, forcing Andrew to move closer to Grace. She pulled her shawl tighter around her, grateful for the warmth Andrew's nearness provided.

"So, Grace, tell me about your life in England. What did you do there, other than teach Sunday school?"

When he watched her with those mesmerizing blue eyes, Grace could scarcely breathe. She tore her gaze away to focus on the water. "I led an exceedingly boring life, I assure you."

"Doing what? Farming? Sheep herding? Opera singing?"

Despite herself, Grace laughed out loud. "Nothing like that."

"Okay, I'll ask a different question. What did you want to be when you grew up?"

She shrugged. "I suppose for a while I fancied becoming a

teacher. But I was still in school when the war broke out. My brother enlisted right away, and my sister was . . . away, working. So it was just Mum and me at home. I finished school and started working at a general store in town to help pay the bills. Mum took in sewing and laundry, but it barely scratched the surface."

"What about your other brother? Peter, was it? Did he enlist as well?"

For the second time that day, Grace absorbed the pain that came with talking about Peter. "He died long before the war began," she said quietly.

She hadn't spoken about Peter's death—ever. It had become a taboo subject in the family. A dark secret, buried deep, where Grace's guilt could fester and grow. Yet she wanted to tell Andrew the truth, or part of it. "Peter died saving my life." *Because of my recklessness.*

His mouth gaped. "How terrible. I'm so sorry."

She shivered just thinking about that awful day.

Andrew moved closer and put an arm around her. Heat from his body spread across her shoulders, yet goose bumps skittered down her spine.

"Are you cold?" he asked. "Do you want to go inside somewhere?"

"No. I'm fine."

"I guess I'll have to keep you warm then." He winked at her.

He was trying to lighten the mood, and she blessed him for it. Anything to avoid admitting her culpability in Peter's death. Anything to calm the nerves his nearness evoked.

"So what did you do while the war was on? Work in a munitions factory?"

"No, though some of the girls in our village did." She paused. "I volunteered at a nearby hospital where the wounded soldiers were taken for evaluation before they were dispersed elsewhere. Helping the soldiers made me feel closer to Owen, and I hoped if he was ever injured, someone would do the same for him."

She was still haunted by not knowing exactly how her brother died. Was it instant? Did he suffer? Had some kind soul helped ease the pain of his final hours?

"That's most admirable. What did you do there?"

"Since I'd had first-aid training, they let me treat the less severe wounds. Bandages and dressings mostly. But I also talked with the men and wrote letters to their families. I did whatever I could to keep their spirits up."

"I don't know what to say. You put me to shame." Under his brow, his eyes were troubled.

"You have nothing to be ashamed about. It wasn't your fault the army wouldn't accept you."

"No, but I still felt guilty for not being part of the war." He pulled his glasses from his inside pocket. "I never thought having poor eyesight would keep me from fighting for my country." He slipped the glasses on.

"How disappointing," she said. "Especially when your brother enlisted with no problem."

"It was humiliating. Because I appeared so healthy, people couldn't understand why I wasn't off with the others. Eventually I got tired of explaining and learned to put up with the rude stares and comments."

Grace bristled. "That's so unfair."

"Perhaps. But it was the reality I lived with, and still do. When I finally accepted that I wouldn't be going overseas, I threw myself into the family business to help fill the void Frank had left."

"Your father must have been grateful. He seems to rely on you a great deal."

"Only by default." Andrew's face grew tense. "He'd far rather be working with Frank."

"What makes you say that?"

He turned his gaze out to the water, a nerve pulsing in his jaw.

After a minute of silence, she laid her hand over his on the railing. "You don't have to answer that."

"No, I want to. It's just that I've never told anyone this before." He took a deep breath. "The day my father received news of Frank's death, I was at my desk. I heard a crash and ran down to Father's office. For some reason, I hesitated outside the door. Harrison Carmichael was with him. My father was weeping. I didn't know what was wrong, but I knew it had to be monumental for him to cry. Then he shouted, 'Why did it have to be Frank?'" The veins corded in Andrew's neck. "He didn't need to say it. I knew he wished it had been me instead."

"Andrew, no." She squeezed his arm. "He probably meant out of all the soldiers fighting, why did it have to be his son? I'm sure it had nothing to do with you."

Andrew turned to her, his expression tortured. "It only confirmed a truth I'd lived with my whole life. My father loved Frank best." He shook his head when she started to protest. "I was the son who couldn't catch a baseball like Frank, who couldn't attract clients like Frank, who couldn't charm the girls like Frank." He closed his eyes, anguish radiating off him in waves. "Who couldn't go to war like Frank. Who couldn't die instead of Frank."

Tears clogged Grace's throat. Unbidden memories of the cruel things her mother had said—and hadn't said—when Peter died came flooding back. Sometimes the things that weren't said could wound deeper than any weapon. She linked her arm through Andrew's, wishing she could do more to ease his pain. "I know a bit about wanting a parent's approval and never receiving it. I looked after my mother for four years, gave up my chance to be a teacher, all in the hopes that one day, she would look at me with affection and say she loved me." Her voice quivered. "That day may never come for me or for you, but somehow we have to learn to value ourselves despite it. To see ourselves as our heavenly Father sees us." She dashed the moisture from her lashes. "I didn't know Frank, but I doubt he could be any finer a man than you."

Andrew looked at her, moisture glinting in his eyes. "Thank you," he whispered. He swallowed, his throat working hard.

His gaze fell to her lips, lingering like a caress. Her pulse stuttered, and for one heart-stopping moment, Grace thought he would kiss her.

Then a loud hiss filled the air, and the crowd cheered.

"They're starting." Andrew pointed to the middle of the lake.

Sure enough, a colorful explosion burst through the dark sky. Immediately, more rockets flew high into the air, erupting in a multitude of greens, blues, and reds. The murmur of the crowd mirrored Grace's awe at the breathtaking display, reflected in the still water of the lake below.

Without a pause, the show continued, each burst of color outdoing the one before.

She'd seen a few amateur fireworks at home, but nothing compared with this astounding exhibition. A residue of tears blurred her vision at the magnitude of the spectacle, and in her heart she whispered a prayer of thanks to be witness to such beauty.

"So, what did you think?" Andrew asked as the crowds began to disperse. "Was it as fantastic as I described?"

He smiled, and she was glad to see a lifting of his previous mood.

"Better than anything I could have imagined. This has been the most wonderful day of my life. Thank you for staying and allowing me to see them." In a rush of gratitude, she reached up and kissed his cheek.

His arm wrapped around her waist. Heat from his hand spread up her back and her pulse shot up, rivaling the fireworks she'd just enjoyed.

"You're welcome." Andrew's husky voice so near her ear sent shivers up her spine. The spicy scent of his cologne enveloped her like a hug.

How easy would it be to give in to temptation and touch her lips to his? But that would mean crossing a line she could never come back from. It could ruin their friendship and put her job at risk.

For once, she tamed her impulsiveness and pulled away to look up at him. The intensity in his eyes stalled her breath. Was he thinking the same thing?

Then his expression changed, and he quickly stepped away. "We'd better head over to the dock. The ferry will be leaving soon."

Grace murmured a response, all the while trying to control her rampant pulse. But it was no use. She could no longer ignore the glaring truth.

Despite her best intentions, she was falling hard for Andrew Easton.

CHAPTER 20

Breakfast the next morning proved to be a tense affair, one Virginia should have expected, knowing how Daddy would react once he learned Grace had joined them at Hanlan Point.

"What were you thinking, inviting the nanny?" he demanded as soon as Andrew sat down. "I thought I made myself perfectly clear on the matter."

Though his glare was aimed at Andrew, Virginia cringed. At least Grace didn't eat breakfast with the family and would be spared the full force of his displeasure. She drew in a breath. "It was my idea, Daddy. Andrew had nothing to do with it."

"Your idea?" His icy attention turned to her. "Why would you suggest such a thing?"

Because Virginia had seen the way her brother looked at their nanny, and the hopeless romantic in her prayed that Andrew would fall in love with Grace. If so, he might challenge their father's archaic social views and open the door for Virginia to be with Collin.

She jutted out her chin. "I consider Grace a friend, and when Basil couldn't make it, I invited her along."

Father huffed. "The woman is still a member of the staff. I'd thank you to keep this *friendship* to the confines of the house. Bad enough she sat with you at the gala—a fact Charlotte Carmichael was all too quick to point out."

An irrational burst of anger swamped Virginia. She didn't give two figs what Charlotte Carmichael or any of those other charlatans thought.

"Excuse me. I feel the need for some fresh air." She pushed aside her plate and, despite the stares of her family, strode from the room.

She continued to the side entrance and closed the door quite forcefully behind her. Her mood since the picnic yesterday had only deteriorated, and Daddy's blustering didn't help matters. She was tired of his unrealistic expectations and his dictatorial attitude.

A walk in the garden might be the only thing to cure her lingering headache and . . . heartache. For if she were being honest, the true source of her turmoil was Collin Lafferty. Seeing him at Hanlan's Point and knowing she couldn't be with him had soured the entire day for her. All she'd wanted was a few minutes alone with him. A stroll along the boardwalk. A ride on the roller coaster. A few treasured memories to tuck away in her journal as a memento of an ill-fated romance.

She plucked a rose from a bush as she passed and brought it to her nose, its fragrance only reminding her of the man she loved but couldn't have, not without exacting a terrible price. If only he and Toby hadn't ruined everything by confronting her family. Collin was supposed to come alone and keep his presence hidden until she managed to get away to meet him behind the roller coaster. A secret part of her had hoped Basil might indeed show up, catch her with Collin, and rescind their engagement. Would that be enough to free her? She didn't know. But it would certainly buy her time to work on her father and make him see that her happiness was more important than any expected social norm.

Instead, everything had gone wrong. Her fingers crushed the petals as a sudden thought occurred. Collin hadn't been too keen on her idea, but she'd worn him down with her pleading. Had he sabotaged her plan on purpose by showing himself to her family?

On a burst of irritation, Virginia flung the rose to the ground. She would not give him up. Not yet. Not until a minister had officially declared her the wife of another man. Until then, she would keep praying something would happen to allow her and that stubborn Scotsman to be together.

Fueled by her growing temper, she marched into the greenhouse and headed straight to the rear where she assumed he'd be working.

Sure enough, he stood with his back to her, digging furiously in a big pot on the table, his shirt sleeves rolled up past his elbows. Soil flew in all directions.

"I see you're taking your frustrations out on that poor plant."

Collin whirled around, a scowl darkening his features. "You shouldn't be out here. Go back inside."

"Not until we clear up a few things." She came to stand beside him, close enough to smell the earthy scent that surrounded him. "You sabotaged our plan yesterday on purpose, didn't you?"

He tossed his tool aside and wiped his hands on a rag. "I did."

A wave of hurt crashed through her at his frank admission. "Why?"

"I never should have let you talk me into such a harebrained idea. You're engaged to another man. We've no business planning any sort of clandestine meetings. It's not right, and I won't be party to any more of your schemes."

"My schemes?" A volcano of toxic emotions spilled through her system, each one more volatile than the last. "*You're* the one who started this, Collin Lafferty. With your smiles, and your compliments, and your roses, and your . . ." She clamped her mouth shut to stem the traitorous tears that clogged her throat.

The hardness left his face. In its place, weariness etched grooves around his mouth. "Believe me, if I'd have known what it would lead to, I never would have spoken to you at all."

Virginia gasped. Pain seared her chest as though he'd plunged his trowel right through her. She sucked in a harsh breath. "Well, I wish to heaven I'd never laid eyes on you." Her legs shook beneath her. "I suppose I should be grateful you never tried to kiss me. At least I won't have to worry about comparing Basil's kisses to yours. Though I'm sure his would prove far superior."

A low growl rose up through Collin's body, matching the fire that ignited in his eyes.

She took a step back, sensing she'd gone too far.

He pounced like a cat on its prey, wrenching her against his chest. A second before he lowered his head, she caught a glint of wildness in his expression. Then his mouth claimed hers in a storm of passion that made her heart beat against her rib cage. Along with the thrill of his kiss came a surge of power, knowing she could make him lose all sense of reason.

Didn't that prove he loved her?

She held on and returned his kiss until her knees went weak. Still, his mouth remained fused to hers, his arms coming around her to hold her up. Finally he pulled away, staring at her with an intensity that rendered her speechless.

"*Mo chridhe.*" The whispered endearment sent shudders through her.

Then he kissed her again, only this time with such tenderness, she feared she might swoon. A tear escaped the corner of her eye and rolled down her cheek.

He released her mouth, brushing the dampness from her face. "Please don't cry."

"I can't help it. I love you, Collin."

A long sigh shuddered through him. "God help me, I love you too." Then he kissed her eyes, her cheeks, her forehead, and returned to her lips.

Virginia's soul sang with the magnitude of her feelings, with the expression of her love at last.

Then, suddenly, he set her away from him. "We can't do this, Virginia. Someone could come looking for you. Are you willing for your father to find out?"

She shook her head. "Not yet. But soon. Just be patient a while longer. I'll figure out a way to make this right."

He stared at her with tortured eyes. "I hope so, lass. Because I don't know how much more I can take."

"Me either." She reached up to kiss him one last time, then

turned and fled from the greenhouse, praying she didn't run into anyone before she made it to her room, for her flushed face and swollen lips would surely give her away.

With a loud exhale, Andrew threw his pen on the desktop and leaned back in his chair. He couldn't seem to concentrate on anything this morning, torturing himself by reliving every moment at Hanlan Point with Grace. Her smile, the sparkle in her eyes, her expression of wonder at each new sight. He'd enjoyed every second they'd spent together, especially the time alone watching the fireworks, yet the undeniable truth remained. The day had been nothing more than a brief respite from reality. A fantasy. A taste of forbidden fruit, so to speak.

Because that's exactly what Grace Foley was to him—forbidden.

Heat swept up his neck at the memory of Grace's lips on his cheek. The overwhelming desire to grab her close and give her a real kiss had been so strong, he'd had to physically restrain himself and step away. Kissing the nanny would be wrong on so many levels, he couldn't begin to list them all.

Although his father certainly could. Oscar Easton's code of acceptable conduct was the creed they all lived by.

Andrew forced himself to recall the painful memory of his father's face after the last terrible fight with Frank over Rose—the one where Frank had stormed out of the house for good. Never did Andrew wish to see his father in such pain again. And he certainly would never be the one to cause it.

He swiveled in his chair to face the window and look out over the city. This was his world, the place he belonged. He needed to refocus his priorities, concentrate on making Father proud and earning that promotion. All thoughts of Grace must be firmly stored away.

The door opened. Without looking, Andrew knew who it was.

He turned his chair around. "Hello, Father. What can I do for you?"

"Andrew, I think it prudent that I send you to Ottawa for a few days. There's a property there Harrison thinks might be the perfect location for our next hotel." He crossed his arms over his chest, not bothering to take a seat. "You'll need to meet with the current owner. Check the building to see if it's worth renovating instead of starting from scratch. That could save us a lot of money."

Andrew nodded. Going out of town to work on this important project might be just what he needed to get Grace out of his system. "How soon do you want me there?"

Father's eyes narrowed. "As soon as possible. If the property is viable, we want to put in an offer before it's snatched up."

"Fine. I'll leave on the first train tomorrow. Any recommendation as to where I should stay?"

"The Chateau Laurier, of course. Always smart to check out the competition."

"I thought so. I'll have Martha make the arrangements."

His father studied him for a moment. "I expected more of a protest. Glad to see you're so eager to get going on this project."

"I am eager. I know I wasn't enthusiastic at first, but I've come to believe that expanding our holdings could be a good thing." Sometimes the facts and figures didn't tell the whole story, as the success of the gala had proved.

"Excellent. And if things work out, you could be moving there sooner than anticipated. You might want to mention that possibility to Cecilia."

Andrew kept his gaze even. "I will."

"Good. I'll look forward to your report." He paused. "I know it might sometimes seem I push you too hard, Andrew. But it's actually a compliment. It shows how much I depend on you."

After his father had left, Andrew basked in that tidbit of information for a minute before going to ask his secretary to make the arrangements for his trip. Then he went in search of Edison to apprise him of his plans. As much as he disliked the idea, Edison would have to fill in for Andrew on a few keys issues while he was gone.

Edison's office was empty, and his secretary told Andrew that he and Miss Carmichael were in the conference room. Irritation prickled. What was Celia doing here when the fund-raiser was over? He marched down the hall and entered the room without knocking. At the far side, Edison and Celia sat close together, their heads almost touching. At the sound of the door opening, they broke apart.

Cecilia jumped up from her chair. "Andrew, you decided to join us after all?" Her cheeks flushed with what looked suspiciously like guilt.

"Join you? I wasn't invited."

She frowned. "Paul, I thought you told Andrew about the meeting."

"Didn't I?" Edison rose, a blasé expression on his face. "I could have sworn I told you Cecilia was coming in today to finalize the loose ends from the gala."

"I can fill you in later, darling," Cecilia said quickly. "We're almost done here anyway."

"I'm afraid it will have to wait." He glanced at Edison. "I came to tell you I'm heading to Ottawa first thing tomorrow. I'll be gone four or five days."

"What's going on in Ottawa?" Suspicion darkened Edison's features.

A brief flare of satisfaction filled Andrew's chest. He knew something his rival didn't—something Father hadn't felt the need to tell Edison about.

"A project my father is working on." He turned to Cecilia. "I'll explain when I get back. Maybe we can meet for dinner then?"

She brightened. "That sounds wonderful. I assume you'll be back in time for the party?"

"What party?"

"Your mother's birthday. Don't tell me you forgot that too?" Her laugh echoed over the room.

Annoyance crawled up Andrew's neck. How did these two always manage to make him feel incompetent? He did a mental calculation of the dates and realized the celebration would likely be on the night he returned. "We'll set a date for dinner when I return then."

"Set a date." She wiggled her brows. "I like the sound of that."

CHAPTER 21

September 10, 1917

Oh, Grace, my heart grows weary with this war. I wonder if I will ever see Frank again. Three long years we've been apart with nothing but letters to keep us going. Who ever imagined this fighting would go on so long? I pray God gives me the courage to endure this agony until Frank comes home to me.

Grace shifted Christian on her hip as she climbed the back staircase, a tug of regret dimming her usual good humor. She'd been looking forward to Andrew's return from Ottawa today and hearing all about his unexpected trip at dinnertime. She'd missed him more than she thought possible. Was it a coincidence or a deliberate choice that this trip occurred right after their day at the amusement park?

She would have to wait to find out because tonight the family was hosting a party in honor of Mrs. Easton's birthday. A party Grace was not invited to attend.

So instead of dinner in the dining room, she'd brought the baby down to the kitchen and grabbed a quick bite with the other staff before the guests began to arrive. She would likely not see Andrew at all, and the long evening ahead in the nursery suddenly seemed very lonely.

Her presence—correction—Christian's presence had been requested by Mr. Easton, who'd asked her to bring the boy down so he could introduce him to their friends. For that, she had donned one of her good Sunday dresses, not wishing to appear before everyone in her nanny's apron.

In order to keep Christian awake later than usual, Grace spent time playing with him and reading him a story. At the allotted hour, she made sure the boy's nappy was dry and that he was dressed in his best outfit. Then with a last peek in the mirror, Grace carried him down the rear staircase. A host of butterflies swarmed her stomach as she neared the bottom of the stairs. The sound of laughter and muted conversation drifted out from the various rooms in the house. She entered the back hall and kept to the shadows where she would await a cue from Mr. Easton to enter the parlor.

A few seconds later, however, Andrew appeared. He came to a sudden halt when he noticed her. "Grace? What are you doing here?"

The momentary thrill that surged through her upon seeing him evaporated under the weight of his frown. Was he not pleased to see her?

"Your father asked me to bring Christian down. I'm waiting for him to come and get me."

"I suppose he wants to introduce his new grandson to the world." Andrew gave a tight smile, yet lines of tension remained around his eyes.

What had happened to the relaxed man who'd watched the fireworks with her?

"How was your trip?" she asked softly, pulling Christian's little hand away from her face.

"Productive. We're thinking of opening another hotel there."

"How exciting." She smiled, happy to see a glimmer of enthusiasm replace the strain on his face.

"Yes, it is." He shifted from one foot to the other, his gaze staying trained on the baby.

Grace lifted her chin. Something had definitely changed between them, and for the life of her, she couldn't understand what. Did he regret opening up to her the way he had on the island?

He took a step forward, and her traitorous pulse leapt.

"I'll take Christian inside. I'd welcome the chance to spend some time with him." Andrew held out his arms for the baby. "I'll bring him back when we're through."

That suited Grace just fine, not having to be on display among all those fancy guests. Yet in a way, it felt like a dismissal. She handed Christian to him, and the boy snuggled into Andrew's shoulder.

When he remained silent, she forced a smile. "Well, have a good night."

"Grace, wait." His husky tone vibrated with regret. "Why don't you come down once Christian's asleep? Mother would be happy to see you."

She held his gaze for a beat, unsure of what she saw in those captivating blue depths. Longing? Remorse? Her throat clogged. Did he really want her there or was he simply being polite?

A movement behind him caught Grace's attention. Clad in a vibrant blue dress, Cecilia Carmichael marched toward them.

"There you are, Andrew darling. I was wondering where you'd gotten to." She walked up and wound her hand through his arm, her eyes colder than the jewels that glittered at her neck.

Had she heard Andrew's invitation?

A closed look came over his face. "Father wants to introduce Christian to the guests." He nodded to Grace. "Thank you for bringing him down."

At his complete change in demeanor, something inside Grace withered. When she'd shared the holiday with the Eastons at Hanlan Point, Grace had almost begun to feel like part of the family, but now her true place became exceedingly apparent.

"You're welcome," she said. "I'd better get back to the nursery." *Where I belong.*

The tension returned to Andrew's face. "I'll have Virginia bring Christian upstairs later. Good-night, Miss Foley."

There was no doubt about this dismissal.

Grace lifted her chin. "Good-night. Please wish your mother a happy birthday for me." Without acknowledging Cecilia, she turned and headed back to the servants' staircase.

After four days away, Andrew had almost managed to stop thinking about Grace, but that had all been undone the second he laid eyes on her again. Coming upon her with Christian in her arms, every good intention had flown from his head. What had he been thinking, inviting her to join the party? Thank goodness Cecilia had shown up when she did, or who knows what he would have done next.

He blew out a long breath. He needed to stay strong, focus on his goal to keep his family intact, and avoid Grace as much as possible.

After seeing him talking to Grace, Cecilia had clung to his arm most of the night, until thankfully she'd been drawn into a conversation with some of the ladies about her contributions to the gala. Andrew had been more than relieved to have a minute to himself and had escaped to the front step for a bit of fresh air.

Now, as he reluctantly returned, he made sure his smile was in place before entering the crowded parlor. He crossed to the solarium where his mother held court in her favorite chair. She was clearly in her element, laughing at something one of her friends said, and for that reason alone, Andrew would endure the false niceties and whispered gossip of the guests. Ever since he'd been turned down by the military, he'd been the recipient of constant condemnation. Nothing he ever did was good enough in society's eyes.

"Can I get you anything, Mother?" he said as he came up beside her. "Another glass of punch perhaps?"

She grabbed his hand. "There you are, dear. We were just talking about you."

"All good things, I hope." He winked at Mrs. Cherry, an old friend of his mother's.

The plump woman chuckled, causing her chin to wobble. "Lillian was telling me how you've taken on the responsibility of raising your nephew. That's very noble of you."

"I consider it an honor to raise Frank's son. I only hope I can do a good job."

"I'm sure you will, what with your family to help."

"That's true. Now what can I get you ladies to drink?"

Two hours later, the party showed no signs of ending, and Andrew found himself longing for the solitude of his bedroom. If he had to smile any more, his face muscles would surely freeze.

He was about to enter the dining room to fetch yet another glass of punch for one of the guests when a shrill voice rose above the others from inside.

"I hear Cecilia suffered quite a disappointment on Dominion Day. Is it true Andrew didn't attend your annual celebration?"

"It is." Mrs. Carmichael's terse response froze Andrew's feet to the floor. "Even worse," she continued, "he spent the day in the company of the family's dreadful British nanny."

"Unheard of! Who brings the nanny on a family outing?"

"Word has it," a third person chimed in, "that Lillian and Virginia left early, and he stayed to watch the fireworks with the nanny—*alone*."

Heat built in Andrew's chest. How on earth could they know that? Were there spies following him around, reporting back to the Carmichaels?

"He's taking an awful chance. It could ruin everything."

"You're so right. If he doesn't make his intentions known soon, I wouldn't be surprised if Cecilia ended up with that handsome Mr. Edison."

"Frankly," Mrs. Carmichael said, "he might be a better match. Mr. Edison is clearly more ambitious than Andrew, who—let's be honest—has had everything handed to him by his father."

Icy chills of rage raced through him. Before he could stop himself, he strode into the dining room, his gaze narrowing on the women by the sideboard.

The two ladies with Mrs. Carmichael gasped, but Cecilia's mother remained as cool as ever. She merely raised a brow as if daring him to say anything.

This time Andrew would not hold his tongue for propriety's sake. He speared them all with a sharp glare. "I hope you ladies are having a good time at my expense. For the record, I invited Cecilia to come to Hanlan's Point with my family on Dominion Day, and she turned me down. So if she was disappointed, it was her own fault."

He waited a beat while the two women murmured abstract apologies. Mrs. Carmichael only stared.

"Furthermore, my relationship with your daughter is private. I'd thank you to keep your opinions to yourself and not stoop to the level of a cheap gossipmonger."

That time he got a reaction. Charlotte's eyes widened and she pressed her mouth into a tight line. Before she could unleash her sharp tongue on him, Andrew stormed from the room.

He'd hear about his rudeness tomorrow from Cecilia and his father, but right now he didn't care. He'd had enough of the endless criticism, the whispered gossip behind gloved hands, the disapproving stares.

Andrew strode out the side door and headed to the rear of the house, pulling his tie loose as he went. Suffocating. That was the perfect word to describe his life. Bound at every side by family obligations and outrageous expectations. If only he could take Christian far away where no one knew him, where no one censured his every action.

The humid night air surrounded him like a shroud as he made his way to the center of his mother's garden, where the heavy fragrance of roses scented the space. He thanked the heavens—and Collin Lafferty—that the bushes were tall enough to conceal his presence from anyone looking out from the solarium. Right now he craved anonymity and solitude, willing the serenity of the night to rid him of his toxic anger. Above him, the clouds shifted, revealing an almost full moon, illuminating his path as he walked.

When he reached the fountain, tension still snapped through his stiff muscles. He picked up a pebble, rubbed its smoothness between his fingers, then hurled it into the water. A tide of ripples swelled out to the edges. As he stared into the pool, his reflection became fractured, distorted—just like his life.

Expelling a long breath, he sank onto the stone ledge and dropped his head into his hands. Why was he so conflicted lately? The family he'd worked so hard to keep intact after Frank's estrangement was slowly healing. His career had improved. His father was ready to entrust him with the expansion of the new hotel, which meant he would finally get to do more than balance the ledgers. If things went well with the Ottawa project, Andrew could make a real difference to the Easton holdings. Earn his father's respect and be considered the loyal son and rightful heir to the family fortune.

So why did his soul seem to shrivel up as each day passed? Why did it feel that the progress he'd made with his father could easily disappear with one wrong word, one misstep?

Like refusing to marry Cecilia.

Andrew's shoulders sagged. Prior to Christian's coming into his life, his path had been clear. Marrying Celia was a logical decision. Not only would a sophisticated wife be an asset to his career, their union would restore his family's honor, a matter of extreme importance to his father.

But Cecilia's lack of support concerning Christian had created a fissure of uncertainty that now seemed as wide as a chasm. Andrew had tried to be understanding, giving her time to adjust to the new development in his life. But she still showed no sign of softening toward the boy.

And then Grace had come along with her gentle ways and her unconditional love for Christian, embodying everything he'd hoped Cecilia would be for his nephew. Faced with such a comparison, he'd been growing less and less enthralled with the prospect of committing himself to a woman who didn't seem to share the same vision for their lives.

Andrew looked upward, his eyes drawn to the amazing array of stars visible in the night sky. As a boy, he used to believe the stars were actually God winking down at him from heaven, proof He was watching over him. Maybe Andrew needed to take his problems to the One with all the answers. But how to begin after so long?

He focused on a star near the moon, and just like he'd done as a boy, lifted his thoughts to the Almighty.

Forgive me, Lord. I know my faith is weak. I've been struggling ever since Frank deserted us. Even more so since his death. Now you've given me the precious gift of his son to raise. But the truth is, I'm not sure I can do this on my own, and it doesn't seem Cecilia will be the mother Christian needs. Lord, please show me what's best for Christian. Help me to know your will for my life, and I will do my best to follow it.

The earnest prayer echoed in Andrew's heart, and for the first time in a long while, a measure of peace spread through him. This was what he needed to do. Turn his life over to the Lord and let Him direct his path. Surely he couldn't fail if he listened for the Lord's guidance.

Andrew remained seated on the edge of the fountain for some time, loathe to leave the peace and solitude. Just when he decided he should rejoin the festivities, a soft humming broke the stillness. He looked around to see where it had originated.

Several yards away, Grace came into view, strolling among the rosebushes. Andrew almost forgot to breathe, so mesmerized was he at the sight of her. In the moonlight, she seemed as ethereal as the graceful statue in the fountain. Her hair, normally pulled back in a roll, now flowed over her shoulders with a few strands left loose around her cheeks. She plucked a flower from the bush and held it to her nose, closing her eyes as she inhaled its fragrance. A soft smile teased her lips.

Andrew's mouth went dry. He rose from the ledge, his movement capturing her attention.

Her eyes widened. "Andrew. What are you doing out here?"

"Getting some air. And you?"

"I-I wasn't tired and thought a stroll in the garden might help." She twisted her fingers together, almost crushing the flower. "Christian is fast asleep. I checked before I came down." She glanced around the area, as though expecting someone to jump from the bushes. "Well, if you'll excuse me—"

"Wait." He hated this awkwardness between them. After all they had shared, she deserved so much better. "I'm glad you're here, because I owe you an apology for the way I treated you earlier. I acted like you were—"

"Your employee?" She raised a brow.

His breath whooshed out. "Yes."

"That's because I am."

He took a step toward her. "You're much more than that, Grace. I'd like to think we're friends at least."

She held his gaze for several seconds. The evening breeze stirred her hair, lifting it from her shoulders. "I don't think Miss Carmichael would be happy to hear that."

"Let's leave Cecilia out of this, shall we?" he said quietly.

"Very well. I accept your apology." The guarded look left her eyes, and she came closer. "So why are you really out here? Weren't you having a good time?" She tilted her head to study him.

He gestured for her to sit and then took a seat beside her. "The truth is, I detest social events. I feel hypocritical, putting on a fake smile, making inane chit-chat about topics I don't care about. And I can't abide the gossipmongers." He scowled, recalling the main reason he'd come out here.

"Did you overhear something unpleasant?"

Her astuteness never failed to astonish him. "I did. And I probably made matters worse by confronting the woman."

Grace plucked at the petals of the rose she still held. "Maybe all will be forgotten by tomorrow."

"You don't know Charlotte Carmichael. She never forgets a thing."

"You're right. Though she's probably the one who owes you an apology."

He gave her an admiring glance. "You're a smart woman, Grace Foley."

She laughed. "I call it being observant. You can learn a lot from staying in the background and watching people." She leaned back and trailed her fingers through the water in the fountain. "For instance, why does Mrs. Carmichael seem to dislike you?"

Andrew sucked in a breath. "You don't beat around the bush."

"Too personal?"

"No, just honest." He ran his hand over his beard. "Ever since Frank broke off his engagement to Cecilia, Charlotte has held a grudge against our family. But because her husband and my father are good friends, she's forced to put up with us."

"How did you end up courting Cecilia then?"

He squirmed under her direct stare. How could he explain it even to himself? "When the Carmichaels heard about Frank's death, they came to pay their respects. The bad feelings seemed to have mended, and Cecilia started going out of her way to talk to me at church and social functions. Our relationship sort of evolved from there."

"Are you happy about it? The relationship I mean."

His usual glib reply died on his tongue at the sincerity in her eyes. "I thought I was. But when Christian came into my life, I started noticing a few problems. I'm hoping they'll resolve themselves in time." How had he ended up discussing his feelings for Cecilia with Grace of all people?

"May I give you a piece of advice?" she asked softly.

"Be my guest."

She shifted to face him more fully, her expression earnest. "Don't base any important decisions on the expectations of others. You deserve to live your life the way you want. The way God intends for you."

Andrew went very still. The words of the prayer he'd uttered right before Grace had come into the garden rang in his ears. *Help me to know your will for my life, and I will do my best to follow it.* Had God used Grace as an instrument to get His message across?

"I know it's none of my business, but you see, I have this terrible character flaw." She gave a slight shrug. "I need to make sure everyone is happy."

"Actually, I find your honesty refreshing. And I'll keep your advice in mind."

Grace smiled at him, the lights from the fountain reflecting in her eyes. He could stare into their depths all night.

Probably not a good idea.

With effort, he tore his attention away and pointed at the sky. "Have you noticed how bright the stars are tonight?"

She tilted her head back. "They're amazing."

"I used to love coming out here as a boy. I'd lie on the lawn and watch them for hours. Sometimes I'd even fall asleep out there."

"Sounds wonderful."

"Would you like to see my favorite viewing spot?" His mouth seemed to operate independently from his brain. But after enduring the falseness of his parents' guests all evening, Grace was a breath of fresh air.

"I'd love to."

Andrew held out a hand to her, regretting the tentative expression in her eyes. But she placed her hand in his, and they rose. He led her out of the garden to the long stretch of grass beyond. Immediately, the lush darkness surrounded them, enveloping them in hushed stillness. When they reached the large maple tree he loved to climb as a boy, Andrew stopped. "This is where I used to come," he said. "I would lie out here under the tree for hours."

But they couldn't do that now. Not in their good clothes. So he tugged her farther along to the gazebo and pointed to the steps. "Not quite the same view, but a lot drier than sitting on the grass."

"This will do nicely." She smiled as she smoothed her dress under her on the top step.

He sat beside her, careful to leave an appropriate distance between them. "If you look straight up, you can sometimes see the Milky Way."

Her lips parted as she gazed upward. "It's breathtaking. It feels as though God is sharing the beauty of heaven with us."

"That's what I always imagined too." He found himself caught up in the wonder of the heavens on display. The immense universe spread out before them, splashed with hundreds of thousands of dancing lights.

They sat together in perfect harmony, staring into the sky, content to drink in the magic of the night. A sense of oneness filled him. Never could he remember being so at peace with himself and the world. His soul sang as though he'd found his perfect match.

Someone who valued the same things he did.

Someone who understood him as no other.

After a few minutes more, Grace rubbed her arms and glanced over at him. "I'd love to stay longer, but I really should get back."

Reluctantly, he held out a hand to help her up. "You're shivering. Here, take my jacket." He removed it and draped it around her shoulders. But somehow he couldn't make his arms drop away. Instead, he tugged on the lapels to pull her closer.

Her soft gasp and the quickening of her breath made his pulse thunder. When she lifted her face to stare up at him, he was undone.

"Do you know how beautiful you are?" he whispered.

She shook her head, her eyes never leaving his.

The chorus of crickets serenading them faded to the background, while the scent of roses and fresh grass filled his senses. He lifted a finger to caress her silky cheek. At that moment, there was nothing he wanted more than to kiss her. Slowly, he moved closer until their lips met. He lingered there for a second before easing back to make sure she wanted this too. Her eyes burned with longing and perhaps a touch of indecision. Yet when he lowered his mouth again, she wound her arms around his neck and kissed him back with a passion that astounded him. His chest expanded and filled with heat. Every nerve in his body hummed with electricity.

It seemed all the stars in the universe had aligned for this precise moment.

The joining of lips. The merging of hearts. The union of souls.

He cupped the back of her head and wrapped his other arm around her, pulling her closer. The silken strands of her hair teased his jaw as his mouth found the sweetness of hers once again. She tasted of honey and freshness and hope.

A groan rumbled through his chest. Before he lost complete control, he broke the kiss, but kept his arms around her. She fit against him perfectly, his chin resting lightly on top of her head. His heart beat an unsteady rhythm while his breathing fought to even out. He'd never experienced such a perfect moment in time. If only he could stay cocooned in this bubble of joy for the rest of his life. Then Andrew could die a happy man.

CHAPTER 22

Grace pressed her face into the silkiness of Andrew's shirt, inhaling the spicy scent of his cologne. Despite an attempt to gather her wits about her, her frantic pulse rate refused to slow. She'd never experienced anything quite like Andrew's soul-stirring embrace. Now, resting in his arms, she'd never felt so safe, so cherished.

When he tilted her chin and pressed his lips to hers again, she responded willingly, her heart thumping loudly in her chest.

"Andrew? Are you out here?" Mr. Easton's booming voice rang out over the stillness of the night.

Andrew sprang back, his expression panicked. "We can't let him find us together," he said. He scanned the dark expanse of lawn between them and the garden. "Wait here till I've gone inside."

Her spirits plummeted faster than a falling star. Of course Andrew wouldn't want to be seen with her. Being caught with the nanny would be a transgression of the worst kind. One Mr. Easton likely wouldn't forgive.

"Promise me, Grace. He'll fire you if he finds you here." The urgency in Andrew's voice brought the strength back to her knees.

"I-I promise."

He guided her into the gazebo. "I'm so sorry. I'll talk to you tomorrow." With a last tortured look, he took off at a run across the lawn and soon disappeared behind the bushes.

Grace leaned back against the wall of the gazebo, her breath still coming too fast. She touched her fingers to her lips. Had Andrew really kissed her or had she dreamt the whole thing?

She closed her eyes, reliving the feel of his arms around her, his warm lips, the brush of his beard against her cheek. If she'd believed she was falling for him before, that embrace had magnified every sensation, fanning her feelings into a roaring inferno.

Yet underneath this moment of bliss lurked the hard reality. Andrew was still involved with Cecilia. She should have pushed him away. Demanded he never touch her again.

But instead she'd kissed him back with reckless abandon.

Reckless. Irresponsible. Just like her mother always claimed.

A groan escaped her. How would she ever face Andrew after this?

Andrew slowed his breathing and stepped from behind the bushes. His father had come down from the verandah, the glow from his cigar bobbing as he walked.

"There you are. Why are you out here all alone?" Father scanned the property behind him.

Andrew prayed Grace had stayed hidden. Neither of them needed the grief that would follow if his father discovered them together. "I needed some air. Why?"

"The Carmichaels are leaving. You need to see them out."

Of course. Heaven forbid he miss saying good-bye. One more thing for Mrs. Carmichael to complain about.

"I didn't realize they'd be leaving so soon." Andrew went to straighten his sleeve and froze. He'd left his jacket draped around Grace's shoulders. How was he going to explain that?

At the same time, his father's eyes narrowed. "Where is your jacket?"

A bead of sweat snaked down Andrew's back. "I must have left it by the fountain. You go ahead. I'll be right in."

His father stared at him. "I hope you're not foolish enough to bring another woman out here. Not with Cecilia waiting for you."

"Don't be ridiculous." The denial sounded defensive even to

him, almost an admission of his guilt. Andrew clenched his hands into fists. "Tell her I'll be right there." He turned and strode away, praying Grace was still where he'd left her.

Otherwise how would he ever explain the disappearance of his jacket?

How long had Grace been waiting? Long enough for Andrew and his father to have gone inside? Certainly long enough for her to miss the warmth of Andrew's embrace.

She shivered in the cool breeze and rubbed her arms. At the feel of the scratchy wool, she gasped. Andrew's suit coat. Would he come back when he realized he'd forgotten it?

From inside the gazebo, Grace peered into the darkness. Above the bushes, all she could see was the faint glow of lights from the solarium. With no way to tell if Andrew and Mr. Easton were still out there, Grace would have to leave the jacket here and hope Andrew would find it after she'd gone.

She slipped the coat off her shoulders and laid it on the bench seat.

"Grace."

She jumped at the hoarse whisper and whirled around.

Andrew entered the gazebo, a curious mix of relief and anguish flooding his features.

Without a word, she handed him the jacket.

"Thank you," he said in a low voice. "I wish I could stay, but I have to get back before they send out a search party." He put on the coat and adjusted the sleeves.

"I understand." She'd love nothing more than to be able to sit by the fountain with him. Maybe he'd hold her hand or even kiss her again.

But it was not meant to be.

"I enjoyed our time together." He took her hand and brought it to his lips. "We'll talk tomorrow." With a quick smile, he turned and ran back toward the house.

Grace stood alone in the darkness, more chilled than ever without his jacket. Without his reassuring presence. Though it was silly, she couldn't help but feel abandoned. Finally, when it seemed enough time had elapsed, she made her way back to the house, keeping to the shadows until she reached the servants' entrance.

Thankfully, she encountered no one on the way up to her room. She shut her door without a sound and leaned against it, her spirits sinking. How had she gone from the most wonderful experience of her life to sneaking back to her room like a criminal?

What a fool she'd been to think she could ever ignore her feelings for Andrew. His kiss had changed everything, and now their relationship would never be the same.

A sharp tug of guilt sliced through her as the faint chime of the grandfather clock registered. She'd only meant to spend a few minutes in the garden, but instead had spent far more time away than she'd planned, gazing at stars and kissing her employer, letting her own selfish desires outweigh her responsibility.

Her mother was right. She *was* reckless. Untrustworthy. Tears fought their way into her eyes. Would she ever learn her lesson?

She entered the nursery through the connecting door, not daring to breathe until she peered into the crib. The baby was sleeping peacefully, his thumb in his mouth.

Grace exhaled softly. *Thank you, Lord.*

She would never have forgiven herself if anything had happened to him while she was gone.

Without a sound, she slipped back into her room, leaving the door slightly ajar so she could hear him if he woke. Her gaze fell on the end of her bed, and she frowned. The corner of the quilt was sticking out as though tucked in with great haste. She was certain she hadn't left it that way when she'd gone downstairs.

Prickles of foreboding raced along her arms. Had someone been in here?

Grace moved toward the bed and pulled the quilt free. An object flew out and landed on the floor. Slowly she bent to pick it up. A large blue stone surrounded by a circle of diamonds dangled from a gold chain. Instinctively, she knew this piece was no imitation.

A jolt of anxiety streaked through her, along with a thousand thoughts pinging through her head. Someone had purposely hidden it in her bed. But why?

Muffled voices sounded from the corridor. She froze, the necklace seeming to weigh like a brick in her palm. Harried footsteps followed, then a deep voice filtered through Grace's door.

"You're being ridiculous, Celia. It probably slipped off somewhere downstairs." Andrew sounded exasperated.

"I'm not being ridiculous. Someone took it. You'll see." Cecilia's petulant voice grew louder. "That nanny of yours was staring at it earlier when she brought the baby down."

Two sharp knocks sounded on her door. "Grace, are you awake? I need to speak with you."

Grace's heart stalled in her chest. She couldn't make her mouth open to answer him. Maybe if she stayed silent, they'd believe she was asleep and leave her be. But Andrew would know she was awake. It hadn't been that long since he left her in the gazebo.

How was she ever going to explain this necklace?

CHAPTER 23

In the corridor outside Grace's room, Andrew held his breath and prayed she wouldn't answer his knock. He didn't know if she'd had enough time to make it back from the gazebo yet, but if he could convince Cecilia that Grace was asleep and that he'd confront her with this ridiculous accusation in the morning, it would buy him time to determine how best to handle the situation.

On the other hand, if Grace was here, Andrew could make a perfunctory search of her room and prove she had nothing to do with the disappearance of Celia's necklace.

Andrew clenched his jaw. He couldn't begin to comprehend why Cecilia was so insistent Grace had stolen her pendant. Most likely, the clasp had come loose, and the piece had fallen off. The maids would find it when they cleaned up after the guests left.

He turned to Cecilia. "I'm sure Grace is long retired for the night. I'll speak to her first thing tomorrow, if the maids don't come across the necklace in the meantime."

Her thin brows crashed together. "That is unacceptable."

Then before Andrew could stop her, she twisted the doorknob and pushed into the room.

Grace stood by the end of the bed, still in the dress she'd been wearing earlier. A fleeting look of panic flickered in her eyes. "What is the meaning of this?" She clutched the bedpost with one hand, thrusting the other behind her back.

Cecilia advanced on her. "Hand over my necklace, you thief. I know you took it."

The blood drained from Grace's face, and for a moment, Andrew feared she would faint.

Then her features hardened as she glared at Cecilia. "You mean the one you stashed under my mattress?"

Cecilia's mouth fell open. "Of all the nerve—"

Grace sidestepped Cecilia to stand in front of Andrew. "When I returned to my room earlier, I noticed my bed was untidy, not like I'd left it. I pulled out the quilt and found this." Grace held out her hand, revealing the sapphire and diamond pendant. "Someone came in while I was gone and put it there." She shot a hard look at Cecilia.

Cecilia's nostrils flared. She snatched the necklace from Grace's hand. "A liar as well as a thief. This would have fetched a pretty penny for someone of your station. I've a good mind to call the constable."

Despite Grace's bravado, her bottom lip trembled. She turned her wide brown eyes on him. "Surely you don't believe that, Andrew."

He almost groaned. She'd called him Andrew, not Mr. Easton. With that tiny slip, Grace might have fueled Celia's ire and sealed her fate.

His stomach twisted at the unfairness of the situation, for even with the evidence in her hand, Andrew knew Grace would never take anything that wasn't hers. Everything in him wanted to shout her innocence. That she couldn't have stolen the necklace, because she was with him outside. But if he admitted they were alone together at the gazebo, it would ruin her reputation.

And he couldn't risk upsetting Cecilia even more. Not with so much at stake.

His hesitation became evident to both women, each looking equally unhappy. He needed time to figure out how to protect Grace from whatever was happening here.

"Let's all calm down," he said. "Celia, you have your necklace back, and your parents are waiting for you. Let's sleep on the situation and deal with it in the morning."

"And give her time to disappear? I think not."

Grace whirled on her. "Why would I disappear when I've done nothing wrong?" She turned to Andrew. "I would never abandon Christian. Never." Her eyes shone with moisture, beseeching him to believe her.

"Those tears aren't fooling anyone," Cecilia scoffed.

Andrew's stomach churned. Any minute, Cecilia would storm down the stairs and accuse Grace of theft, leaving his parents with no choice but to call the authorities.

"That's enough," he snapped. "Grace isn't going anywhere. We'll handle this tomorrow." He took Cecilia firmly by the elbow and guided her toward the door.

She shot another glare over her shoulder at Grace. "Don't think you've heard the last of this."

Grace pressed her lips together. The anguish in her eyes nearly undid him, but there was nothing he could do at the moment. If he told everyone about meeting Grace in the garden, their time together would be misconstrued, and her future would be destroyed.

He needed more time to come up with a solution that would satisfy everyone involved.

With a silent look of apology, Andrew closed the door and followed Cecilia down the hall.

Andrew's mind whirled, reaching hard for logic to override his heightened emotions. He required a clear head to diffuse the situation. If he went down those stairs to face both their parents, he had no doubt Grace would become a sacrificial lamb in Cecilia's drama. They might even have Grace arrested. He couldn't take the chance of that happening. He had to get to the bottom of this before he let Cecilia wreak havoc below.

Gripping her arm, he propelled her past the staircase to an alcove at the far end of the hallway, where there would be no chance of being overheard.

"What are you doing?" She pulled her arm free. "My parents are waiting for me."

He kept his eyes trained on her. "I need to clear up a few things first."

"What things?" A trace of unease passed over her features.

He paused to collect himself, forcing a calm he didn't feel in order to pry the truth from her. "There are several holes in your story, Celia. For one, I saw you minutes before I went outside to get some air, and you were still wearing the necklace."

She crossed her arms. "So?"

Andrew took a gamble and prayed it would pay off. "While I was out by the fountain, Grace happened to come along. We chatted for a while. Quite a while, in fact." He paused to let the implication of his comment sink in.

Celia's expression grew thunderous. "How convenient! You were probably planning a *rendezvous* when I saw you both in the hallway."

Andrew fought to keep his temper under control and not think about the amazing kiss by the gazebo. "A pure coincidence, I assure you. But the point is, Grace couldn't have taken the necklace and hidden it in her room, because she was in the garden with me. Besides, how would she have gotten it off your neck in the first place without you knowing?" He pulled himself up to his full height and gave her a stern look. "You put it there, Celia. Admit it."

She pressed her lips together and looked away. Her silence was all the proof he needed.

"How could you do something so cruel to a woman who's never done anything to you?"

Her eyes flew to his, anger glittering in their depths. "Can you not guess? Or are you so besotted with her you can't see straight?"

Her harsh words stung, but he forced himself not to flinch. "I am not besotted."

"Oh really?" She paced the alcove like a caged animal. "Do

you imagine I don't see how you follow her every move, how your ear is attuned to her every word while I sit unnoticed beside you? How do you think that makes me feel?"

Guilt sliced neatly through his chest. Had he been that obvious? A landslide of images flew to mind. Dancing with Grace at the gala, enjoying her company at Hanlan's Point, and most damaging of all, kissing her tonight under the stars. He'd never felt so alive, so uplifted as when he spent time with her. "So, out of jealousy, you planned to have Grace fired to remove her from my life?"

Her bottom lip trembled. "I had to do something. I could feel you slipping away from me more and more each day. And then seeing you together in the hall with that baby, looking like a real family, something just snapped." A tear slid down her cheek, and she brushed it away. "I won't lose you the way I lost Frank. Do you have any idea what his rejection cost me? I could never endure such humiliation again." All her bravado fell away, leaving only raw emotion.

Compassion mixed with guilt as Andrew handed her his handkerchief. Despite everything, she did have legitimate cause for her insecurity. Was he such a cad that he could ignore her pain?

And for what? One perfect kiss in the moonlight with a woman he could never have?

He rubbed his temples where a headache grew in intensity. "I'm sorry, Celia. Sorry I've been so . . . distracted lately. You're right. I haven't been fair to you."

She blew her nose and sighed. "I'm sorry too. For lying about the necklace."

A recollection flashed through his mind of Celia as a young girl, chasing him, Frank, and Ginny around the back lawn, her blond braids flying out behind her. They'd been so young and carefree back then. How had things gotten so complicated?

"What do you intend to do now?" she asked quietly.

Andrew released a weary breath. Maybe if he tried harder to involve Celia in his life, to include her on outings with Christian, she would form a deeper attachment to them both. And in turn, maybe his feelings would strengthen. "If you drop your accusation against Grace," he said. "I promise to make more of an effort in our relationship."

It was the least he could do to ensure Grace's reputation remained untarnished. Especially since this whole situation was his fault. If he had to sacrifice himself to do so, then so be it. He should be used to it by now.

Cecilia sniffed. "You're not just saying that to guarantee my silence?"

Faced with the naked vulnerability in her blue eyes, Andrew couldn't bear to hurt her again. "I give you my word."

A smile fluttered on her lips. "Then I will try harder with Christian as well."

"Thank you. That would mean a great deal to me."

The pressure eased in his chest. He'd saved Grace for now and hopefully taken steps to solidify his connection with Celia. Maybe he could make this work after all.

He led her out of the alcove toward the stairs, his resolve firming. He'd known all along that his attraction to Grace was inappropriate. Pursuing it would be wrong and would only result in the ruin of many lives, Grace's included.

It was time to be a man and accept the truth. Cecilia was his future.

After a sleepless night spent alternately pacing the floor of her room and reading her Bible, Grace dressed for the day ahead with wooden movements. She'd stayed up for hours in the hope that Andrew would come back to tell her that he believed her and that he'd put Cecilia in her place. But he never returned, leaving Grace's imagination to run wild with what might have happened.

Now with the household beginning to stir, Grace feared that at any moment Mr. Easton would call her down and fire her. Or worse, turn her over to the police. Because unless Andrew had succeeded in getting Cecilia to change her mind about accusing her of theft, this would be Grace's last day in the Eastons' employ. The last day caring for Christian. Her heart hitched at the thought. How would she ever say good-bye to that precious boy?

On a deep inhale, Grace attempted to shake off her worries, and entered the nursery to check on Christian. She was glad to find he was still asleep. His late-night appearance at his grandmother's party had likely tired him out. She would go down to the kitchen and get his morning bottle prepared because when he awakened, he would be hungry.

She stepped into the hallway and found Andrew waiting by the top of the stairs. Her heart leapt into her throat. How would he treat her today after everything that had transpired?

"Good morning, Grace. May I have a word with you downstairs, please?"

Her tongue tangled at his serious demeanor, and she could only nod. She forced her legs to carry her down the staircase.

"Let's sit in the solarium," he said when they reached the main floor.

She followed him into the spacious room filled with sunlight and plants, where only a few stray balloons bore evidence of the festivities that had taken place the previous night.

Andrew gestured for her to take a seat on one of the wicker chairs.

She did so and waited while he paced to the windows overlooking the rear yard.

At last he turned, his expression haggard. "I owe you an apology. Two apologies, in fact." He paused. "First, for taking liberties with you last night at the gazebo." Color crept into his cheeks. "I had no right to kiss you. Not when I'm courting another woman. I hope you can forgive me for overstepping the bounds of our . . . friendship."

Hurt stole her breath. Was that all he considered her to be?

She held his gaze. "Well, I don't regret it. Not for a minute."

He actually flinched, then moved to the other side of the room where he fingered the leaves of a potted fern. It seemed he couldn't even bear to look at her.

A burn of indignation heated Grace from the inside out. It was glaringly obvious that their kiss, which had changed everything for her, meant nothing to him. She'd been foolish to believe anything else. She pressed her lips together to keep from saying anything rash. One reckless deed was enough.

"The second apology is for that stunt Cecilia tried to pull." The sun shone through the windows, surrounding him in a wash of light.

Grace went still. "Does this mean you believe me? Because last night I wasn't sure you did."

He whirled around. "Of course I believe you. I know you'd never do anything like that." He was saying all the right things, but his eyes remained shuttered. "Cecilia told her parents we found the necklace in the hallway and apologized to everyone for overreacting."

Relief crashed through her with such intensity that for a moment she lost her breath. "So I won't be going to jail?"

"No." A hint of a smile touched his mouth.

She rose from her seat, too unsettled to remain still. "Why did she do it?" she asked.

Yet as the words left her mouth, she remembered the iciness of Cecilia's words when she'd seen Grace with Andrew in the hallway. Had she suspected Andrew's interest in her and followed them out to the garden? Grace's stomach churned at the idea of being spied on in such a manner.

"She was making a point in her usual dramatic fashion." His brow furrowed. "Ever since Christian became my ward, Cecilia has been angry. She resented the attention I gave him and the time I spent away from her."

"Well, you have a nanny now. She should be happier."

"Except that the nanny also seems to claim a great deal of my attention." He gave her an intense look.

Heat scorched her cheeks as emotions seesawed through her. "If I've done anything to make you think—"

"No, Grace. You haven't." He moved in front of her. "You've

done nothing except be the wonderful person you are. How could I not want to spend time with you?" The huskiness of his voice drew her gaze to his face, where his eyes flashed with an undefinable emotion. "The fault was all mine for forgetting my place. Forgetting my commitments. I'm truly sorry if I gave you the wrong impression."

Grace's lungs felt like they were collapsing. "What are you saying?"

"I haven't been fair to you—or to Cecilia." His gaze slid away as he shoved his hands in his pockets. "I'm going to do my best to make it up to her."

"I see." Coldness settled in the pit of Grace's stomach. Despite what Cecilia had tried to do, he was remaining loyal to her. Grace had been foolish to ever imagine she held any sway over him. That his kiss meant he'd choose her. She couldn't look at him, afraid he'd see too much. "If you'll excuse me, I need to get back to Christian." She turned to leave before her emotions got the best of her.

He reached for her hand. "Forgive me, Grace. I never meant to hurt you."

She went still, anguish tightening her chest. With enormous effort, she tugged her fingers free. "You've made your position very clear. From now on, I'll remember my place."

CHAPTER 24

November 30, 1917

It's a miracle, Grace! Frank has been granted permission to come home. His commander has allowed him a special leave to visit his family due to his mother's poor health. He will be home in time for Christmas and will stay until spring. By then, I pray the war is over and he'll never have to leave me again.

Grace peered out the window of the automobile. "This is it. Number 233."

Toby guided the automobile to a stop in front of Mrs. Chamberlain's boardinghouse.

Hours after her conversation with Andrew, Grace had been unable to shake the depression that suffused her soul and, yearning for the comforting presence of her dear friend, had requested Toby's services to take her there for a visit.

After he set the brake, Toby came around to open Grace's door and reached in to give her a hand. With Christian on one shoulder and a bag on the other, she appreciated the assistance.

"Thank you." She struggled to regain her composure. The intense way Toby had been watching her on the way over had unnerved her more than a little.

"I'll be back in two hours, if that's enough time for you." His green eyes were solemn beneath his chauffeur's cap.

"That would be fine. Thank you."

"My pleasure, Miss Foley." He gave a low bow, then rushed to open the small iron gate.

She passed him with a nod of thanks.

Before she reached the steps, the front door flew open and Mrs. Chamberlain rushed out, her dress blowing around her legs.

"I've been watching for you ever since you called to say you were coming." She wrapped her arms around Grace and the baby. "How I've missed you, Grace dear."

"I've missed you too." The woman's warm embrace felt like coming home. A soothing balm to her bruised soul.

"Let me look at this darlin' boy. My goodness, how he's grown since I saw him last." Mrs. C.'s voice quivered. "When I think of how thin he was when the Eastons took him, I can scarcely believe it's the same child. Rose would be so proud."

The tension in Grace's shoulders eased. It was a relief to be able to talk freely about Rose and not to have to pretend she wasn't related to Christian.

"Come in and tell me all about that fancy house you've been staying in. The tea's already brewed, and I have warm muffins right from the oven."

Five minutes later, Grace sat at the kitchen table as though she'd never left, sipping tea from Mrs. C.'s china cups, with Christian content on her landlady's lap.

"Things must be going well if this boy is any indication." Mrs. C. nuzzled Christian's head while deftly making sure he didn't grab anything off the tabletop.

Grace set down her cup. "I'll admit the Eastons have turned out to be a surprise. Except for Mr. Easton. He's as terrifying as Rose described." She laughed. "But Mrs. Easton and Virginia have both been very kind. And Andrew . . ." She paused, hoping she could speak about him without breaking down. "Family is extremely important to him, which is why he's taken on the responsibility of raising his brother's son."

Mrs. C. eyed her thoughtfully. "He seems to have made quite an impression."

The dreaded heat climbed into Grace's cheeks, but she remained silent. There wasn't anything she could add that wouldn't get her into trouble.

"Well, now that you know Christian has a family who loves him, what are your plans? Will you keep working for them?"

Grace's hand stilled on her cup. "Of course. Christian has grown very attached to me. I could never abandon him now." The mere thought of leaving the precious child made her throat grow tight. "I'll continue as his nanny for as long as I can."

For as long as my heart can bear it.

"I see." Mrs. C. patted Christian's back, the boy now half asleep on her shoulder. "What about your mother? Won't she be expecting you home at some point?"

Grace startled, a flood of guilt rushing through her. She'd written to Mum a few times since she arrived, but had asked her not to send any mail to the Eastons, too afraid someone might intercept the letter and determine she was related to Rose. Other than that, she'd tried not to think about her mother much, finding the time away from her caustic tongue a welcome reprieve. "She's probably upset. But I can't go home yet."

"Why not?"

Grace picked at her muffin. "Andrew is seeing a woman. Someone I don't think will be a good mother to Christian. Until I know for certain what he plans to do, I can't leave."

Mrs. C. aimed a shrewd gaze at Grace. "Is it the baby you're concerned about . . . or Andrew Easton?"

"Christian, of course." Grace squirmed on her seat, heat blazing in her cheeks. Were her feelings for Andrew so transparent? "Andrew and I are just friends." She lifted her chin.

Mrs. C. stood up to rock the baby in her arms. His thumb went into his mouth, a sure sign he would soon be asleep. "Speaking of friends, that nice Mr. Miller from the Newcomers group came by the other day with a telegram for one of the boarders. He asked about you. Seemed very disappointed to learn you weren't living here any longer."

"Oh dear." Grace hated that she'd forgotten all about him. "I did say I'd drop by his office sometime. But my day off is Sunday and the telegraph office is closed then."

Mrs. C. nodded. "Maybe the next time you come to church with us, you'll see him there and can make plans to get together."

Grace held back a groan and shook her head.

"What's wrong?"

"I'm afraid that would give Mr. Miller the wrong idea. That I'm interested in more than friendship."

Mrs. C.'s eyes narrowed. "Grace Abernathy. I hope you're not judging that poor fellow by his looks. He may not be the handsomest of men, but there's no one finer. He's a kind, hardworking Christian who would make any girl an excellent husband."

"That's just it, Mrs. C. I'm not looking for a husband. My only interest right now is Christian." The falseness of that statement echoed in Grace's ears, as her traitorous thoughts flew to the kiss she'd shared with Andrew under the stars. Ever conscious of her friend's scrutiny, Grace pushed back her chair and busied herself with sweeping the crumbs from the tablecloth.

"I hope you truly mean that, dear, because harboring any illusions about someone like Andrew Easton will only lead to disaster. Remember what happened to Rose when she got involved with one of them."

"How could I forget?" Grace gathered the dirty dishes and carried them to the sink. Then she turned to look at her sleepy nephew. "I think Christian is ready for a nap. Is there somewhere I can put him down?"

Mrs. C. patted the boy on her shoulder. "I'll take him. You can read your mail while I'm gone." She pointed to the envelopes on the counter. "I've been saving it until I saw you."

Grace's insides twisted as she moved to retrieve the mail. She sat back down at the table, staring at her mother's familiar script. Finally, she forced herself to open one, bracing herself for whatever she would find inside.

The first letter bore all the anguish of her mother's grief after learning of Rose's death. Somehow, in the process of pouring out her anger and sorrow, Mum found a way to indirectly blame Grace.

If you'd have left for Canada when I asked, you might have been in time to save our Rose.

Grace clenched her teeth together. Would her mother's words ever lose their power to fill her with resentment and guilt?

She broke the seal on the second envelope, written after receiving Grace's letters. Mum was at least somewhat cheered by the fact that Grace had found Christian, though she was incensed he was living with the Eastons. By the end of the third missive, her harping tone rang through.

What are you waiting for, girl? Hurry up and bring my grandson home. Only the hope of seeing Christian's face is giving me the will to go on. Don't wait too long, like you did with Rose. I may not be here when you return.

Grace exhaled and let the paper drop to the table. No matter how disagreeable the woman was, Grace *had* promised to bring her grandson home. But to keep her word to Mum, she would have to inflict the worst kind of pain on the Easton family. Andrew, Virginia, and especially Mrs. Easton would be devastated. They didn't deserve to lose any more family members.

But then neither did her mother.

Grace lowered her head to her hands. *Lord, grant me your wisdom to deal with this situation. Help me do what's right for everyone and not lose myself in the process.*

CHAPTER 25

March 30, 1918

Today my heart broke as I said good-bye to my husband once again. Mrs. Easton's health recovered, which leads me to suspect she may have exaggerated the severity of her illness. But the fact that it brought Frank home, even for a few short months, is all that matters.

Mr. Easton refused to speak to Frank, even knowing he would be returning to the front. Please pray hard for the end of these terrible hostilities, Grace, for I suspect a baby may be on the way. If so, I'll need my husband at home with me. I cannot imagine giving birth without him.

Two days later, Grace stood at the crib, her hand on Christian's forehead as he writhed and whimpered. Just as she suspected, the heat radiating from him seared her palm. The fever, one she had attributed to teething, had worsened overnight, clearly not due to incoming molars.

A tremor of fear clutched her. Could it be the flu, like the one that had claimed his mother?

Dear God, please don't let it be so.

"I'll be right back, sweetheart," she said aloud. "We need to get the doctor to see you."

Pushing aside a wave of panic, Grace headed downstairs to the dining room where the family would be eating breakfast before heading out to church.

She dreaded having to face Andrew. Ever since their kiss and the awkward conversation in the solarium, he'd been avoiding her like the bubonic plague.

Grace sighed and continued down the stairs. No point in dwelling on that now. Andrew had made his decision, and she would have to accept it.

Squaring her shoulders, she stepped into the dining room. "Good morning. Andrew, may I have word with you, please?"

All heads swiveled in her direction except for Mr. Easton, who kept his back to her. "What is it, Miss Foley?" he said. "You may speak in front of everyone."

She swallowed. "It's Christian, sir. He has a high fever. I think it would be prudent to have a doctor examine him."

Andrew's chair scraped back as he rose. "I'll call Dr. Ballard right away."

"Thank you. I'll be in the nursery."

Grace's gaze collided with Virginia's, hoping for some type of reassurance. The girl gave a slight shrug, then stared back at her plate.

Strange currents of unease hovered in the air. Surely Andrew hadn't said something to Virginia that would make her rescind their friendship?

Grace turned and walked quickly to the rear staircase, half hoping, half dreading Andrew would come after her.

But he didn't.

Forty minutes later, Andrew admitted Dr. Ballard to the nursery. "This is Grace Foley, Christian's nanny," he said.

"Good day, Miss Foley." The doctor set his bag on the floor and took out a thermometer. "How long has the child had the fever?"

"It started yesterday."

The doctor gave her a sharp look. "And you're only contacting me now?"

"It was mild at first. I thought it was due to teething, but this morning it became much worse." Grace gripped her hands together and risked a glance at Andrew.

He stood, not looking at her, his jaw tight.

The doctor examined the baby, and when he straightened his face was grim. "I believe it's the flu. What strain I can't yet tell. For now, we will treat the fever with cool baths and compresses."

"I'll have a tub sent up." Andrew disappeared into the hall.

"And I'll get a basin of water." Grace hesitated in the doorway, dread pooling in her chest. "It's not the Spanish flu, is it, doctor?"

The man's features softened. "I don't believe so. That strain has more swift and dire consequences. He would be much sicker than this, or worse, already dead. Still we can't rule it out completely."

Grace pushed back the cold clutch of fear and focused on what she needed to do to help Christian.

The next twenty-four hours passed in a blur. The doctor instructed her in the proper method of bathing and using cool compresses on Christian's forehead. Most of the time she had to hold the cloth in place, as the boy thrashed and cried, dislodging the fabric from his brow.

Grace alternated bathing times with rocking the child in her arms. As far as she was concerned, nothing beat a mother, or in this case, an aunt's loving arms. She sang to him until he dropped into an uneasy sleep and at such time, managed to catch a few winks of sleep herself in the chair.

Andrew and Virginia took turns keeping vigil with her, but despite their insistence that she get some rest in her room, Grace would not leave Christian's side, certain if she did, he would worsen.

When the fever raged on the next day, Andrew sent for the doctor again. The physician checked the boy and pronounced him no better, but no worse.

"At this point, even that is good news," he told them. "Continue with your treatments and I'll come by again tomorrow."

Grace did not think it was good news. Not at all. She sat up all night in the rocker with her Bible in hand, praying harder than ever before, refusing to close her eyes lest Christian slip away.

In the predawn hours, she got up and checked him again. Still too warm. She bathed his head and limbs with water from the basin. He squirmed and whimpered in protest, but she persisted until he at last dropped into a fitful sleep.

At that point, though her body ached all over, Grace knelt by the side of the crib, head bowed. She couldn't shake the feeling that she was responsible for this. Had she exposed Christian to some contagion on one of their outings? Had she not dressed him warmly enough in the pram?

"Please, Lord," she said aloud. "Christian has to recover. I can't be responsible for another life, not after Peter. I'll do whatever you wish, just please let him get better."

After almost forty-eight hours without sleep, exhaustion weighed her down, and the strength seemed to seep from her body. She sagged over her knees, dropped her face in her hands, and wept. Tears ran through her fingers, her hands muffling her sobs.

Through the haze of her distress, she became aware of someone entering the room. Strong arms lifted her and placed her gently in the rocking chair.

"Don't cry, Grace. Everything's going to be fine."

She opened her eyes to see Andrew's concerned face hovering over her.

"You must rest," he said, "or you'll become ill yourself."

She wanted to protest, but with no strength left, she merely laid her head back. Perhaps she'd close her eyes, just for a minute.

Andrew stared down at Grace's limp form in the rocking chair. Her spiky lashes highlighted the translucent purple smudges below her eyes. Tears stained her pale cheeks, and her hair had come loose, framing her face. Concern for her well-being tightened his muscles.

"You need a proper sleep in your bed," he said. "You won't do Christian any good if you take ill."

She opened her eyes, anguish shining in their brown depths. "I can't leave him," she whispered. "Something bad will happen if I do."

He fought the impulse to carry her next door himself, conscious that he didn't need any more hints of impropriety. He'd been doing so well lately, spending most of his spare time with Celia, barely sparing a thought for Grace.

Until now.

"I'll stay with him until you awaken. I promise." He studied her anxious features, the lines of fatigue around her mouth. "No matter what happens, Grace, you are not responsible for Christian's illness, do you understand?"

She shook her head. "It's my job to keep him safe and healthy, and I failed. Now he might die. Just like Peter."

Andrew kneeled beside the chair and took one of her hands in his. "Christian isn't going to die," he said firmly. "And you weren't to blame for Peter's death either."

"You're wrong. It was all my fault." Fresh tears welled in her eyes.

He couldn't bear the agony on her face. "How was it your fault? You were only a child."

"I was twelve. Old enough to know better."

"What happened?" he asked softly. Perhaps talking about it might lessen the guilt festering inside. He couldn't do much for her, but he could maybe bring her a measure of peace.

She grasped the arm of the rocker, her knuckles whitening. "We were on holiday in Brighton. My parents warned us not to go near the cliffs. But the view was so beautiful up that high. One night, my sister and I snuck out. I dared her to walk along the edge of the cliffs with me. I was doing fine until I heard my brother shouting at us. Then I lost my balance and fell into the ocean."

Andrew went still. "You fell off a cliff?"

"Yes. Peter knew I couldn't swim and jumped in to save me."

Andrew rubbed his thumb over her cold hand. His chest ached at what he knew was coming.

"He managed to drag me to the shore, but all that time in the cold water had worn him out. The next day, he took ill, and it quickly turned to pneumonia." A sob rose in her throat. "He died three days later. He was only seventeen."

"Oh, Grace." He squeezed her arm. "I can't imagine the guilt you went through, even though it wasn't your fault."

"If I hadn't been so reckless, if I'd listened to my parents, Peter would still be alive." Tears spilled down her cheeks.

"It was a horrible accident, nothing more." He handed her his handkerchief, wishing he could do more to ease her pain.

"My father was never the same. He died two years later. And my mother . . ." She bit her lip. "She never forgave me. She blames me to this day." Her chin trembled.

A wave of protectiveness rose in Andrew's chest. What kind of a mother would let a child bear such a burden? He ached to hold her, to offer her the love and comfort she'd so long been denied. But he had no right to do so. "I'm sorry you've had such tragedy in your life. You deserve so much better than that." From what Andrew knew, she'd lost everyone she loved, except a bitter mother who obviously didn't treat her well.

Her shoulders slumped, as though the life had drained from her. "Perhaps I will lie down after all." Her dark eyes stood out against the paleness of her skin. She got slowly to her feet, glancing once more at the crib.

"I'll be right here with Christian if you need me," he said.

He wished he could tell her nothing would ever hurt her again, but that was a promise he couldn't keep.

Hours later, Andrew jerked in the rocking chair, awakened from a light doze. He scrubbed a hand over his beard and stretched his stiff limbs. During the entire time Grace had been sleeping, Andrew had stayed by Christian's side, even when Ginny joined his vigil.

Muscles aching, he pushed up from the chair and checked on Christian, pleased to note that he looked to be sleeping more peacefully. Then he looked at his pocket watch. There hadn't been a sound from Grace's room in over twelve hours. Andrew hoped she hadn't become ill herself.

He crossed the carpet and knocked on her door. When she didn't answer, a thread of anxiety wound through him. He opened the door wide enough to see into the room, worry overcoming his guilt at taking such a liberty.

The room was bathed in shadows, but he was able to make out her form beneath the covers. Andrew moved closer, his eyes trained on the curve of her cheek. A tendril of hair vibrated with each shallow breath. His fingers itched to feel the silkiness of her hair, the satin of her skin. Instead, he rubbed at a persistent ache in his chest. When he looked at her, he felt the same overwhelming emotions as he did with Christian. The desire to cherish her, nurture her, protect her from all harm. This was more than a mere physical attraction, more than a forbidden summer dalliance. The truth rose up to fill every cell of his body.

"I'm in love with her," he whispered.

From the moment he saw her sitting forlornly on the curb, nursing a sprained ankle, Grace had captured his heart. Her kindness, her ability to find beauty in the mundane and to bring joy to everyone around her, these were the qualities that continued to amaze him. In addition, she saw only the best in him. In her eyes, he was clever and capable and never lacking. Not only did she accept him for who he was, she admired him.

Was it any wonder he'd fallen in love with her?

But to what avail?

Lord, why would you bring her into my life and allow me to love her when I'm obligated to marry someone else?

He lingered a minute longer until he could no longer bear the exquisite torture. Then with a last glimpse of her lovely face, he returned to the nursery.

"There you are." Virginia's voice startled him.

He stopped short, heat climbing up his neck. "I was just checking on Grace. She's still sleeping."

Virginia gave him a knowing smile. "No need to explain. I'm worried about her too."

Andrew had told his sister about finding Grace in such a distraught state, and she'd praised him for convincing her to get some rest.

"I think I have good news." Virginia leaned over the crib and placed a hand on the baby. "It might be my imagination, but he feels cooler to me. What do you think?"

Andrew felt Christian's forehead and cheeks. "You're right. Definitely cooler." A two-ton weight lifted from his shoulders. "Grace will be so relieved."

"As will Mother. She's been fretting about him, but Father won't let her come near for fear she might contract the illness."

A fear Andrew shared. That any one of them, Grace and his mother in particular, could fall ill.

Virginia turned to him. "I came to tell you I'm going out for a while. I have to meet Basil to discuss the engagement party his parents wish to throw for us."

"Of course. You go on."

"Do you want me to have one of the maids relieve you for a spell?"

"No thanks. I promised Grace I'd stay with him." He rubbed his gritty eyes. "But you could have Mrs. Hopkins send up a sandwich and some coffee."

"I'll do that." Virginia crossed to the door. "If Grace wakes up, tell her I'll be back later."

"I will. And Ginny?"

"Yes?"

He moved closer so he could look her in the eye. "Is everything all right?" Lately, something about his sister's demeanor had changed. An almost defeated air surrounded her.

"Of course. Why wouldn't it be?" Her gaze fell away from his. "I have to go," she said in an overly cheerful voice. "Mustn't keep Basil waiting."

Once she'd left, Andrew shook his head. Something definitely wasn't right with Ginny, but what could he do if she wouldn't confide in him?

After checking on Christian again, he sank into the rocker and laid his head back. How tempting it would be to give in to sleep. But nothing would make him break his promise to Grace. He straightened on the chair and bent to examine the quilt Grace was making. Her depth of devotion to the boy continued to astound him. What nanny would go to such lengths for a child not even her own?

As he fingered the colorful fabric, his gaze fell on Grace's Bible, which had slipped down the side of the basket. She'd prayed continually through this whole ordeal. Her steadfast faith, which she relied on in every circumstance of her life, was another reason why he loved her.

Andrew lifted the book and ran his palm over the worn leather cover. Curious to know which passages she had marked as her favorites, he fanned through the pages. As he did so, a picture fell to the floor. He picked it up, and the laughing faces of two young women stared back at him. One was definitely Grace. He smiled at the unbridled joy on her face. She seemed so young and happy, so carefree.

Then he looked at the other woman and froze.

The air in the room seemed to thicken. Why would Grace have a picture taken with Frank's wife?

He turned the photo over. A neat script flowed over the back. *Rose and Grace, April 1914.* Shivers of foreboding pricked his skin. He opened the cover of the Bible and found the same handwriting inside. *Grace Abernathy, 24 Sheepshead Lane, Sussex, England.*

His hands shook. The book fell from his fingers and landed with a thud on the floor. His lungs squeezed the last bit of air from his chest.

She'd been lying to them this entire time. She wasn't Grace Foley at all.

She's Rose's sister. Christian's aunt.

He shot up from the rocker, disbelief roaring through his system.

Raking his hands through his hair, he replayed their conversations and everything that had happened since Grace had come to Fairlawn. He recalled then the first time she'd held the baby, the tears in her eyes now making sense. No wonder she loved the child so deeply.

Anger, raw and deep, settled in the pit of his stomach, the taste of betrayal bitter on his tongue. How could she deceive him like this? Worm her way into his family and make herself indispensable to Christian's well-being? Why wouldn't she have told him who she really was?

Andrew looked into the crib at his sleeping nephew. His thoughts swirled in a continual loop of unanswered questions. Everything he thought he knew about Grace now seemed tainted, spoiled by her lies. He'd been duped by a pretty face, a false virtue that hid her true duplicitous nature.

Thank goodness he'd never told her he loved her. How ridiculous would he feel then?

Nausea rose in his throat as he bent to snatch the Bible from the floor. Clutching it in his hands, he vowed to get to the bottom of this unholy deception.

He would let nothing—and no one—jeopardize his relationship with his nephew.

CHAPTER 26

Grace awoke to find her room in shadows. She blinked, trying to chase the cobwebs from her brain. What time was it? Memories of Christian's illness flashed through her. She bolted upright in the bed, smoothing down her wrinkled skirt. More images rose in her mind. Andrew picking her off the floor, carrying her to the rocker, comforting her while she bared her soul to him.

What must he think of her? She'd been an emotional mess, a state she rarely, if ever, found herself in. When she saw him again, she would apologize for her display and assure him it wouldn't happen again.

Squaring her shoulders, she entered the nursery, relieved to find Virginia instead of Andrew.

Virginia rose from the rocker. "You're awake at last. I hope you're feeling better. Andrew said you weren't quite yourself."

"I'm much better, thank you."

A smile bloomed on Virginia's face. "You'll be pleased to know Christian's fever broke this morning, and Dr. Ballard has pronounced him on the road to recovery."

Grace joined Virginia at the crib and laid a hand on the sleeping boy's forehead. Cool to the touch. She closed her eyes and breathed a prayer of thanks. "Has he taken his bottle?"

"He drank about half of it. And it wore him out. The doctor

said it would take a few days before he's back to normal and that he'd likely be fussy, off his usual schedule."

"As long as he's going to be fine, I don't care how fussy he gets."

Virginia put her arm around her. "I know what you mean. I've never been more scared in my life. I don't know what we would do if we ever lost him."

The words curled around Grace's heart, tugging with the weight of guilt. What would Virginia do if she knew Grace had been considering taking Christian to England? She still hadn't completely ruled out the idea if Andrew asked Cecilia to marry him.

"You must be hungry yourself," Virginia said. "You slept almost round the clock. I'll stay here if you want to get something to eat."

"Thank you. I believe I am hungry." She laughed, her taut muscles loosening at long last, now that she knew Christian would be all right.

Before she reached the door, Andrew entered the room. Grace's pulse kicked up at the sight of his handsome face. Yet her smile froze when his eyes didn't warm in greeting as they normally did.

Instead, his gaze bounced off her and settled on Virginia. "How is he doing now?"

"You heard what the doctor said. He won't have his usual energy for a few days yet." Virginia picked up a knitted blanket from the rocker and folded it. "Grace is feeling much better after her sleep, so between the two of us, we can look after him. You don't need to feel guilty about going in to work."

Andrew straightened, his expression darkening. "Actually I need to speak to Grace before I leave. In the library, please." Without waiting for her reply, he walked out of the room.

Grace's stomach swooped at his flat tone. Had he decided Christian's illness was her fault after all, that she'd been negligent in her duties? And if so, would he dismiss her?

She shot a desperate glance at Virginia, who only shrugged.

"I'll be back as soon as I can." With trepidation beating in her chest, she headed down the stairs.

Andrew stared out the window in the library, his thoughts consumed with the conversation he was about to have, one he dreaded more than his father's lectures. If Grace admitted what Andrew knew to be true, he didn't see how he could possibly keep her on staff. Part of him held out a slim hope that she might offer a plausible explanation for what he'd discovered, yet what possible reason could there be?

His emotions wavered between anger and despair, further proof he'd lost all perspective when it came to Grace. Without intending to, he'd let down his guard and allowed her into his heart. But it was all a lie, a huge deception.

She'd used Virginia to obtain an interview for the job and manipulated his emotions—as well as his family's—to ingratiate her way into their lives. Was it her plan all along to make him fall in love with her in the hope that he'd marry her and thereby gain access to Christian? His temple throbbed with the agony of thoughts plaguing him. He didn't even hear the door open.

"Andrew? Is everything all right?" Grace's quiet voice filled the room.

He squared his shoulders and turned to face her, keeping his expression stony. "Sit down."

He waited until she was seated before taking his father's chair, which creaked as he leaned forward. Despite his erratic heartbeat, he did his best to maintain a calm outward demeanor. It wouldn't do to let his anger get the best of him.

Grace's hand fluttered to the neck of her blouse as she waited for him to speak, her face pale.

"I want to know," he said slowly, "why you've been lying to us—to *me*—all this time."

Her mouth fell open, her eyes widening with a hint of fear. "I . . . I don't understand."

Without a word, he pulled her Bible from the top drawer and slid it toward her, then waited for her reaction.

"My Bible," she said. "Where did you . . . ?" A frown creased her brow, and then as realization dawned, horror flooded her features.

"Why didn't you tell us who you really are?" He slipped the photo from the book and tossed it down in front of her. "That you're Rose's sister. Christian's aunt." With effort, he held his anger in check. "What kind of game are you playing, Miss *Abernathy*?"

She flinched, then picked up the picture and ran a trembling finger over the glossy surface. When she lifted her head, tears shimmered in her eyes. "I'm sorry. It was the only way I could think of to get close to Christian."

"Other than what? Telling the truth?"

She tilted her chin, brown eyes flashing. "What do you think your father would have done if I'd shown up at your door and said, 'Good day. I'm the sister of the woman you despised. I'm here to establish a connection with my nephew'? Do you really think he would have welcomed me with open arms?"

A flush heated Andrew's cheeks, for he couldn't dispute her point. "Maybe not right away. But I'm sure once he got used to the idea—"

Grace scoffed. "You know very well he would never have let me in the house, much less allow me to be part of Christian's life. Even now, after months of living here, he barely tolerates me."

She had a valid point. Andrew let a few beats of silence pass. Long enough to let both of their tempers settle.

"How did you know what my father's reaction would be?" he asked at last.

"Rose wrote me every week. She told me how badly your family treated her." Defiance glowed in her eyes. "How they disowned Frank for marrying her. How your father fired her from her job at the hotel, and how when Frank left to go overseas, she couldn't afford to keep their flat and had to go back to the boardinghouse."

Despite his anger, Andrew's heart sank. He'd never considered what life had been like for Rose with Frank away for so long.

"When she found out she was expecting, she hid her pregnancy as long as possible, but once her employer learned of her condition, he let her go. Rose had the baby, and they lived on the charity of a stranger." Tears squeezed from beneath Grace's closed lids. She drew a handkerchief from her apron and dabbed her face.

Andrew stifled another surge of guilt, hardening himself to her pain. "For the sake of the baby, Rose should have swallowed her pride and come to us."

"And what do you imagine your father would have done?" Grace's eyes snapped with anger. "Rose was terrified he'd take the baby from her, and what recourse would she have had against such a rich, powerful man?"

Andrew went still for he again couldn't deny the truth of her statement. Yet it didn't excuse what Grace had done. "So you came to seek revenge for your sister's mistreatment? Is that it?"

Grace jerked up from the chair, her mouth pinched. "I won't dignify that with a reply." She grabbed her Bible and headed for the door.

"Just a minute." Andrew hated the desperation in his voice.

She half turned and stood waiting while he rose slowly from his chair.

"I need to know. What was your real intention when you followed Virginia to the park?" He was bluffing, assuming she'd done just that.

Her cheeks reddened, and she let out a breath. "At first, I only wanted to catch a glimpse of Christian. To make sure he was all right. But when the opportunity of the nanny position presented itself, I couldn't pass it up. I promised Rose . . ." Her voice cracked. "I promised I would take care of her baby if anything happened to her. I had to be sure your family wasn't as terrible as she'd made out in her letters."

"And if we were?"

Her gaze faltered and she shrugged. "I don't know."

Somehow he didn't quite believe her. Had she planned to challenge him for custody of the boy?

"You've lived with us for two months now. You saw how much

we love Christian, how well he's cared for. Why didn't you tell me the truth then?"

The distinct tick of the desk clock matched the cadence of his heartbeat.

"I was too afraid," she whispered.

"Afraid of what?" He held his breath, praying for her to say something that would make him understand.

"That you'd hate me. Like you do now." She pressed her handkerchief to her mouth.

Andrew exhaled loudly and ran a hand over his beard, conflicting emotions battling within him.

"What are you going to do?" she asked softly. "Will you tell your parents?"

Every instinct told him he should order her to leave immediately. But staring at her profile, the delicate curve of her cheek, the sweep of her lashes, he couldn't bring himself to do it. Silently he cursed his weakness. "I haven't decided."

She took a step toward him, a glimmer of hope brimming in her eyes. "Nothing has to change. I still want to be Christian's nanny."

The muscles in his neck seized. How could she expect him to pretend nothing had changed when everything had?

"I love him, Andrew. He's my nephew too. The only thing I have left of my sister. Don't I have a right to be part of his life?"

Her pleading expression was more than he could endure. He turned to stare out the window before he caved in and granted her request. "The problem," he said without looking at her, "is that I no longer trust you. And if I can't trust you, how can I let you be responsible for Christian?"

"I would never do anything to harm him." Her voice quivered. "Even if you can't forgive me for lying, surely you must believe that."

He wanted to believe her. To be able to say he forgave her. But he couldn't force the words from his mouth. "I need time to think. I'll have an answer by tomorrow. In the meantime, Virginia will look after Christian."

Andrew heard a sharp intake of breath and what sounded like a quiet sob. He clenched his hands into fists, not daring to look at her for fear that witnessing her tears would weaken what little resolve he had left.

Still facing the window, he didn't move a muscle until the door had clicked shut behind her.

CHAPTER 27

May 1, 1918
Dear Grace,

It's official. You are going to be an aunt! Sometime in late November if the doctor is right. I pray Frank will be back in time to see his son or daughter come into this world. If only you could be here, Grace. I'd feel so much less alone.

Grace could not face Virginia. Not with a flood of tears dripping from her cheeks. She needed time to recover her equilibrium before she went back to the nursery.

Seeking the solitude of the garden, she slipped out the rear door and crossed the yard. Once within its sanctuary, she sank onto the fountain ledge and let the full extent of her despair pour out. Her shoulders heaved with the force of her sobs, so deep she could barely catch her breath.

Andrew had discovered her secret and he now despised her. Could barely stand to look at her. And when he did, the contempt in his blue eyes made her heart shrivel in her chest.

It was only a matter of time before he'd demand she pack her bags and leave. He'd already admitted he didn't trust her. How could she ever think he would let her stay after her dishonesty?

If only she'd told him the truth before he found out.

She gulped in a huge breath, her tortured lungs expanding within her chest. She had no recourse left to her. All she could do was await his mercy—or his punishment—for her transgression.

Perhaps once Andrew's anger cooled, he'd realize that she was right. That his father would never have let her near Christian if he'd known her true identity. And that she hadn't lied for any harmful purpose, only to honor Rose's request.

Are you certain of that? Her conscience nagged her with a fresh sense of guilt.

If her intentions were completely honorable, she'd never be entertaining the idea of taking Christian from the Eastons.

No, not from the Eastons. From Cecilia Carmichael's harmful influence.

Grace twisted the limp handkerchief between her fingers. If Andrew was planning to marry a kind woman, one who actually cared about Christian, she'd have no qualms leaving the baby in their care. But she couldn't risk Cecilia inflicting severe emotional damage on the boy with her cold indifference.

Lord, I need your help. I'm in a terrible predicament, and I don't know how to fix it.

Above her, the birds continued to twitter in the trees, oblivious to her distress. If only she had such a carefree existence and could fly away from all her problems. But she couldn't. She'd have to be brave and face the consequences of her lies. She dried her eyes, took a deep breath, and got slowly to her feet. All she could do was pray for forgiveness and see what God—and Andrew—had in store for her next.

The next morning, Andrew knocked reluctantly on Grace's bedroom door. He'd spent several agonizing hours trying to decide what to do with the knowledge of her true identity. His heart and his pride still stung at being taken in by her deception, but despite everything she'd done, he knew she loved the boy as much as he did. And in the end, he found he simply couldn't stomach the idea of ripping one more maternal figure from Christian's life.

Grace answered after a few seconds, adjusting the sleeve of her blouse. Her hair flowed in a shining mass over her shoulders.

He swallowed hard and focused on her chin. "I won't take much of your time. I wanted to let you know my decision."

"Very well." She clasped her hands in front of her.

"For Christian's sake, I've decided to keep your secret—for now."

Relief crashed over her features, and she bit her bottom lip.

"But know that I'll be watching your every move. If you give me the slightest provocation, I won't hesitate to terminate you."

"I understand." She opened her mouth, closed it again. "Thank you, Andrew."

He flinched at the use of his name. She didn't deserve such intimacy, not after her betrayal. "From now on, you should address me as Mr. Easton. I've allowed too much familiarity with a staff member."

She winced as though he'd slapped her. "As you wish," she whispered, hurt shining from her eyes.

He hardened himself to the pain on her face, yet he couldn't seem to force his feet to move away. When she closed her door with a soft click, he shoved his regrets down deep and headed for the stairs.

As he descended to the foyer, his thoughts turned to Cecilia, and it struck him with astounding force that perhaps she'd been right about Grace all along, and he'd been too blind to see the truth. He'd built Grace up in his mind and his heart as a paragon of virtue. The perfect woman. But it had been nothing more than an illusion, a figment of his imagination. Grace was just as flawed as Cecilia.

At least Celia didn't try to hide who she really was. For all her faults, Andrew knew exactly where he stood with her.

Seated in the Carmichaels' sitting room, Andrew drummed his fingers on his thighs, trying to dispel his restless energy. Mrs.

Carmichael's haughty white cat stared at him from her perch on the back of the sofa as though daring him to invade her territory.

In a strange way, discovering Grace's true nature had set Andrew free. His daydreams were over. He was back to reality. Without the false hope of a possible life with Grace, he could finally take the steps necessary to secure his future.

After coming to a decision at last, Andrew had already spoken with Mr. Carmichael this morning in his study. Now he waited while Cecilia got dressed. He should have realized she wouldn't be up and ready at this early hour. Another aspect of her life that would have to change once they were wed. Andrew was an early riser. Lying in bed until noon, wasting half the day away, didn't sit well with him.

"Goodness, Andrew. What are you doing here at the crack of dawn?" Cecilia came into the room with a swirl of her skirt. Her blond hair lay loose over her shoulders.

"Nine o'clock is hardly the crack of dawn." He rose to greet her with a kiss on the cheek.

"It is on a Saturday." She took a seat on the sofa and gestured for him to sit.

"I wanted to speak with you before I go into the office."

She groaned. "Honestly, Andrew, must you work every Saturday? It's called the week *end* for a reason."

"Funny, I always thought you admired my ambition."

She passed a hand over her forehead. "I have no wits for sparring this early. What is it you want?"

He rubbed his damp palms on his thighs. "I've spoken with your father, and he has given me his blessing to speak to you today."

Sudden interest brightened her eyes. "Does this mean what I think it does?"

"It might—provided you can allay my one concern." He held her gaze.

"Christian."

"Yes. I need to know you can accept him as part of our family."

Her lashes swept down. "I understand how much he means to you, and I promise to try harder where he is concerned."

Andrew nodded. It was a start, one that would surely grow with time. He reached into his pocket. "As long as we're clear, then I believe I can give you this." He opened the box and took out the ring—a family heirloom passed down from his grandmother—which sparkled under the lights.

Eyes wide, she pressed a hand to her mouth.

"Though I can't promise you romantic babblings or false words of love, I *can* promise to be a loyal and dedicated husband, if you'll have me."

"Oh, Andrew." Her lip quivered as she moved closer. "Of course, I'll marry you." She held out her hand, and he slid the ring onto her finger.

His chest tightened at the sight of it on her hand. Would his grandmother approve of his decision? She was a woman who had done whatever she deemed necessary to secure their family's position in society. Surely she, of all people, would understand his actions.

Celia reached over to press a kiss to his lips. He tried to put some effort into the embrace, but her eyes clouded over as they parted, proving he hadn't done a very convincing job. He prayed that in time his feelings would strengthen.

He rose from the sofa and walked to the fireplace, where a low ember burned. "There's another matter we need to discuss. My father has put me in charge of a new hotel we're opening in Ottawa. Which means we'll have to move there once we're married."

"How marvelous." She came up beside him at the mantel.

"So you wouldn't be opposed to living so far from your family?"

She hesitated, then lifted her chin. "A wife's place is with her husband. Besides, we'll have lots of time to figure out the details."

"Not exactly. I'm needed in Ottawa by early September. Your father wants the wedding to take place before then so you can come with me."

"That soon?"

"Unfortunately, yes." He took her hand. "Is it enough time for you to prepare?"

He could almost sense the wheels turning in her head as she considered her options. "I think it will be, as long as the date is available at the church."

"What about your dress? The flowers?" What else did a bride need?

"Mother and I have been preparing for my wedding for years." She gave a light laugh. "Besides, if I can pull off a gala at your hotel in mere weeks, a wedding shouldn't be a problem."

"Then it's settled. We'll be married at the end of August, which will give us time for a honeymoon before our move." Instead of easing, the band of pressure across his chest increased.

She threw her arms around his neck and hugged him. "You've made me so happy, Andrew. You won't regret this, I promise."

As he drew her close, Andrew did his best to push aside all doubts. For now, he would take consolation in Celia's joy, and strive to put Grace's face out of his mind—once and for all.

CHAPTER 28

Later that afternoon, Andrew joined his family on the back verandah overlooking the gardens where they were enjoying a peaceful interlude before the dinner bell summoned them. He took a vacant seat at the wrought-iron table and paused to inhale the warm summer air. A soft breeze stirred the leaves in the garden below, bringing the heady floral scent up to greet him.

Seated in her favorite lounge chair, Mother wore a large floppy hat to shield her complexion from the sun. Father, still dressed in his business attire, had made a slight concession by removing his suit jacket and sitting in his shirtsleeves and waistcoat. Andrew did his best to enjoy the tranquility of the moment, but with the announcement he was about to make, he couldn't seem to relax.

Virginia, who'd apparently just returned from a walk in the park, carried Christian up the stairs and joined them at the table. "Here, Daddy. Hold Christian for a while." Without waiting for his consent, she sat the baby on his lap.

Remarkably, Father accepted the boy with a smile.

Andrew fought the temptation to look around for Grace. Correcting old habits had become a bit of a challenge, so he was relieved that Grace seemed bent on avoiding him as much as he avoided her. When he was certain she hadn't followed Virginia onto the verandah, he turned his attention to the rare sight of his father enjoying time with his grandson.

The boy made a grab for the chain of Father's pocket watch, and instead of becoming annoyed, his father chuckled and pulled out the timepiece for Christian to hold. Father bounced his knee, eliciting a stream of giggles from the baby. Mother and Virginia laughed along with him.

Andrew marveled at how quickly Christian was growing. Now almost eight months old, he was already attempting to crawl whenever he was on the ground. Soon he would want to test his newfound mobility and would no longer be content to sit on their laps. Andrew would miss those times a great deal.

"There's something about a child that brings a family together." Father's gruff voice drew Andrew's gaze. He was surprised to see such raw emotion on his face. "Having this little fellow here certainly helps ease the sting of loss."

Virginia moved to Father's chair and hugged him from behind. "You're right, Daddy. I feel like Frank's with me every time I pick up his son."

For once Father didn't shrink at the mention of Frank's name. "I know what you mean. It's uncanny how much he reminds me of Frank."

Christian gave a delighted shriek and kicked his plump legs, almost as if he understood what they were saying. They all laughed again.

Andrew's throat thickened at the idea of his nephew almost ending up a ward of the Children's Aid. If Reverend Burke hadn't been privy to the identity of the baby's father, they might never have known Frank's son.

A twinge of guilt surfaced as his thoughts turned once again to Grace and the lengths she'd gone to in order to get to know Christian. How devastating it must have been to arrive in Toronto expecting to see her sister only to learn that Rose had died. He swallowed hard to dislodge any trace of sympathy that might lessen his outrage. He needed to remain angry with Grace to keep any lingering feelings for her at bay.

He cleared his throat. "Mother, Father. I have some important news."

"Oh?" Mother peered from under her hat's wide brim.

"News that I hope will please you both." He made a deliberate attempt to relax his shoulders and smile. "This morning I asked Cecilia to marry me, and she accepted."

"Oh, Andrew. That's wonderful." Mother clapped her hands together.

Father wore a broad smile. "That's the best news I've heard in a very long time." He rose, handed the baby to Virginia, and came forward with his hand outstretched. "Congratulations, my boy. I knew I could count on you to restore honor to this family."

Andrew stood and shook his father's hand. In the look they exchanged, a shimmer of understanding passed between them, and for a brief moment, Andrew basked in the glow of his admiration.

Mother came over to hug him. Her wide smile and the sparkle in her eyes brought back happier times. Andrew's chest swelled. At last, he'd achieved what he'd set out to accomplish. He'd united his broken family and brought happiness back to them. The Eastons would overcome their loss and pain, and forge ahead to reclaim their rightful place as the city's most influential family.

Only the disapproving stare of his sister marred his exuberance.

Father must have picked up on her silence. "Virginia, aren't you going to congratulate your brother?"

Shifting Christian to her hip, she walked forward to join them by the rail. The breeze stirred her dark curls, lifting them away from her troubled eyes. "Congratulations, Drew." She leaned up to kiss his cheek. "I hope you'll be very happy." Though the words sounded sincere, the life had gone out of her expression.

"Thank you, Ginny. That means a lot."

"So I take it Cecilia was agreeable to the quick wedding?" Father asked.

Andrew's stomach sank. He'd hoped he'd have time to talk to Ginny privately and explain the necessity for having the wedding while she'd be away in Europe.

"It was a bit of a shock, but she rallied to the challenge." Andrew laughed, trying to dispel the impending storm sure to come. "With

Charlotte's help, I'm certain they will have everything organized in time."

Mother didn't seem the least surprised, leading Andrew to believe that Father had discussed the matter with her.

Virginia moved closer, heedless of the baby's growing restlessness. "Just how soon are you talking about?"

"The end of August." He smiled brightly. "Cecilia and I will be moving to Ottawa right after the honeymoon so I can oversee the new hotel."

The color left Virginia's cheeks and her features crumpled with disbelief. "You're getting married while I'm away?" Tears formed in her bright eyes. "How could you after what happened with Frank?"

Andrew groaned. He'd forgotten how much weddings mattered to Virginia. "I'm sorry, Gin. Truly. If there was any other way . . ."

"There is another way. Wait until I return. It will only be a few more months."

"Nonsense." Father lifted a squirming Christian from her arms, as though he feared she'd drop the child. "Andrew needs his wife by his side as he begins his new life. Besides, once you get back, you'll be engrossed in wedding plans of your own."

One of the maids approached them. "Excuse me, sir. Miss Foley sent me to get Master Christian. His supper is ready."

Andrew ignored his family's pointed stares. It seemed they too had noticed Grace's marked absence from their lives, since she'd started taking all her meals with the staff in the kitchen. But no one had come right out and asked him about the sudden change.

"It's all right, Serena," Virginia said. "I'll bring him up." She threw Andrew a dark look. "Suddenly I'm not very hungry."

His gut clenched as she turned away quickly, but not fast enough to hide the tears rolling down her cheeks.

Virginia sat on the sofa in the darkened parlor, the only light coming from the low embers in the hearth. She'd waited until the house had quieted for the evening before coming down to the kitchen for some toast and tea, knowing no matter how upset she was, she'd never last until morning without something in her belly.

Now in the darkness of the empty room, she set her teacup aside and allowed herself to examine the true source of her despair. It wasn't just that she would miss Andrew's wedding, although that surely bothered her. No, her utter desolation was due to the fact that Andrew's announcement had destroyed her last hope of ever being with Collin.

Virginia had been so sure Andrew loved Grace. She was counting on him to ignore Daddy's wishes and marry her, which would have opened the door for her and Collin.

But something terrible had happened. Something that had changed the dynamics between her brother and Grace. One minute, he'd been consumed with worry about Grace catching Christian's illness, barely getting a wink of sleep. The next, he'd become distant and angry, making certain he was never in Grace's presence unless absolutely necessary.

And now, after months of hesitation, he'd suddenly proposed to Cecilia and planned to marry her in a matter of weeks. Drew knew how she'd despaired over missing Frank's wedding. How could he turn around and do the same thing to her? Tears burned the back of her eyes.

"Virginia?" Grace's voice whispered into the room. "Is everything all right?"

Virginia swiped at her eyes and rose from the sofa.

"I could tell something was bothering you earlier. Do you want to talk about it?" Grace moved into the faint light from the fireplace.

Virginia's response died in her throat at the look of concern on her face. If anyone would commiserate with her pain, it would be Grace. And she deserved to know the truth. Perhaps she already did.

Virginia let out a long sigh. "You might as well know. Andrew announced his engagement tonight. He and Cecilia are getting married at the end of August."

"Oh my." Grace sank onto a cushioned seat near her, staring straight ahead. All the life seemed to drain from her.

"I'm so sorry, Grace. I can't believe he went through with it."

"I can." Her words were wooden. Her eyes seemed hollow.

"What happened between the two of you? Everything changed after Christian's illness. Suddenly you two can't abide being in the same room together."

Grace plucked at the string of her apron. "It's complicated."

"Did Andrew do something inappropriate?" Though Virginia couldn't imagine her brother doing anything improper, she had to ask.

"No, of course not." Grace swallowed. "This is all my fault. You mustn't blame him."

"What could you possibly have done to deserve such treatment?" Indignation on her friend's behalf burned through her.

"I lied to him." She said it so quietly that Virginia thought she must have misunderstood. Then Grace raised anguished eyes to her. "I lied to all of you. I'm so sorry, Virginia. I never meant to hurt anyone."

A sliver of alarm crept through Virginia's veins. "It must have been a whopper to be so unforgivable."

"To Andrew it was." A tear slipped down Grace's cheek.

Virginia took a breath. Grace was her friend, and friends stood by each other through thick and thin. She reached over to squeeze her arm. "Whatever it is, you can tell me. I promise it won't matter."

Grace dabbed a handkerchief to her eyes. She'd dreaded this moment ever since Andrew had discovered the truth. She knew then it was only a matter of time until Virginia found out too. She licked her lips and swallowed hard. "Andrew found out that my real name is Grace Abernathy. I'm Rose's sister."

Virginia's mouth fell open and her eyes widened. "You're Christian's aunt?"

Grace nodded, twisting the handkerchief between her fingers. "I never set out to lie. But when you mentioned the nanny position, it was the only way I could think of to spend time with Rose's son."

Slowly Virginia crossed the room and stood staring into the fireplace. "So you didn't just happen to run into us in the park."

Her lifeless tone wrenched Grace's heart.

"No." She hung her head. "I'd been watching the house for days, trying to catch a glimpse of the baby, so I'd know he was all right. That day, I happened to be outside when I saw you leave with the pram. I followed you to the park. I never dreamed the opportunity of working for your family would arise. But when it did, I knew it was the only way I could be part of Christian's life."

Virginia turned around. A multitude of emotions flickered over her face. If only Grace could tell what her friend was thinking.

"I came to Canada," she went on, "because Rose asked me to help with the baby. But when I arrived, I was devastated to learn she'd passed away a few weeks earlier. I couldn't go home without finding out how my nephew was faring. I had to know whether the people who'd rejected his mother could really love him and treat him well."

Virginia sat in the chair across from her. "So you didn't come here because you learned of Rose's death?"

"No. I had no idea she was even ill."

"Oh, Grace. You must have been shattered." Virginia's lips quivered.

"I was. I hadn't seen Rose in five years. I'd so looked forward to seeing her again, to getting to know my nephew and . . ." She stopped. It would serve no purpose to tell Virginia that she'd intended to bring them back to England. "Never mind. You don't need to hear my whole sad tale. But please believe that I had no malevolent intent when I became Christian's nanny. And I certainly never expected . . ." *To fall in love with your brother.* She clamped her lips together, then straightened her shoulders. "I never expected to become so fond of you. I value our friendship a great deal, Virginia. I only hope that you can forgive me for lying to you." She blinked hard to stem the rise of tears.

Virginia shook her head sadly. "I wish you'd told me sooner," she said. "I wish you trusted me enough. But I can't really blame you for hiding your identity, knowing what Rose must have told you about our family."

"I wanted to tell you—and Andrew. But I suspected how he would react." Grace sniffed. "And if I told you, I knew you'd have to tell him too."

"You're right. I could never keep such a secret from Drew." Virginia's brow puckered. "It doesn't mean I agree with how he's handled things though."

Grace stared at her, a faint hope dawning. Her heart beat loudly in her chest. "Are you saying . . . ?"

Virginia leaned forward and reached out to grasp Grace's hand. "I know you love Christian, Grace, and the fact is, he's your flesh and blood too. I forgive you, and I hope we can still be friends."

Grace shot up from her chair and threw her arms around Virginia. Her whole frame shook as she hugged her.

When Virginia pulled back, they both swiped tears from their cheeks.

"You don't know how much this means to me," Grace said. "I couldn't bear to lose you too."

"Never." Virginia hugged her again, then pulled her over to the sofa. "We need a plan. My brother is being a complete ninny, as you would say. And it's my job to make him see reason."

At the determined look on her friend's face, Grace dared to believe Virginia might be able to soften Andrew's heart. At this point, Grace would even be grateful for the absence of hostility. "What do you intend to do?"

"I don't know yet. But hopefully something will come to me soon."

CHAPTER 29

"Miss Virginia. How nice to see you." Father's secretary smiled up at Virginia as she approached the desk.

"Thank you, Martha. It's been a while since I've dropped by." She gave the woman her brightest smile, tilting her head to show off her stylish new hat. "Is my brother in his office?"

"I believe so. Would you like me to tell him you're here?"

"No need. I know the way." Virginia headed down the hall toward Andrew's office, praying he was alone. This was a conversation that needed privacy, which was another reason she'd chosen to come to the hotel instead of risking being overheard at home. Besides, Andrew would be less likely to shout at her in the middle of the office.

His door was ajar so she poked her head inside. He was in his chair, facing the window. Virginia could just make out his profile.

"Working hard, I see." She stepped inside and closed the door behind her.

Andrew whirled around in his chair. "Ginny. This is a nice surprise." He rose and came to kiss her cheek. "What are you doing here?"

"Do I need a reason to visit?"

His expression changed from pleased to wary. "If you've come to lecture me about my engagement, you can save your breath."

"I've come to have a rational discussion with my brother, whom

I love." She flopped onto one of his guest chairs, her purse on her lap. "And I hope he'll be honest with me."

The scowl deepened, but he returned to his seat. "Dare I ask what I haven't been honest about?"

She gave him a long look, measuring her words before she spoke. "I want you to explain why you're marrying Cecilia when you're clearly in love with Grace."

His eyes went wide, then his brows crashed together. "I am not in love with Grace. The farthest thing from it."

She knew that stubborn set to his jaw. "You're deceiving yourself, Drew. You may be angry with her, but deep down, you know you're in love with her."

"The topic is not up for discussion. I've made my decision, and it's final."

At that moment, he sounded more like their father than ever before. She'd expected resistance, but not downright refusal to discuss the situation.

"I realize Cecilia is not your favorite person," he continued, "but you're going to have to find a way to tolerate her, because she will be my wife by the time you return from Europe. And I'm sorry our wedding will take place while you're away. But both Father and Mr. Harrison agree—"

"For heaven's sake, Drew, aren't you tired of always bowing to Daddy's wishes?" She pushed up to pace the room, frustration humming in her veins. "Why can't we make our own decisions? Would the world really stop revolving if we did?"

He crossed his arms over his chest. "I sense there's more to this than just my wedding. Does this have something to do with your own engagement?"

Virginia huffed and sat back down. He always could see through her. "Indirectly, I suppose. But this is more about your happiness." She leaned toward him. "Drew, if you love Grace, why shouldn't you marry her? This whole idea that we have to choose a partner within the same class is archaic. And why does Daddy get to dictate whom we marry?"

Andrew came around to sit on the edge of the desk. "Is there someone else you wish to wed, Ginny?" he asked softly. "Someone you think Father won't approve of?"

She bit her lip to control her emotions. Somehow this conversation had gotten out of hand. She was supposed to be talking about his romance, not hers. She leaned toward him. "What if there were? What if we took a stand and both told Daddy we were marrying who we wanted?"

Andrew stared at her. "Do you really think he'd just accept it?"

"He'd have to. Surely he wouldn't disown both of us."

He looked down at her with eyes that seared her soul. "I'm afraid he might, Gin. And have you considered what that would do to our mother? Her health couldn't withstand another shock like that."

Virginia's stomach sank to her shoes. "It would kill her to lose both of us, as well as Christian." She stared into his haggard face, noting for the first time the network of lines around his eyes. "You're doing this partly for her sake, aren't you?"

"It's the right thing to do. The honorable thing. I've led Cecilia to believe I was courting her with the intent to marry. I can't go back on my word and reject her, like Frank did. Nor can I let our parents down again." He released a breath. "I have a duty to them and to our family. One I can't ignore."

Virginia pressed her lips together, blinking back the tears that burned beneath her lids. "You are the most honorable man I know. I suppose I can't expect you to do anything less."

A wave of relief passed over his features, easing the furrows on his forehead. He pulled her into a hug. "Thank you for understanding. And I promise I'll make up for my hasty wedding by celebrating doubly at yours."

She swallowed the lump of raw emotion constricting her throat and squeezed him harder. "In the meantime, will you at least try to forgive Grace? For Christian's sake, if nothing else."

His eyes widened. "She told you?"

Virginia nodded. "I was hurt at first too, but I understand why she did it."

The stiffness returned to his shoulders, and he appeared ready to argue.

"Never mind. I'll leave you to think about it." She kissed his cheek. "We're quite the pair, aren't we?"

"That we are." He pulled one of her curls, an act reminiscent of their childhood.

"Don't forget the engagement party at the Flemings' next Saturday. I suppose you'd better invite Cecilia too."

"I will." His face changed and he pulled her close in another hug. "Everything will work out for the best, Gin. You'll see."

In that instant, with nothing else she could do, she chose to believe him.

"I hope you're right." She mustered one last parting smile as she left him.

With a huge sigh, she continued down the hall. Their conversation had not gone at all the way she'd hoped, but at least she and Drew understood each other better.

And, with time, she knew he would forgive Grace. Maybe that was all she could expect.

Andrew poured himself a glass of water and drained it in one gulp. His insides were as twisted as a bedsheet that had just passed through a wringer. He couldn't believe Ginny knew about Grace's lies and had actually forgiven her.

He closed his eyes. Maybe he'd be able to forgive her too, if he weren't in love with her.

Leave it to Ginny to figure out his true feelings. Yet he'd denied it to her face. *Who's lying now, Easton?*

With a thud, he set the glass back on the sideboard.

A knock sounded on his door. He turned as Paul Edison stepped into his office.

Andrew suppressed a groan. Just what he needed. Another confrontation.

"I'd like a word, if you have a minute." Edison stood very still, hands in his pockets.

Gone was his usual swagger and bravado. Instead he looked beaten down, subdued. His face was unshaven and even his hair lacked its usual luster.

"Have a seat." Andrew gestured to the guest chairs.

"I'll stand, thanks. This won't take long." Edison squared his shoulders and inhaled. "I came to apologize."

Andrew crossed his arms and studied the clearly uncomfortable man. "For what exactly?"

"First of all, for flirting with Cecilia." He moved farther into the room, his gaze falling somewhere in the vicinity of Andrew's shoulder. "I'll admit I brought her to work here, hoping she'd come to prefer my particular brand of charm over yours. I knew you were courting her, and I had no right to intrude on that." He lifted his head and met Andrew's gaze. "She's made her choice now, and I want you to know you don't have to worry about me interfering again." His face twisted with what looked like a mixture of regret and sorrow.

"I appreciate that. Thank you."

Noise from the hall filtered in through the partly open door.

Edison shifted his weight. "Secondly, my overly competitive nature has not been in the best interest of the company." He cleared his throat. "This is hard to admit, but I was jealous of your relationship with your father. Of the faith he has in you." He shrugged. "I never knew my own father. So it was an honor when Oscar took me under his wing. But I didn't repay him the way I should have by respecting his son."

Andrew frowned. Was this sincere or was Edison after something? He moved behind his desk, studying him. "What brought about these startling revelations?"

"You're skeptical. I understand that." Paul gripped the back of a chair, his knuckles whitening. "Losing the woman you love forces you to take a long hard look at yourself. And when I did, I didn't care for what I saw."

Losing the woman you love. So he wasn't just trying to win over Cecilia out of some sense of competition. He truly cared for her.

"I know I can never take your place with Oscar, but I promise to ensure things run smoothly here. And to keep you informed of all pertinent matters that arise."

Andrew leveled Paul with a hard stare. The man didn't flinch or break eye contact. "I appreciate you saying all this. It takes courage to admit when you've done something wrong." He held out his hand across the desk. "It will be good to have someone I can trust at my father's side when I'm gone."

The lines in Paul's forehead eased as he shook Andrew's hand. "No hard feelings?"

"None."

Paul smiled. "That's a relief. I wasn't sure if I'd be looking for a new job after this."

"As far as I'm concerned, everyone's entitled to a mistake as long as they learn from it."

"Thank you. You won't regret this."

As Paul exited the room, Grace's face flew to mind. She'd seemed sincerely remorseful for her mistake when Andrew confronted her. If he could be magnanimous with Paul, couldn't he show her compassion as well?

Andrew slumped back against his chair. Maybe Virginia was right.

Maybe it was time he considered forgiving Grace.

CHAPTER 30

On the night of her engagement party, Virginia sat ramrod straight in the front seat of Basil's automobile. He had chosen to take her home himself instead of using his driver, perhaps hoping to have a moment alone before the busyness of the next few days overtook them.

The party had been a combination of a congratulations on their engagement and a *bon voyage* before the family left for Europe. Though the Flemings were nice enough, Virginia still felt out of place in their home. Basil's sister, Bettina, who would be her maid of honor, was a somber girl, who tended to regard Virginia as an interloper. His much older brother, Martin, was a staid fellow with a mousy wife and three rather irritating children. Virginia wished Grace could have been there, but realized it wouldn't have been appropriate. At least her friend had agreed to see her off at the train station in the morning.

Virginia couldn't believe that tomorrow she'd be taking a train to Halifax, and from there boarding a steamship to Britain. Then they would spend the next two and a half months traveling all over Europe. What would her world look like when she returned?

Andrew would be married to Cecilia, and he and Christian would be living in Ottawa. It hurt Virginia's heart just to think about not seeing that darling boy every day. She would have to make a point of visiting them often so he wouldn't forget his Aunt Ginny.

And without Christian, Grace would be gone as well. Virginia had no idea if Grace would stay in Canada or return to England to care for her mother. Very likely, Virginia would lose the closest thing she'd ever had to a sister.

The car jostled her as Basil drove up the driveway toward Fairlawn. He stopped in front of the house and set the brake. "Well, my dear, this is the last time I will drive you home for quite some time."

"So it is." Her heart pinched. The thought of leaving Fairlawn, even for a few months, released a flood of nostalgia and regret—along with a large measure of unease, traveling so far from home with a man she didn't really know. No better time to change that and hopefully clarify a few things between them.

She turned in her seat to face him. "Basil, there's something I wish to discuss, if you don't mind."

"What is it?" His expression became wary.

"We haven't really talked about . . . children." Each time she'd tried to broach the topic, he found a way to change the subject. "You do want a family, don't you?" The question hung in the air as Virginia awaited his reaction.

His brows drew together. "This isn't about your nephew again, I hope."

"No. I've resigned myself to that situation. But Basil"—she leaned over to place a hand on his arm—"once we're married, I would like to start a family right away. After all, I am almost twenty-five, and—"

"I'm afraid that's out of the question. For the next year or two, my work will require extensive traveling, and I will need you by my side."

Her mouth fell open, her heart thumping hard.

He must have noticed her distress for he patted her knee. "Once things settle down in a couple of years, we can revisit the idea of having children."

Virginia's insides clenched. She knew that condescending tone, the one he used when he wanted to placate her. She had the dreadful premonition that when the time came, Basil would find yet another excuse why children would not be convenient.

"Come now, darling, don't pout. The future will take care of itself. You'll see." He pulled her closer and kissed her.

Virginia closed her eyes, trying to relax into his embrace. She'd have to learn to enjoy his kisses—and more—if they were to have children.

He broke away with a laugh and trailed a finger down her bare arm. "You'd better go inside before I forget myself."

A chill invaded her body at his possessive manner. What would he be like when they were legally joined?

When he made no move to accompany her to the house, she opened her door. "Good-night, Basil."

"Sweet dreams, darling. I'll see you bright and early tomorrow."

She hurried up the stairs and inside the front door, waving briefly before closing it and leaning back against the solid wood surface. Her erratic breathing bore testimony to her unsettled emotions.

Lord, am I doing the right thing? Is this trip, this marriage, your will for my life?

In the silence of the foyer, the loud ticking of the grandfather clock was her only answer. She pushed away from the door and headed toward the stairs, but before she reached them, the sound of raised voices from the direction of the library waylaid her.

Surely Daddy and Andrew weren't having a row? Virginia marched down the hall to find out. As she reached the library, the door flew open.

Collin strode out, a deep scowl etching his features.

Her heart flopped in her chest. "Collin, what's the matter?"

"Not a bloomin' thing." He jammed his cap on his head and continued toward the rear of the house.

Rarely had Virginia seen him so upset about . . . anything. She bit her lip, indecision wreaking havoc. She couldn't go after him now—it wouldn't be seemly. But she could find out from her father what they'd been arguing about.

Virginia entered the library and quietly closed the door. Her father sat in one of his armchairs, staring into the fire. The overpowering smell of his cigar hung in the air.

She took a seat beside him. "What was that about? Collin looked ready to punch someone."

A nerve jumped in her father's jaw. He took a drink from the glass of amber liquid in his hand but said nothing.

"Well? Why were you two arguing?"

"If you must know," he bit out, "Mr. Lafferty just tendered his resignation."

Virginia went rigid. Her lungs squeezed, as though a vice had gripped them. "He quit?"

"I believe that's what I said."

"Why would he do such a thing? He loves it here."

"He claims his sister is ill and needs his help. But I don't believe that's the real reason." Her father turned to level her with a pointed stare.

Virginia gripped the wooden armrest, her mind whirling. "His sister lives in Scotland. Is he going back there?"

"It appears so. He's agreed to stay until Andrew's wedding and do the flowers as promised. After that, he'll be gone."

The air in the room closed in on her, suffocating and dense.

Daddy drained the glass and set it on the side table. "I'm going to bed. I'd advise you to do the same. You'll want to be well rested for tomorrow." He trudged off, appearing suddenly older than his years.

Virginia remained in the chair until the squeak of the stairs told her he'd gone up.

Her heart felt trapped in her chest, as if the simple act of beating had become too burdensome a task.

Collin was leaving. In a few weeks, he'd be on a ship bound for Scotland.

And she'd be away on a trip with a man she didn't love. A man who gave little regard to her wants or needs. A man who might never give her the children she craved.

This was not how her life was supposed to be. Not one thing about it felt right.

Nervous energy propelled her out of her chair.

She had to do something to fix it before it was too late.

The cool August night air bit at Virginia's arms as she crossed the lawn toward the garage where Collin and Toby shared the upper apartment. What would they think of her knocking on their door at this hour? A wave of shame threatened to stall her feet, but she pushed on, her mission too important to worry about her reputation.

As she passed the greenhouse, her heart lurched. She couldn't imagine another man tending the plants Collin had nurtured from mere seeds. She remembered all the beautiful roses he'd created for her, the first inkling she'd had that he cared for her in a romantic way. Until their recent kiss, he'd never done anything forward, always the perfect gentleman. But his simple act of making sure she had her favorite flowers in her room each day had filled her with warmth and had made her take note of the humble gardener.

She blinked at the low light coming from the rear of the greenhouse, realization dawning. Of course Collin would go there. If anything could soothe his mood, it would be his beloved plants.

Changing direction, she strode to the greenhouse and slipped inside. She needed to see him, needed to convince him not to leave the country.

For as long as he remained at Fairlawn, there existed hope.

On silent feet, she made her way to the rear work area. She could already picture him, sleeves rolled up, hands in the dirt.

He hadn't turned on the overhead lights. Only the glow of a single lantern lit the interior. He stood with his back to her, working.

She entered his sanctuary, inhaling the smell of earth and greenery, a scent she always associated with him.

"Is it true?" she asked quietly. "Are you really going back to Scotland?"

Collin jerked around, knocking over a clay pot and spilling dirt onto the table. He scowled, his brow wreathed in furrows. "You shouldn't be here, Virginia. Go back to the house."

"Not until you take back your resignation."

He crossed his arms, nostrils flaring. "That's not going to happen."

She moved closer. "You can't leave, Collin," she whispered. "You can't."

"You know why I have to go." His eyes bore into hers.

"But I'll be gone. You can continue doing what you love without me here to bother you."

A harsh laugh escaped. "And what about the times you come home with your *husband*? Or bring your children to play in the yard? How am I supposed to feel then?"

Virginia winced. "I didn't think of that."

"No, I guess you didn't." He turned back to scoop up the spilled dirt. "You're doing what you have to, and so am I. Though even with an ocean between us, I'm certain the pain will be every bit as great." His fingers stilled. "Do you have any idea how hard it is to watch you with another man? I can't keep torturing myself this way."

A shaft of agony sliced through her. She hadn't considered his pain, only thinking of her own. Now, the magnitude of his suffering created a wall around him, one she would never be able to breach. Tears blurred her vision, spilling down her face unchecked.

This really was good-bye. He was walking out of her life forever.

He flicked a glance at her, and the pain in his eyes mirrored her own.

"There's nothing I can do to change your mind?" she whispered.

"You know what would make me stay, but I doubt you have the courage to do it."

His bold stare challenged her, dared her to prove him wrong.

Her gaze dropped to the ground, hope leaking out of her like air out of a punctured tire. He was right. Deep down, she was a coward, too afraid to risk her father's wrath to claim Collin's heart. Too afraid to be cut off from the family she loved, as Frank had been.

"I'm sorry," she choked out. "I wish things could be different." She brushed the tears from her face and forced herself to meet the agony in his hazel eyes. "Good-bye, Collin. I pray that one day you'll find happiness."

Because at least one of us should be happy.

She took in his beloved face one last time, then turned and walked away.

CHAPTER 31

July 16, 1918
Dear Grace,

I'm back living with Mrs. Chamberlain again. I couldn't manage to keep up with the rent and had to let our flat go. So many happy memories there. But I pray Frank will be home soon, and we can start making new memories together.

"Thank you, Serena. I appreciate you doing this." Standing beside the crib, Grace smiled at the young woman.

"No trouble at all, miss. I enjoy looking after this wee one. You go and give Miss Virginia a great send-off on her trip."

"I will." Grace tried to muster more enthusiasm for her friend's grand adventure. However, Virginia had been her main ally in the house—a buffer from Andrew's still-palpable animosity. Grace would miss Virginia terribly, and in fact, she didn't know if she would even be here when she returned. Now as she headed down the hall, she hoped to catch her friend for a few private moments before they had to leave for the train station.

Though it was still early, Grace suspected Virginia would be up and about, too excited to remain in bed. Grace's steps slowed as she passed Andrew's bedroom. Regret clawed at her throat. Before he'd discovered her secret, this day would have been filled with delight at sharing a few stolen moments with him. But now, with Andrew barely speaking to her, the little send-off party was sure to be awkward. For Virginia's sake, Grace would have to make the best of the situation.

She continued on and knocked on Virginia's door. No response. Surely she wouldn't still be asleep on such an important day.

"Virginia. It's Grace. Do you need any help with your bags?"

When no answer came the second time, Grace cracked open the door and peered inside. The room was empty, Virginia's bed neatly made. A closed steamer trunk sat against the far wall. Grace had anticipated a last-minute flurry of excitement with final items to be packed. Never had she expected this unearthly quiet.

Grace walked into the room. The beautiful pink dress Virginia had worn to the engagement party last night was strewn over a chair in the corner. One shoe peeked out from under the bed. A tremble of alarm surfaced. Something about this scene didn't seem right.

Grace crossed to the vanity where her gaze fell on an envelope propped against the mirror. Andrew's name was written in Virginia's lovely script. Then she noticed a small velvet box, one that might contain an engagement ring. A chill of foreboding swept through her. With trembling fingers, she lifted the lid of the box. Virginia's stunning diamond ring sat within the velvet interior. She snapped the lid shut. Underneath it, another envelope was visible, this one addressed to Basil. Grace sank onto the stool by the vanity, her legs shaking. There could only be one explanation for this.

"Oh, Virginia. What have you done?" Grace pressed a hand to her mouth, her mind spinning. Speculation was pointless.

She'd bring the letter to Andrew. He would know what to do.

Andrew fiddled with his tie and grimaced at his reflection in the mirror. For some reason, the knot seemed extra tight today, jabbing at his Adam's apple. Or perhaps it was the idea of Ginny traveling halfway around the world—away from her family and those who loved her—that was strangling him. She'd miss Andrew's wedding, something he regretted deeply. He hadn't fully realized the stabilizing effect her presence had on him and what a blessing she would be to have around on that day.

Someone rapped sharply on his door.

"Just a minute." Probably Father making sure he was coming with them.

When he opened the door, his mouth fell open at the sight of Grace standing in the hall. Despite the strain in their relationship, his pulse took off like a sprinter at the start of a race.

He blinked as the anxiety on her face registered. "Grace? Is everything all right?"

"I don't know." Her brown eyes filled with misery. "I just went to check on Virginia and she wasn't there. I found this." She thrust an envelope at him.

He frowned, a thread of alarm buzzing through him.

"She left her engagement ring and another envelope for Basil as well." Grace twisted her hands together. "Oh, Andrew. I think she may have run away." Her slim frame shuddered.

"Come and sit down." He guided her to the chair just inside the door.

Then he ripped open the envelope, pulled out the notepaper, and scanned the rows of Ginny's precise handwriting. The more he read, the farther his stomach sank.

Dear Drew,

I am so sorry to burden you with this; however, you are the only one I trust to handle the situation.

Right now, my heart is being torn in two. I simply cannot go away on an extended voyage with a man I do not love, and whom I fear does not and will not ever love me. Not the way I wish my husband to love me. And so I am breaking off my engagement to Basil.

The truth is, Drew, I'm in love with Collin. I tried to say good-bye to him last night, but afterward I couldn't sleep, filled with anguish knowing I would never see him again. So after I finish this note, I'm going to go to him, and if he's willing, I will marry him. If he's not, then I'll go away for a while until things calm down.

Please don't hate me for this. I know how much Frank's betrayal cost you, and I feel terrible for putting you in a similar position. I only pray Father has learned from the past and will be able to understand my actions. Tell Mother I love her.

Your affectionate sister,
Ginny

P.S. If you could have the chauffeur deliver the other letter to Basil, I will be in your debt.

"I don't believe it." He raised his head to stare at Grace. "She says she's in love with the gardener."

Grace released a breath and nodded.

"You don't seem surprised. Did you know about her feelings for him?"

"Yes." She twisted her fingers together. "When I first suspected, I tried to talk to her about it, but she said that her father would never let her marry an employee."

"She's right. He wouldn't." Wasn't that exactly why he could never be with Grace?

Andrew ran a hand over his beard and paced the floor, the full horror of the situation slowly sinking in. It was Frank all over again. His shoulders ached as though two rocks had dropped onto them. "How am I ever going to tell my parents?"

He wasn't sure he'd said that out loud, until he felt the touch of Grace's hand on his arm.

"I'm so sorry, Andrew. I wish—"

"It's not your fault." If anyone was to blame, it was his father, who refused to allow his children to live their own lives. A sudden thought struck. "Maybe we can stop her before it's too late."

"How? We don't know where she's gone."

"I have an idea where they might be." He pulled out his watch. "By the time we arrive, the courthouse may be open."

"Courthouse?"

"Where else would you go to get married in a hurry?" His certainty grew. "If I know Ginny, she'd want the deed done so Father couldn't foil her plan."

"Shouldn't you check Collin's quarters first? In case he turned her down?"

Andrew grunted as he shoved the letter into his pocket. "Highly unlikely, but you're right." He led Grace into the hall. "I'll be back as soon as I can. If I'm right, I'm going to head over to the courthouse." He paused as a troubling thought occurred. He doubted he'd be able to sway Ginny, but Grace seemed to have a way with her. "Virginia might listen to you. Will you come with me and try to make her see reason?"

Indecision splashed over her features, but then she nodded. "If you think it will help."

"Thank you." He hated having to rely on Grace. Hated that his traitorous heart still beat harder in her presence.

But he would do whatever it took to keep his family intact. To keep his sister from inflicting further damage. They'd only just started to heal after losing Frank, and Andrew wouldn't let anything tear them apart again.

After searching Lafferty's quarters, Andrew headed back to the house, his mood growing more sour by the minute. Most of the gardener's clothes, as well as his immigration papers and his billfold, were missing, leading Andrew to believe that Lafferty had indeed left with Ginny.

Andrew entered the dining room. His father was seated at the table, reading the morning paper while he sipped his coffee. Andrew's gut twisted, hating that he was about to impart news that would ruin his father's life—again.

Father laid his paper down and smiled. "Good morning, Andrew. Are you still coming to see your sister off?"

Andrew moved forward to grip the back of a chair. "I'm afraid there's been a change in plans," he said quietly.

The smile turned to a frown. "What are you talking about?"

"Virginia is gone. She left this note."

Father snatched the paper from Andrew and scanned the page. His face became ashen, and he appeared to age ten years before Andrew's eyes.

The letter drifted to the table. "How could she do this to us? After everything we went through with Frank."

Andrew's chest tightened at the agony on his father's face. He didn't even dare imagine his mother's reaction. "There's a chance they went to the courthouse," he said. "I'm heading there now to try and stop her. Do you have any contacts you think might help?"

His father's eyes brightened. "I'll call Judge Ashford. Maybe he can stop this farce of a wedding before it begins."

"Good idea. I'll let you know as soon as I find her."

CHAPTER 32

October 19, 1918

Telegram from Mrs. Harriet Chamberlain, Toronto, Canada to Mrs. Helen Abernathy, Sussex, England. Rose's husband killed in battle. STOP. Rose overcome. STOP. In hospital.

The Toronto courthouse stood tall against the bright morning sky. The clock on the high stone tower chimed nine o'clock. With Andrew whisking her up the cement steps, Grace had little time to appreciate the dulcet tone of the bells, nor the majesty of the building's architecture.

She darted a glance at Andrew's tense features as they walked, wishing she could say something to comfort him, but knowing he wouldn't welcome her overtures. He'd told her that Mr. Easton was going to telephone his friend, a Toronto judge, to see if he could somehow stop Virginia from marrying Collin. Between the judge and Andrew, perhaps they might succeed.

When they reached the office they'd been directed to, Andrew paused. The clerk's hours were printed in gold letters on the frosted-glass window. 8:30 a.m. to 4:30 p.m. Monday to Friday. 8:30 a.m. to 12:00 p.m. Saturday.

The office had already been open for half an hour. Would that have been enough time for the couple to get a license?

Grace didn't know what to feel or what to hope for. Part of her cheered for her friend's bravery in marrying the man she loved. Yet, knowing the ramifications her actions would cause for Andrew and his family, Grace half hoped they'd be in time to stop her.

With a grim set to his mouth, Andrew opened the door and crossed to the long counter where a woman stood, sorting papers.

She peered over her glasses. "Can I help you, sir?" Then she noticed Grace and her eyebrows rose. "Don't tell me you want a marriage license too? That will be my second this morning."

Grace inhaled sharply and gripped the handle of her purse.

"I don't need a license," Andrew said. "But I'm looking for a young woman who might have come here this morning to obtain one. Virginia Easton is her name."

The woman blinked and removed her glasses. "Yes, she and her fiancé were here waiting for the office to open."

"Was the man's name Lafferty?"

"Yes." She frowned. "Is there a problem?"

"Did you grant them a license?"

"I did indeed." The woman turned to glance at the clock on the wall, and her features brightened. "If you hurry, you might catch the ceremony. They're in Courtroom A."

"Next! Virginia Easton and Collin Lafferty."

Virginia's knees shook as she and Collin took their place in front of the magistrate. Collin handed the man the freshly inked marriage license, which he looked over and set aside.

She could hardly believe this was really happening. After she'd left the greenhouse, she'd spent a sleepless night pacing her room and praying, and had finally come to the conclusion that she couldn't imagine her life without Collin. She'd packed her things, written letters for Drew and Basil, and under the cover of predawn darkness, had gone to see Collin. He hadn't been thrilled to find her at his door, nor had he initially been receptive to the idea of an elopement. But in the end, she'd stood her ground.

"Either way, I'm leaving, Collin. You can come with me, or I'll go on my own."

"Don't be daft, Virginia. Where would you go?"

"It doesn't matter, as long as it's far away from my father and Basil Fleming."

She stared him down, until he ran a hand through his already disheveled hair and heaved a sigh. "I guess you leave me no choice."

"Isn't that the romantic declaration every woman dreams of?"

His face had softened then. "Are you sure about this? We don't have to marry. I'll go with you anyway to keep you safe."

"Don't you want to marry me, Collin?" For a moment, she'd feared she'd been wrong about his feelings after all.

"Aye, lass, you know I do. Just not this way."

"There is no other way. My father will find out and put a stop to it. If we do it now, he won't have any recourse, and in time he'll come around. I know he will."

"What if he doesn't? What will we live on until I find another job?"

"I have some savings that should tide us over for a while."

His dark brows had crashed down. "No, Virginia. I won't take your money."

"Is your pride worth more than a future with me?" She'd gambled that it wasn't.

Collin had stared at her for several seconds before expelling a loud breath. "Give me a moment to change."

He'd emerged several minutes later, dressed in his Sunday suit and carrying a small bag. Since it was too early for the clerk's office to be open, they'd taken a cab to the train station, stowed their luggage in a locker, and ridden the streetcar back to the courthouse. Everything had gone smoothly from there, with the issuing of their license and being able to get a magistrate to marry them almost immediately.

"Please join hands." The commanding voice of the official jolted Virginia from her thoughts.

She smoothed down her green Sunday dress, wishing she could be standing before Collin in the fabulous wedding gown Mother had commissioned her dressmaker to create for her. But that dress was meant for another life. She held out her hands to Collin, willing them to stop shaking.

Collin took her fingers and began to tug at the cotton gloves she wore.

"What are you doing?" she whispered.

"We're about to join our lives together. I won't have any barriers between us." He removed the gloves, stuffed them both in his pocket, then took her hands firmly in his warm, solid ones. "Much better."

Nerves jumbled around in her stomach, yet the heat from his fingers steadied her.

"I wish I could have made a bouquet for you. You deserve flowers on your wedding day."

"I have you. That's all I need." She meant it with all her heart.

He smiled, crinkles forming at the corners of his eyes. In his good suit, with his dark hair slicked back, he looked incredibly handsome, so steadfast and strong.

The magistrate tapped his Bible. "If you're ready, let's begin. Do you have any witnesses?"

"No, sir," Collin said.

The man turned to a woman sitting at a table near the side door. "Mabel, call Trudy in, please. We'll need you both as witnesses."

As soon as the two women returned, the court official opened a book and began to read. "We have come here today to join Virginia Lillian Easton and Collin Michael Lafferty in marriage. If anyone objects to this union, let them speak now or forever hold their peace."

He glanced around the empty room and shrugged. "A formality." He cleared his throat. "Do you, Collin, take Virginia to be your lawfully wedded wife? To have and to hold, for better or for worse, in sickness and in health, and forsaking all others, keep only unto her so long as you both shall live?"

Collin gazed deeply into her eyes and nodded. "I do."

Virginia's gaze, fastened on his, grew misty.

"And do you, Virginia, take Collin to be your lawfully wedded husband? To have and to hold, for better or for worse, in sickness and in health, and forsaking all others, keep only unto him so long as you both shall live?"

She drew in a deep breath. "I do."

"Do you have a ring?"

Virginia opened her mouth to say no, when Collin took his hands from hers. He pulled a gold signet ring from his finger.

"It's not much, but it'll do until I can buy you a proper wedding ring."

She bit her bottom lip and nodded, blinking back the tears forming. Basil's ostentatious engagement ring did not come close to the meaning of this simple offering.

"Place the ring on her finger and repeat after me."

Collin slid it on. "With this ring, I thee wed."

The huskiness of his voice sent shivers up her spine.

She gazed into his eyes, and the power of the emotions shining there nearly robbed her of breath. This was what she'd been searching for. A lasting love, deep and true, on which to forge her future.

"By the powers vested in me by the City of Toronto and the Province of Ontario, I now pronounce you husband and wife."

They stood smiling at each other, as if they couldn't quite believe it.

"You may kiss your bride," the official said. "Unless you don't wish to."

"Oh, I wish to." Collin took her face in his hands and lowered his lips to hers.

Virginia's heart stuttered and then soared in her chest. She returned the kiss in equal measure, happiness spreading through her system like warm molasses. They'd done it. They were legally married. There was nothing her father could do to stop them now.

Collin pulled back, his eyes serious. "I love you with every breath in my body, Virginia. And I will do my best to give you the life you deserve."

"I love you, too, Collin. Forever."

He bent to kiss her again, and the official cleared his throat. "I don't mean to rush you, but I have another wedding scheduled soon. If you could sign the register with the witnesses, I'll have Trudy file the paperwork. Congratulations to you both. May you enjoy a long and happy life together."

Andrew raced down the corridor, his only thought to stop Virginia before she ruined her life and devastated their parents.

Please, Lord, let me be in time.

At the end of the hall, a sign over the double doors read *Courtroom A*. Andrew yanked one door open, glanced back at Grace who had fallen behind, and rushed inside. He came to an abrupt stop at the sight of his sister walking toward him on the arm of Collin Lafferty.

Her mouth fell open, and the color drained from her cheeks. "Andrew? What are you doing here?"

He speared Lafferty with a glare, then focused on Virginia. "Tell me I'm not too late. That you've come to your senses."

She tilted her chin in that stubborn way of hers. "I have come to my senses, but not how you mean. I realized I couldn't go off with Basil when I'm in love with Collin." She turned to smile at the traitor.

"He's filled your head with nonsense, Gin. Think sensibly. What type of life will you have with him? Cut off from the family with no money. Living above a garage or at the back of a flower shop."

Collin's hands fisted. Virginia tugged at his arm.

"It doesn't matter, Drew. Collin and I are already married. And we'll have a good life together because we love each other."

Collin moved forward. "I didn't want it to be this way, believe me. I wanted to speak to your father, but Virginia forced my hand.

Said she was running away with or without me." He shrugged. "I couldn't let her set off on her own."

"We'll give Daddy a chance to cool off," Virginia said, "and then we'll try to make things right."

The blood pounded through Andrew's head, pulsing at his temples. "Make things right?" His voice thundered over the cavernous room. "Things will never be right again. How could you do this to them? To me?"

The court official walked toward them, frowning. "Excuse me, but I'm going to have to ask you to leave. We have another wedding in five minutes."

"Andrew." From beside him, Grace's soft voice penetrated the haze of his anger. A slight pressure on his arm had him turning to face her. "There's nothing to be done now," she said in an infuriatingly calm tone. "They're married."

Grace stepped forward then and embraced Virginia. "Congratulations. I hope that you will be very happy together."

"Thank you, Grace. I only wish you could have been here."

"I do too." Grace smiled. "Take good care of her, Collin."

"I intend to do just that."

"Ginny." Andrew clutched at her hand. "Come home with us, please. We can fix this mess somehow. We'll have the marriage annulled."

She shook her head, her gray eyes filling with tears. "I'm sorry, Drew. Tell Mother I love her. I'll write a letter explaining everything—"

"It won't matter. He'll cut you out of our lives. You know he will." Desperation leached into his system. He was losing her. Just like he'd lost Frank.

"Maybe. But I'll always keep trying to change his mind." She reached up to kiss his cheek. "Good-bye, Drew. Be happy. You deserve it."

Then she took Collin's arm and left the courtroom.

Andrew's legs wouldn't move, his mouth so dry he couldn't even call after her.

Grace slipped her hand in his. Warmth enveloped his chilled fingers. "Let's go home, Andrew. Your parents will need you to be strong for them now."

He swallowed the bitterness at the back of his throat as the terrible truth dawned. All his efforts to heal his family—to bring some measure of happiness back to their lives—had been for nothing. Once again, he was left to pick up the pieces of their broken hearts and shattered dreams.

He looked down at Grace's pretty face, her worried eyes filled with sympathy, and for one dark moment, he wished that he'd been the one to defy his father. That he was the one heading off on a train to anywhere but here.

Instead, the shackles of duty chaining him had just become ten notches tighter.

CHAPTER 33

October 30, 1918

I'm sorry I haven't written sooner, Grace. By now you know my Frank is gone. And with him my heart is too. I don't know how I will go on without him. Or if I even want to. But for the sake of our unborn child, I have to try. Pray for me, Grace. For both of us.

Two weeks later, Grace sat in the park, trying to enjoy the beautiful summer day, yet her jumbled thoughts continued to create unrest in her mind. The Easton house had not been the same since Virginia's elopement. Upon hearing the news, Mrs. Easton had collapsed and had taken to her bed, claiming she could never show her face in public again after another scandal. Dr. Ballard had checked on her daily, and each time he emerged from her room, shaking his head, saying there was nothing he could do. He believed her ailments were mostly psychological, rather than physical.

Grace had done her best to calm the woman, bringing Christian to her room for a period of time every afternoon in an attempt to bring her out of her dark mood. Yet nothing helped.

Mr. Easton had holed himself up at the office, coming home barely long enough to sleep and then go right back again the next day. Andrew too had thrown himself into his job. The only thing that seemed to bring him out of his despair was the time he spent with Christian each night. Grace would leave them alone, praying the child would soothe the Andrew's hurt at what he considered his sister's betrayal.

What bothered Grace the most was his complete withdrawal from her—again. It was almost as if on top of her deceiving him about her identity, he resented her for not holding the same grudge against Virginia. But Grace saw no point in condemning her friend. If anyone could understand acting on impulse, it was Grace. And though she missed her greatly, she prayed Virginia and Collin would find happiness together and that someday the Easton family would be reconciled.

"Well, Christian, I suppose we'd best get back." She smiled at the boy sitting on a plaid blanket on the grass. His chubby arms waved in the air as he reached for the rubber ball that had rolled away from him. He was getting so big now. Soon he would outgrow his pram, and she would have to find another way to continue their daily outings.

Grace attempted to ignore the ache in her chest, one that felt like it increased in intensity with each day that passed. In addition to the gloomy mood permeating the Easton household, Grace was haunted by the uncertainty of her future. Even if by some chance Andrew wanted her to continue as Christian's nanny after the wedding, she simply couldn't do it—no matter how much she dreaded being separated from Christian. The mere thought of sharing a house with Andrew and Cecilia, of having to witness Andrew's married life with that woman, made her soul cry out in protest.

Yet how could Grace stand to lose contact with her nephew, her last tie to Rose?

She dashed useless tears from her eyes. In this time of turmoil, she had to trust God and remain steadfast in her faith that He would provide an answer for her. Even if she couldn't imagine how.

"Good day, Miss Foley. Is everything all right?"

Grace looked up. Toby McDonald stood on the path near the bench she occupied. "Everything is fine, thank you." She jumped up to retrieve Christian's ball and hand it to the boy. "What are you doing here?"

"I was looking for you. Might I have a word?"

For some reason, Grace's heart began to thud loudly in her ears. Why would Toby seek her out like this instead of speaking to her at Fairlawn?

He must have noticed her bewilderment. "I wanted to be sure our conversation wasn't overheard, and this seemed the best way."

"Please have a seat." Grace smoothed her skirts under her as she resumed her spot on the bench.

Toby sat at the opposite end.

"What can I do for you, Mr. McDonald?"

"For starters, you might call me Toby." He removed his cap, then ran a hand through his hair, causing his flattened curls to spring back to life.

Was he nervous about something?

"Very well, Toby." She sat with her hands folded.

"I wanted to talk to you about your plans now that Mr. Easton will be marrying and moving to Ottawa. Do you intend to go with them?"

Though he wasn't looking directly at her, Grace sensed his tension, waiting for her response.

"No, I don't."

"Has he not asked you to stay on as wee Christian's nanny?"

Grace shifted on the bench, averting her gaze to the baby on the blanket. How did she begin to explain the complex situation she now found herself in? "I imagine he wants Miss Carmichael to care for Christian once they"—her throat tightened—"once they're wed."

"I see," he said quietly.

Grace didn't dare look at him for fear her feelings about that would be visible on her face.

"So what do you intend to do then?"

"I suppose I'll have to look for another post."

"You won't be heading back to England?"

"Not right away. But if I can't find work, I'll have no choice."

He turned toward her on the bench. "I want you to know you have another option available."

Christian let out a squawk of frustration. He'd rolled onto his stomach and pushed up on his knees, but could neither go forward or backward. Before Grace could react, Toby reached over to scoop him up and handed him to her.

"Thank you. He gets impatient when he can't go where he wants." She gave a nervous laugh and settled the boy on her lap.

She half hoped Toby would forget what he'd been about to say.

But he turned back to her. "I've admired you since the first day I met you, Grace. And if you ever found yourself in need, I would be more than happy to do whatever I could to help."

She swallowed, not entirely sure what he was offering. "That's very thoughtful."

"What I'm trying to say, and doing a bad job of it, it seems, is that I'd be honored if you'd consider marrying me."

Her mouth fell open. The blood rushed to her cheeks. "I . . . I don't know what to say."

"Now that Collin is gone, there'd be plenty of room in the apartment for the two of us. I know it's not fancy, but we could fix the place up the way you like." He paused to catch his breath.

For a brief moment, Grace considered what it would mean to marry Toby. To have someone to share her burdens—both financial and emotional. To have a means to stay in this country where she could keep tabs on Christian, even from afar, on how well he was doing with Cecilia Carmichael as a stepmother.

But that wouldn't be fair to Toby because, though she liked him, her heart belonged to another.

She looked him in the eye. "I'm very flattered, Toby, truly I am. But I'm afraid I can't marry you."

He stared at her, the intense green of his eyes flashing like emeralds. "There's someone else." His flat tone indicated that he already knew the answer. That her refusal had only confirmed it.

She rose abruptly and laid Christian in the pram. "I'm sorry," she said as she grabbed the ball and blanket from the grass. "But I really must be getting back."

And before he could confront her about her feelings for Andrew, she set off down the path.

CHAPTER 34

November 12, 1918

The war is over at last—bittersweet news, to be sure. If this had happened a month ago, my Frank might still be alive. Mrs. Chamberlain has been most kind, allowing me to stay here until the baby is born. After that, only time will tell. Now that the fighting has ended, would you consider coming to visit? Please, Grace. I need you here.

On the eve of Andrew's wedding, Grace sat in the darkened nursery, rocking Christian in an attempt to get him back to sleep. He'd awakened, fretful and crying around nine o'clock, something he hadn't done since her early days of caring for him.

Perhaps he sensed the tension that coiled through every cell in her body, brought about in part by the knowledge that Cecilia and her family, along with thirty other guests, were gathered in the parlor below. They had just returned from the wedding rehearsal at the church, and Mr. Easton had gone all out with a lavishly catered meal for those who came back to Fairlawn afterward.

Grace closed her eyes and laid her cheek against Christian's head. His deep even breathing told her he'd fallen asleep at last. "What's going to happen to us, sweetheart? Both our lives are about to change drastically, whether we like it or not."

The thought of never seeing Andrew or Christian again created a giant hole in her chest, one that nothing seemed to fill, not her constant stream of prayers nor her extra time spent reading her Bible every day. Grace was waiting for some sign as to what the Lord expected of her next, but so far, the silence had been deafening.

Soon, her heart whispered. Something needed to happen soon.

Without warning, the door to the nursery opened. Grace's pulse skipped like a pebble over a pond. But it wasn't Andrew who entered.

Cecilia Carmichael strode in and stood staring at Grace. Her upswept hairdo showcased her long neck and patrician features, and a low-cut red dress hugged her figure.

"Miss Carmichael." Grace swallowed the dread rising in her throat. "Is there something I can do for you?" She kept her voice low so as not to disturb the boy's slumber.

"I'd like a word, if you please." The tone was more of a command than a request.

Grace nodded. On some level, she'd been expecting this confrontation, certain after the failed necklace debacle that Cecilia would want a final word at Grace's expense. "Let me put the baby down." She rose and laid Christian in the crib, thankful she'd become adept at transferring the boy without waking him. "Why don't we step into my room so we can talk more freely."

"Fine."

Once Cecilia had entered the room, Grace closed the connecting door. She smoothed a hand over her apron, conscious of the wrinkled fabric, then turned around, her head high. "What is it you wish to discuss?"

Cecilia wandered around the room, running her fingers over the footboard of the bed. "As you know, Andrew and I are to be married tomorrow."

A wrench of pain invaded Grace's heart. "I'm aware of that."

"I'm not sure if Andrew has been clear on the matter of your employment. But in case he hasn't, once we return from our honeymoon, your services will no longer be required."

Grace held herself perfectly still. She would not give the woman the satisfaction of reacting. "I assumed as much."

"Good. Then we understand each other."

Grace's heart thudded so hard she could barely hear above it. For Christian's sake, she had to swallow her pride and stay in control. "May I ask what your plans are for Christian?" she asked. "Will you get a new nanny?"

"That's really none of your concern, is it?" Cecilia crossed her arms, her blue eyes cold.

Grace lowered her head. This was it. Her punishment for claiming Andrew's attention for even a second. "I only ask because I care about that little boy very much. I pray you want to be a real mother to him and give him the love he deserves." With difficulty, she held on to her composure.

Cecilia moved to Grace's nightstand and picked up the Bible. "That's why we have nannies. Once we're settled in Ottawa, I will hire someone of a more suitable age in that role."

"A nanny can never fill the need for a mother's love. Won't you even try to be that for him?" Grace hated begging, but for Christian she would grovel if she had to.

Cecilia stared at her as though she'd sprouted horns. "That child is nothing to me. And if Andrew and I are blessed with children of our own, I certainly wouldn't want them thinking of him as a sibling."

The blood rushed from Grace's head, leaving her dizzy. "But Andrew loves Christian and plans to be a true father to him," she whispered.

"He'll get over it when he has children of his own. As soon as the boy's old enough, I intend to send him off to boarding school." She raised a brow. "I hear there are some wonderful ones in Europe."

The air backed up in Grace's lungs. She clenched her fingers around the wooden post to keep from screaming. "You know Andrew would never allow that."

Cecilia tossed the Bible back on the nightstand, her mocking laugh echoing in the room. "Haven't I already proven I can get

Andrew to do whatever I want? He shaved off his beard for the wedding, didn't he? It may take me a while, but I always get my way." Her features hardened. "And don't bother going to Andrew about this. He'll never take your word over mine."

Tremors attacked Grace's body, rushing from her spine down her limbs. The urge to fight back burned hotly in her chest, but for once she knew enough to rein in her reckless side. It would serve no purpose to further antagonize this woman. Christian would only end up paying the price.

"Now that we understand each other, I will be off. I have a big day ahead." Cecilia crossed to the door and paused to give her one last withering look. "If I were you, I'd catch the next boat back to England. There's nothing for you here."

The door slammed behind her.

Grace waited until the sound of her footsteps had faded before sinking onto the bed. Her whole body shook uncontrollably. She fisted her hands in the fabric of the quilt and squeezed as hard as she could. It was bad enough to know she'd lost Andrew, but that woman's plans for Christian made her physically sick.

Grace had been clinging to the slim possibility that despite Andrew's marriage, she could somehow manage to be a part of Christian's life. She'd hoped Virginia would be her ally in that regard, but now with her estrangement from the family, she couldn't be much help.

Grace would likely never see her nephew again.

A sob rose in her chest, and the tears she'd done so well at suppressing now leaked out from beneath her lids. She dropped to her knees at the side of her bed.

Dear Lord, I can't bear to lose Christian like everyone else in my life. What am I going to do now?

Early the next morning, after a sleepless night, Grace dressed and brushed her hair. The tidal wave of dread building inside her gave her some idea how a prisoner might feel on execution day. Grace laid down the brush and paused to stare at her lifeless reflection in the vanity mirror. Wooden eyes stared back at her, hollowed out from the misery of the previous twelve hours. Her whole world was crumbling around her, and she seemed powerless to stop it.

Today was Andrew's wedding day. Would he actually go through with this?

Of course he would. All he'd ever wanted was his father's approval, and to back out of this wedding—the one the papers were calling the union of Toronto's royal families—would not only devastate Mr. Easton, it would surely destroy his mother. In her already fragile condition, the woman would never withstand another shock like that. This wedding was the only thing that had finally coaxed her from the self-imposed exile of her bedroom.

Grace exhaled, trying to rid herself of the toxic emotions building inside her. She wound her hair into a knot and pinned it in place with a little more force than necessary. This pointless rumination would get her nowhere. She'd best keep herself busy and see to Christian.

When she stepped through the connecting door into the nursery, she froze. Andrew sat in the rocking chair, feeding Christian a bottle. The homey sight brought a shaft of pain to her heart.

Then, for one irrational moment, hope filled her lungs.

Maybe he'd changed his mind and was waiting here to tell her the good news. Waiting to declare his love for her and to tell her he wanted the three of them to be a family.

A bubble of anticipation expanded in her chest, making breathing nearly impossible.

Then Andrew lifted his head to look at her, his features carefully schooled.

Grace frowned. He seemed different somehow. A small gasp escaped. His jaw was bare! Then she remembered what Cecilia had said. He'd shaved off his beard at her request.

"Good morning," he said. "I took the liberty of getting Christian up earlier than usual since I won't see him later today." His gaze slid to the wall behind her. "I'll be gone for a week, and I wanted to spend a little time with him before I go."

Reality hit her like a cold ocean spray, shocking her out of her stupor. He wanted to see Christian before he got caught up in the wedding frenzy. She stiffened her shoulders, pressed her lips together, and remained standing by the door, unable to force any words from her dry throat.

He rose from the rocker and set the bottle on the dresser. With practiced ease, he rubbed the boy's back to induce a burp.

Nerves jumped in Grace's stomach as she gathered her courage. This was her last chance to speak to him alone. She couldn't pass up the opportunity to appeal to his senses—for Christian's sake, if nothing else.

"It's not too late, Andrew," she said softly. "You don't have to go through with this. Cecilia won't make you happy, and she certainly won't be a good mother to Christian."

He went still, then closed his eyes. Deep grooves formed around his mouth. When he opened his eyes again, they revealed a world of pain. "I have no choice. My parents are counting on this marriage, and I can't let them down. Not after the toll Virginia's elopement has taken." He set Christian on the carpet near a basket of toys. The boy immediately made a grab for his favorite wooden train.

Grace squeezed her hands into fists as she crossed the room. "Doesn't your father care about your happiness? About his grandson's well-being?" Her voice was becoming shrill, but she didn't care. She had to get through to him. To the part deep inside that loved this little boy more than even his father's approval.

"Of course he does. He wants what's best for everyone, and he believes this is it."

"Best for whom? This marriage certainly isn't what's best for Christian." Unable to tamp back her growing frustration, she closed the gap between them. "Cecilia wants to cut me out of his life for good. Are you going to allow her do that?"

Misery swept over his features. "Grace, I—"

"Do you know she intends to ship Christian off to boarding

school as soon as he's old enough? That she will never consider him as one of your children? She told me so last night and appeared to take great delight in delivering the news."

A muscle twitched in his jaw. "You know I'd never allow that. When the time comes, I'll handle Cecilia."

"Really? Like you've been able to handle her so far?" She pointed to his naked chin. "You couldn't even manage to keep your beard. You always end up giving in . . . to everyone." She sucked in a shaky breath. It wouldn't do to insult him or challenge his pride. That would only make him dig in his heels even more.

He pushed his hands through his hair, then paced to the window and back. "I have a duty to my family. I cannot go back on my word." His eyes met hers, and his expression softened. "For a very brief while, I imagined I could, but after the pain my parents have been through, I realized . . . I simply can't." His shoulders drooped. "I guess I'm not as brave as you imagined." Regret and sorrow swirled through the blue depths of his eyes.

She held his gaze for several seconds, absorbing the pain and disillusionment, then shook her head. Why had she ever imagined he'd choose her? They'd shared some meaningful conversations and a few stolen kisses in the moonlight. At no time had he ever promised more.

She squared her shoulders, mentally erecting a wall to shield herself from any further pain he might inflict.

"I've provided a month's wages for you," he continued, "as well as a letter of reference. I've left them on Father's desk. You shouldn't have any trouble finding another job."

He came toward her then, close enough for her to catch the scent of his aftershave. "I want you to know that I've forgiven you, Grace. Once I got over my anger, I was finally able to understand why you had to lie, and I can't really blame you for it. " He stared at her, holding her in place with just his eyes. As much as she wanted to, she couldn't seem to make herself move away.

"I pray that one day you'll be able to forgive me too." Slowly, he reached out and placed his palm against her cheek.

She closed her eyes against the heat of his fingers on her skin. Against the exquisite torture of his touch. Then he removed his hand and the warmth vanished.

"What will you do when you leave here?" he asked sadly.

With immense effort, she pushed back all her feelings and allowed a cold detachment to settle over her before she opened her eyes. "Actually, your loyalty to your family has reminded me of a promise I made to my mother before I left home. A promise I intend to keep."

"So, you'll go back to England then?" The defeat in his tone threatened to unravel her carefully held composure.

"Yes."

He froze for a split second, then nodded. "It's probably for the best." His eyes held her captive, regret alive in their depths. "Good-bye, Grace. I wish you every happiness for the future."

She opened her mouth to respond, but the words lodged in her throat. To wish him the same would be an exercise in futility, for she knew with every fiber of her being that he would never be happy with Cecilia.

In the doorway, he gave her a final lingering look, and then he was gone.

CHAPTER 35

December 7, 1918
Dearest Grace,

How my heart bursts with joy and sorrow in equal measure. Two days ago, I gave birth to a son. A beautiful baby boy who will never know his father. I endured eighteen hours of labor, but when the midwife put him in my arms, it all became worthwhile. Never have I felt such overwhelming love. I named him Christian Francis—Christian in honor of the faith that sustains me—and Francis after his father. If only Frank could be here to meet his son.

While the entire household was in an uproar with preparations for the wedding, Grace sat numbly in the rocking chair, watching Christian play with his toys on the rug, and tried not to imagine Andrew dressing for his bride. Her stomach twisted every time she thought of him shaving off his beard to please Cecilia and not wearing his glasses for the same reason.

Did he not see that he was denying his true self by marrying her?

And what did that mean for Christian?

Grace no longer held any illusion that Andrew would be able to keep Cecilia from going through with her plans for the boy. The woman was right about her ability to get her own way, even if she had to resort to underhanded tactics to achieve it. Somehow Cecilia would convince Andrew that boarding school was best for Christian.

The more Grace thought about it, the more certain she became that for the sake of Christian's well-being, she had to take action. And it would have to be today when everyone was too distracted to notice the nanny and her ward.

By 10:40, the house would be empty, since even the servants were going to the cathedral to watch the wedding. The ceremony would take about an hour, at which time the staff would return to Fairlawn and resume their workday, while the other guests attended the wedding reception in the ballroom of the Easton Towers Hotel.

By then, Grace and Christian would be gone.

Grace bided her time until Christian went down for a nap, then she pulled a small valise from the top shelf of the closet. With shaking hands, she filled it with as much of the baby's things as it could contain and stored it back in the closet.

Leaving the connecting door open, Grace gathered her own things, most of which she had already packed in her suitcase, knowing she would be leaving Fairlawn in the near future. For once she was grateful for so few belongings.

She'd just returned to the nursery when the door opened, and Serena entered.

She observed Grace's attire with a frown. "Mrs. Easton sent me to see if you'd be bringing Christian to the church."

With effort, Grace kept her expression neutral. She'd rather poke a fork into her eye than witness Andrew pledge his life to another woman, but Mrs. Easton didn't know that. "Christian has been fussy all night. He has a bit of a fever and may be teething. I think it's best to keep him home."

Serena hesitated in the doorway. "Very well. I'll let her know."

"Thank you, Serena. Enjoy the wedding." How Grace managed to fib so smoothly and then smile about it, she had no idea. But she was banking on the fact that no one would challenge her decision an hour before the wedding.

She was right. No one else bothered her, and finally, after the flurry of footsteps in the hall died away, the main door slammed shut. Grace waited a few seconds, then crossed the hall to the guest room and peered out the window that overlooked the front of the house. From there, she watched the entourage leave the property. When everyone had departed, she waited another ten minutes in case someone had forgotten something, and then returned to her room.

She removed her apron, folded it and laid it neatly on the bed, then pinned her straw hat in place. As she donned her wrap, she took one last look around the room she'd lived in for the past several months before collecting her valise and returning to the nursery. Thanking her good fortune that Christian had awakened from his nap in a good humor, she picked him out of the crib, grabbed his small bag, and checked the room for anything she might have forgotten. The photo of Rose and Frank on their wedding day stared back at her.

"I'm doing this for you, Rose," she whispered.

On impulse, she grabbed the picture and stuffed it in the satchel she wore over her shoulder. A lump rose in her throat. How she would miss this room, where she'd experienced such a sense of peace and love. With a last fortifying breath, she pushed back any traces of regret. There was no point in dwelling on what could never be.

"Ready for an adventure, sweetheart?" She kissed Christian's cheek and walked out of the nursery for the last time.

Grace chose the rear staircase on the off chance that someone might return. Her footsteps echoed in the empty stairway, making her painfully aware they were alone in the house. She wished she'd had the chance to say good-bye to Mrs. Hopkins, who had been so kind to her. She would have liked to have seen Mrs. Easton too, but how could she face the woman, knowing she was taking away her grandchild—the only reminder of her son?

Think about Cecilia, Grace. And the horrible life she has planned for Christian. You're doing this for him and for Rose. Remember that.

Before leaving, there was one more thing she needed to do. On tiptoe, she made her way down the corridor leading to the library. The loud ticking of the grandfather clock reverberated through the main floor. Grace entered the room, crossed quickly to Mr. Easton's desk, and scanned the neat desktop. As Andrew had promised, an envelope bearing her name sat in plain view, bulging with her last wages and what she expected was likely a bonus. She stuffed it into her satchel and headed to the side entrance. Once outside, she inhaled the now familiar scent of roses that drifted over from the garden, one she would forever associate with Fairlawn and with Andrew.

Christian was already becoming heavy in her arms. How she wished she could take the pram, but it would only end up being a hindrance, another way for them to track her down.

"Grace! Why are you not at the church?" Toby's loud voice rang out behind her.

She froze. Cold chills shot through her body. What was he doing here? He was supposed to be outside the church, waiting to drive the Eastons to the reception.

She pasted on a smile as she turned, willing her knees not to shake. "Christian is a little cranky. I didn't think they needed a wailing baby to interrupt the ceremony."

Toby came closer, frowning. "He looks happy enough now. I could drive you over if you'd like." He seemed to be studying her. Did he suspect something?

Panic clutched at Grace's throat. She didn't have time to waste. If she missed the eleven o'clock streetcar, she'd have to wait thirty minutes for the next one. "Thank you, but no. I'm going to take him for a walk. The fresh air always makes him feel better."

There was no way around it now. She'd have to take the pram.

Toby followed her over to where the baby carriage was parked. "I could come with you. I don't have to be back to the church for a while."

"I don't think that's a good idea, Toby." She laid Christian in the pram and arranged the blankets over him, then she placed the bags in the boot of the pram. She turned to face him. "If you'll excuse me." Everything depended on her getting rid of him as soon as possible.

He stared at her satchel and the other cases she'd stowed in the pram. "If you're just going for a walk, why do you have so many bags?"

Bile rose in the back of her throat. She tried to appear nonchalant. "I'm going to visit Mrs. Chamberlain, and I thought I'd bring some of the things I won't be needing over to the boardinghouse. Less to move later on."

"That's a long way away." Suspicion laced his words.

Of course he would remember driving her there once before. Her hands shook as she lifted the brake and pulled the carriage out onto the walkway. "A nice long walk is exactly what I need today."

"It's Andrew, isn't it? He's the one you're in love with."

Grace stilled, her heart battering her rib cage. If Toby had figured it out, did everyone else know as well? She raised her eyes to his, neither confirming nor denying his claim.

He stared at her for a second, then nodded. "I thought so. No wonder you don't want to go to the church."

At the pity on his face, the emotions she'd worked so hard to repress swirled through her chest. "I really need to get going."

His hand clamped down on her arm. "Don't do anything foolish, Grace. Something you can't take back." His green eyes bore into hers.

She jerked her arm away from him. "Please forget you ever saw me, Toby. It will be better for everyone that way."

Blinking hard, she pushed the pram into motion and headed down the drive at a fast clip. Before she passed through the iron gates, she peered over her shoulder.

Toby stood motionless where she'd left him, watching her go.

Andrew paced the floor of the anteroom in the cathedral, his nerves stretched to a thin line. His two work colleagues, who would serve as groomsmen, laughed at something on the far side of the room. Watching them, Andrew had never felt more alone. His thoughts turned to Ginny. How he missed her wit, her quirky sense of humor, her unwavering support. Despite the residual anger at what she'd done, Andrew wished she could be here to share his wedding day. What words of wisdom would she have given him to help him through these last few minutes before he committed his life to a woman he didn't love?

A humorless laugh rose in his chest, but he quickly stifled it. Neither she nor Frank would ever have found themselves in such a position. They had married the people they loved, despite the obstacles in their way.

Too bad Andrew didn't have that luxury.

His father poked his head inside the door. "Everything under control in here?"

As Andrew's best man, Father was keeping busy by making sure all the details on the groom's side were handled.

"We're fine. Is the church filling up?"

"Filled to the rafters." His father beamed. "According to the society page in the *Star*, this will be the wedding of the season. After Virginia's elopement, I never thought the press would report anything favorable about us again, but fortunately, these events sell newspapers. We must remember to let them take your photograph after the ceremony."

Andrew attempted a smile, but couldn't quite manage it. Still, he was grateful he had given his parents this day of happiness. After the fiasco with Virginia, he'd worried that his father's heart might give out under the strain, and that his mother might never leave her room.

"I'll go and check on your mother again, and then it will be time to start. The car arrived with Cecilia and her parents a few minutes ago."

Andrew's stomach churned. "I'm ready whenever she is."

Liar.

He turned to the small rectangular window that overlooked a

side garden. Too small to provide any manner of escape. Through a clear section of the refracted glass, he could see an array of rosebushes that lined the fence. Immediately, an image of Grace in the garden came to his mind with haunting clarity—the way she'd smiled as she held the rose petals to her nose. The way the moonlight had cast its spell over her flawless features. The way she'd filled his world with joy.

A dull ache radiated out from his chest. *I'm doing the right thing, aren't I, Lord? Honoring my father and mother?*

Then why did he feel so wretched?

A knock sounded on the outer door, jarring him from his foolish memories.

"Come in."

Toby McDonald stepped inside. He pulled off his chauffeur's cap and ran his fingers around the brim, his eyes darting around the room. "Excuse me, Mr. Easton. Could I have a brief word with you?"

Andrew frowned. "What could be so important that you would interrupt me minutes before I'm to be married?"

McDonald glanced at the two other men. "It's a personal matter, sir."

"Then I suggest it can wait for a more appropriate time. Or you can take it up with my father while I'm on my honeymoon." Anger churned like acid in his gut. He strode back to the window.

"It's about Miss Foley."

Andrew stiffened, each vertebrae solidifying to send pain shooting through his body. He couldn't bear to talk about Grace today.

"You should know that she's in love with you," he said quietly.

Andrew jerked his head around. He opened his mouth to speak, but nothing came out. How the devil could Toby know that? And even if it were true, it was much too late now.

"That's not all," Toby went on. "I have some important information that I need to tell you in private."

Andrew glared at the man. The last thing he needed right now was any more drama.

"Please. Two minutes is all I'm asking."

Andrew blasted out a breath. "Charlie, Brent, could you give us a minute?"

When the two had left the room, he turned to the chauffeur. "Spit it out."

Toby gripped his cap, wetting his lips before he began. "You've a right to know the type of woman you're about to marry."

"How would you know anything about Cecilia? You've never even spoken to the woman."

"Oh, but I have. On the night of Mrs. Easton's birthday, Miss Carmichael approached me in the kitchen. Said she had a job for me." He paused. "She offered me a sizable amount of money to seduce Grace. She wanted to ruin Grace's character so she'd be fired."

Andrew's jaw fell open, his brain grasping to process what he'd said. "I don't believe you."

"What reason would I have to lie?" Toby's eyes were steely. "When I refused her offer, she was furious. But then she said she'd figure out another way to do it. Whatever that meant."

Andrew clenched his back teeth together. His mind flew to the incident with the necklace in Grace's room. Had that been her alternate plan when Toby wouldn't cooperate? Celia's tears and pleadings had convinced Andrew she'd made a mistake, but had it all been an act just to mollify him?

"If you're in love with Grace too," Toby continued, "I thought you should have the chance to do something about it before it's too late."

Andrew threw out his hands in exasperation. "It *is* too late. There are five hundred people in that church waiting to witness my marriage."

"So rather than face embarrassment, you'd marry a woman who could be that deliberately cruel to another person?" Toby gave him a look of disgust, then rammed his cap back on his head. "Probably just as well. You don't deserve someone as fine as Grace."

He stalked toward the door, opened it, and then stopped. Slowly he turned, his brow wreathed in a frown. "I don't know why I'm bothering to tell you this, but I ran into Grace and the baby outside Fairlawn. She had two bags stored in the pram and was acting very nervous. I'm not sure what's going on, but don't say I didn't warn you." Seconds later, the door slammed behind him.

Andrew stood alone in the center of the anteroom, a maelstrom of emotion sweeping through him. This was a nightmare. An unmitigated disaster. He'd always known Cecilia was flighty and vain, but was she as cold and calculating as Toby implied?

Do you know she intends to ship Christian off to boarding school as soon as he's old enough? That she will never consider him as one of your children? She told me so last night and appeared to take great delight in delivering the news.

Andrew hadn't taken Grace's accusation seriously, but now he realized Cecilia wasn't just issuing idle threats. She most likely intended to follow through with her plan, which meant she'd been lying to him all along about trying to forge a bond with the boy. How could he stand at the altar before God and pledge his life to such a lying, manipulative person? Worse yet, how could he subject Christian to her hatefulness? The idea literally turned his stomach.

And now Toby said Grace had her bags stowed in the baby carriage. Surely she would never do something like . . .

Andrew bolted to the door, panic flowing through him like a surge of electricity. He ran into the vestibule, his glance falling briefly on the people milling about, then he raced out the front door, praying Toby hadn't left.

The chauffeur sat in the car in front of the church.

Andrew ignored the greetings the guests called out to him and jumped into the passenger seat. "Take me to Grace."

CHAPTER 36

Fifteen minutes later, Andrew ran into the nursery, his lungs near bursting. Before blindly scouring the city streets, he decided to check the house first, in case Grace had come back.

But she wasn't there, and the crib was empty.

Toby had said they were about to go for a walk when he'd seen them. Yet it was an unusual time of day. They normally went to the park in the afternoon.

An uncomfortable feeling niggled at Andrew's subconscious. Something was different. He scanned the room. Frank and Rose's wedding picture was gone. Had the maid moved it? Or perhaps broken the glass?

His gaze fell on the basket by the rocking chair, the one that held the quilt Grace was sewing. All the fabric was gone. Andrew's breathing grew raspy. He opened the dresser drawers. Nothing seemed amiss, except maybe they weren't as full as usual.

Still . . .

He knocked on the door to Grace's room and when there was no response, pushed it open. The room was dim, the drapes pulled across the window. Why hadn't Grace opened them? He did so now and looked around the room. Instantly, he noticed a difference. Grace's Bible was missing from her nightstand. The vanity top sat bare, her hairbrush and pins strangely absent. Andrew opened the closet, trepidation clawing up his spine.

Empty!

He moved to the dresser and yanked open the drawers. They had been cleared out completely. Except for the apron on the bed, the room held no evidence Grace had ever lived here.

Andrew's heart beat too fast in his chest.

Grace was gone. Surely, she wouldn't . . .

No. She would never do that to him. To his mother.

He raced out of the room and down the stairs. The echo of his footsteps in the eerie silence reminded him that everyone was at the church. Surely there had to be one staff member left to manage things.

He rushed into the kitchen, where a young maid stood at the sink.

"Have you seen Miss Foley or Master Christian?" he shouted, certain he must resemble a wild-eyed fanatic.

"No, sir. They haven't come down here."

He gulped in a breath, trying to slow his mind. He needed to think logically. "If she returns, ask her to wait in the parlor for me."

"But, sir, aren't you supposed to be getting married now?"

He didn't bother to reply. Before the baffled girl could ask him anything else, he ran back up a flight of stairs and out the side door. He knew the route Grace usually took on her outings. He'd follow it and probably find them sitting in the park enjoying the day.

There had to be a perfectly good explanation why Grace's things were gone.

He ran down the street and headed toward the park, scanning all the pedestrians as he went. Up ahead, a woman pushed a baby carriage.

Grace! Waves of relief flooded his system. It had been innocent after all.

Andrew jogged around a couple strolling on the sidewalk and ran up behind her, grasping her elbow. "Grace. Thank goodness. I've been looking—"

The woman turned, and Andrew's mouth fell open.

She yanked her arm free. "I think you have the wrong person, sir."

Andrew peered into the carriage at a baby in a pink bonnet.

The blood pounded in his ears. "I-I'm terribly sorry. I thought you were someone else."

The woman nodded and continued on her way.

Andrew just stood there, attempting to regulate his breathing and pull himself together, as people pushed by him. Then, with grim determination, he returned to his search.

As he neared the streetcar stop, something caught his attention. Andrew slowed, his heart rolling in his chest. A familiar handle protruded from the greenery. Christian's pram had been purposely shoved between the bushes.

Andrew reached inside and rifled through the blankets. Empty.

He blew out a ragged breath, his lungs constricting. There was no denying it now.

Grace had taken Christian and in all likelihood was headed to England.

He bent over the handle of the pram, chills and heat rushing through him.

Lord, I need your help. How am I ever going to find them now?

Andrew pulled his car to a stop outside the cathedral, not caring if he blocked anyone else's. He wouldn't be here long. Only long enough to let his parents know what had happened and explain to Cecilia why he had to leave. Despite his disillusionment with her, he owed her that much at least.

Andrew rushed into the vestibule, ignoring the curious looks of the people standing around.

The first person he saw was his father heading toward him. "Andrew, thank God. We've been worried sick."

"I'm sorry, Father. I'm afraid I have unfortunate news." He slowed his pace only slightly. "Christian is missing. I'm going in search of him, but first I have to speak to Cecilia."

"What do you mean missing?" His father's eyes bulged.

Andrew stopped outside the women's anteroom. "I'll explain later. Time is of the essence."

He rapped once and stepped inside without waiting for an answer.

The women gasped. One of them leapt up from her chair. "He's here, Celia! I told you he would never desert you."

Andrew focused on his bride. She looked like a true princess, from the tiara on her head to the waves of satin and lace that surrounded her slender frame.

"Andrew. What are you doing? You can't see me before the ceremony." For once her blue eyes held no guile, no secrets—just confusion and yes, fear.

"I need to talk to you. It's urgent." He turned to the other girls. "Could you give us some privacy, please?"

The women scurried from the room. Andrew could only imagine the gossip that must be flying among the guests.

Cecilia rose from her seat. "You're scaring me, Andrew. Is someone unwell?"

"No, at least I don't think so." An idea dawned that maybe Christian had fallen ill again and Grace had taken him to the hospital. That might explain their absence. He'd check there first. "Christian is missing."

"How do you know that?"

"I don't have time to explain. It's possible Grace has taken him. All her things are gone too. I have to find them before she leaves the country."

Celia's mouth fell open. "Do not tell me you're planning to leave me here." Her bottom lip trembled.

"I'm sorry. . . ." Guilt twisted his insides.

"No, this is not happening." She marched over and jabbed a finger at him. "Let the authorities handle it while we go on with the wedding."

He threw out his hands. "I can't just stand at the altar and pretend nothing's wrong. I have to look for him."

Her nostrils flared, red patches of anger staining her cheeks. "Is it really the baby, or are you more upset that Grace is gone?"

Guilt and frustration bubbled up, because he couldn't totally deny her accusation. Still, it was Christian he cared about most. "Can't you understand that in every way that matters, I consider Christian my son?"

"He's not your son." Her shrill voice echoed through the chamber, loud enough to be heard outside, he was certain. "He's the son of that English whore and your faithless brother."

The bitterness of her words struck him as hard as a slap. "Is that why you wanted no part of him? You blame an innocent child for something he had nothing to do with?" It all made sense. Why she wouldn't even attempt to bond with Christian.

Her chin darted upward. "That doesn't matter. Right now, we have five hundred people out there waiting for us. So it comes down to this. What do you choose to do, Andrew? Marry me—or give up everything to run after the nanny and that child?"

The smug look on her face indicated she thought she knew his answer. She didn't realize that she'd bluffed and lost.

"I'm sorry, Celia. But if you force me to choose between you and Christian"—he shook his head—"I choose Christian."

She gasped, and tears pooled in her eyes.

Knowing there was nothing he could say to fix the situation, he pulled the door open.

A jumble of wide-eyed stares flashed before him.

"I'm terribly sorry," he said to no one in particular, "but due to a family emergency, I'm afraid I have to cancel the wedding." Over the heads of the guests, Andrew met his father's agonized gaze. "Could someone please notify the authorities? I believe my nephew has been kidnapped."

CHAPTER 37

January 5, 1919

Motherhood is hard, Grace, harder than I ever imagined. The baby cries for hours at a time. I feel like such a failure. What kind of mother can't comfort her own child? The noise is disturbing the other tenants at Mrs. Chamberlain's. I fear I must find somewhere else to live, and a means of making a living. If I could, I'd come home to England. But even if I had the money, an ocean voyage is extremely dangerous for an infant. I can't risk Christian's health. I beg you, Grace, please come to Canada. We need you.

"Are you sure this is the right address?" Grace peered out the window of the taxi cab at the tall building across the street.

"Yes, ma'am. Sixty-nine Yonge Street. The Canadian Pacific building."

"I thought this was the telegraph office." She rechecked the address on the business card Ian Miller had given her months ago. The information matched the number on the sign.

Grace's stomach fluttered at the risk she was taking, coming here in the hopes that Ian had meant what he said about helping her if she ever needed it.

"The telegraph office is on the second floor." The cab driver grinned over his shoulder. "Handy thing, actually. You can buy your train ticket on the first floor and go upstairs to send your telegram right after."

"Handy indeed." Grace's heart picked up speed. That was perfect. She'd come to ask Ian's assistance in obtaining a train ticket for her. He wouldn't even have to leave the building to do so—if he was working today. Being a Saturday, she wasn't sure he would be.

"Do you know if the telegraph office is open?" She fished for money in her handbag.

"I believe so. Would you like me to wait for you, just in case?"

Grace shifted Christian on her lap as he bounced and squirmed. "No, thank you." She passed the driver the bills to pay her fare and included a nice tip.

He pocketed the money and jumped out of the car. "Let me help you with those bags."

He hefted them out of the back seat while Grace got out with the baby. Then they crossed the street and the man accompanied her inside the main door.

"Thank you," she said as he set the bags down. "You're very kind."

"No trouble at all, ma'am." He tipped his cap. "Good luck with sending your telegram."

She was about to correct him, but thought the better of it. Instead she thanked him again, then waited until he'd gone before looking around in awe at the two-story marble lobby. At the far side, several people stood in line at the ticket office. Grace could buy her own ticket, but hoping to stay as inconspicuous as possible, she'd decided that it would be better for Ian to purchase one on her behalf. That way, if anyone questioned the ticket sellers, they wouldn't remember a woman and baby.

The large brass clock on the wall chimed quarter past the hour, startling her. Andrew's wedding would have started by now. She couldn't waste any more time. She picked up her bags, shifted Christian on her hip and walked to the elevator. A directory on the wall indicated the telegraph office was indeed located on the next floor. She took a deep breath as the elevator opened and stepped inside.

A man in a suit got on with her. He smiled. "Let me help you with those bags. You have your hands full with that little one."

"I'm only going up one floor," she protested, though Christian was growing heavier in her arms.

"So am I. I work in the office there."

Seeing no way to refuse, she simply smiled. "Thank you then."

The elevator soon stopped and the doors opened. She stepped out and the man followed.

"Do you by any chance know a Mr. Miller who works here?"

"I do indeed. His office is right next to mine."

"Would he be in today?"

"Knowing Ian, I imagine so. Follow me."

Still carrying her bags, he led her down a long corridor to an open door. He knocked and entered without waiting for an answer.

Grace's palms were damp, and she was very glad for the gloves she was wearing. What would Mr. Miller think of her showing up unannounced at his workplace? But he had insisted that if she ever needed help with anything to call on him.

"Ian, you have a visitor. A mighty pretty one at that." The man's laughter boomed through the hallway.

Heat rushed in Grace's cheeks, but she held her head up.

Seconds later, Mr. Miller came into the hall. He wore a striped shirt and bow tie, and a pair of red suspenders held up his pants. A quizzical smile lit his face when he saw her. "Miss Abernathy! This is an unexpected pleasure." He glanced at the baby and frowned. "What brings you by?"

She glanced at the man behind Ian, who had deposited her bags on the floor. "May we speak in private?" she asked.

"Of course." He turned around. "Thanks, Richard. I'll handle it from here."

Richard nodded at Grace. "Have a pleasant day, ma'am."

"Please come in." Ian gestured for her to enter his small office, which held a desk and two chairs. "And who is this young man?" he asked as he plucked his jacket from the chair and slipped it on.

"This is my nephew, Christian." Grace took a seat and began to undo the ties of the baby's bonnet. "Do you remember me telling you about my sister, the one I came to Canada to see?"

Ian's face clouded. "The one who had recently passed away."

"Yes. Well, this is her son."

He took a seat behind the desk, still watching her with a curious expression. He glanced at the bags inside the door and back at the baby. "It looks as though you're going somewhere. Is that why you're here? You need to send a telegram?"

Grace swallowed and pasted a smile on her face, praying he wouldn't detect her heart nearly thumping out of her chest. "Actually I was hoping to take you up on your offer."

"My offer?"

"You said if I ever needed help with anything to call on you. Well, I really need your help now."

An hour later, Grace paced the small office, bouncing Christian on her shoulder. He'd grown tired and fussy, and she was about at her wits' end. If Ian didn't return soon with the tickets and the food he'd promised to get for her, she doubted she'd be able to keep the child from screeching.

"Shh, sweetheart. I promise this is only temporary. Once we get through this, everything will be fine."

She tried giving him a bottle, but with nowhere to heat it, he'd objected to the cold milk. She hoped Ian would be able to procure something the baby could eat, some applesauce or pudding perhaps. Then, as soon as he got back, she would either head right to the train station or if the earliest train to New York wasn't leaving until tomorrow, she'd find a room for the night and set out in the morning.

Fortunately, Ian seemed to accept her story that the boy's family had allowed her to take him on a trip and hadn't questioned her overly about why she was heading to New York. She'd told him that she'd always wanted to see the Statue of Liberty and the Brooklyn Bridge, which in itself was a true statement. She simply left off the part about catching a steamship to England once she got there.

She figured that by sailing from New York instead of Halifax, the way she'd arrived, she might throw the Eastons—and whoever else might be looking for her—off her trail.

Tension screamed in her shoulders and neck. This small space was feeling more like a prison cell by the moment. But would a ship cabin be any better? How would she keep an active baby occupied, fed, and happy during an entire ocean voyage? Her stomach twisted. She really hadn't thought this plan through. Once again, she'd reacted in the panic of the moment and let her impulsive nature take over.

The door opened, and Ian entered the office. Her immediate relief was short-lived because of the bleak expression on his face.

"Were you not able to get the ticket?" she asked.

He set a grocery bag on the desk, then turned to look at her. "Please forgive me, Grace, but you were acting so strange, I felt something was wrong. So I brought someone to speak with you."

Chills broke out over Grace's body. Surely he hadn't contacted the police?

"Hello, Grace." Reverend Burke removed his hat as he entered the office. "Ian feels you might be in some sort of trouble and asked me to come."

She whirled to face Ian. "I trusted you," she hissed. "Why wouldn't you help me like you promised?"

"I'm sorry." His features were etched in misery. "I'll let you two have some privacy." He shot the minister a troubled look, then walked out and closed the door behind him.

Grace's whole body began to shake. Blood pounded at her temples, giving her an instant headache.

Reverend Burke lifted the baby from her arms. "Have a seat, dear."

With her legs so unsteady, she had little choice but to comply.

"Ian tells me you're taking a trip." Reverend Burke's brows rose in question as he sat down with Christian.

"That's right." She lifted her chin, still unwilling to admit defeat. "I'm bringing Christian home to Mum."

"Without the permission of the boy's guardian, I take it." He studied her with no hint of judgment, only curiosity.

Her shoulders slumped, as the full magnitude of her actions hit home. "Yes."

"The last I heard from Harriet, it seemed things were going well at the Eastons'. What brought you to this point?"

She drew in a shuddering breath and released it. "Andrew is getting married today to a woman who is cruel and selfish. Last night, she told me she would ship Christian off to boarding school as soon as he was old enough. That she would never be a mother to him." She gripped her hands together. "I couldn't let that happen. Not when I can give him all the love he deserves." Tears blurred her vision, but she held them back.

"Tell me, Grace, what do you think it means to really love someone?"

She glanced over at him, then back at her lap. "I suppose it means you want the best for them. That you put their life and their happiness ahead of your own." Something no one except Peter had ever done for her.

"And is that what you're doing for Christian?" he asked gently.

"Of course." She bristled at his insinuation that she was being selfish. "I'm doing this for him."

"But have you thought about what his life will be like with you? I gather money isn't too flush back home. How will you support the child? Your mother is too ill to care for him. Who will watch him while you work?"

Grace closed her eyes. She'd never really thought past the moment when she would place Christian into her mother's arms, at last fulfilling her promise, releasing her from her guilt. Had she really been putting Christian first or had her actions been fueled by her own selfish need for her mother's absolution?

"There's something else to consider." Reverend Burke shifted the boy on his lap, bouncing him lightly. "Christian is an Easton, heir to a grand fortune. Despite the stepmother you speak of, he would have the best possible education and unlimited opportunities to do whatever he wanted with his life. Plus, you'd be denying Andrew the chance to raise the child, as well as depriving Christian's grandparents of their only grandchild."

A sob escaped Grace's dry throat. She'd done all she could not to picture Andrew and his family's pain at learning of Christian's disappearance. Would this be the final straw that pushed Mrs. Easton over the edge?

"I'm also sure I don't need to remind you," Reverend Burke said gently, "that you're about to commit a serious crime."

She shook her head, then bit her lip to stop the tremors.

"Soon the authorities will be looking for you. They'll be checking the train stations and bus depots. It will be hard to stay unnoticed, carrying your bags and an infant. And asking Ian to help you would make him guilty by association. I don't think you'd want to put him in that type of position, would you?"

Her stomach roiled. Once again, her reckless actions had created chaos. She'd put Christian and two other dear people in possible jeopardy, all because of her impulsiveness. Instead of raising her nephew, she could be facing a long prison sentence. Defeat erased the last trace of her courage. "I only wanted to bring Mum her grandson. So she'd finally forgive me." She dropped her face into her hands, unable to stop the tide of emotions sweeping through her. All the fear, anger, and uncertainty of the last twenty-four hours released in a flood of tears.

Reverend Burke moved his chair closer and draped an arm around her shaking shoulders. "There now, child. You let it all out."

She leaned into him as she wept, relishing his warmth and the homey smell of pipe tobacco, accepting the comfort she didn't deserve.

When her tears subsided at last, the minister pressed a handkerchief into her hand. "I've given you a lot to think about, Grace. I'll be praying that the Lord gives you the courage to do the right thing." He rose and handed her back the baby with a meaningful look.

As she stared into Christian's blue eyes, so innocent and trusting, doubts rose up to plague her. Was she really being fair to the child? Or would her actions cause him more harm than good?

Grace sucked in a quick breath, sudden certainty flooding her every cell. "Thank you, Reverend, but I don't need any more time to think. What I do need is your help to bring Christian home."

A wide smile split his face, easing the lines of worry. "I'd be more than happy to take you."

Grace stood with the baby and straightened her spine. "But first, if you don't mind, I need a moment with Ian. I owe him a huge apology for my selfish actions." She only hoped Ian would forgive her. The way her life was unraveling, she couldn't afford to lose another friend.

"Certainly." The minister bent to pick up her bags. "I'll wait for you in the lobby."

His easy acceptance of her transgressions without judgment or criticism humbled her. She laid a hand on his arm. "Thank you for helping me come to my senses before it was too late."

"All part of the job, my dear." He winked at her. "I'll send Ian in to see you."

Seated in the library, Andrew stared at the flames in the hearth. A log shifted, sending embers shooting outward. Even in the summer, Father always liked to keep a fire going in here.

Andrew raised his aching feet onto the footstool in front of him. He'd just returned from filing a report on his missing ward at the police station. It was a last resort after looking everywhere he could possibly think of. He'd searched the hospitals, churches, boardinghouses, bus depots, and the train station. He had no idea where to look next, and so he had decided to bring the police in to track Grace down.

Unfortunately, they hadn't taken the situation very seriously, convinced that the nanny had just taken the child on an outing and would bring him home at the end of the day. Andrew had finally lost his temper with the constable in charge, but at least now they seemed to be paying more attention.

Andrew scraped a hand over his lightly-stubbled jaw. He still wasn't used to not having his beard—felt naked without it. Why had he ever given in to Cecilia's demand to shave it off? It would ruin the wedding photograph, she'd said. Of course she cared more about the appearance of perfection than she did about him. Cecilia always did things to suit herself, never considering anyone else's feelings.

Just like Grace, as it turned out.

Andrew scowled at the ashes in the grate. The acrid smell of burned wood filled his nostrils. He'd thought Grace was different, but in the end, she was no better than Celia—worse, in fact. His mood darkened further. How could she take Christian like that? Ripping him from the arms of his family, away from everyone who loved him?

Away from him.

He pushed out of his chair to pace the area rug. Andrew had gone back for a second time to Mrs. Chamberlain's boardinghouse, hoping that although the woman hadn't seen Grace that morning, perhaps later in the day Grace might have made contact. She couldn't simply disappear, not with an infant in tow. Yet Mrs. Chamberlain swore she'd had no word from Grace at all. The worry in her eyes made Andrew believe she was telling the truth.

Where would Grace have gone?

Andrew rubbed his stiff neck muscles to no avail. Because no matter what he did, he couldn't erase the magnitude of his failures. Despite all his efforts, all his sacrifices, he'd failed his father on every level possible.

He'd failed to keep his family intact. Failed to keep Christian safe. Failed to guard his heart against a woman who could so easily betray him.

Why, God? Why has this happened?

The library door opened, and his father entered.

Andrew stifled a groan. He did not need a lecture right now, nor additional guilt for not going through with the wedding. Marrying Cecilia was the last thing on his mind. All he could think of was getting Christian back.

His father walked to the table in the corner and lifted the decanter of brandy. He poured a good amount into a crystal tumbler and swallowed it in one shot, banging the glass on the table when he finished. "This is one devil of a mess, Andrew." He narrowed his eyes. "Of all my children, I never expected you to let me down this way."

Andrew sighed, exhaustion and anxiety fraying the last edges of his nerves. "What would you have me do? Go ahead with the ceremony as if nothing was wrong? I couldn't do that. Not with time being of the essence in finding Christian."

"A lot of good that did. We still have no idea where that woman has taken him. I knew it was a mistake to hire her. What kind of unstable nanny kidnaps her charge?"

Andrew let out a breath. He'd kept Grace's secret this long, but there was no point in hiding the truth any longer. "There is a reason Grace took Christian. A personal one." He hesitated, wishing for some way to soften the blow. "Grace isn't just his nanny. She's his aunt. Rose's sister."

Father's face went white. He closed his eyes briefly, the lines around his mouth deepening. "Is that how she got you to hire her? With a big sob story about her dead sister?"

Andrew flinched. "No. I didn't know until a few weeks ago, when Christian took sick. At first I was furious, but she explained that she only wanted to get to know her nephew."

His father scowled. "Why didn't you fire her on the spot? None of this would be happening if you had." He splashed some more brandy in the glass and drank it down. "She won't get away with it. He's my grandson, and I'll hunt her down to the far corners of England if I have to."

There was nothing Andrew could say to help matters, so he stayed quiet.

They sat in silence for several minutes until Father turned to him. "Tell me, Andrew. How do you intend to fix this situation with Cecilia?"

Andrew straightened on his chair. Had his father not heard Celia's outburst at the church? He couldn't expect him to marry her now.

"I'll apologize to the Carmichaels," he said. "But I won't be marrying Cecilia. This whole situation with Christian has made things very clear. I've had my priorities all wrong. Being a good guardian to that boy has to be my main goal."

Father studied him for a moment. "It's made things clear to me as well, Andrew." A fleeting expression of pain passed over his features before his jaw tightened. "I've decided to give Paul Edison the Ottawa position."

"You can't be serious."

"I need someone reliable at the helm, who will give all his attention and energy to the job. That man isn't you."

Andrew leaned over his knees, trying to catch his breath. Everything he'd worked so hard for was slipping away. He'd lost his bride, his nephew, and his promotion. Once again, his father had deemed him unworthy.

What had he done to warrant such utter failure?

Nothing but attempt to please everyone else in his life—everyone except himself—and perhaps God.

Maybe it was time to quit worrying about his father's approval, which clearly he would never get, and figure out what God really wanted. Maybe this wasn't His plan for him after all.

With icy calm, Andrew pushed to his feet. "If that's the way you feel, Father, then I'll save us both a lot of frustration and disappointment." He stared at him. "I quit."

His father's eyes widened, his mouth pressed into a hard line.

Andrew stalked to the door.

"Where are you going?" His father's voice barely registered.

"To keep looking for Christian. Beyond that, I have no idea."

CHAPTER 38

February 23, 1919
Dear Grace,

Reverend Burke has found me another place to stay. One of his parishioners, an elderly widow, has offered me room and board in exchange for work around her house. She's a dear soul who doesn't mind Christian's crying. Please pray for me, Grace. I don't know how I'll get through these darkest of days. If anything happens to me, promise you'll raise Christian. And that you'll never let the Eastons have him. I couldn't stand for them to raise my precious child.

Grace held Christian tightly on her lap as Reverend Burke's car swung up the lane toward the Fairlawn estate. The sight of the magnificent house brought up a rush of homesickness along with an attack of nerves. She had loved being part of this family, even for so short a time, making memories she would cherish for the rest of her life.

But what would await her now when she walked through those doors? If only Virginia were here to help her parents understand the panic that had fueled Grace's impulsive actions. But no one knew where her friend was or if she'd ever be back.

Grace looked out the window at the sky, attempting to ascertain what time of day it was. Judging by the sun, it was likely late afternoon or early evening. Would Mr. and Mrs. Easton be back from the wedding or would the reception still be in full swing? No matter what, she needed to have an honest conversation with them before she left their house for good. If they weren't home, she'd wait in the nursery until they returned.

At least she wouldn't have Andrew to contend with since he would have already left on his wedding trip by now. Her spirits sank even lower.

Reverend Burke slowed to a stop near the front door and set the brake. "Maybe I should come in with you. As a mediator, in case things get heated."

Grace shook her head. "Thank you, Reverend, but I must face the consequences of my actions alone." The very real possibility loomed that if someone had noticed she'd taken the baby, she could be charged for her crime. She prayed that the Eastons would be magnanimous and show her mercy. "I'd ask you to wait, but I don't know how long I'll be."

"I don't mind waiting." He reached over and squeezed her arm. "I'm proud of you, Grace, for having the courage to do the right thing."

She blinked back the sting of tears. "I don't feel very brave right now. I wouldn't blame them if they never let me see Christian again." A tear escaped and landed on the baby's sleeve. "If that's the case, I don't know how I'm going to say good-bye." She laid her cheek against his tiny head.

"God will give you the strength, child. And I'm sure the family will come around eventually and be grateful to you for returning their grandson."

"I hope you're right." On a deep exhale, she opened the door and got out. With Christian in one arm and his bag in the other, she climbed the stairs to the front door and knocked.

A few seconds later, Mrs. Green appeared. Her mouth fell open. "Grace? Master Christian? Oh, my goodness. Come in." She glanced nervously down the hall as Grace stepped into the entry.

The woman's reaction made Grace's heart sink. It was clear their absence had been noticed.

"Are Mr. and Mrs. Easton home?" she asked. "I'd like to speak to them, if I may."

"They're in the parlor. I'll tell them you're here."

"Thank you."

Grace set the bag on the floor and looked around the grand entrance, committing every detail to memory—from the burgundy flock wallpaper to the ornate silver candlesticks on the hall table. Hugging Christian tightly to her, she walked over to the gallery of paintings that graced the long corridor wall. As usual, Andrew's portrait claimed her attention. The artist had done an excellent job of capturing his noble air, the aristocratic angle of his head, the twinkle in his deep blue eyes. Her pulse quickened, and despite the circumstances, she wished they could somehow get past all the animosity and resume their friendship. But he was married to Cecilia now, and he'd never forgive her for what she had tried to do.

"You may come in, Grace." The housekeeper reappeared in the hall.

"Thank you." Shifting Christian on her hip, Grace took a deep breath and walked into the room on shaky legs.

Mrs. Easton sat in her usual seat by the fireplace. As soon as she spotted Christian, tears brimmed over and streamed down her face. Mr. Easton rose slowly from his chair, his face ashen, staring at Grace with an anguished expression. As she suspected, Andrew was absent, which was for the best.

"You have some nerve, miss." Mr. Easton came forward, and Grace feared he would snatch the baby from her arms.

Before he could, Grace crossed the room and placed Christian gently on Mrs. Easton's lap. Then she loosened the strings of his bonnet and removed it, smoothing down a few stray hairs.

"Thank you," Mrs. Easton whispered. "Thank you for bringing him back."

Grace bit her lip to contain her own rising emotions. She had much to say and needed to remain in control. "I want to say how deeply sorry I am. I acted in haste, out of fear and misguided intentions, but it doesn't excuse what I did."

Mrs. Easton swiped at her cheeks, staring at her grandson with such love that a wave of pure remorse washed over Grace at the pain she'd inflicted.

"I do, however, have one request in entrusting Christian back to you."

Mr. Easton came to stand beside his wife. "You are in no position to make demands of us. I have half a mind to call the constable right now and charge you with kidnapping."

Grace choked back a protest. It would do no good to antagonize the man.

Mrs. Easton seemed to collect herself. "There's no need for that, Oscar," she said firmly. "All that matters is she brought him back. Now, Grace, what is this request?"

Grace hesitated. Insulting their new daughter-in-law would earn her no favor, yet she couldn't remain silent. "I'm asking that you keep Cecilia from ruining Christian's life."

"Why would you say that?" Mr. Easton demanded.

Grace gripped her hands together. "Last night, she came to the nursery to tell me about her intentions for Christian. How she was going to send him off to boarding school in Europe as soon as he was old enough."

Mr. Easton's face darkened. "Andrew would never allow that."

"That's what I said. She only laughed and told me that she always gets her way." Needing to move, Grace crossed to the mantel to stare at a group of family photos. Her focus stayed on the image of Andrew as a boy. "I couldn't bear to think of Christian being raised without love, shoved away like an unwanted toy. Not when I could give him all the love he'd ever need." She inhaled. The time had come for the truth. She owed them that much. Grace turned back to them. "There's something else you should know. Christian is my nephew too." She paused. "I'm Rose's sister."

A beat of silence followed. Neither of them looked surprised.

"Andrew told me earlier today." Mr. Easton scowled. "I knew my instincts were right about you."

"Hush, Oscar. I want to hear what she has to say."

Grace nodded to Mrs. Easton, who suddenly didn't seem quite as fragile. "After Frank died, Rose made me promise I would look after her son if anything happened to her. A promise I took seriously." She moved closer, keeping a wing chair between them. "Rose had her faults, but she loved your son more than her own life. In fact, I believe it was grief over Frank that ultimately led to her death. She just didn't have the will to go on without him." Grace gripped the back of the chair. "I came here prepared to detest Rose's in-laws, the people who had rejected her without giving her a chance. But instead I grew quite fond of you all." She shot a glance at Mr. Easton, whose expression remained stony. "I discovered a group of people who, despite their differences, were committed to each other, loyal to a fault at times. I had no doubt Christian was well-cared for—until Cecilia became part of the picture. To be fair, I don't believe Andrew had any idea what she intended. I think she only showed him the side she wanted him to see."

"I'm confused, Miss Abernathy." Mr. Easton came forward, his steely gaze pinning hers. "What does all this have to do with anything?"

Her stomach fluttered, still not immune to his intimidation tactics. "I'm trying to explain my state of mind when I came to work for you. I didn't come here with the intention of taking Christian."

"That doesn't change the fact that you *did* take him, subjecting us all to incredible distress, even for a short period of time. You knew what that type of upset could do to my wife."

Grace reached deep for her composure. "Again, I'm truly sorry. I thought I was doing what was best for Christian."

Mrs. Easton rose with Christian in her arms. "It takes courage to admit your mistakes, Grace. I'm only grateful you came to your senses in time." She smiled. Her eyes were clear, and she looked much stronger than she had in weeks.

Grace smiled back, then fixed her gaze on Christian, who

squirmed in his grandmother's arms. This could be the last few minutes she got to spend with her beloved nephew. She bit her lip, trying to gather the courage to say good-bye.

Footsteps sounded in the hallway.

Grace's heart flew into her throat. She'd know that tread anywhere.

Seconds later, Andrew strode into the parlor, a frown creasing his brow. "Is that Reverend Burke sitting outside in his car?" His focus landed on Grace, and he slammed to an abrupt halt.

The color drained from his face, giving his eyes a hollow look.

"Hello, Andrew," she said quietly.

"Grace." His vivid blue gaze, filled with a swirling mixture of angst and anger, captured hers. Every nerve ending vibrated across her body.

Then he immediately crossed the room to his mother. "Christian," he said in a strangled voice. He lifted the child from his mother's arms and hugged him tightly against his chest, resting his cheek on Christian's head. "Thank you, Lord." Andrew's eyes squeezed shut, the tick in his jaw giving evidence to the extremity of his emotions. When he opened his eyes, a world of pain glistened there, rending Grace's heart even further.

She twisted her fingers together to keep them from visibly shaking. Her whole being yearned to go to him, to beg his forgiveness, but her feet remained rooted to the floor. "I've apologized to your parents, but I want you to know how terribly sorry I am. I panicked and reacted out of fear." She paused to draw in a breath. "I hope one day you can forgive me for any anxiety I caused."

His features hardened as he handed Christian back to his mother. Then he speared Grace with a hard look. "Can I speak to you in the library, please?"

Grace's stomach clenched. Perspiration dampened her palms. "I'd like a minute more with your parents, if you don't mind."

He gave a terse nod and strode from the room.

Grace went to stand in front of Mrs. Easton. She rubbed a hand down Christian's back. "Thank you for everything, Mrs. Easton.

I've enjoyed my time here very much." She kissed the baby's chubby cheek. "Good-bye, sweetheart. Be a good boy for your grandma. And remember, your Aunt Grace will always love you." Swallowing back her tears, she gave his soft head one last caress.

Mr. Easton stared at her with an unreadable expression, his eyes not quite as hard now.

Despite the urge to bolt, she held her ground. She couldn't pass up this chance to give some much-needed advice. "Before I go, I want to remind you how fortunate you are to have such a wonderful family. I'd give anything to have my father or my siblings back, even for just a moment." Her voice cracked and she cleared her throat. "Please remember that when Virginia returns. She loves you all very much. Don't make the same mistake with her as you did with Frank."

She glanced at Mr. Easton, trying to gauge his reaction. Would he shout at her and order her to leave? But he remained silent, his guarded expression giving nothing away.

With a resigned sigh, she gave her nephew another kiss, then went to face Andrew for the final time.

Andrew threw open the library door, letting it bang against the far wall, and stalked over to the window. A thousand emotions waged war inside him, spinning through his system until he didn't know whether to laugh or cry or hurl his father's decanter across the room.

His throat tightened as the walls seemed to close in on him, and he knew the room was too confining for this conversation. He needed open air and wide spaces. As he stepped back into the hall, Grace appeared.

"Follow me," he said tersely.

Without waiting to see if she obeyed, he headed to the rear door and strode outside. The first pull of fresh air into his lungs loosened the muscles in his chest. He led Grace to the fountain where they would have a measure of privacy from anyone in the house.

Andrew stood with his back to her, his shoulders stiff with tension. His gaze landed on the old maple tree, calling to mind the night when the two of them had watched the stars together. When everything had seemed so right but then had turned so terribly wrong.

That night felt like a thousand lifetimes ago after all that had happened since.

He still couldn't believe Grace had come back. All the things he'd imagined saying to her jumbled together in his head. At last, he turned to face her. She looked like a lost waif, her expression so forlorn that his heart pinched. But he wouldn't soften. Not this time.

"Do you know what your actions have cost me?" he bit out. "I had to abandon Cecilia at the church in order to search for Christian, which of course infuriated my father. So much so that he gave my promotion to Paul Edison." Andrew gave a harsh laugh. "I have lost everything because of you—my bride, my promotion, and my father's respect."

"I'm terribly sorry, Andrew." Tears welled in her eyes, magnifying the amber flecks within. "I never intended to ruin your wedding. I didn't plan much further than getting Christian away from Cecilia." She looked up. "Can you reschedule the ceremony for another day?"

Andrew squeezed his hands into fists. "In light of Cecilia's reaction to Christian's disappearance, I've come to realize that marrying her would not be in his best interest." He hated to admit that Grace had been right about his fiancée when the raw wound of Grace's treachery still gaped in his chest.

"How could you?" he hissed. "How could you take Christian from us like that? You knew that losing him would devastate me. Not to mention my mother. I thought we were—" He clamped his mouth shut before he said too much.

Grace's frame stiffened. "I thought we were too, Andrew, yet you chose to cut me out of Christian's life for no reason other than Cecilia demanded it. How fair was that?"

Andrew closed his eyes, her words striking hard at the core of his guilt. He *had* been unfair to her, letting her go not only to please Cecilia, but because it would be easier for him not to have Grace under his roof. "I guess we both made mistakes," he conceded. "But at least I didn't break the law."

"I'm sorry," she repeated. "Sorry my impulsiveness caused you and your family pain. I only wanted to place Christian in my mother's arms so she could meet her grandson before she died." She paused to dash tears from her lashes. "I hoped it might make up for losing Peter, Owen, and Rose."

He stared at her, steeling himself against a wave of compassion before he did something ridiculous like take her in his arms and comfort her.

A bird landed on a branch behind Grace, its cheerful twitter seeming to mock their pain.

"I hope that one day you might be able to forgive me, and perhaps . . ." She lifted tear-filled eyes to his. "Let me visit my nephew."

Heat flared in his chest. "You must be joking."

A flash of pain crossed her features. "I wouldn't need to be alone with him. Someone else could be present at all times."

He shook his head. "I doubt my father will ever let you set foot in the house again."

She took a shuddering breath. "If you change your mind, I'll be at the boardinghouse. I'll be staying there until I decide what to do."

"You aren't heading back to England?" His traitorous heart thudded, awaiting her reply. He told himself he needed to know in case they decided to press charges.

"I'm not sure. Without a job, I don't know what I'll do." Lines bracketed her mouth, sorrow seeming to weigh her shoulders down.

Andrew suppressed an oath. He'd been so busy counting his own misfortunes, he hadn't considered hers. In fairness, she'd suffered as much as he. She'd lost her sister, and Christian, and now her job. The only tenuous connections she had in Toronto were her former landlady and her minister. At least he had his family, a beautiful home, and, though he'd lost out on the promotion, he was fairly sure he could still have his old job if he chose to take it back.

And now he had Christian, which was all that really mattered. He made an effort to relax his shoulders and soften his expression. "Despite everything, I do appreciate you bringing him back. Not only for my sake, but my mother's. I know it couldn't have been easy, so . . . thank you."

"You're welcome." She stared at him for a long moment. Then her gaze darted toward the house. "I should go. I've kept Reverend Burke waiting too long as it is."

Unable to find the appropriate words, he gave a stiff nod.

"Good-bye, Andrew." The wind blew tendrils of hair across her face as she turned away.

He watched until she disappeared from view, then sank onto the stone ledge of the fountain and closed his eyes. All the anger drained from him, leaving him limp and exhausted. Though he tried hard to hold on to his outrage, he couldn't seem to hate her for what she'd done.

If only he could, he might be able to forget how much he loved her.

CHAPTER 39

Virginia paused at the foot of Fairlawn's iron gates. Had it only been a few weeks since she'd left her home, sneaking out in the predawn hours to marry Collin? It felt far longer.

A hundred emotions coursed through her, making her head spin. She still couldn't believe Drew hadn't gone through with the wedding. This morning, determined to see her brother get married, Virginia had waited across the street from the cathedral, planning to slip in the back of the church once the ceremony began. Instead, she'd been privy to Drew's odd comings and goings. Once he left the church for good—without his bride—she'd sent Collin over to casually ask some of the guests what had happened. They'd explained the necessity to postpone the wedding due to a possible kidnapping by the nanny. Virginia had been shocked by the news, and knowing her family would be devastated, she came to support them, whether she was welcome or not.

A tiny sliver of guilt surfaced that she might have an ulterior motive, hoping that in the midst of their distress, her parents might be more willing to forgive her.

She was desperate enough to try.

A familiar hand touched her shoulder. "Are you sure you want to do this, sweetheart?"

"I'm sure." She brought her husband's hand to her cheek. "No matter what happens, at least we'll know where we stand."

Collin entwined his fingers with hers. "Let's go then. But know that I'm going in with you. I'll not let you face them alone."

Collin's fierce frown dragged a smile from her. She adored his protectiveness. It was one of the many facets of his love she'd come to cherish. "Very well. I only hope there's been news of Christian. I still can't believe Grace took him. I never thought her capable of such a thing." Virginia knew Grace's connection to the baby, and that she had feelings for Andrew. Even so, kidnapping Christian seemed a bit extreme.

"I can't pretend to understand it," Collin said. "One thing I'm sure of, however, is that she loves that child."

At the front door, Virginia hesitated for a second, then turned the handle and went inside. She would not knock on her own door. Not until she'd been formally banned from her home. Her stomach swooped with a case of wild nerves. What would Daddy say when he saw them?

The familiar smell of her father's pipe tobacco mingled with Mother's perfume, and a pang of homesickness knotted her chest. She prayed Daddy would be open to accepting her marriage. But no matter what, she would never regret following her heart.

The sound of soft voices drifted into the hall.

With Collin on her heels, she crossed to the parlor, took a deep breath, and entered.

She had a vague impression of her father standing by the window, her mother in her usual chair by the hearth, and Andrew holding—

"He's back!" Virginia flew over and enveloped her brother and nephew in a hug. Then she rained kisses on Christian's cheeks. "What happened? Where did you find him?"

Andrew gave a tight smile, though his eyes remained haunted. "Grace brought him back about an hour ago."

"Thank the Lord." She blinked hard to keep the tears from forming. "But why did she take him in the first place?"

"It's a long story. All that matters is that he's back where he belongs."

Virginia stroked Christian's back. She couldn't seem to stop touching him, to ensure he was real. "Where is Grace now?"

Andrew's features hardened. "Gone." His tone brooked no argument, but his eyes remained shadowed in pain.

"Drew—"

"If you'll excuse me, I need to take Christian upstairs." He gave her a pointed look and a subtle nod toward their father. "I'll talk to you later if you're still here." He leaned down to kiss her cheek. "It's good to see you, Gin. Collin." He glanced at her husband before leaving the room.

Virginia longed to follow him, to pepper him with questions about the status of his relationship with Cecilia. But first she needed to face her parents and try to make amends.

She turned to look at her father. He'd come to stand behind her mother's chair, his expression serious.

"Daddy, may we speak with you and Mother?"

"I don't see what there is to say. You humiliated us as well as the Flemings."

"Sir, if you'd allow me, I'd like to apologize." Collin, who had been standing quietly beside her, moved forward. "When Virginia came to me that night, I wanted to wait and speak to you, man to man."

Virginia took his arm. "And I told Collin you'd never listen. That you'd find a way to prevent us from being together."

"The only reason I finally agreed to the elopement," Collin continued, "other than the fact that I love Virginia more than life itself, is that she was going to leave, with or without me. I couldn't bear the thought of her out there alone. So, faced with an impossible choice, I took the path that would ensure her safety and her happiness." Collin stood tall and strong, but not imposing.

Her father's eyes narrowed. "Perhaps we should have that man-to-man talk. Let's adjourn to the library."

Virginia grabbed her father's arm. "Daddy, please don't—"

He gave her a sharp look. "Don't what?"

"Just . . . be nice."

"When am I ever nice?"

"There's always a first time."

The slight twitch to his lips gave Virginia hope that he might be in a more receptive mood.

"I suspect you ladies have a lot to catch up on," Daddy said. "We'll be back shortly."

Collin gave her a quick kiss, then followed her father out the door.

"Oh, Mama." Virginia went to her mother, who stood up to envelop her in a tight hug. Virginia inhaled her familiar scent and melted into her embrace. "I hope you can forgive me for eloping. At the time, I couldn't see any other way."

"Of course I forgive you." Her mother pulled back to lay a hand on her cheek. "I'm only sorry you couldn't tell us how you really felt."

"I thought I could marry Basil, I really did. But the longer our courtship went on, the more I realized he wasn't the man for me. And when Collin said he was going back to Scotland, I couldn't let him go."

Her mother looked her in the eye. "Does he make you happy, Virginia?"

"Oh yes." She couldn't stop the smile that spread over her face. "He's thoughtful and kind and very protective. He does whatever he can to please me."

"Then that's what's important." Her mother's brow creased. "But how is he supporting you? I've been so worried about where you're living."

"Right now we've rented a room in town, but as soon as Collin finds work, we'll get a better place."

"I'll speak to your father. Have him give Collin his job back." From the determined set to her mother's chin, Virginia knew she'd do it.

She shook her head. "Thank you, Mama, but I don't know if Collin's pride would allow him to accept, even if Daddy did change his mind."

Her mother led her to the sofa, and they both sat down. She took Virginia's hand in hers. "Listen to me. Losing Christian even for such a short time has had a profound effect on your father. It was almost like losing Frank all over again, and reliving that pain has made him realize what's truly important—though he might never admit it to anyone but me." She smiled. "Now that Christian is back, it wouldn't surprise me if he views things in a much different light."

"Oh, Mama. I hope you're right." Virginia lifted a silent prayer that the Lord might soften her father's heart and allow him to finally accept his children as they were—the good with the bad—and value them still.

If so, then maybe they could truly be a family again.

CHAPTER 40

April 14, 1919
Dearest Grace,

You're coming at last! You don't know how happy I am! Mrs. Gardiner has assured me you're welcome to stay here until we find a place of our own. I know once you're here, I'll finally feel whole again. Able to regain my strength and become the woman God meant me to be. Safe travels until we meet again. . . .

One week after leaving Fairlawn for the last time, Grace pushed the supply cart down the aisle of Holy Trinity Church, its wheels rattling over the wooden floors. The comforting scent of flowers and candle wax washed over her. When Reverend Burke had learned that she wanted to stay on in Toronto for a while, he'd been kind enough to give her part-time hours cleaning the church and the rectory until she could find a permanent job.

She paused to gaze up at the stained-glass windows, her focus resting on the one with Mary holding baby Jesus.

This was the time of day Grace would have taken Christian on his daily outing to the park. Where she would sit with him on the swings and play with him in the grass. Her heart ached with missing the boy—and with missing Andrew.

The utter disillusionment in Andrew's eyes that night by the fountain still haunted her. The only positive outcome from the whole fiasco was that Cecilia Carmichael was now out of Christian's life for good. It seemed Andrew had finally realized the woman was not right for them. Unfortunately, that realization had come too late for Grace, but at least she had the comfort of knowing Andrew would always take good care of her nephew.

Her thoughts turned to her mother and the unfinished letter that lay on the desk in the boardinghouse. Each time she started writing, she couldn't find the words to explain why she wouldn't be bringing Christian home. That he would be staying in Toronto, and she'd likely never get to meet her only grandson.

Once again, Grace had failed her mother.

Another reason why she was in no rush to return home.

With a sigh, she pulled the cloth from the cart and began to polish the wooden pews. Focusing on her task of making the Lord's house shine was the only way she could free her mind from regrets and recriminations, and in some small way allowed her to feel like she was giving back for the grace and mercy she'd received.

When she was about halfway through, she looked up to see Reverend Burke coming toward her, with Mrs. Chamberlain following close behind. Grace slowly straightened, a chill of foreboding running up her spine. From the grim look on their faces, it appeared they had unpleasant news.

She wiped her hands on her apron and went to meet them. "What is it? Something's wrong, I can tell."

Mrs. Chamberlain pulled a piece of paper from her handbag. "This telegram just arrived for you, dear. Ian Miller delivered it himself. I figured it must be important, so I came right over."

Grace froze. Telegrams usually meant bad news. Her hands shook so hard, she stuffed them in her apron pocket. "C-Could you read it for me please, Mrs. C.?"

"Are you sure, dear?"

She nodded.

"All right then." She opened the envelope and unfolded the paper within. "Your mother has taken a turn for the worse. STOP. You need to come home ASAP. STOP. Violet."

Grace gripped the back of a pew. Mum must be on her deathbed for Aunt Vi to spend money on a telegram. The words of her mother's last letter sprang to mind, infusing her with fresh guilt. *Don't wait too long like you did with Rose. I may not be here when you return.* If only Grace could bring Christian home with her. Seeing her grandson might give Mum the incentive to get well. Without him, she had little left to live for.

Mrs. C. came forward to embrace her. "I'm so sorry, Grace. Is there anything we can do to help?"

Tears stung the back of Grace's eyes, but she held them back with stubborn determination. "Not really. Except I'll need to book my passage home to England." As the words left her mouth, a pang of sorrow squeezed her chest. Leaving Toronto meant severing her last ties with Christian—and with Andrew. She'd likely never see either one of them again. She bit down on her bottom lip and blinked hard.

"Why don't you come to my office?" Reverend Burke said gently. "I can help you make the arrangements."

Grace took a deep breath and nodded.

"I'll stay here and say some prayers for your mother," Mrs. C. said. "When you're ready, we'll go home together." She gave Grace another hug.

For a few brief seconds, Grace soaked in the comfort of her embrace, then turned and followed the minister out of the sanctuary.

Fifteen minutes later, Revered Burke hung up the receiver. "The tickets will be held for you at the train station. You can pick them up whenever you're ready, or wait until the day of departure. Whatever's more convenient."

Grace had taken his advice to sail out of New York, rather than Halifax, since a ship was leaving in four days.

"Thank you, Reverend. I only hope I can make it home in time to see Mum again." She twisted her hands together. "Long enough to grant me her forgiveness at last." Maybe then Grace would finally have the peace that had eluded her for so long.

The minister frowned. "What is it you think you need forgiveness for?"

Grace shook her head. "For so many things." Quietly, she relayed the story of Peter's death, which had led to her father's demise. "I came here to bring Rose back, hoping to make it up to Mum by doing so, but I was too late. Now I've failed again with Christian." Silent tears rolled down her cheeks. She pulled out a handkerchief and dabbed them away.

Reverend Burke came around to sit in the chair beside her. "Do you believe in God's forgiveness, Grace?" he asked quietly.

"Yes, of course."

"Then that's all that truly matters. Knowing that God has forgiven you for everything."

"I know He has." She sighed. "I just wish Mum could forgive me too."

He waited until she lifted her head to meet his kind gaze. "Only God can change a person's heart, Grace. All we have control over are our own feelings and actions." He gave her arm a light squeeze. "Perhaps you've been seeking forgiveness in the wrong place. Perhaps, my dear, it's time to forgive yourself."

Andrew waited in the Carmichaels' parlor for Cecilia to come downstairs. He hadn't spoken to her since their wedding day, and though he dreaded it, he owed her a more formal apology. Technically, they were still engaged, and until they had a candid conversation, Andrew wouldn't be able to close that chapter of his life and move forward.

Forward to what, he didn't know. His future yawned before him like a gaping chasm.

Too restless to sit, he walked to the large window that overlooked the front yard. The first signs of fall could be seen in the changing of the leaves. Soon the street would explode with color—vivid yellow, red, and orange. It was ironic that the changing of the seasons seemed to mirror a change within Andrew as well. Ever since Grace had left Fairlawn, he'd felt a subtle shifting inside, as though nothing in his life made sense anymore.

He should be furious that Paul Edison had already moved to Ottawa to oversee the new hotel, yet all he felt was mild disappointment. As for Cecilia, he bore her no ill will. Instead, he sympathized with her position. It couldn't have been easy to face all those guests and explain why the wedding was cancelled. Her pride would have been severely damaged, which was partly why he'd given her time to nurse her wounds before confronting her.

"Hello, Andrew. I wondered how long it would be before you came."

He turned to find Cecilia standing in the doorway. She looked as beautiful as ever in a striped dress, her blond hair perfectly coiffed. But instead of the icy expression he'd expected, there was softness about her features he hadn't seen in a very long time.

"I should have come sooner." He walked toward her. "Though nothing I say can make up for it, I want you to know I'm sorry for what happened, and I deeply regret hurting you."

She gave him a long look. "But you'd do it again if the circumstances were repeated, wouldn't you?" The statement held no hint of condemnation.

He hesitated, wishing he could dispute her claim, but he couldn't lie. "Yes."

"I thought so." She moved to the sofa and sat on the edge, smoothing her dress over her lap.

"It doesn't mean I don't feel terrible. It's just that Christian's welfare—"

"—comes first. I know." She studied him without calculation, also something new.

Andrew had been prepared to receive the full brunt of her outrage. This calm, composed Celia left him flummoxed.

"I've done a lot of thinking since that day, Andrew, and I've come to some important realizations about myself." She lifted her eyes to his. "I need a husband who will dote on me. One who puts my needs first—something you haven't been able to do." She held up a hand to halt his response. "Secondly, though it might sound selfish, I really don't see motherhood in my future, and since I know how much having a family means to you . . ." she gave a delicate shrug. "I feel it would be best to part ways."

This was the last thing he'd expected. Tears, threats, ultimatums, yes, but a quiet surrender? This was not the Cecilia he knew. His gaze moved to the bare fingers on her left hand and back to her face.

She reached into the drawer of a side table and drew out a small box, then rose. "I'm returning your ring. You should have it back since it's a family heirloom." She held it out to him.

Frowning, he took the box, opened it to see his grandmother's ring inside, and snapped it shut. "I don't know what to say."

"It's for the best really. I doubt we would have made each other happy in the long run." She laid a hand on his sleeve. "You deserve someone who will love you for who you are, not who they want you to be. Someone who can give you the family you want." She arched a brow. "Someone like your nanny perhaps?"

The words seared through his chest like a knife. "Grace is not Christian's nanny anymore. Not since she took him."

"But she brought him back. That should count for something."

"It doesn't erase her crime. I could never—*we* could never trust her again."

Cecilia turned to face the fireplace. "I can't help feeling this is my fault." She sighed. "The night before the wedding, I went to see Grace."

"I know. She told me the next morning. She also told me that you would never accept Christian as your son. That you threatened to send him to boarding school."

Cecilia whirled around. "She did? And you were still willing to marry me?"

He shrugged, not proud of his blindness where Grace or Cecilia was concerned. "I told her I'd never let you do that. And I wouldn't have." The clock on the mantel chimed the hour. He took in a breath. "Since we're being honest, I should tell you my chauffeur came to inform me that you offered to pay him to seduce Grace. I suspect framing Grace for stealing your necklace was your backup plan."

Guilt slid over Celia's features, and she hung her head. "I'm sorry, Andrew. It's just that I was desperate. . . ."

"It doesn't excuse what you did."

"No, it doesn't." Cecilia lifted her chin, a bit of her sass returning. "So is that the reason you came? To tell me what a horrible person I am?"

"To hold you accountable, yes. And to resolve matters between us."

A resigned expression settled over her features. "Well, consider yourself relieved of your obligation to me. You're free to do whatever you want with your life. As am I." She twisted a curl around one finger, avoiding his gaze.

He stared at her profile, her conciliatory attitude making sudden sense. "It sounds as though you've already made plans."

"As a matter of fact, I have." She walked to the window and pushed aside the curtain. "Paul Edison has asked me to marry him . . . and I said yes."

Heat blasted through Andrew's chest as old feelings of resentment rushed to the surface. "Are you doing this to punish me?"

She let the curtain fall as she turned back. "I never understood the rivalry between you, but no, Andrew. This has nothing to do with revenge and everything to do with love."

His mouth fell open. "You love him?"

"Is that so hard to believe when you're obviously in love with Grace? And don't bother to deny it. I think I knew before you did, which is why I was so determined to get rid of her. Now I understand the futility of trying to control another person's emotions. Paul helped me see that." She gave a rueful smile. "Once I got over my wounded pride, I found I was actually relieved the wedding never took place. So you see, in reality, you did me a favor."

Andrew shook his head, unable to fully comprehend the complete change in her demeanor.

"Paul loves and accepts me for who I am, which is a rare gift. If you've found that with Grace, don't let a mistake on her part rob you of the life you could have together. No one is perfect, not even her."

Andrew remained silent, unable to deny the truth of her words. Grace had always accepted him for exactly who he was. Her admiration had made him feel like he was the man God had intended him to be. But was it enough for him to ignore what she'd done?

He scrubbed a hand over the new growth of beard and nodded slowly.

Cecilia gave him a small smile. "Don't overanalyze the issue, as you tend to do." She raised herself on tiptoes to kiss his cheek. "May you find happiness, Andrew."

"Thank you, Celia. I hope you'll be happy too."

As Andrew left the Carmichael estate, his thoughts swirled in his head like the leaves blowing about his feet. Before he could come close to making any decisions about his life or his future, there was a long-overdue stop he needed to make.

CHAPTER 41

Andrew stood before the mammoth family headstone in the St. James Cemetery. Dappled sunlight filtered through the remaining leaves on the trees, bathing the granite marker in a soft glow. He scanned the engraved names of his ancestors until he came to the one he sought.

Francis Oscar Easton
1891—1918
Killed in action
Taken too soon

Andrew removed his hat and stared at the stone, not entirely sure why he'd come, only knowing that he had to in order to finally have peace.

He hadn't had the chance to reconcile with Frank before he went off to war, and even when he came home on leave, Andrew hadn't made amends. Why hadn't he tried harder to bridge the gap between them when he knew his brother might never return? He'd allowed years of bitterness and jealousy to harden his heart, when he should have put their differences aside and reached out to him.

"Forgive me, Frank. I never should have let my resentment come between us. It wasn't your fault that Father loved you more. I always envied your charisma, your passion for life. But you broke our parents' hearts, and I'll admit I hated you for that."

The wind picked up, blowing Andrew's hair across his forehead. "I'd always lived in your shadow, and the fact that your death put me in Father's good graces added to my guilt. Guilt that I was alive and you weren't, that I actually benefited from your death." A shudder went through him. "I should have tried harder to get Father to accept your marriage instead of basking in his attention for the first time in my life."

He paused to watch a flock of sparrows fly by overhead and land in the nearby trees. Andrew clutched his hat harder as the wind whipped his overcoat against his legs.

"I hope you can forgive me too for not doing better by Rose. Maybe if I had, she'd still be alive today." He brushed away the moisture gathering in his eyes. "I've kept one promise, though. I'm looking after your son. And no matter what happens, Christian will always be my priority. I love you, Frank. And I'm truly sorry. For everything."

He swallowed hard against the lump in his throat. So much wasted time. So much unnecessary anger and bitterness. If he'd realized this sooner, would things have been different?

Movement to the left caught Andrew's attention. He turned, astounded to see his father coming up the path, a bouquet of flowers in his arms.

Andrew fought to push back his raw emotions. He'd barely spoken to his father since he'd quit his job and still hadn't sorted out his feelings about him giving Edison the promotion.

"Andrew." His father lacked his usual confident stride. "If I'm intruding, I can come back later."

"No, I'm finished here." Andrew stepped away from the headstone.

Father laid the flowers at the base of the stone, then shoved his hands in his coat pockets. "Your mother feels I need to make peace with Frank. She suggested I start here. I have a feeling she thought you might be here too. The woman has a sixth sense sometimes."

An uncomfortable sensation fluttered through Andrew's stomach. He'd had enough emotional disclosure for one day. "Well, I'll give you some privacy."

"Andrew, wait. Since you're here, there are some things I need to say. Things I've put off for too long."

His father motioned to a bench under one of the large oak trees. Reluctantly, Andrew followed, and they both took a seat. Above them, the leaves rustled in the fall breeze. A raven's lonely cry rang out overhead, but no answering call sounded.

Father stared out over the rows of gravestones, the lines around his mouth making him look older than his years. "I want to explain why I gave Paul the promotion instead of you," he said at last.

"I think you made that clear. Apparently, I'm not reliable enough."

The comment still rankled, since Andrew had always prided himself on being the most reliable one in the family.

"That was said in the heat of the moment." Father shifted on the bench. "The real reason, the one I couldn't admit even to myself, is that I want you here with me. I lost Frank and Virginia. I can't lose you too."

Stunned, Andrew could only stare.

"I hope you'll reconsider your resignation. The hotel needs you." He cleared his throat. "I need you. I can do without Paul Edison, but I can't do without you, son."

Something uncurled within Andrew, loosening the tension in his muscles. He swallowed hard. "I don't know what to say."

"Say you'll think about it."

A tentative decision now solidified in his mind. "I don't need to think about it."

"I see."

"I never really planned on leaving. Like you said, it was the heat of the moment."

The lines in his father's face eased. His lips lifted in a rare smile. "I'm glad. Your mother will be relieved as well."

Andrew looked his father in the eye. "You should know I officially ended my relationship with Cecilia today. Turns out she's going to marry Edison."

"I know. I spoke to Paul this morning."

"This won't hurt your friendship with Harrison, will it? He won't pull his investment out of the new hotel?"

His father frowned. "You thought our alliance hinged on your marriage? I may be a ruthless businessman, but I'd never manipulate my own son for the sake of a deal. If you believed that, then I've been a worse parent than I thought."

It seemed Andrew had been mistaken about a few things. "This isn't all your fault. I've made some wrong assumptions based on issues from my childhood." He twisted the brim of his hat. "All my life I've felt second-best because I thought you loved Frank more."

A pained expression flitted over his father's features. "Not more. Just differently. I always knew you'd have a fine career ahead of you. You were smart, studious. You had a college degree. Frank was a charmer, but could never seem to commit to anything, to settle into a job. I tried my best to mentor him, but nothing worked." Regret shone from his father's eyes. "If I made you feel inadequate, son, I'm sorry."

Warmth spread through Andrew's chest, clogging his throat. Had his own insecurity colored the way he'd viewed his brother and his father? "I'm sorry too, Dad."

His father grabbed him in a rough embrace and clapped him on the back. "What do you say we mark this day as a fresh start—for all of us?"

"I'd like that."

Father gave him a long look. "I'll say one thing about that nanny of yours. At least she owns up to her mistakes—something I've been too stubborn to do until now. And she gives some pretty good advice." He smiled. "Let's go home and spend time with Christian. I'll have your mother invite Virginia and"—he rolled his eyes—"Lafferty for dinner. We can celebrate a new beginning for the Easton family."

All of Andrew's pent-up guilt and resentment finally evaporated in the crisp fall air. "That sounds like a good idea." He rose from the bench. "I'll see you back at the house. There's something I need to take care of first."

When his father left the cemetery, Andrew went back to the family plot, an idea taking shape in his mind. With a final glance at the names on the stone, he knew what he needed to do to make amends to Frank.

A gesture he hoped might please Grace as well.

Holy Trinity Church was as small and quaint as the cathedral was grand. With its plain wooden benches and simple altar, Andrew could immediately see how it would appeal to Grace and remind her of her hometown. He scanned the length of the main aisle, wondering if she still worked for Reverend Burke or if she'd found a new job yet.

His heart ached just thinking about her. Andrew's anger had faded once Christian was back at Fairlawn, and without his righteous indignation to cloud his judgment, he found he could empathize with the desperation that had fueled Grace's actions. If he'd been faced with similar circumstances, would he have done the same thing?

He'd like to think not, but he couldn't be one hundred percent certain.

Figuring Reverend Burke would be at home at this time of day, Andrew headed over to the rectory and knocked on the door.

The man himself answered. "Mr. Easton. This is a surprise. Please come in."

"Thank you." Andrew stepped into the narrow hallway. "I'd like to speak to you about a somewhat delicate matter."

"Is this about Grace?"

Even just hearing her name sent more shafts of regret searing through him. "Actually it's about her sister."

The minister gave him a puzzled stare. "Why don't you come in to the parlor and we can discuss what brought you here?"

An hour later, Andrew found himself on the sidewalk in front of Mrs. Chamberlain's boardinghouse, indecision wreaking havoc with his nerves. He had not intended to see Grace again, but the unsettling news Reverend Burke had told him mere minutes ago had shaken him to the core.

Grace's mother was dying, and she was leaving to return to England.

For good.

That knowledge had unleashed something inside him. Something he hadn't taken time to examine, instead rushing right over to the boardinghouse. All the way over, Cecilia's words kept running through his mind. *Don't let a mistake on her part rob you of the life you could have together.*

Now he halted outside the small gated walkway. Insecurity held him rooted in place. Perhaps it was the fear that he might have missed his chance to see her before she sailed across the ocean. Perhaps it was the uncertainty of what he'd do if she was here.

His insides twisted. The tea and scones he'd eaten at Reverend Burke's threatened to come back on him. He raked a hand through his hair, his coat now making him overwarm in the mild September afternoon.

"Is there something I can help you with, Mr. Easton?"

Andrew froze.

Mrs. Chamberlain came down the stairs, peering at him. "You've been pacing back and forth for nearly twenty minutes."

Andrew squirmed in his shoes. The only time he'd met the woman, he'd been less than cordial, grilling her about Grace's whereabouts when Christian was missing. "I was wondering if I might speak with Grace."

She reached the gate and swung it inward. "I'm afraid she's not here."

His spirits sunk faster than a lead-bottomed boat. He licked his lips that had gone bone dry. "She hasn't left for England yet, has she?"

"Not until tomorrow." She wiped her hands on her apron,

frowning. "I hope you're not here to make her feel worse. She's been terribly hard on herself already."

A flush of heat rose in his cheeks. "No, ma'am." He exhaled. "I'm not entirely sure why I'm here. Except that when Reverend Burke told me Grace was leaving, I couldn't not come."

Not even to please his father. Surely his family would understand when they found out why he hadn't made it back for dinner.

Mrs. Chamberlain nodded. "I think I understand." She leaned closer. "If you really want to see her, I happen to know where you might find her."

"You do?"

"She's out at Hanlan Point. Seems she has fond memories of the place and wanted to visit it again before she left."

His heart threatened to burst from his chest. Did that mean Grace still cared for him, despite everything that had happened between them?

"It's a lovely day for a ferry ride, don't you think?" She winked at him.

He smiled as hope bubbled to the surface. "It is indeed."

CHAPTER 42

Grace lifted her face to the sun, relishing the warmth on her cheeks that contrasted with the cool breeze blowing off the lake. She stood in the exact spot where she and Andrew had watched the fireworks display on Dominion Day. Instead of the crowds that had lined the boardwalk that night, today the island seemed almost deserted. The amusement rides now only operated on the weekends and would soon close down for the season. She never did get her ride on the roller coaster, but the memories she held of that day were worth far more than the thrill of one ride.

For it was right here she'd realized she was in love with Andrew. She couldn't leave Toronto without coming back to relive the wonder of that day. She hugged the memories to herself, trying to memorize every sound, every smell, and hold them to her.

Tomorrow she would board a train for New York City where she would then catch the steamship home. Part of her yearned to see the shores of England again, to return to her small village where life was so much simpler. Yet deep down, she knew it would never be the same, because she was not the same.

Too much had happened. Too much had changed.

"I'm sorry I failed you, Rose," she whispered. "I didn't keep my promise after all. But I hope you know Christian is loved and that the Eastons aren't as bad as you feared. They'll take good care of him."

Especially now that Cecilia was out of the picture—the one good thing that had resulted from her costly mistake.

She let out a soft sigh and pulled her jacket more firmly about her. The afternoon was waning. She'd better head back to the ferry—after one last walk around the park. She retraced her steps, passing the area where they'd all shared the picnic lunch. A couple sat at a picnic table, holding hands, their heads close together, oblivious to everything and everyone around them. Grace pushed aside a sharp jab of envy and continued on to the arcade, pausing in front of the shooting gallery.

A man appeared from the back of the booth, and his eyebrows rose when he saw her. "We're not open till Saturday, miss. But if you want, I can give you a practice shot."

Memories rose up to swamp her. She shook her head, her throat too tight to speak.

"Come on. Give it a try." He winked at her. "You got nothing to lose."

"What's the matter, Annie Oakley? Lose your nerve?"

Grace froze, every muscle stiffening. Her imagination had to be playing tricks on her. Very slowly, she turned around, and her pulse skyrocketed as though a hundred fireworks had exploded inside her.

Andrew stood a few feet away, watching her with an enigmatic expression. He wore a navy blue jacket, which made his eyes appear even brighter. His hair blew across his forehead, and his beard had almost fully grown back.

"Andrew," she said slowly. "What are you doing here?" Her bewildered mind couldn't make sense of his presence. It couldn't be a coincidence that brought them here at the same time, could it?

Lord, why are you torturing me this way?

Andrew came a few steps closer. "I went to see you at the boardinghouse. Mrs. Chamberlain told me you were here."

What could be so important that he would track her down on the island? Instant panic clutched at her. "Is Christian all right?"

"He's fine. Though I daresay he misses his nanny."

Fresh grief clawed at her insides. "If you've come to make me feel bad, you needn't bother. I couldn't feel any worse than I already do."

She turned to walk down the sidewalk, the day suddenly ruined. Why couldn't he have stayed away and allowed her to keep her happy memories intact?

"Grace, wait. That's not what I intended." He ran up beside her. "I wanted to talk to you about something that concerns your sister."

Her steps slowed. "What about her?"

"Can we sit by the water a minute? I need to explain a few things." His earnest expression proved difficult to resist.

"Fine." Pressing her lips together, she followed him over to a bench and gingerly sat at the very end.

He sat beside her and stared out over the water, fiddling with the cap in his hands. The breeze off the water lifted his hair, making it dance around his forehead. "I went to Frank's grave today and made my peace with him. But it occurred to me that I owe you an apology." He paused. "The truth is I didn't do everything I could to help Rose after Frank died."

She frowned, unsure where the conversation was headed.

"Frank wrote and asked me to look out for Rose. He told me she was expecting and that if anything happened to him, he wanted me to take care of her."

Grace closed her eyes on a fresh wave of sorrow. Even amidst the horrors of war, Frank had protected Rose. He must have been a kind and considerate man. One who loved her sister more than anything.

"I did go to see her once after Frank's death. She wouldn't speak to me. Slammed the door in my face, in fact." He frowned and looked away. "I'm ashamed to admit I was relieved. I could ease my conscience. Tell myself that I'd tried." He shook his head. "But I should have gone back until she accepted my help. If I had, maybe she wouldn't have fallen ill and Christian would have his mother." Tears stood out in his eyes. "I'm sorry, Grace. Sorry I didn't do more for her."

Grace gripped her hands together to keep from reaching for him. She knew firsthand the type of guilt he was experiencing. "It's all right, Andrew. All the 'should haves' in the world won't change anything. I would know." She blinked back the moisture in her own eyes.

"While I was at the cemetery, I had an idea for a way to make things right for Frank and for Rose. I hope you'll allow me to do it."

"What do you mean?" She dashed at the tears on her lashes, unable to imagine anything that could accomplish that.

"I want to move Rose's remains to the Easton family plot and have her name engraved below Frank's. His body was interred overseas, but we did bury some mementoes in a small casket, so that part of Frank would be there when we visited. It's only fitting that Rose be buried there too. Frank would've wanted it that way."

A lump blocked Grace's throat as she remembered the unmarked grave in the Holy Trinity Cemetery. The parishioners were still saving money toward a stone. Perhaps they could donate the funds to another worthy cause instead. "That's a wonderful idea. Rose would have wanted that. And when Christian's older, he can visit both his parents at the same time."

The lines in Andrew's forehead eased. "I'm glad you agree. I didn't want to do anything until I had your blessing. Now I can tell Reverend Burke to go ahead."

Grace nodded. "Thank you for coming all this way to tell me. I'll be able to let Mum know when I get home . . . if I make it in time."

"Reverend Burke told me about your mother. I'm so sorry, Grace."

"Me too." The sun had disappeared behind a cloud, making her shiver. She rose from the bench. "Well, I'd better get back. I have a lot to do before I leave tomorrow."

"Wait." He leapt up and snatched her hand. "There's something else."

She stared down at their joined fingers. Heat from his hand curled around hers, and she didn't have the strength to pull away.

"It's taken me a long time, but I want you to know that I'm

finally seeing things clearly. And I realize that everything you did, you did with the best of intentions. I'm sorry I didn't see it sooner and that I've been so unforgiving."

She couldn't think, couldn't speak. What did all of this mean?

With his free hand, he tipped up her chin until she had no choice but to look at him. His eyes were filled with a mixture of hope and longing. "You've changed me, Grace Abernathy. Because of you, I've found the courage to stand up for myself, to be the man I always wanted to be. A man I hope is worthy of someone as kind and loyal as you."

The air stalled in her lungs. Tingles danced down her arms.

"What I'm trying to say is that I'm in love with you, Grace. It took me a long time to admit it. I was so determined to keep my family together that I was blind to everything else. I should have listened to you. I should have fought for you. For us." He brushed a finger down her cheek. "I know I don't deserve it, but I wondered if there was any chance you might . . . love me too?"

Grace could scarcely believe her ears. Tears blurred her vision. Her heart broke free from its chains and soared in her chest. "Oh, Andrew, I've loved you from almost the first moment we met."

His lips came down on hers. Every nerve came alive inside her as though an electric current had traveled through her. In that moment, time stood still. All that mattered was the heat of his arms around her, the insistence of his lips. Her heart swelled with such bliss that she feared her knees might give out. She clutched the sleeve of his jacket to steady herself, wishing the kiss would never end, but knowing it must.

The instant he broke for air, she put a hand to his chest. "I have to go home, Andrew. My mother is dying. I can't let her down again."

"I understand," he said softly. "I'm not asking you to stay." He searched her face. "Only that you'll come back to me one day soon."

Joy and regret warred within her. "I can't make any promises. I don't know what I'll be facing when I arrive home."

He pulled her back against him and kissed her again, as though he couldn't bear to be separated from her for even a moment. She returned his embrace, fighting to memorize every sensation coursing through her. The graze of his beard, the scent of his skin, the shelter of his arms spreading warmth through her whole body.

When at last he released her, she looked up at him, wishing things could be different. Wishing the timing had been right for once. But she'd trusted God all along on this crazy journey. She had to trust He had a plan for her now.

Andrew took her hand. "I'll walk you to the ferry."

"Thank you." She smiled, relishing the warmth of his fingers on hers. She still couldn't believe he loved her. Yet his declaration proved bittersweet, because these would be their last cherished moments together. She had to see her mother again and attempt to fix the brokenness between them before it was too late. She'd regret it forever if she didn't.

Who knew if she'd ever be back?

"It's just occurred to me," Andrew said as they approached the dock, "that perhaps I should take some time off work. Go on a little vacation after everything that's happened."

Grace frowned. "What about Christian?"

"I'd take him with me, of course. Though Mother would probably love the chance to look after him while I'm gone."

Why was he telling her this? Tormenting her with details of his life she wouldn't be here to share?

"As a matter of fact, I think I'll take Christian overseas. To see his mother's homeland. Maybe visit a few relatives while we're there."

Grace came to an abrupt halt, almost tripping in the process. "Wh-what are you saying?"

The twinkle in his eyes belied his serious expression. "I was hoping we might bring Christian to meet his grandmother, if you think that's a good idea." A slow smile spread across his handsome face.

Grace pressed a hand to her mouth, but nothing could contain the emotions bubbling up inside. Tears so near the surface spilled unheeded down her cheeks.

Andrew pulled out a handkerchief and dabbed at her face. "This wasn't supposed to make you cry. I hoped you'd be happy."

"I am happy. So very happy." She hiccupped, joy and disbelief rioting through her. Perhaps she could do this one last thing for her mother after all. "But how can you be ready on such short notice? The train leaves tomorrow morning."

"I'm extremely resourceful, as you may have observed. I'll take care of everything as soon as we get off the ferry. But there's one more very important thing to consider."

Her mind swirled. "What could that be?"

Smiling, he brought her fingers to his lips. "Should we get married before we leave or wait so that your mother can attend the ceremony?"

EPILOGUE

"I'm going to murder my brother." Virginia flounced into the anteroom at Holy Trinity Church. "A few hours' notice is not sufficient time to prepare for a wedding. What was he thinking?" She draped a garment bag over a chair in the corner of the tiny room.

Grace looked up from the vanity mirror, still unable to believe she was about to be married. "You mustn't blame Andrew. It was my decision to get married before we left." Nerves buzzed in her stomach. She wasn't about to let anything interfere this time. Even if the ship were to sink, at least she'd have the comfort of knowing she was Andrew's wife.

Virginia grinned. "Can't say that I blame you after everything you've been through. I'm glad I could come up with a suitable dress on such short notice." She unzipped the bag and removed the gauzy ivory creation. "This was part of my trousseau for Europe, though I must say it doubles nicely as a wedding gown."

Grace rose from her seat. "Are you sure about this?"

"Absolutely. There's no one I'd rather see wear it." She winked. "Come on. You'll look fabulous."

With Virginia's aid, the dress slid into place with a whisper. As Virginia fastened the tiny buttons at the back, Grace risked a glance in the mirror. "Oh, my. Is that really me?"

She'd never seen a more gorgeous dress. Its softly draped bodice, edged with embroidered lace and pearls, met a high waistband and flowed down in a sea of satin.

The door opened. Mrs. Chamberlain stepped inside and stared. "Grace dear, you look like an angel." She came forward with two bouquets of flowers. "These are from Mr. Lafferty." She laid them on the table. "And this note is from Andrew."

Grace's hand trembled as she took the paper.

"Go ahead. I'm sure it's a love letter." Virginia laughed as she picked up the veil and spread the netting around.

Mrs. Easton had been kind enough to offer Grace the use of her veil that she'd preserved all these years for Virginia. What better blessing could she receive on her marriage to Andrew?

Grace sat on the stool in front of the vanity and opened the note.

My darling Grace, you've made me the happiest of men by agreeing to marry me tonight. I promise to spend the rest of my life loving you, cherishing you, and ensuring your happiness. Together we'll share the privilege of becoming Christian's parents. I cannot wait to begin our lives as man and wife. All my love forever, Andrew.

Grace closed her eyes and pressed the paper to her chest. *Thank you, Lord, for your mercy and grace, and for granting me the love of such an amazing man. I promise to do everything I can to be worthy of such a gift.*

A knock sounded on the door. Mrs. Chamberlain went to answer it.

"That was Andrew's father," she said. "Reverend Burke is ready any time you are, dear."

"Thank you, Mrs. C. And thank you, Virginia. I don't know what I would have done without you both."

"I'm just grateful to be here. Grateful my parents have accepted my marriage to Collin." Virginia fastened the veil to the crown of Grace's hair with pearled combs. "And it's all thanks to you."

"Me. How?"

"You opened my father's eyes to how wrong he was about Frank and Rose and helped him see that it's not so terrible to follow your heart." She smiled. "Who knows? By this time next year, my parents could be welcoming another grandchild, or even two, into their lives."

Grace turned to pull Virginia into a warm hug, her heart filled to overflowing with gratitude. "I'm so glad you're my friend, and that now you'll be my sister too."

Mrs. Chamberlain bustled over and handed Grace the flowers. "No tears allowed. We don't want a puffy-eyed bride." She adjusted the veil around Grace's shoulders. "Now, go marry that man."

At the foot of the altar, Andrew shifted from one foot to the other. If the women didn't hurry, he might jump right out of his skin.

A warm hand squeezed his shoulder. "Relax, son. Women always take longer to get ready. Though considering Grace only had a few hours, it will be a miracle if she's ready at all." His father's easy laugh loosened the bands of tension in Andrew's chest.

"Thanks, Dad. I'm honored you agreed to be my best man."

"I'm only sorry it took me so long to see the light." He cleared his throat. "I don't want to ever lose you, son. Or your sister. You and that young lady of yours have shown me the true value of family. I promise to do my best not to forget that in the future." He reached into his pocket and drew out an envelope. "This just arrived today. I was going to save it for later, but go ahead and open it now."

Andrew couldn't imagine what his father was giving him. He pulled out a slim brass plate. Engraved in flowing script were the words *Andrew Easton, Vice President*. Dumbfounded, he looked at his father, who smiled.

"I figured this promotion could make up for missing out on Ottawa."

Andrew couldn't speak against the lump in his throat. "Thanks, Dad. You have no idea how much this means to me."

The organ music swelled, and the doors at the back of the church opened.

"Time to get married." His father winked and took the envelope. "I'll have this installed by the time you return. I wish you every happiness, son. You deserve it."

Virginia appeared in the doorway, wearing a pink flowing gown. She held a bouquet of pink and white roses, no doubt arranged by her husband. She started up the aisle, and seconds later, Grace came into view.

Andrew's breath tangled in his lungs. No bride could have looked more beautiful. She glided toward him, her arms filled with an array of multicolored flowers. Despite the late hour, the church glowed with the light of a hundred candles, giving the building an ethereal effect. Almost like looking up at the stars.

Grace reached the foot of the altar, and Andrew stepped forward to meet her. The blinding smile she gave him made his chest swell. She took his arm, and together they turned to face Reverend Burke.

"Dearly beloved, we are gathered here tonight in the sight of God and these witnesses to join together in holy matrimony Grace Agnes Abernathy and Andrew Gerard Easton."

The minister's opening words flew by, and minutes later, Andrew turned to face the woman he loved. With great solemnity, he pledged his life to hers. From the corner of his eye, he saw his mother in the front row with Christian on her lap, wiping her cheeks.

Andrew gazed deeply into Grace's warm brown eyes and smiled, certain that Frank and Rose were looking down on them with love, thrilled at the merging of their two families—this time in perfect harmony.

"I now pronounce you husband and wife. What God has joined, let no man put asunder." The minister paused and smiled. "You may kiss your bride."

Andrew lifted the veil and pulled Grace close for their first married kiss. A holy union, binding their troth.

"I love you, Mrs. Easton," he whispered. "And I'll spend the rest of my days proving it."

A smile bloomed on her lips. "As long as you keep up those kisses, Mr. Easton," she teased, "that shouldn't be a problem."

Then, not caring who might object, Andrew kissed his wife once again for good measure.

ACKNOWLEDGMENTS

It has been a true pleasure writing a story set in my own country and getting to know my history in more depth. Toronto is truly a fascinating, multicultural city. Exploring its old buildings and houses has been a real treat.

I'd like to thank my agent, Natasha Kern, for giving me a gentle push when needed! Her prodding at a time when I was feeling burned out made me buckle down and come up with the proposal for Canadian Crossings.

Thank you to David Long and Jen Veilleux, my editors at Bethany House. Your suggestions and attention to detail are very much appreciated. A special thank-you to Jennifer Parker and the creative team who design the amazing covers that grace my books. They are truly awesome. And thanks to all the wonderful staff who work so hard on our behalf. I am so honored to be a Bethany House author.

As usual, my sincere gratitude goes to my amazing critique partners, Sally Bayless and Julie Jarnagin, who are most generous with their time and advice. I'm so happy to be sharing this career with you both!

Thank you, as always, to my husband, Bud, and my children, Leanne and Eric, who support me every day.

Once again, I must thank my wonderful readers. I was so grateful to have the chance to meet quite a few of you at the past two Christian Fiction Reader Retreats in Nashville and Cincinnati. I appreciate you all so much!

And my most gracious gratitude goes to God for the inspiration and stamina required to bring these characters and stories to life. I could never do this alone!

With hugs and good wishes always,

Susan

Susan Anne Mason describes her writing style as "romance sprinkled with faith." She loves incorporating inspirational messages of God's unconditional love and forgiveness into her characters' journeys. *Irish Meadows*, her first historical romance, won the Fiction from the Heartland contest sponsored by the Mid-American Romance Authors chapter of RWA.

Susan lives outside Toronto, Ontario, with her husband, two children, and one rather plump cat. She loves red wine and chocolate, is not partial to snow even though she's Canadian, and is ecstatic on the rare occasions she has the house to herself. Learn more about Susan and her books at www.susanannemason.net.

Sign Up for Susan's Newsletter!

Keep up to date with Susan's news on book releases and events by signing up for her email list at susanannemason.com.

More from Susan Anne Mason

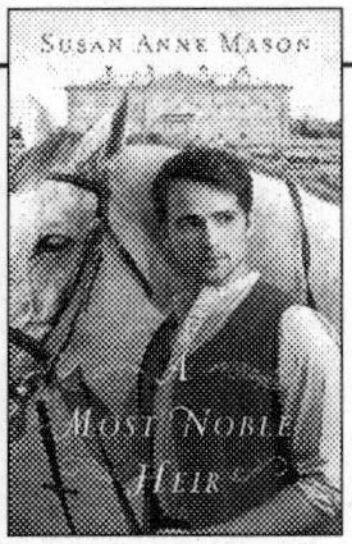

Stable hand Nolan Price's life is upended when he learns that he is the heir of the Earl of Stainsby. Caught between two worlds, Nolan is soon torn between his love for kitchen maid Hannah Burnham and the expectations and opportunities that come with his rise in station. He longs to marry Hannah, but will his intentions survive the upstairs–downstairs divide?

A Most Noble Heir

You May Also Like . . .

Seeking justice against the man who destroyed his family, Logan Fowler arrives in Pecan Gap, Texas, to confront the person responsible. But his quest is derailed when, instead of a hardened criminal, he fin an ordinary man with a sister named Evangeline—an unusual beauty with mismatched eyes and a sweet spirit that he finds utterly captivating.

More Than Meets the Eye by Karen Witemeyer
karenwitemeyer.com

Amid the glamour of early 1900s New York, Dr. Rosalind Werner is at the forefront of a ground-breaking new water technology—if only she can get support for her work. Nicholas Drake, Commissioner on the State Water Board, is skeptical—and surprised by his reaction to Rosalind. While they fight against their own attraction, they stand on opposite sides of a battle that will impact thousands of lives.

A Daring Venture by Elizabeth Camden
elizabethcamden.com

Forced to run for her life, Kit FitzGilbert finds herself in the very place she swore never to return to—a London ballroom. There she encounters Lord Graham Wharton, who believes Kit holds the key to a mystery he's trying to solve. As much as she wishes th she could tell him everything, she can't reveal the trut without endangering those she loves.

A Defense of Honor by Kristi Ann Hunter
Haven Manor #1
kristiannhunter.com

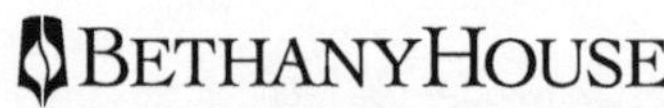